MALORY'S KNIGHTS of ALBION

DARK NORTH

PAUL FINCH

Abaddon
Books

WWW.ABADDONBOOKS.COM

An Abaddon Books™ Publication
www.abaddonbooks.com
abaddon@rebellion.co.uk

First published in 2012 by Abaddon Books™, Rebellion Publishing
Limited, Riverside House, Osney Mead, Oxford, OX2 0ES, UK.

10 9 8 7 6 5 4 3 2 1

Editor-in-Chief: Jonathan Oliver
Desk Editor: David Moore
Cover art: Luke Preece
Design: Simon Parr & Luke Preece
Creative Director and CEO: Jason Kingsley
Chief Technical Officer: Chris Kingsley
Malory's Knights of Albion created by
David Moore and Jason Kingsley

UK ISBN: 978-1-907992-88-9
US ISBN: 978-1-907992-89-6

Printed in the US

NORTH

C ES1

"I'VE COME ALL this way for such as you?" Lucan said. "I wouldn't normally sully my steel. But too many good men are groaning in the darkness, waiting for justice."

He drew *Heaven's Messenger* back for the final stroke – and it was taken from him.

Snatched from his hand.

By something that had descended from above.

Some *thing*.

It was essentially female, in that it had a head with long, streaming hair, and arms, legs and breasts, but in place of hands and feet were eagle's talons, and in place of skin it had a hard rind of greenish scales. It was immense in size; twice the height of a normal man, its bat-like wings spanning maybe fifteen feet. Its face was its most repellent aspect: a grotesque visage with bunches of bone sprouting from its brows and cheeks, a jutting chin and nose, and jagged spades for teeth. With an ululating shriek, it lofted skyward with its prize, a mane as wild and green as seaweed billowing around it.

At first the men could only gape, Briton and Roman alike.

Maximion, incredulous, shouted: *"Stymphalianus!"*

WWW.ABADDONBOOKS.COM

MALORY'S KNIGHTS OF ALBION

The Black Chalice
The Savage Knight
Dark North

Dedicated to my children, Eleanor and Harry,
who were my very first audience.

INTRODUCTION

FOUND IN A church vestry in 2006, the Salisbury Manuscript (British Library MS Add. 1138) is the only existing copy of *The Second Book of King Arthur and His Noble Knights*. Apparently a sequel to Thomas Malory's *Le Morte D'Arthur*, the best-known and most influential version of the story of King Arthur and his Round Table, the *Second Book* has caused enormous controversy throughout the academic world.

Following negotiations with the manuscript's owner, Abaddon Books won the rights to modernise and publish the stories for the mainstream market in early 2010. *Dark North* is the third title to be released to the public.

For more information about the Salisbury Manuscript, and themes and notes from this story, see the Appendices at the rear of this book.

My son,[1]

When I am gone you will inherit nothing but my bad name, this fur and this sword. Do not underestimate their power. In particular, do not underestimate this sword, for it is the embodiment of our strength. Wield it, and those who come against you will fall like stalks of grass. Do not think this an evil thing, for you will be lord and protector of many lands. While countless will die by your sword, countless others will live by it.

God rules this world and His people thrive, not because He is good but because He is strong. Christians once died like cattle, men, women and children hunted down and put to death in torturous ways. They only came to safety the day they struck back. At the battle of the Milvian Bridge, General Constantine destroyed the pagan horde of the pig Maxentius with blood and iron. This is the only lesson you need learn. The men of the One God rule because they are mightier than those of many gods. Do not be fooled by the wittering of priests and monks. Strength matters. Spare those who oppose you, and they will kill you and your children. This gift of rage I bequeath to you in the form of this sword, which has delivered death to more foes than I can count, and must continue to.

Worship God, serve your overlord, and vanquish your enemies – vanquish them utterly. There is no law but your own. God respects those who conquer and triumph in His name. Your enemies are His. Cleanse the world of them.

> – Duke Corneus of Penharrow,
> Dictated on his death-bed

---

[1]Taken from lines 612-627 of the "Noble Tragedie." See Appendix 2 for a discussion of this passage within Malory's greater work.

PROLOGUE

Lucius Julio Bizerta[2] did not care a great deal for the Imperial purple. Nor did he stand on ceremony, not even when there were matters of state to discuss. As such, on that unseasonably mild February evening when he received twelve honoured guests in the audience chamber of the Episcopal Palace at Ravenna, he was wearing a simple tunic, breeches and sandals. There were no laurel leaves on his brow; there was no sceptre in his hand; the only ring on his hands was the royal seal.

The chamber was tall and spacious, and built from polished white marble, but aside from its simple New Testament frescoes, and the heavy ermine curtain drawn across its single casement, it was devoid of ornamentation. The hearth was bare – the hot-water pipes under the tiled floor provided adequate warmth, and numerous candelabra cast an orange glow. Twelve cushioned seats were arranged for the guests; as they included two consuls, three senators, several high churchmen, and various representatives of the capital's wealthiest patrician families, they might have expected greater extravagance, but less was always more where Emperor Lucius was concerned. He didn't address them flanked by flunkeys, but with only a single scribe to keep a record of their meeting. He awaited

---

[2]The apparently fictional "Emperor Lucius" first appears in Geoffrey of Monmouth's *Historia Regum Britanniae*, although he may have been based on either of the Emperors Glycerius or Tiberius II Constantine. See Appendix 2.

their arrival behind a broad teak desk rather than seated on a gilded throne; a desk layered with books and quills, which revealed more than words ever could the enquiring state of his mind and his dedication to personal industry.

The Emperor was not tall – about middle height, but with a strong, stocky frame, and possessed of curly red-gold hair, and a light red-gold beard and moustache. His complexion was unusually ashen for one born in Capua, far to the south, but he was a handsome man with a steady smile, a straight aquiline nose and bright green eyes. From his simple attire, restless air and tireless movement, one might have thought him an artisan, a talented but humble fellow who strove tirelessly for a good greater than his own glory but drew pride and satisfaction from it nevertheless.

"Gentlemen," he said, once his guests were seated. He walked around his desk and stood in front of it, arms folded. "It always reassures me to summon such august company, and see it arrive with such a dignified lack of haste. Only conspirators hasten to their Emperor's presence."

There was a mumble of polite laughter.

"The only conspiracy here, Caesar, is to sing your praises," Consul Rascalon replied. "Because of you, the world will soon be Roman again."

Lucius shook his head. "No. Not the world, just the parts of it that were Roman before. Gentlemen... we live in a bustling age. Powers rise and fall, some of them righteous, some of them vile. There has been much chaos, much bloodshed. But there have also been achievements – in the arts and sciences, in culture and philosophy. One cannot, and indeed must never, belittle the successes of those who were left to gather up the pieces when the Empire collapsed."

"Those who kept the candle of civilisation burning during those dark years are to be honoured," Consul Rascalon said. "But alas, these became small voices in a wilderness of barbarism, much of it heathen. It is you who have brought the light back to the Empire, Caesar. Glory to your name!"

Cheering filled the audience chamber. Fists stabbed the air.

Lucius acknowledged this with a patient smile, but gestured for peace.

"This isn't about conquest for its own sake, gentlemen. Or even reconquest. I'm sure you'll agree I have gone out of my way not to tyrannise. Things must never be allowed to revert to the way they were in the bad old days... of Gaius Caligula's reign, for example, when the Emperor made whores of his best friends' wives simply because he could. Or the days of Nero, when fear and superstition led the Palatine gardens to be lit by Christians smeared with pitch and made into living torches."

The guests fell silent in mute recognition of these tragic events. The bishops among them nodded their skull-capped heads sagely.

"What I wish to restore to our provinces is the light of learning and love," Lucius added. "Rome as a parent, a firm father and caring mother, a guiding hand for those who, since our departure, have come to wallow in ignorance and squalor."

"No-one has ever doubted this, Caesar," Rascalon stated.

"This is why we have christened our resurgent empire 'New Rome.' We are proud of our past, but there are many reasons why we also need to break from it."

His audience listened intently.

"So let us consider what New Rome has so far accomplished." Lucius clapped his hands and two attendants entered carrying a display board, which they set up alongside their master's desk. A map of the Empire was pinned to it; the eastern provinces were marked in gold, the western ones in red.

Bishop Severin Malconi, in whose own palace they sat, regarded the map warily. He was a plump, sunburned man of fifty years, whose close-cropped white hair belied his youthful looks. As a boy, he would never have dreamed to see Roman hegemony restored to so many disorderly regions. The notion that the Mediterranean Sea could ever again be a 'Roman lake' would have amazed and enthused him, and yet how quickly these staggering events had come to pass.

Lucius continued: "We have now recovered in full the provinces of Italy, Africa, Spain, Gaul and Aquitaine. In some cases they are still controlled by their original potentates, but now they pay fealty and taxes to us."

Malconi glanced sidelong at his young nephew, Felix Rufio, who was present both as a patrician and as a tribune in the army. Rufio was handsome and dark-eyed, his short hair so black it was almost blue. Unlike many of his age, he was clean-shaven. As he was fond of saying when in his cups: "Why hide looks like mine beneath a baggage of unsightly, perfumed bristles?"

The Emperor was still addressing the business at hand. "Of course, things are never straightforward. Those provincial rulers who had lapsed into pagan traditions have been advised to... reconsider their ways. Religious missions have been sent, and churches and monasteries restored."

Proclates, the Bishop of Palermo, spoke up. "Time is an issue here, Caesar. Dangerous beliefs have taken root. Might I enquire at what stage we can expect to see more persuasive methods used? In those corners of Empire which have strayed *far* from the light?"

Bishop Proclates was an athletic, blond-haired hawk of a man. He might affect the trappings of religion on state occasions, but he was young and virile, and known to be as fond of the feast and the hunt as he was the cloister or the chapel. He was also known for his vaunting ambition. Malconi smirked. There had been much talk recently that valuable archbishoprics would be up for grabs in the re-acquired provinces – if only the local leaders the Emperor spoke of could be persuaded to tolerate them.

"I've discussed the matter with His Holiness," Lucius replied, "and we've decided that at this early stage there is no need to be too provocative. Particularly in those cases where renewed loyalty has been bought rather than enforced. To use a plebeian phrase, we see no need to upset the applecart just yet."

Proclates looked disgruntled, but said no more.

"Religious issues aside," the Emperor continued, "not

everything is rosy in New Rome's garden. You'll notice that the one glaring omission from this list of recaptured territories is Britain."

Rufio clutched Bishop Malconi's arm. The young tribune stared excitedly at the map, and at the boot-shaped island in the corner. Malconi sighed. The follies of youth knew no bounds.

"It is my intention," the Emperor said, "to send a new embassy to Britain. And I would like you twelve to go as my official representatives."

Rufio released his uncle's arm and clenched his fist in triumph.

"A number of you were present on the last embassy I sent to King Arthur's court, so you know what to expect. I've written to Arthur several times since, pressing my claim, but always I get the same intransigent response."

Quintus Maximion, another tribune in the army, stood. He was a much older man than Rufio, but tall and muscular, with solemn features and iron-grey hair.

"Lord Caesar," he began, "Arthur's kingdom is stable and prosperous. I can think of no reason why he would see benefit in becoming a client-king of the Roman Empire."

Lucius laughed. "That's the reason why I've assembled twelve of the brightest minds in Rome. Together, I'm sure you can enlighten him."

"Forgive me, Caesar," Maximion said, "but I was part of that embassy, six years ago. The country was in a more fragile state in those days. There were many recalcitrant elements that Arthur had to deal with. But even then he saw no advantage in bowing to Roman rule. Why would he see things differently now?"

Rufio also stood. "Tribune Maximion has a very defeatist attitude. I was there also, and I detected divisions among Arthur's nobility. I did not see him as the invulnerable sovereign his propagandists claim."

"Gentlemen, please!" Bishop Malconi said, standing. "May I...?"

He gestured gently at the two soldiers, and reluctantly they sat.

"We all know Arthur to be a strong and confident ruler,"

Malconi said. "We also know that he has the full support of his people, magnates and peasants alike. He is to be respected, certainly... but let us not get carried away. By no stretch of imagination can we put him on the same pedestal as our own revered ruler."

There was hearty agreement, and Tribune Maximion shook his head firmly, as if to dispel the very possibility.

"Well spoken, my lord bishop," Lucius said. "Please continue."

Malconi wove his fingers together, a pose he used in the Senate when he felt he was on secure ground. "The main difference, as I see it, between this embassy and the last is that, increasingly, we have right on our side. And the whole of Christendom will recognise..."

Maximion stood up again. "Forgive me, your grace, but how can it be right to steal another man's freedom?"

There was a disbelieving silence. Malconi looked around at his opponent as if he couldn't quite believe that anything so blasphemous had been uttered in the presence of a Roman Emperor. Maximion flushed a little, perhaps realising that he'd gone too far. He turned to his master, although it was difficult meeting the Emperor's cool, green-eyed gaze.

"Tribune Maximion, your opinions are welcome," Lucius said. "That is why I summoned you here. But I think you misunderstand our purpose. We are not denying anyone their freedom; we are merely seeking to bring order to the world. Bishop Malconi is quite correct. With the rest of the Western Empire settled, and only one unruly state remaining, it could even be said that we now have a moral obligation to intervene in British affairs..."

"And I say again, Caesar..." Maximion looked troubled by the stand he was making, but he persisted. "When I look at Britain, I see no unruly state. In our absence, Camelot has become the cultural heart of northern Europe. The people are content to work and play under a ruler who does not oppress them. Surely this is something we should encourage, not punish?"

"And what of the devil, Merlin?" Bishop Proclates wondered.

Maximion shrugged. "I've heard that Merlin has left Camelot."

"You've heard, but do you *know*?" Proclates's voice was scornful. "And even if Merlin *has* left, Arthur's power was built on his druidic magic. The pagan influence is everywhere. You only need wander Britain's woods and fields to see standing stones, ancient temples..."

"Yes," Maximion retorted. "In an equal state of disrepair to those in Rome."

Proclates sneered, but had no immediate riposte.

"It's good that we're having this debate," Lucius interrupted. "This is exactly what I was hoping for when I assembled you." He turned to Maximion. "But while I think you speak from the heart, tribune, I fear you underestimate what Roman citizenship can bring to a nation. Britain may be a happy land at present, under its kind king. But I see few roads there, and even fewer cities. I see no system of education for the people of the country, no organised civil service. Much of the land is still covered by wild forest. Britain could be so much more than it is today. Surely you don't dispute that?"

"No, my lord, I don't. But if they don't want it..."

"When you say *they*, who do you mean, tribune? *They* as in Arthur and his court, who enjoy all the liberties and luxuries of any nobility? Or *they* as in the people on whose backs that nobility rides?"

Maximion sat down, knowing when he was beaten.

Malconi broke the brief silence that followed. "Tribune Maximion's concerns are understandable, Caesar. Those who matter in Britain will not wish to be made servants in their own land, no matter how cleverly we argue at the negotiating table. They *will* resist us."

Lucius nodded sadly, as if reluctant to accept.

"They may also, my lord," Malconi added, "appeal to the Vatican. Arthur is a Christian monarch. His knights were famous for their battles against heathen powers."

Again Lucius nodded. "All of this is acknowledged by the

Holy Father. For which reason he will always seek, in public at least, to steer a middle course. But at heart he shares our worries for the common good of the British people, and in addition has concerns of his own. He feels that Christian teaching in Britain is in need of reform. It may even be straying into the realms of heresy – not purposely, but through a lack of communication.[3] Britain is on the fringes of our known world. Like fruit at the end of a tenuous vine, it is withering. Pope Simplicius sees it as our duty to nourish this fruit. And to do that, we must first enclose it in our own vineyard."

Malconi smiled. He'd known Pope Simplicius[4] since he was a lowly deacon called Castinus, and even then he'd been an astute man. Imagining heresy was only one of many tactics he could use to divide and conquer, though his machinations often ran much deeper than that.

"Only this afternoon, a legate arrived from Rome," Lucius added. "He brought something that I think will reassure even the most anxious among you."

He clapped hands, and another attendant scurried into the room, carrying a pole from which a great pennon hung: a pair of crossed black keys on a white weave. It was the papal gonfalon, and the other guests could only regard it blank-faced. Malconi glanced knowingly at his nephew, who visibly suppressed a smile.

"Caesar, I'm confused," Consul Rascalon said. "Why do we need a military standard if we are only going to Britain on a diplomatic mission?"

"Because, my lords..." the Emperor replied, moving towards the curtain, "I'm not a fool. I'm fully aware that any negotiation with this self-proclaimed King of the Britons will prove to be a waste of time. It's important that we at least

---

[3]In fact, after the fall of Rome, the monasteries of the British Isles – in particular Ireland – were widely respected for their preservation of Classical knowledge. But in Malory's time, Roman orthodoxy was ascendant once again, and England was becoming known as a home for heresy and dissent.

[4]St. Simplicius was Pope from 468 to 483 CE.

go through the motions – certainly as far as the Holy Father is concerned – but we know what Arthur's response will be. Therefore, *this*..." – he pulled a cord, which drew back the curtain on its brass runner – "...will be my response."

They had all seen the Roman army marching before.

But never in darkness; never in complete silence.

At first it was difficult to work out what the immense mass of bodies snaking north along the highway actually signified. There was no fanfare of trumpets, no banging of drums or cymbals. But at length they made out moonlight glinting on helmets, and the tips of spears, and the heavy overlapping plates of the legionaries' body armour, as they trundled past the palace in rank after rank, cohort after cohort, legion after legion.

It was anyone's guess how long they had been marching for – hours maybe, and still there was no end of them in sight. Little wonder that Emperor Lucius's normal mask of rational affability briefly slipped, revealing an expression of fierce, almost deranged joy.

"As my official ambassadors, gentlemen, you will carry no banners to Britain; neither papal, nor Imperial. But in due course, *these* fellows will."

ONE

"THE PENHARROW WORM, O God!" the vagrant priest cried by the roadside. "Spare us the Penharrow Worm! It terrorises our land. O Lord in Heaven... grant Earl Lucan the strength to bring us its head!"

"The 'Penharrow Worm,'" Lucan said, frowning down from the gatehouse battlements. "They make it sound like a dragon, yet it's only taken sheep and goats."

"The villagers are frightened," Turold replied. He was seated in one of the embrasures, strumming on his lute. "They fear for their children."

"As lord of these lands, I suppose it's my duty. But I wouldn't have called this hunt today were it not for Alaric's birthday."

"I'm sure he's grateful, but he'd be more grateful to be knighted."

"Everything in the right time, Turold." Lucan pulled on his leather gauntlets and strode to the top of the ladder.

Earl Lucan, marcher-baron of this region and Steward of the North, was an imposing figure, taller than most men, broad-shouldered and barrel-chested, but also craggy-faced and scarred; a testimony to his many years in the King's service. He had a shock of unruly black hair, which even though he'd seen nearly forty winters, was not yet shot with silver. His eyes were grey-blue, and capable of an icy, penetrating stare which could put the hardiest opponent on edge.

Below them, the hunting party trickled through the gatehouse onto the open ground in front of the castle. There was much noise and ribaldry. Like Lucan and Turold, the earl's retainers were clad for holiday rather than war, in cloaks and tunics, all brightly coloured and richly embroidered. Lucan himself sported a pale green pelisson and a darker green shoulder-cape, complete with hood and square-cut scallops. Turold, his *banneret*,[5] and a much slighter figure with long golden locks and almost girlish good looks, affected a more fashionable thigh-length gypon and hose, quartered in Harlequin style, pearl-blue alternating with peach-yellow.[6]

They were greeted at the foot of the gatehouse stair by Wulfstan, a hardened oldster with a bald head and thick white beard. Lucan's chief scout and tracker, Wulfstan was clad more practically in cross-strapped breeches and a heavy sheepskin doublet. He had three grooms with him, and a trio of destriers in readiness, each noble brute loaded with spears, hunting-bows, and quivers of fresh-fletched arrows.

Lucan had sixty other household knights aside from Wulfstan and Turold, and each one held at least one squire in training. Those who weren't already mounted up were hastening to do so, all the while boasting and mocking each other. In addition to these, many of the earl's tenant knights, with their own manor houses and retainers on his estates, had arrived; rather than wait outside, a number of them had ridden straight into the castle to greet old friends, swelling the disorder. Hounds yapped frenziedly; pages and servants scampered back and forth with sacks of food and skins of wine.

Wulfstan eyed the scene with weary resignation. "I thought we were only celebrating Alaric's birthday tonight? Most of

[5] A noble knight. While Turold is Lucan's vassal, he is entitled to lead his own vassals into battle under his own banner.

[6] *pelisson:* a fur-lined waistcoat; *scallops:* a projecting collar on a cape or cloak; *gypon:* a padded doublet or tunic. The emphasis on Lucan's and Turold's lavish dress emphasises England's sophistication, belying the New Romans' perception of the English as uncultured barbarians. See Appendix 2.

these fools are at the feast already."

"Let them enjoy their sport while they can," Lucan said. "It won't be as much fun when they're out in the woods."

Bows were flexed and hunting-horns put to the test. Turold slung his lute over his back, swept off his feathered hat, leaned from the saddle and grabbed a buxom serving lass, giving her a kiss. "The sight of you is more bewitching than any basilisk's gaze, my love," he laughed.

She hurried away, scarlet-cheeked.

It seemed that little order could be brought from the chaos. But when Lucan mounted up and galloped beneath the portcullis, there was a race by the merry company to follow.

Their laughter echoed around the great bastion that was Penharrow Castle.

Penharrow – a name to stir relief in some, fear in others, awe in all.

It stood on a ridge at the head of a valley filled with wild, rugged forest, which, this being only the first day of spring, was still shrouded in spectral mist. On all sides, the valley was cradled by mountains, their snow-capped peaks scraping a sky as blue as cut steel. It made a majestic setting, yet Penharrow Castle was a cruel edifice: a bleak, oppressive stronghold, towering tier upon tier. Though many handsome, heraldic pennons fluttered from its towers and parapets – Lucan's own black wolf, King Arthur's red dragon, and the many hawks, bears and leopards of the household men – its outer walls were built from crude, cemented stone, sheer and unbroken, save for the occasional cruciform arrow-slit.

The track that wound down from the castle was lined with village folk, who cheered to see their overlord riding to do battle with the enemy that had tormented them. The vagrant priest – one of many of his kind who wandered the roads of Arthur's realm, commanding penitence and calling doom on evil-doers – was standing on an upturned pail. He wore a sackcloth robe tied at the waist with a knotted rope. His bare feet were cut and dirty, his beard unkempt; his matted hair straggled down either side of a thin weasel-face. He held aloft a crucifix.

"Praise God for Earl Lucan," he called, "whose wrath the foul serpent shall taste!"

Further down the road, beyond the bridge over Wintering Beck, Lucan's own chaplain, Father Belisarius, stood beneath a yew tree, his two altar servers flanking him. Compared with the vagrant, he was resplendent in a hooded black habit, snow-white tabard and matching gauntlets. He, too, was praying, incanting in Latin, incense smoke curling from his thurible. A few yards on, Lucan's wife, Countess Trelawna, and five of her ladies were seated side-saddle on their palfreys. As it was a cold day they wore woollen gloves, taffeta cloaks over their tightly-fitted kirtles, and wimples and veils tied in place with bands of silk. Countess Trelawna was eight years younger than her husband, but now in the full flower of womanhood. Her hair was honeyed gold, and, when uncoiled, descended in tresses to her slender waist. Hers was a serene kind of beauty, very gentle, very childlike. Her nose was slightly upturned in a fetching elfin way, her lips full but soft. Her eyes were as blue as her husband's, yet infinitely kinder.

As Lucan rode by, their gazes met, and she smiled in her distant, wistful manner. Her ladies were more demonstrative. Those knights who weren't married would gallivant up to them in search of favours, which, in honour of the day, they were showered with.

"I suspect the countess fears for your safety, my lord," Turold said, a little embarrassed, as always, by his chatelaine's coolness to her husband.

Lucan was unmoved. "She needn't. Were I worried, I'd have called the host for battle."

"Loving wives rarely see such reality. Not when their husband's safety is at stake."

"Aye," Lucan grunted. "So I've heard."

He drew the broadsword from his hip and transferred it to the scabbard on his saddle, then kicked his horse forward, riding to catch up with those leading the hunt, many of whom were already spreading out into the wildwood. The gamekeepers beat their drums and blew their horns, spreading out in a line, the hounds gambolling ahead of them. Riding just behind them were Lucan's squire, Alaric, and his two closest companions, Benedict and Malvolio, respectively Turold's and Wulfstan's squires.

At eighteen, Alaric was the oldest and most serious-minded of the three. He was tall and spare of limb, but after his years of knightly training, had developed a strong, wedge-shaped body. He kept his brown hair short and his face clean of bristles. He was a fresh-faced lad, not exactly handsome, but for all his youth there was a manliness about him, which the local village girls had noticed. At sixteen and fifteen, Benedict and Malvolio were boys in comparison, the former thin and rangy but clean and handsome of aspect, the latter short and dumpy and somewhat less appealing. They wore their hair long but cut square at the shoulder as was the fashion at Court.

"YOU UNDERSTAND, ALARIC?" Malvolio chided him. "In these days of peace, there's no call for knights. If Earl Lucan were to knight you, it would cost him dear. A horse to call your own, an equestrian seal, full armour, full weaponry, a bed in the knights' hall. Why make such expense when all you'd be doing is exactly what you do now – loafing about the castle? Surely it would be more cost-effective to leave things as they are?"

"Alas, it's true," Benedict said. "The only time a knight is needed is when he must die heroically in battle. Isn't much of a life we've chosen for ourselves."

"It isn't much of a life Alaric has chosen," Malvolio said. "How often has he made that tiresome trip to Camelot, and had to stand in the ante-hall while his master is honoured at the Round Table... and yet here he is, unfit even for his master's table?"

Alaric smiled. It wouldn't be a normal day if they didn't

rile him, though there was often some truth in their jest. For all his success in the tourney – and Alaric had proved himself many times with sword and lance in sport – he knew his master believed that only war could test a man's true mettle. And Alaric had never yet fought in one. The last major crisis to afflict the kingdom had occurred when a vast horde of Danes had invaded along the River Humber. Arthur had triumphed, though it had seen a terrible slaughter on both sides. By nightfall, the crows were picking at five Danish kings, along with eight Knights of the Round Table, and maybe thirty thousand other men and ranks. Earl's Lucan's left eyebrow was still bisected by a hard, white scar where a Danish war-axe had cloven his helm.

But that had been a decade ago, when Alaric was still a lad. With so many widows and orphans made, it seemed wrong to wish for such perils to revisit the kingdom purely so that he might benefit. Instead, Alaric had hoped that with the advent of his eighteenth birthday, Earl Lucan might make an exception to his normal rule, but it seemed not.

He attempted to laugh. "At least I get a hunt to celebrate my coming of age."

"Aye," Malvolio agreed. "The Penharrow Worm would have been allowed to slither across the land, ravaging every farmstead, if it hadn't been for your birthday. The good people of the North owe you a boon for being born on the first day of March."

A call went up from along the line. The three squires steered their horses towards the call, ducking under low boughs, wading to the fetlocks through clumps of dew-soaked bracken. When they arrived, the earl's keepers were leaning on their quarterstaffs. In their midst, a foul fetor rose from a pile of fleshy organs and glistening, semi-liquid pulp. Splintered bones and cartilage were visible, woven into the mess along with scraps of black and white hide. A single hoof jutted out on a slender, fleshless shank.

One by one, the rest of the hunt gathered. At last, the men stood aside to allow Earl Lucan to dismount. He stood in silence, regarding the obscenity. When Wulfstan arrived, he sank to his haunches for several long moments, before standing up and searching the surrounding area. The circle of spectators widened to accommodate him.

At last he came back. "This is what it does, my lord – regurgitates its food."

"Regurgitates?" Lucan said.

There were grave mutters. The atmosphere of gaiety had diminished somewhat.

Wulfstan scratched his beard. "Evidently, it swallows its prey whole... but it would take a long while to fully digest a beast of this size. It would become sluggish and might even curl up and sleep, which would leave it vulnerable out here in the open. So it absorbs what it can, and then, as I say, vomits up the remains and continues on its way."

Silence filled the glade. Men cast nervy glances over their shoulders.

"How long since it was here?" Lucan asked.

Wulfstan probed the rubble with his finger. "There's more than a whiff of decay. I'd say a day, maybe a day and a half."

"Plenty of time for it to re-ensconce itself."

Wulfstan nodded grimly.

"Can you track it?"

"Yes, my lord. Now that we have a starting point. The last place it attacked was the hamlet at Hubblewell. That means it's heading due northeast... for the Flint Axes.

"Over the last few weeks livestock was destroyed at Godhall, Langbourne and Wathby. Those are also within easy striking range of the Axes."

"You're thinking what I'm thinking?" Lucan said.

"I believe so, my lord. It's using Dungeon Ghyll as its lair."

There were sharp intakes of breath among the knights.

The borderland between Arthur's kingdom and the pagan realm of Rheged was mainly wilderness. From Penharrow to Hadrian's Wall, from Carlisle to Durham, it consisted almost entirely of trackless moor, foggy mountain and fathomless wood. There were many ways for an unwary traveller to die out here, but there were also places that even local folk would avoid – places like Dungeon Ghyll.

It was a geographical oddity even in this land of extremes: a labyrinth of crags, defiles and deep, water-filled caverns, covering about six square miles. It was much overgrown with trees and vegetation, many of its channels so narrow and so thick with undergrowth that they were almost impassable. It occupied high ground at the far northern end of Penharrow Vale, and was accessible in various ways, though on the south it was bordered by the so-called 'Flint Axes,' a row of three towering rock forms shaped like the blades of axe-heads.

"Very well." Lucan swung up into the saddle. "This changes things. We advance to the Ghyll, but there are many paths through it, and we need to cover them all. So we divide into separate groups when we arrive there. No party is to have less than five men."

There were muted protests from some of his knights, who, though they weren't girt for war, were still affronted by the suggestion that this monster might be too much for them. Lucan called them to silence, pointing at the mass of festering offal.

"This was once a full-grown cow. Up to now we've been told only of sheep and goats, but clearly that was wrong. No group is to consist of less than five men. You people on foot..." He turned not just to his beaters and keepers, but to the villagers and foresters who'd followed with bills and reaping hooks. "None of you are to enter the Ghyll. Instead, blockade as many of its exits as you can find. And no noise from this point. We aren't going to frighten this creature out into the open, so we've a better chance coming on it unawares. From here on, we keep the pack to the rear."

They proceeded more stealthily. The mist seemed to thicken, and icy dew dripped from the interlaced branches overhead. Within an hour they'd reached the Flint Axes, which towered over the treetops as they approached. All joy of the hunt had fled. Every man felt a discomfiting distance from home. In silence, they formed their separate groups.

There were various ways to enter the Ghyll, either through low clefts or high passes. Two routes led through the Axes themselves, parallel passages cluttered with scree. It was one of these that Lucan opted for, now in company with Turold, Benedict and two other knights.

"Good luck, everyone," Lucan said, as they went their separate ways.

He and his party filed through one tight, V-shaped valley. In some parts it was barren, in others thick with thorns. There was silence, save for the cawing of crows or the skittering of pebbles dislodged from, on high. Their eyes roved in every direction. Veils of mist continued to pass over them.

The same experience was shared one valley over by Wulfstan, Alaric, Malvolio and two other house-men. Their path descended deeply. Grykes appeared to either side: yawning fractures in the cliff-sides, from below which they heard an immense churning of water. What few trees there were, were bent and gnarled. Underfoot, a shifting moraine could snag a hoof or snap an ankle, and indeed, when an eagle screeched as it lofted overhead, Alaric's mount panicked and turned sharply, from which point it developed a limp. Examination revealed that it had thrown a shoe.

"You'll have to proceed on foot," Wulfstan said, in the tone of irritation he used with all the squires. "Either that or go back."

Alaric stiffened. "I'm not going back."

Wulfstan climbed into his saddle. "We won't be racing ahead. It shouldn't be too hard to stay in touch. But don't slouch."

Malvolio watched sympathetically while Alaric tethered his horse to a bough, took his bow and a hunting spear, and slung a quiver of arrows over his shoulder. They continued in single file. Only a slice of sky was visible between the parapets of rock overhead. It grew colder as the path meandered downward; soon they were pressing through mist so dense that the horsemen ahead of Alaric became dim silhouettes. When the passage suddenly broadened out and he found himself slogging through knee-deep water, his companions were rendered indistinguishable from the skeletal outlines of willows, which clustered around them, their bony fingers trailing in the pools and bogs.

"Everyone mind your footing," Wulfstan muttered. "Particularly you, Malvolio. Malvolio? Malvolio... where are you?"

There was no response, though a heavy splashing could be heard to their left. Or was it behind them? It was difficult to tell.

"Damn!" Wulfstan snapped. "Where are you, boy? Blast it! The rest of you, hold up!"

They wheeled their animals around as they searched for the errant squire. Alaric couldn't believe it. They'd only just entered this swampy area; it seemed impossible that in so short a time even a buffoon like Malvolio could have got himself lost.

IN FACT, MALVOLIO didn't consider that he was lost – not as such.

He'd veered away from the others in order to take advantage of the broader passage, only to find himself deeper in the marsh. His horse, a wilful young mare with the unlikely name of Rosebud, had taken it on herself to find drier ground. She'd plunged another ten yards to their left, found firmer footing and proceeded uphill despite his best efforts to turn her round again. The next thing he knew, he was pushing through matted thickets, which clawed at his clothes and face. It seemed to take minutes to reach higher, flatter ground, where the mist abruptly melted away.

He had entered a woodland clearing, sheltered beneath a mighty oak but with a cliff face at its far end, in the centre of which a cave yawned. He managed to rein up, and glanced over his shoulder. Vapour ebbed through the meshed branches behind him. He wanted to call out, but something stopped him. He glanced back at the pitch-dark cave. Cautiously, he dismounted and approached on foot, one hand gripping the hilt of his sword, and halted about ten yards away. He peered further into the depths, seeing a low, jagged ceiling mottled with lichen, an earthen floor strewn with dried branches. A stale smell seeped from the cave – the dankness of the underworld, no doubt. He pictured endless caverns, their slimy walls thick with fungus and spider-webs.

Then two things struck him.

Firstly – he was being watched. From somewhere in the bowels of that cave, a baleful gaze was fixed on him.

Secondly, what he'd thought were dry sticks were actually bones.

Malvolio sensed the thing coming down the cave before he saw it. And he heard it too: a sudden rushing of air; a whisper of leathery flesh; and a savage *hisss* like a jet of gas erupting from the earth. He turned and fled across the clearing – only to find that Rosebud, evidently more sensitive to these things than he was, was already capering off through the trees. From the corner of his eye, he glimpsed an enormous shape emerge into the daylight. As he ran, Malvolio screamed.

LUCAN HAD SEPARATED from his own group to give his mount fresher water to drink. He was in the saddle alongside a burn running downhill through a steep gorge. Thirty yards below him, the others had made temporary camp among a stand of pines.

At first he thought he'd imagined the distant, echoing cry. Curious, he manoeuvred his animal around.

There was a second, louder cry. He glanced down to the pinewood. Turold and the others were moving on. He shouted, but the acoustics in the enclosed place were difficult; he couldn't be sure whether they'd heard him or not. But there was no time to waste. He urged his horse up the boulder-strewn passage. At the top, he crossed the burn. When he reached the other side, he heard a third cry. This one was clear and high-pitched. Lucan cursed; it could only be Malvolio. He spurred his horse to a gallop, weaving through the thickets until he spied open ground.

Lucan's first thought on entering the clearing was that he should have called the retinue out for battle rather than a holiday hunt. He also wished that he was riding Nightshade, his great warhorse, rather than this easy-natured brute. Because what he now faced was a vastly more terrifying opponent than any of them had expected.

The rambling nonsense they'd heard from the few frightened farmers who'd seen the creature had referred to "an ungodly demon, with hunger both for man and beast" – a common enough exaggeration, in complete contrast to the physical evidence, which had suggested that the so-called Penharrow Worm had sought to prey on smaller animals. And yet this monster was perhaps fifty yards long – its coils almost filled the clearing, and it was as thick around the middle as a beer keg. It had a tough, scaly hide, tinged muddy brown, with a white diamond pattern running down its spine. It was now rearing up towards Malvolio, who, though he'd already climbed high into an oak, was clearly about to be dragged to his death.

Lucan's mount went wild with fright, and it was all he could do to pull it to order. He didn't bother nocking an arrow; from this range, he was unlikely to penetrate its armour-plated skin. Instead, he cast his bow aside, drew his hunting spear and shouted at the top of his voice as he galloped across the clearing, veering around and behind the monster to distract it away from the boy.

It spun to face him.

Its countenance was truly devilish – it was flat-headed and broad-mouthed, and its eyes were soulless baubles of emerald hate. With a deafening *hisss*, its jaws gaped, revealing a flickering forked tongue and cavernous mouth that were both jet-black, and a pair of fangs that were at least a foot long and curved like sabres. Yellow fluid bubbled from their tips.

Lucan closed on the serpent's flank, and it turned to face

him. Shrieking in terror, his horse vaulted over its body, before he pulled it deftly to the right, now galloping straight for the oak tree. As he did, he hurled his spear, but it caught the beast at a poor angle and glanced harmlessly from its thick scales. Of all the horrors he'd faced in Arthur's service, there'd been nothing of this magnitude. Without his armour, Lucan felt no shame in admitting that it was time for flight rather than fight.

"Jump, lad!" he roared. Malvolio was perched directly overhead. "Behind me!"

Malvolio had watched bug-eyed as Lucan had navigated around the clearing. He'd seen the monster loop back on itself, but its vast, sinuous body had now shifted position, and it was coiling to strike.

"My lord!" he wailed as he descended.

Lucan leaned forward, pressing into the pommel of his saddle. Malvolio fell heavily into position behind him. The horse, shocked by the impact, squealed and bucked, giving the serpent all the delay it needed. Thrusting itself in a blur of motion, it snapped its jaws shut, a single fang puncturing the right sleeve of Lucan's pelisson, sinking into his shoulder and lodging there. With his horse driving onward, Lucan was yanked sideways from its back. Malvolio was almost buffeted from the saddle as well, but managed to hang on. The next thing Lucan knew, the leafy ground had struck him, driving the wind from his body. In the process he became detached from the serpent's tooth, and rolled away.

Again its massive jaws slammed shut, this time missing him by inches.

He leapt to his feet and doubled back, running alongside the monster's trunk, leaping over it as it twisted in pursuit. He grasped at his hip, only to find an empty scabbard. He swore; he'd left his sword on his horse.

He glanced back to see the serpent bunching for another strike, its tongue flickering. Beyond it, the diminutive shape of Malvolio struggled to stay on the terrified horse as it bounded off into the wood.

Lucan cast around for something else he could use. Nothing lay nearby, not even a stone or rotted branch. To his left was the yawning mouth of the cave; evidently the creature's lair. Aside from that, it was a rugged rock-face coated with thorns and briars – not climbable in the time he had.

He swung back to face the monster.

It slid towards him, its head low. Its gaze was almost hypnotic.

Lucan locked eyes with it. It seemed to hesitate, and he couldn't help wondering if it was relishing the moment. Did it understand that he was the ruler of these lands? Did it realise the extent of its victory, and was it pleased?

For Lucan's own part, he felt only regret: that he hadn't done better things in his life; that there weren't kinder words he could have spoken to his friends, and above all to his wife. It was a familiar sensation. He'd known it from a hundred battlefields past, when he'd thought he was facing death. And he responded now in the way he always did – standing tall, shoulders back. He clawed his hands as though ready to grapple his way through his final minutes, although he knew it would be futile. As did the serpent.

It struck with numbing speed, lashing its entire body forward – and at the same time it was hit in the left eye by an arrow, slanting down from the top of the rock-face.

The eye burst in a welter of green putrescence.

The monster reared to a colossal height, its black tongue rigid in its gaping maw and its prolonged *hisss* taking on a painfully shrill note. It whipped back, folding over itself, and crossed the clearing, its body writhing and twisting in agony, loops passing from its snout to its tail.

Lucan turned, and saw Alaric scrambling down a steep crevice in the rocks, tripping and sliding through the briars and mulch. As he reached the ground he threw aside his bow, hefted his spear and launched it. It struck the serpent squarely in the open mouth, piercing its head clean through, driving the flat head backward and pinning it to the bole of the oak.

"My... my lord!" Alaric cried, seemingly stunned by his success.

"Sword!" Lucan roared. *"Sword!"*

Alaric, flushed and gleaming with sweat, took a moment to realise what his master had asked; he drew his sword and threw it. Lucan caught it and dashed across the clearing. Alaric pulled a hunting-knife from his boot and stumbled after him.

The transfixed monster thrashed its body, throwing such immense coils of muscle and scale at them that a clean blow would have crushed the marrow from their bones. But Lucan was elusive, darting to and fro as he ran, and – once he was upon it – chopping and hacking, his gleaming blade rending through scaly flesh and pink sinew, ignoring the blood that spurted over him, ignoring the yellow venom that gurgled from either side of the monstrosity's open mouth – until at last, with a sickening *crunch*, its spine came apart. Abruptly, it dropped in a heap, the tip of its tail quivering for a moment before lying still. Lucan didn't halt, sawing and slicing until, with a little help from Alaric, he'd entirely separated the head from the torso.

Seconds passed before they turned and regarded each other, breathing hoarsely. Steam enveloped them both, rising from their own sweat rather than the blood that spattered them, which had never been warm in the first place.

Alaric crouched and tentatively peered into the rents in the serpent's body.

"If you're looking for your friend, he's quite safe." Lucan rested his hands on the pommel of the sword. "He made sure of that himself."

Alaric stood up and mopped the sweat from his brow.

"We had to spread out to find him," he explained. "It's a good thing I was on foot. Sir Wulfstan sent me to look up there along the ridge. Otherwise, I'd never..."

"It's also a good thing you were brave. Not to mention quick-thinking."

"To be honest, my lord, I acted without thinking."

"That's the way it should be with a warrior."

Alaric now saw the hole ripped in the upper sleeve of Lucan's pelisson, and fresh blood coursing over his hand.

"My lord, you're hurt."

"It's nothing. A nick."

"If that creature bit you..."

"It's a nick." Lucan smiled – or attempted to. He was ash-pale. "So how does it feel to be eighteen *and* a hero? Until now only Arthur has been able to answer that."

"My lord, I think the venom..."

"It's not important. You realise you've just saved your lord's life, Alaric?"

"Erm, yes... I suppose." Only now was it striking the squire what he'd done. He'd prevented the death, not just of his lifelong friend and mentor, but of a full-fledged Knight of the Round Table.

"So now I have to reward you," Lucan said. "I wonder what might be a suitable accolade." His complexion had worsened. Faint shudders passed through him as he spoke. "Why don't we put it to a vote at tonight's birthday banquet?"

"Of course, my lord, but I..."

"Very well." Lucan wiped the sword on a clump of grass, and handed it back. He held out his hand for Alaric's hunting-horn, and blew a long blast on it, though it lacked his normal gusto.

"My lord, I think you need to rest."

"Nonsense." Lucan indicated the serpent's head, still speared to the tree. "And be sure to bring your trophy. Without the evidence, they'll have us down as story-tellers."

"They'd never believe that of you, my lord."

"But they might of you." Lucan smiled again, but it was strained. When Alaric lugged the spear free, and Lucan tried to catch the serpent's head, he winced in agony, clutching his wound. "No matter." He laughed, though his face was a sweat-soaked grimace. "You're a man now, Alaric. *You* can be my strong right arm."

Alaric knew that his master spoke in jest, but there was something disturbing in that notion. More than he could possibly say.

TWO

Countess Trelawna and her ladies were resting by Wintering Beck, enjoying their noon picnic. Servants had brought a wickerwork hamper from the castle, and the ladies were enjoying sweetmeats and fresh crusty rolls, and sipping from goblets of watered wine. The sky was clear, the sun high, and at last there was a modicum of warmth. The Countess reclined on a blanket amid the roots of an ancient willow. Next to the stream, two of her ladies tittered as they played *jeu de paume*.[7]

Gerta, Countess Trelawna's long-serving handmaid, was seated on a lichen-covered stone, her wizened features narrowed in concentration as she worked at her embroidery. The rest of the ladies were seated on the grass. They passed a book between themselves, reciting tales from the *Chansons*.[8] Countess Trelawna, a devotee of the *Cult d'Amor*, closed her eyes and dreamed of foreign courts in sun-drenched climes: of magnificent, tile-roofed chateaux, their grand halls and galleries done in white and gold plaster, their balconied apartments overlooking vineyards and orange groves, or green

[7] Literally "the palm game." The medieval forerunner of tennis. In Malory's time, *paume* was still played empty handed or with gloves; racquets would start to appear in the next century.

[8] The *Chansons de Geste*, or "Songs of Deeds," were a genre of epic French poetry, telling the stories of great heroes of the past. Again, Malory is emphasising England as a home of culture, at odds with the Romans' perception of the country as backwards and barbaric.

lawns decked with the pavilions of adventuring troubadours, who had travelled from far and wide to win the hearts of blushing damsels.

Currently, Annette was reading: "'And when the joust was complete, Sir Yvo stood before the royal banner, quartered with its blue dragon, golden hind, crimson lion and milk-white unicorn, and made each of his vanquished foes – great knights and barons all – bow once to the north, once to the south, once to the east and once to the west in honour of his lady, who was far away, but closer to his heart than she had been in many a long year...'"

Trelawna was easily lulled from the reality of her world; the harsh, snow-capped mountains and dark, pine-filled valleys, and the rugged stronghold that was her home. A home where the only ornaments were hanging weapons and antlered skulls, where animal hides were needed to maintain warmth in the winter, and a smothering, kiln-like atmosphere pervaded in summer. In truth, it would not have taken the gilded words of a *jongleur* to lure her away from all that.

"My lady, I think something is wrong," Annette said, closing the book.

Trelawna glanced towards the forest, and saw the first of the hunting party emerge. She rose to her feet. "So early?"

Even from a distance, little celebration could be seen. Men rode slowly or led their horses on foot. Hounds walked with their masters. There was no singing, no triumphal shouting. A chill touched the countess that had nothing to do with the melt-water flooding down Wintering Beck.

THOUGH HE WAS loath at any time to be seen an invalid, Lucan struggled not to fall from his destrier. The serpent's severed head, now bound in a leather sack and drawn behind him on a cart, was all but forgotten. The men's voices became muted as their overlord swayed in his saddle. Only when he was a few yards from them did Trelawna and her entourage recognise him; one or two of the ladies stifled squeals. He was spattered with gore, both his own and the serpent's, but he'd paled to a ghostly hue and his hair was matted with sweat.

"Ladies," he said, reining up with a courtly gesture. "My lovely wife..." And he tumbled from the saddle, only the diligence of his men preventing him striking the ground. Trelawna grabbed her skirts and dashed forward, but already her husband was fighting his way back to his feet. He tried to smile as she took his hands, but was in too much pain. When others assisted, he became irritable, shrugging them off.

"The Penharrow Worm, my lady," Turold explained. He stepped aside as his overlord pushed past him, determined to walk to the castle unaided. "It caught him with its fang."

Trelawna gasped.

"I doubt there's anything to fear, ma'am," Wulfstan said, dismounting. "It's only a small wound. He's suffered much worse in the past."

Trelawna gazed at the object on the cart. The neck of the sack had fallen open, and the serpent regarded her with its one remaining eye, which even glazed with death was hypnotic in its lustre.

"How... how did this happen?" she stammered. "Someone tell me... Alaric!"

Her husband's squire was leading his limping horse by the bridle. He, too, was pale and daubed with blood. He described the event as best he could, playing down his own role.

"You were present when my lord was bitten?" Trelawna asked, clasping his shoulders.

Alaric nodded awkwardly. He didn't like to meet her gaze these days, for fear it would reveal too much. She'd always behaved with him the way a mother would, fond and fussing, but Alaric didn't regard her so in return. He was on the cusp of manhood, and his adolescent adoration of Trelawna was increasingly replaced by a confused but fierce yearning. "It's true what Sir Wulfstan says, my lady. The serpent only caught him a glancing blow."

From further up the track came gruff shouting, as Lucan insisted that people take their hands off him. He pushed his men away, growling like a bear. This was not the way Lucan routinely treated his vassals, and those who witnessed it knew for certain that he was more badly hurt than he was admitting.

"This monster?" she said. "He stood against it alone?"

"He killed it, my lady," Alaric replied. "It was the greatest act of bravery I ever saw."

"My lady, forgive me," came another voice. It was Benedict, now struggling with several horses whose masters had hurried off on foot to assist their lord. "Alaric does himself an injustice. It was *his* arrow that pierced the monster's eye, *his* hunting spear that pinioned it to a tree. As Earl Lucan saved Malvolio's life, so Alaric saved Earl Lucan's."

Trelawna gazed wonderingly from one lad to the other.

"I know this to be true," Benedict added, "because your husband proclaimed it so."

"You saved my husband, Alaric?" she asked.

Alaric shrugged. "I was only doing my duty, ma'am."

Her sad smile betrayed a mother's pride, which tore at his insides. "There are many who have used that phrase to disguise evil deeds, Alaric. You, however, grace it. As your deeds grace your birthday. Today is your coming of age in many ways."

She planted a kiss on his brow, before turning to an attendant who had brought up her palfrey. She climbed onto the saddle, and trotted away.

Alaric hung his head, cheeks burning.

"Beware, my friend," Benedict said. "Unrequited love is always the worst."

Alaric glanced round at him. "So speaks the voice of experience?"

"Of course. I love *all* women, but only a few reciprocate. Hence I know what I'm talking about."

"You're being presumptuous, Ben."

"I've got eyes, haven't I? And so have others around here. You need to be careful."

Alaric assisted him with the horses. "You think I would do anything improper?"

"The heart is a treacherous master."

Alaric gripped his wrist. "My master is Earl Lucan, Steward of the North! I would never do anything to dishonour him!"

Gingerly, Benedict disentangled himself from the bloodstained paw. "Let's hope he lives long enough for you to keep that promise."

THREE

Despite Lucan's orders that Alaric's birthday feast should go ahead, it was not to be.

For the rest of that day, a severe sickness struck the injured nobleman. On his return to Penharrow, Trelawna herself attended to his wounds. During her many years on this wild border, she'd lost count of the number of times she'd stitched him. Thanks to the tutelage of Morgan Tud, a famed physic of the Royal Court, who had studied at Salerno, she knew how to draw poison from a freshly infected wound, but in Lucan's case the point where the serpent had bitten him was already so putrid that she dared not touch it, neither with needle, nor knife, nor hot iron.

She washed the wound as gently as she could, an experience her husband bore through with gritted teeth, and patched it with clean linen and a poultice. She advised that Lucan rest, but he had other ideas, insisting on striding around the castle, ordering fresh rushes to be laid on the floor of the main hall, having the fires built up and advising his kitchen-staff and his minstrels that tonight would be an opportunity for them to impress him with their talents. He alternately sweated and shivered, and if it was possible – and some, appalled, said it was not – he grew even whiter of hue. When he attempted either to eat or drink, he suffered bouts of dizziness.

"I swear to you, Alaric," he said, "tonight your heroism will be proclaimed."

Alaric nodded and smiled, secretly horror-struck by his master's pale face and unfocused eyes. Trelawna watched from behind her husband's back, the fingers of both hands laced tightly.

It seemed only fitting that the serpent's head should take pride of place during the feast. After all, this was the first real trophy Alaric had participated in capturing. But it was a grisly object, still dribbling its vile fluids, its jaws locked open in a yawning gape that could swallow a man whole. Some of Countess Trelawna's ladies felt faint on looking at it; a serving maid shrieked and a dropped a tray of crockery. Lucan thus decided that it could be shut in the ice-house until the following morning, at which point tanners would be summoned from one of the villages so the ghastly shape could be rendered and mounted. But the servants were loath to touch it, so the earl opted to carry it out himself, at which point his shoulder gave way. The pain that lanced through his upper body took the breath from his lungs, and it was all he could do to keep his feet. Again, sweat streamed from Lucan's face; blood, freshly shed but brackish with impurity, burst through the poultice and drenched his loose-fitting tunic.

Trelawna took charge and ordered that he be conveyed to his bed.

For the rest of that day he lay stripped to his braies, insensible. Trelawna had no option but to defy his orders, and delay the evening celebrations. In response, he only mumbled, his eyelids fluttering. At length, she closed the door on the chamber and turned to the small group of officials assembled in the adjoining passage.

There stood Father Belisarius, Godric, the chief steward, Hubert, the earl's chamberlain and treasurer, and Brother Oswy, his scribe and chronicler. Of the fighting household, Turold was present, along with Wulfstan and Gerwin, Lucan's knight-commander, who had ridden in from his own estate, and Guthlac, captain of the Castle Guard. Also present were Cadelaine and Brione, the castellans of the earl's subsidiary fortresses at Grimhall and Bullwood.

"There is no point in my lying to you," she said, regarding them with the cool authority she'd seen her husband adopt in times of crisis. "You know Earl Lucan well enough to recognise that he is seriously ill. As we speak he is gripped by a frightful fever. It may break during the course of the night, but at present it is impossible to make predictions. All we can do is watch and wait. Father Belisarius, your prayers would not go amiss."

The chaplain nodded soberly.

"My lady," Turold said, "among the White Canons at Thornbrook Abbey there is a certain Brother Callisa, a skilled surgeon and physician who trained in the same schools as Morgan Tud. He is elderly now and a recluse, but he worked among the wounded on the River Humber, and achieved miracles."

"Thornbrook Abbey is two days ride from here," Trelawna said. "But in the absence of any other choice... Wulfstan, send a rider to Thornbrook."

Wulfstan nodded and withdrew.

The countess fixed the rest of the group with a stern eye. "In the meantime, we sound no death-knells yet. Turold, I hear they are donning mail and weapons in the Knights' Hall. They must desist at once. No vigils are to be held tonight. It was the Penharrow Worm who lost the fight today," Trelawna reminded them, "no-one else. Earl Lucan is strong, and we have Father Belisarius and Brother Oswy to sing a Mass by his bedside."

Once the remainder of the party had been dispatched to their quarters, she admitted the two clerics to the bedchamber, where they burned purification herbs in the grate – honeysuckle, rhubarb and dried rose-petals – and lit candles of healing. Even when the holy men began to chant, their overlord did not stir. He lay in deep sleep, glazed with icy sweat. Even by the dull red candle-glow, he remained shockingly pale. At last Trelawna withdrew to one of the guest-chambers, where Gerta prepared her for sleep, which did not come easily.

She dreamed that she was fleeing through the gnarled trees cramming the nooks and channels of Dungeon Ghyll, and that something dreadful was following her – something vaguely like a man though several feet taller than any man had ever been, and covered with a shaggy pelt of silver-grey fur. It roared and snarled, uprooting tree-trunks and snapping boughs, while Trelawna struggled to make any headway, her night-gown and hair catching on twigs. Her pursuer's Herculean roars echoed through the twisting ravines as it drew closer. The thudding impacts of its feet sounded right behind her –

And then she realised the truth, and her eyes snapped open.

She rose from her pillow as Annette entered her chamber unbidden. "Forgive me, my lady. There's a matter of some importance."

"My husband?" Trelawna asked.

"Not your husband... he still sleeps. But a messenger has arrived."

"What hour is it?"

"Shortly before three, ma'am."

"A messenger, at this time?"

"He carries the Royal Seal."

Trelawna drew on a shawl, and hurried to the courtyard gantry. Torches burned below, where a groom led away a lathered, steaming horse. Its rider was pacing distractedly. He'd removed his feathered cap, to let loose a hank of blond, sweat-soaked hair, and wore a green, travel-stained cloak over a doublet, hose and leather riding-boots. An empty scabbard hung over his back – his sword must have been surrendered to the gatekeepers on arrival. Members of the Night-Guard stood close by, spears brandished. Turold had also been roused. He wore breeches, slippers and a cloak, and had buckled on a sword-belt.

"Who are you?" Trelawna asked, descending.

The newcomer turned abruptly. He was a youngish man, ruddy-faced but unshaven, an indication of the time he had spent on the road. Briefly he seemed captivated by the sight of her. This may have been because he had been expecting the earl, though it was often the response of men who had never met Countess Trelawna before. In her night-time attire, wearing only a simple woollen gown cinched at her narrow waist, a shawl around her shoulders and with her long, honey-gold hair hanging in a single braid, her beauty seemed that much more homely.

He bowed. "My name is Crispin, my lady. Of the family Roncesvalles. If you are Countess Trelawna – and forgive me, you could only be she – I have urgent news for your husband."

"You have ridden all the way from Camelot?"

"Yes, my lady. I have barely stopped these last five days."

"Five days?" Trelawna was astonished. "Have you eaten, slept?"

"I've ate the few supplies I carried whilst on the road, ma'am. As for sleep, I took naps in haystacks and cowsheds."

"I think we can do better than that." Trelawna turned. Godric, sleepy-eyed and looking even more corpulent than usual in a voluminous night-shirt, had now arrived. "Our steward will provide you with..."

"My lady, there is no time," Crispin interrupted. "I must speak with your husband."

Trelawna regarded him carefully. "This is a serious matter?"

The messenger seemed discomfited. He scanned the gantries, clearly seeking Earl Lucan, but finding no-one. Finally, he opened a pouch and produced a scroll, tightly bound with the royal emblem. "I have an Extraordinary Summons for your husband, ma'am. He is to attend a Royal Council straight away."

"I'm afraid my husband is in no fit state to make such a journey."

The messenger's face fell. "He is ill?"

"A hunting accident yesterday."

"Ma'am, the King has issued an *Extraordinary* Summons, which means that..."

"Which means that only in the most extreme circumstances may it be refused. I'm fully aware of this."

"Forgive me. Is your husband very badly hurt?"

"We fear he may die."

There was a brief silence during which the messenger's face visibly fell. "These... these are grave tidings."

"Your kindness is appreciated. But Crispin, you seem inordinately affected. Did you know my husband?"

"I know his quality, and the truth is the King has need of him."

"How so?"

"Ma'am. I am only a messenger. It's not my place to..."

"I am Earl Lucan's official representative, so any message you had for my husband will be safe with me." Crispin regarded her nervously, torn by indecision. "Crispin!" Her voice hardened. "If you will not give me the message, I would deem it a politeness if, at the very least, you would explain why you deem it such a disaster that my husband is ill."

"That part is simple, ma'am. Your husband commands the North. That's an easy phrase to utter, of course, but in Earl Lucan's case it is actually true. His lands buttress all the central region of this northern border, which is perhaps the most difficult to govern in the whole of Britain..."

"In my husband's absence, I command the North, Crispin. As he cannot attend this Royal Council, I shall do it for him."

Crispin looked startled. "Ma'am?"

"As you doubtless know, we were not blessed with children. My husband has no son or heir. Therefore I will take his position."

Crispin glanced at the earl's steward and *banneret*, who both regarded him steadily.

"If this is a War Council," Trelawna said, "I will not and never would presume to take my husband's seat at the Round Table. But I see no additional document to call a muster, so I must assume we are not at war. If you are merely seeking the advice of the North, I am the only person qualified to give it."

"What's this?" came a voice from the top of the stair.

They glanced up and saw Lucan. He still wore only his braies, though a blanket was swathed around his shoulders. He gripped the balustrade with one hand, but seemed otherwise steady as he descended. His hair and body were damp, but he was breathing easily and, when he alighted in the courtyard, his eyes – so fogged with delirium earlier – had cleared.

"WHAT'S THIS?" HE said again, apparently vexed. But then his face cracked into a broad grin. He even laughed, though it made him cough. "Did any man have so brave a wife?" He approached Trelawna and put his arm around her. "You would go among these lions on my behalf?"

"My lord," she replied, "you seem to have regained your strength."

"I slept well. At least until those priests you stationed in our chamber awoke me with their snoring."

"You've not regained your colour..."

"One can't have everything." Lucan turned to the messenger. "Your name is Crispin?"

"It is, Earl Lucan. I understood you were injured..."

"Don't concern yourself. I'm fit enough to travel. My wife was doing exactly as she ought to in these circumstances. Mind, she should have realised by now that no serpent venom is a match for the blood Corneus."

Trelawna shook her head as if this was boyish nonsense. Crispin nodded curtly, and handed over the scroll. Lucan tore it open and read through it.

When he closed it again, he was smiling. "So the Romans are coming."

"The Romans...?" Trelawna whispered.

"Special envoys will shortly arrive from New Rome," Crispin explained.

"*New* Rome is it now?" Lucan said. "The men from the Tiber think they can disguise their intentions simply by putting on new clothes."

Crispin shrugged. "They say they want peace."

"We already have peace. Do we need their permission for it to continue?"

"The King has been asking the same question. This is why he seeks the advice of his magnates."

"We'll be facing these dogs across the Council chamber, will we?" Lucan said.

"The King hopes the matter can be resolved without acrimony."

Lucan smiled again. "It may be, or it may not. The Romans have recovered much lost territory, but they've met no real opposition as yet. The question is, do they realise that? You perform your office well, sirrah. Godric... make sure this fellow has food, drink and a comfortable bed."

"Your lordship is too kind," Crispin replied. "But I'll be leaving at the first cockcrow. What might I tell the King?"

"Tell him we'll be leaving at the second."

Crispin nodded, satisfied, and allowed himself to be led away. Trelawna put a hand on her husband's chest, and then on his brow.

"Are you sure about this?" she asked.

He rubbed the back of his neck. "Truth is, I'm burned out inside. I don't know what that means exactly. I'm light-headed. Feel like I'm stuffed with hay..."

"It's perhaps to be expected."

"It's an improvement on earlier. Anyway, I'll be fine by morning. If not, what does it matter? I won't be walking to Camelot."

"I'll be coming with you," she said.

Lucan looked surprised. "You fear I may drop dead on the road?"

"I'm your wife, and I'll be with you."

"I'd have no other chaperone," he said, leaning down and kissing her lips. She reciprocated – a little. No doubt his unkempt state was putting her off.

By God, but she was such a beauty. He gazed down on her, awed yet again that he had ever found so handsome a bride, and at the same time stricken to his heart that she could never feel quite the same way about him that he felt about her.

He'd been a much younger man when, in a single-combat between champions, fighting on behalf of Arthur, he had killed Alain d'Abato, the famous Frankish warrior. Trelawna, d'Abato's daughter, was already without a mother, and had been left facing, at best a wardship, at worst destitution. Lucan had done the honourable thing and taken her hand in marriage. Naturally, she'd hated him at first, but time was a healer in many ways. Gradually, as he'd cared for her and given her a new place in the world, she'd come to have affection for him, and certainly to respect him, but love – well, love was not some gift you could bestow upon a person. Either you held it for them, or you didn't.

"I watched from the gantry as you spoke for me," he said. "It made my hair stand on end. 'This isn't just a noblewoman,' I said to myself. 'This is a noblewoman of the North.'"

"You need to rest," she replied.

"No, we've an early start. I must assemble the household."

"You may leave that to me..."

"Trelawna..."

"Am I not chatelaine at Penharrow? When I step into your spurs and couch your lance for the charge, you may assemble our house."

He laughed, while his wife bade servants assist him to their bed-chamber. Lucan assured them he could mount the stair himself, though he still took careful, prudent steps, and the servants, marshalled by Turold, hovered close behind.

GERTA AMBLED FORTH carrying a warmer shawl for her mistress, and a goblet of mulled wine. "A pretty show, my lamb," she said, as Trelawna donned the wrap and drank.

Detecting a tone, Trelawna glanced round at her. "Gerta?"

"The Romans are coming and now we are Camelot-bound."

"Pray, don't misspeak yourself, Gerta. This is a serious matter."

"No doubt. In more ways than anyone can know."

Trelawna handed back the empty goblet, but seized Gerta by the wrist.

"My mother's maid also had the habit of speaking out of turn," she said quietly. "One day, when my mother was a child, my grandfather was vexed by some trivial naughtiness... and whipped her little bottom until it bled. Her maid could hold back no longer and scolded him. By the end of that day, she would never scold anyone again because she had no tongue in her head."

"A harsh lesson," Gerta acknowledged.

"Which any servant may learn at any time," Trelawna said, releasing her.

"So please you... if it will make you feel better about what you are planning."

"I plan nothing except to support my husband in this most urgent matter."

"As you wish, my dove."

"I am not your dove!" the countess hissed. "I am your *mistress*. It's time you remembered that."

"Of course, mistress," Gerta said, curtseying as much as her cynical old bones would allow. "With the marks I still carry on my nipples from your days of greedy suckling, how could I have forgotten?"

FOUR

"THIS WOMAN, NEPHEW," Bishop Malconi said, "the one you think you love...?"

"I *know* I love her," Rufio replied, though he had to shout to be heard over the tumultuous acclaim being heaped on the procession as it wound its way between the tall, timber-and-wattle houses of Camelot's residential district. Some of the thoroughfares were so narrow that they had to move in single-file, though they also crossed open squares and esplanades, lined with fruit trees and hung with banners and bunting, all thronged with onlookers.

"You *know* you love her?" Bishop Malconi raised an eyebrow. "After one night of passion?"

Rufio smiled to himself. "Sometimes one night is all it takes."

It was a stately procession. Its mounted vanguard consisted of three clarion-blowing heralds wearing red and green striped hose, red berets with green plumes and red satin tabards slashed with green. Behind them rode three cavalry officers, unarmed but clad in polished breastplates and greaves over red jacks and open-faced sallet helms with sharp steel crests. The rest of the parade was slightly less formal: the churchmen, with the exception of Bishop Malconi, rode in gilded carriages, but without their vestments or mitres, preferring daytime robes of velvet and taffeta, with skullcaps and chains of office. Rufio, like the other non-clerics in the embassy, had joyfully surrendered to the new Italian fashions, choosing a tight-fitting burgundy doublet over a collarless linen shirt, canary yellow hose and leather ankle-boots with long, pointed toes, an ensemble which girt his trim, youthful figure well.[9]

Lines of Arthur's halberdiers, wearing white tabards embossed with the red dragon, held the excited crowds back. Overhead, folk leaned dangerously from balconies and windows, either to cheer or shower the visitors with spring blossoms. All ranks and classes were present, from ordinary townsfolk – merchants, craftsmen and the like – to scholars from the University, distinctive with their shaven heads and dark robes, novices from the colleges and deaneries attached to the cathedral, and then the lower orders: cottars and free-folk from the towns beyond the city walls, servants, vagrants, and mendicants. To a man and woman, they knew they were supposed to welcome these guests, though the task was made easier when the Romans arrived in the trappings of a nobility the British found familiar rather than behind the standard-bearers in leopardskins of yore, carrying Imperial eagles and purple banners. It also helped that, at the very rear of the procession, three monks in white habits tossed out handfuls of golden coins.

In the midst of this jubilation, it was difficult for Rufio to detect any familiar face in the crowd, though he tried his best, always focusing on the prettier women, of whom there were a great many.

"I understand this special lady is married to one of Arthur's northern barons?" Bishop Malconi said.

"That's correct," Rufio replied.

"In which case she's unlikely to be here in Camelot, wouldn't you say?"

"One can but dream."

"Her husband may be here. Perhaps that's something for you to think about."

[9]See footnotes 6 and 8. The emphasis on fashion and the trappings of sophistication in the "Noble Tragedie" reflects Malory's ideas on culture and morality. See Appendix 2.

"Apparently he's a brutal oppressor of his tenants, not to mention the local plebs."

"She told you that?"

Rufio smiled. "No. That's just the way I imagine him. Actually, she speaks highly of him. Says that he's always been kind to her, but that his manners are those of the military camp. His main flaw, it seems, is that he's unsophisticated."

"And you haven't seen her for...?"

"Six years, eight months, two weeks, four days."

"Great God in Heaven!" The bishop's brow furrowed. "You keep an exact account... hardly encouraging. How can you be sure that after so long in the company of this man, she hasn't become a beldame, a bitter harridan of the north?"

"No-one who wrote such letters could be anything less than a fairy princess."

"Ah yes, the famous letters. Your mother complained to me that for several years after first bedding this... this married woman, you wrote to each other once a month?"

"Mother was always very observant."

"You still maintain this degree of correspondence?"

"Not quite. Trelawna feared we'd become reckless and be discovered. Also, her bower-maid, Gerta, who did most of the to-ing and fro-ing for her, came to disapprove."

"At last, someone in this kingdom with a head on their shoulders."

"No. Gerta likes us. Her main fear was that we'd never meet again, and that her mistress's heart would be broken."

"Hearts break so easily. Especially in times of love *and* war."

"We aren't at war yet, uncle."

"Aren't we? Felix, you must brace yourself for the possibility you may never meet your fairy princess again. Even if she's here, we have more important matters at hand."

"I don't understand this concern." Rufio caught a daffodil and blew a kiss to the young girl who'd thrown it. "Did any Roman embassy ever receive such a welcome?"

"Don't be fooled. In the old days it was quite common for us to be flattered by those we planned to conquer. It's a mindset born of fear – they hope to buy us off with friendship. But King Arthur is no fool. He will pay lip-service to our greatness, and he may even discuss terms with us, but in the end, if necessary, he will show his steel. Our role here is purely investigative, but we must keep our wits about us. The less mooning over a woman who can never be yours the better."

Rufio laughed. "It took New Rome two decades to recapture the old Western Empire's lost provinces, but only one night for Countess Trelawna to capture my heart. Which of those powers is more deserving of fealty?"

The parade entered the Royal Plaza, a wide, smooth-paved boulevard running like an artery through the very heart of the city, and lined with shops of a more esoteric ilk: booksellers, silversmiths, perfumeries. It terminated in front of the magnificent marble basilica of St. Stephen's cathedral, behind which loomed the battlemented edifice of Camelot's palace.

The cathedral was built in the Byzantine style, with turrets, pediments, spires and arches, and a plethora of stained-glass windows; it must have stood two hundred feet at its apex. But the fortress, in whose shadow it huddled, was awe-inspiring, perched on a precipitous man-made mound, from which it overlooked the whole of the city, and doubtless the plains and woods far beyond. Its colossal ramparts and towers billowed with thousands of knightly banners.

The thought that one day New Rome might have to besiege Arthur in this citadel was enough to chill even the blood of an optimist like Felix Rufio.

KING ARTHUR AWAITED his guests enthroned at the top of the basilica's stone steps, a handful of knights and prelates gathered behind him. In honour of the day, none of his warriors were mailed. Instead, they wore hose and slippers and comfortable courtly robes; but in mark of their status they also carried swords at their hips.

"Behold," Sir Cador said, as the embassy embarked from the far end of the Plaza, "the masters of the world."

"At one time that was no idle boast," Archbishop Stigand[10] replied, leaning on his crosier. He was the most visibly delicate among them; a gangling beanpole of a man, who walked with a curious halting gait, rather like a heron. His face was lean, his nose an axe-blade. Aside from his tonsure, his hair was long, white and wispy. He alone was decked in full ceremonial regalia: his white satin tabard and cloak, his silver mitre.

"People should learn not to live on past glories," Cador replied.

"They are without doubt the masters of Christendom," Archbishop Stigand retorted. "Thanks to Emperor Lucius, the light of Christ now shines back into such morally desolated lands as central Gaul and lower Germany, Spain, North Africa..."

"At what price, I wonder?" Sir Bedivere said.

The archbishop affected shock. "Surely no price is too high?"

Cador snorted. "Easy to say when you've not been subjected to the Imperial taxation structure."

"I hear that Emperor Lucius has proved himself a fair and equitable master," the archbishop said. "That he taxes his new provinces heavily, but in return his legions rebuild their roads and bridges, their civic administrations..."

"It's true that even civilisation has its price," Bedivere replied. "There are several Episcopal princes in the party approaching us. I'd imagine each one will have at least half an eye on the many tithes and titles to be had in a kingdom as grateful as ours will be."

Archbishop Stigand pondered this. He was a man who professed great piety, but in reality often searched for new ways by which to cement his position as senior churchman in the British Isles. He lived in constant fear that his rivals at

[10]The eleventh-century Archbishop of Winchester, which Malory identifies with Camelot. Although anachronistic, Stigand – who was excommunicated by five successive popes – may have represented a strongly anti-Roman church to Malory, although he was notorious for using his position to secure personal influence.

Canterbury and York might someday steal a march on him, and as such had spies at every level in the Royal Court which he thought nobody else knew about. He cleared his throat before speaking again.

"My lords, just because we in the Camelot See approve New Rome's reinvigorated Christian mission does not mean we endorse it heartily. This will be, I imagine, a mere fact-finding trip... perhaps an examination of the health and spirit of our nation. I shall be glad to inform our Roman brethren that spiritually we want for nothing, and that our lord, the King, has maintained the *Pax Britannica* as well as any Roman governor who ever held sway in this land."

"Who knows," Bedivere said, "there may be some among them who aren't already aware of this, though I doubt it will make much difference."

The ambassadors were now in close proximity, and at last King Arthur spoke.

"Enough debate, gentlemen." He rose to his feet. "We can save that for the Council chamber. At this moment we welcome our guests with open arms."

Arthur, too, was clad informally. He wore his golden crown, but aside from that his only other royal garment was his sleeveless gold and purple cape, which was draped over a black doublet, tight black trousers, and black leather riding boots. He was trim at the waist but possessed of a broad, strong frame, typical of a man who had spent many long years wielding the broadsword and the battle-axe. He wore his sunny-brown beard and moustache neatly trimmed, but his mane long and cut square at the shoulder. There were nicks and scars on his face, as with all those who had borne hardships in war, but he was as handsome a devil now as he'd ever been; lean-faced and square-jawed, his deep hazel eyes shining with wit and wisdom.

The first ambassador to approach was Bishop Proclates of Palermo, who descended from his carriage with the aid of two pages, doffed his chaperon and bowed.

"Hail Arthur," he said loudly, "son of Uther and Igrane, King of all the Britons, Protector of the Holy Mother Church, Guardian of Chivalry, slayer of demons, devils and heathens... I bring greetings from the court of New Rome, and the seat of his Imperial Majesty, Lucius Julio Bizerta."

"Hail, Bishop Proclates of Palermo," Arthur replied. "Statesman, writer, Librarian of the Fathers, founder of the new Christian universities in Alexandria and Nisibis, scourge of all Vandals and Aryan heretics."

Several of the ambassadors glanced at each other, surprised that the King of the Britons even recognised Bishop Proclates, let alone knew his personal history.

"I TOLD YOU," Malconi murmured to his nephew. "This Arthur is nobody's fool."

"Any fool can send a scribe to research a biography," Rufio replied.

Arthur continued his address: "Hail, Bishop Pelagius of Tuscany, healer of schisms, reliever of famines, and restorer of vanquished monasteries. Hail Consul Publius, senatorial voice of the plebeians, advocate of land reform, master of the judiciary. Hail Lord Ardeus Vigilano, Duke of Spoleto, soldier, sailor, scholar, founder of the Alchemical Order..."

One by one, Arthur addressed them, drawing nods and smiles from each individual, who, even if they didn't demonstrate it, were mildly disconcerted that he had not only known they were coming, but that he knew their pedigree to the finest detail.

"Nobody's fool," Malconi said again. "Remember that, Felix. And it applies equally to his Knights of the Round Table."

"I only see a handful," Rufio remarked. "Where are the rest?"

"They'll be here. And sooner rather than later."

FIVE

THE ROADS LEADING down from the north, what few there were, were quagmires. If this wasn't difficult enough for Lucan and his retinue, winter returned briefly. As they traversed the wilderness of Elmet, with its rugged moors, rocky outcrops and deep, dark forests, they were assailed by wind, heavy rain and flurries of sleet.

Lucan remained weak for the first few days, and was forced to travel in the ornate, flag-draped carriage normally reserved for Countess Trelawna and those handpicked ladies who accompanied her on baronial visits. Flax hangings over the doors and windows, cushions, blankets and pans filled with hot coals kept the interior of the carriage snug, and this enabled Lucan to rest and regain sufficient strength to eventually resume his position on Nightshade at the head of the cavalcade, which otherwise consisted of twenty knights, plus their squires, sixteen mounted men-at-arms and various pages, grooms, cooks and domestic staff.

It wasn't entirely a tale of wearisome travel. Occasional feasts and feather beds made pleasing wayside distractions in inns, monasteries or the castles and manor houses of friends, and within two weeks of setting out, the sun had at last broken through. When they reached southern Albion, the broad meadows had turned a dusty green, the hedgerows were blue and gold with buttercups and tulips, and the woods were misted with new leaves and echoed to the calls of birds.

Lucan had lost some weight, his skin was still pale as ice and his blue eyes were now grey and glimmered eerily; "elf eyes," whispered Annette and the other ladies when their mistress was out of earshot. His hair seemed to have darkened – it was jet-black, and had grown long and unruly. But aside from these matters he was more his normal self, and on the last day of the journey he and the rest of his household replaced their scuffed leathers and dingy, mud-spattered travel-mail with snug black hauberks and crimson surcoats adorned with the black wolf. The official household standard, the 'Black Wolf of Corneus,' was wielded by Turold, who rode at the head of the company, the foot of its pole fitted into a sturdy leather pocket alongside his stirrup.

They entered Camelot that evening, the Captain of the Guard recognising Earl Lucan's livery and allowing him immediate access. From the Royal Gardens behind St. Stephen's, they ascended to the castle by the 'Eagle Road,' a narrow but firmly metalled shelf, which spiralled up around the great mound to the palace. Several more guarded gates had to be passed, and each time the checks imposed by the officers on watch became more stringent. At the final point, where the road turned inward towards the Barbican, a small castle in its own right which controlled the main entrance, Lucan had to display not just his equestrian seal but also his Extraordinary Summons.

Behind the Barbican's portcullis, a fire-lit tunnel passed beneath several murder-holes through which storms of arrows, bolts and boiling pitch could be discharged. Guards in mail and the royal insignia were ranked along the tunnel, wielding spears and halberds, but Lucan's party was only halted by Sir Kay, King Arthur's brother and official seneschal.

Kay was a hulking fellow, with a shock of gold hair and a trim gold beard and moustache. Like his underlings, he was mailed and wore the official white tabard with its red dragon symbol.

"Not before time, Lucan," Kay said gruffly. "The Romans are already here."

"Do they measure up to their reputation?" Lucan asked, dismounting.

"They're a bunch of wily old birds. You can tell that just from looking at them... great Heaven!" Kay peered more closely at him. "Are you unwell?"

"It's nothing," Lucan replied.

Kay shrugged. "A good thing you're finally here. The King has called a pre-Council meeting. We are to attend him in the West Library."

Lucan nodded, and he and his band were admitted to the fortress's reception courtyard. Their animals were taken for stable and feed, and Lucan's retainers sent to one of the great lodge-halls, where, by the light of a few smoky torches, each man would have a pile of straw on which to lay his bed-roll.

"The joys of Camelot," Malvolio remarked as they viewed the gloomy cavern. "In the future, men will write about this magical place and no-one will believe it could be true."

"When we've achieved rank, Mal, we can rest our bones between silken sheets," Alaric said. "Hardships like this will keep us in the trim."

"Of course," Malvolio replied. "Stale air and a cold floor is just the thing to improve a body's reflexes."

Meanwhile, Lucan and Trelawna were conducted to a more comfortable apartment, high in the West Tower, comprising a broad central room, its whitewashed walls lined with woven cloths, with rugs covering the paved floor and a large fire crackling on a hearth. A divan sat in front of the hearth, alongside a table arrayed with sweetmeats, a jug of water, a pitcher of wine and two crystal goblets. The room was airy and lit by candles fixed in iron racks. There were two other rooms: a small privy and a sleeping chamber containing an immense four-posted bed, its mattress, pillows and quilt stuffed with duck-down.

Aching and begrimed from the journey, they sought first to bathe. A porcelain tub was on hand for the countess, which her ladies immediately set about filling. Once they had withdrawn, Lucan watched from the doorway as his wife relaxed into the steaming, scented water. Her tresses drifted on the surface in a golden froth, mingling with the floating petals of many exotic flowers.

She seemed barely aware of him as she rubbed her hands, arms, shoulders, and the pink tips of her breasts with a new creamy lotion from the Orient.

It occurred to Lucan that, should they go to war with New Rome, these eastern delicacies would become a thing of the past. There'd be no more expensive gifts from dark-skinned emissaries, no more merchant cogs from distant harbours, no more trade with the continent of any sort as long as hostilities persisted. But these were fleeting concerns. Now he had thoughts only for Trelawna. During the two-week journey, he had initially been too weak to approach her, and later, when he felt better, she had slept in the carriage with her ladies while he had rested by the campfire with his men. Two whole weeks. His need for a woman was urgent.

He retired to the bedroom, where he replaced his armour with an ermine robe, then returned to the bathroom and pulled up a stool. She acknowledged him with a smile, but continued cleaning her fingernails.

"I understand you're to attend a pre-Council meeting?" she said.

"It can wait," he replied, eyeing the curved form beneath the fragrant water.

"Is that wise?"

"We've just made a tiresome journey. I think the King can spare us half an hour."

"I don't think you should keep him waiting, my love."

Slowly Lucan felt his ardour cool. Yet again she was being stand-offish with him. This had happened from time to time during their marriage, but recently it seemed to happen more often than not. He could always tell when that mood was upon her: she would not sulk or pout, but merely become distant. Sometimes he was able to talk her around, though she'd remain aloof during their love-making, which was no aphrodisiac for him. Of course, as her husband he had the right to take her whether she was willing or not, but he had never done that. It ill became a Christian knight to rape a woman, especially not his own wife. This much he had learned from his mother who, several times in his boyhood, while wallowing in her misery, had advised him that he himself was the fruit of such a coupling. As though to add salt to a wound, she would always append this statement with the view that though the Church would never say he was the child of sin, this was something for God to decide, not Man – so he should seek no comfort from "his father's toadying chaplain."

Lucan rose from the bath-side, tightened his robe with its cord, and left the apartment, descending through the palace's various levels. Throughout his years of increasing power, Arthur had expanded his citadel at Camelot in numerous ways, adding halls, passages, common rooms, more towers, more turrets, more battlemented walks, more gardens, galleries and banquet halls – all crammed and interwoven within the mighty walls of its outer fortification. In these latter days, as peace and prosperity settled on Britain, he had taken account of luxury as well as necessity. The 'steam rooms' were one of the most recent additions; they had been inspired by the swimming-baths of the great Romanesque villas that had dominated the British landscape before the legions left and the barbarians ran riot. The caldarium was the first of these chambers. It was tiled and equipped with marble benches, and running with moisture, heated by furnaces beneath the floor. In the second room, the tepidarium, there were arched niches where the busts of long-deceased Roman lords kept a careful watch, and braziers containing hot coals, which servants wearing only loincloths ladled with cold water, to emit clouds of cleansing steam. In the final room, the frigidarium, it was cooler and there was a plunge-pool. More servants were on hand there to offer soaps and massage.

Lucan worked his way from chamber to chamber, brooding as he sweated. Other palace-guests moved around in the steam. He knew many but lacked the interest to address them. However, in due course one addressed him.

"They told me a northern brute had ridden down here with a band of cutthroats. I could hardly believe it when I heard he'd been admitted to the palace."

Lucan glanced up, and smiled.

His brother Bedivere, Marshal of the Royal Household, sat beside him, sweating and draped in towels. They embraced.

They were not alike. They were half-brothers, sharing the same mother. Bedivere, though older by several years, was leaner of build, almost slender. His hair had always hung in glossy chestnut curls, though these were now cropped short and shot with silver. He was brown-eyed and refined of aspect, with a long patrician nose and high, ruddy cheekbones – and though he, too, bore the scars of battle, he was almost pretty in comparison to his square-jawed, heavy-browed sibling.

"ALL IS READY for tomorrow?" Lucan asked.

"All is ready."

"What of the Romans?"

"The King has quartered them in the university precinct. We're to have no truck with them tonight, although a tournament and pageant are planned for next week if the Council is a success."

Lucan gave a thin smile. "And will both sides be happy to attend this pageant?"

Bedivere shrugged. "If the Romans are merely here to test the water, why not? The knowledge that it would be a mistake to attack us would be as much use to them as the knowledge that it would be safe."

"And if they're not?"

"A new age of darkness will dawn. You look terrible, by the way."

"So I keep being told."

"Anything I should know about?"

Lucan described his struggle with the Worm. Bedivere glanced with fascination at the livid patch of scar-tissue on

Lucan's shoulder. "You say it was Alaric who saved you... your squire?"

Lucan nodded.

"The lad deserves to be knighted, at the very least."

Lucan frowned. "If I were to knight him, he'd have to go questing – find his own way in the world. The household would miss his service."

"He has to build his own career at some point."

Lucan shook his head. "Something tells me he isn't ready yet."

"If he stood against this malevolent serpent..."

"There's more to it than that. Any man can find courage and think quickly on the spur of the moment – well, not *any* man, but any man of quality. Alaric is a man of quality. But there are other things. He seems so young to me..."

"He's eighteen, isn't he? More than old enough."

Lucan rested his chin on his fist. "He wants to be a knight, but he's not bullish about it. It's as though he's content to live out the rest of his days at my side."

"What reason could there be for that?"

"He may just lack ambition. Or confidence. I suppose, in keeping him close, I'm protecting him. I don't know if that's right or wrong."

"Good Christ, you talk as if he's your son rather than your squire."

"I can't help it if I feel that for him, Bedivere. Trelawna certainly does. There are times when she shows Alaric more motherly affection than she shows me wifely love."

"Aah," Bedivere said. "Still haven't managed to win her heart?"

"Forgive me, it's a personal thing. You shouldn't be troubled by it."

"You're my younger brother. I want you to be happy."

"What does happiness mean to men like us? We're here to serve."

"It means everything. We've both achieved greatness in our own way, yet I, for one, would trade much of that for memories of a pleasant home-life."

Briefly, they relapsed into silence.

Bedivere only had vague recollections of the time before his father died. Sir Pedrawd was a Welsh knight by birth, and held a border stronghold in Dyfed. He was renowned for his gallantry on the battlefield and his benign lordship off it. He died while Bedivere was still a young child, and a short time later his beautiful wife, Gundolen, was remarried to Duke Corneus, also recently widowed, who controlled a vast swathe of rugged land on Uther Pendragon's northern frontier, governing it from the notorious Craghorn Keep. Duke Corneus was in every way the opposite of Sir Pedrawd: whereas Pedrawd famously halted the construction of a new manor house because it would interfere with a peasant hamlet, Corneus once repaid a town that failed to pay him homage by destroying it with a horde of rats. This was the new life that Bedivere was dragged into while still a stripling. The first child Corneus fathered by Gundolen died. The second was Lucan. In time, though there were several years between them, the two half-brothers became very close, which was perhaps inevitable given the dangerous world they grew up in at Craghorn.

"A man can't be a warrior all the time," Bedivere added. "There has to be some joy in his world."

"Trelawna makes me happy enough," Lucan said.

"But she doesn't love you?"

"She comes as close to it as she can. I owe her for that."

"You *owe* her?"

"Whatever girlish dreams she entertained about finding a handsome paladin, well... she's had thirteen years to accept that they'll never be more than dreams."

Bedivere looked frustrated. "You're underselling yourself, Lucan. Courage, heroism, loyalty to God and your king... these things can't be measured. There are women all over Albion who'd give anything to be married to a Knight of the Round Table."

Lucan pondered this morosely.

"Unless..." Bedivere paused, and glanced around to ensure no-one was eavesdropping. "Unless she loves another."

Lucan regarded him curiously.

Bedivere spoke quietly but seriously. "We don't know this is a fact, of course – it's just supposition. But it would explain certain confusing things. After thirteen years, she ought to have *learned* to love you. You're her husband. Rather than you owing her, she owes you... for protecting her, honouring her. She ought to have *taught* herself to love you, if for no other reason than to ensure her own survival."

Lucan shook his head. "Love another? How? We live on the Northern March. She never sees anyone else."

"You have a household full of knights. You have landed tenants as well..."

"Country oafs... loyal, stolid enough fellows who can aim a good sword-stroke, but most have no more education than the peasant farmers they supervise, and certainly no wider view of the world."

"It was only a thought." Bedivere shrugged. "In retrospect, it seems unlikely. But there must be a reason for this remoteness she constantly subjects you to."

"As I said before, it's my trouble... not yours."

"Indeed." Bedivere stood up. "We already have troubles enough. Despite their current mission of peace, our spies tell us the Romans are moving large numbers of troops into central and northern Gaul."

"If any monarch can stand up to the new Roman Empire, it's Arthur."

"We're to attend him this evening, in the..."

"I know." Lucan's brow furrowed as he again wondered about his wife's aloofness and the possibility of infidelity.

"Forget what I said about Trelawna," Bedivere said, wondering if he'd done more harm than good by mentioning it. "There is no proof. Not even a hint of suspicion. And even if it *were* true, these other matters are more important."

Lucan nodded in agreement, though his metal-grey eyes told a different tale.

SIX

THE WEST LIBRARY was a suite of barrel-vaulted chambers separated from each other by tall, marble archways. Their walls were inlaid with deep shelves crammed with ancient tomes. A central hearth provided warmth, while rush-lamps provided light. There was a comforting aroma of wood-smoke and old leather.

Again, Arthur opted for informality. He wore only a blue, loose-fitting tunic, black linen breeches, and soft leather shoes cross-banded to the knee. He strode up and down the central chamber, sipping from a cup of watered wine as he made his address.

"Here is what we know, gentlemen. Emperor Lucius is in the process of reconquering what he considers to be his rightful dominion. Like any astute monarch, where possible he will achieve this by words rather than battle. His negotiating skills, and those of his emissaries, are said to be subtle. Many Gallic dukes and princes succumbed to these machinations straight away. They are now *nominal* dukes and princes, but at least they are still alive; that is how most of them regard it. Because, despite this diplomatic offensive, Emperor Lucius is a Roman and – like all Romans before him – he knows that war will not only be necessary at some point, it will be desirable. The only thing that *really* impresses Roman citizens is success on the battlefield. That does not mean Lucius is looking to wage war on us. The last Roman army to invade Britain was vast, battle-hardened and led by a corps of experienced and able commanders. Even so, only by the skin of its teeth did it gain a toehold, and then it had to fight continual exhausting campaigns to expand. Lucius knows this would be an immensely difficult undertaking."

Many of the Round Table brotherhood were now present: Lancelot, Bedivere, Kay, Lionel, Cador, Caradoc, Claudin, Griflet, Tristan and others.

It was Lancelot who spoke up. Son of King Ban and the only Frankish-born warrior present, he was a huge, brawny, thickset fellow, with a tawny mane like a lion's and a thick beard and moustache. He was Arthur's champion, but he interrupted the King's discourse freely; *all* Arthur's knights were encouraged to speak their minds.

"Nevertheless, sire, Emperor Lucius has consciously manoeuvred himself into a position where, if he were to back down from a fight with us now, it would cost him face. He has told his people that he will deliver the Western Empire. Not to do so because it would involve war with Britain would be a humiliation, from which, politically, he might never recover."

Arthur nodded. "I agree. We have spies all over Gaul, and have seen his legions assembling. So we can be under no illusions. But at present I think a war between New Rome and Britain can only occur as an end-game. There may be ways to divert it. For example, one thing we do not know is where the Holy Father stands. If New Rome were to invade Britain tomorrow, it would be a blatant act of aggression by one Christian power against another. Pope Simplicius should condemn it outright."

"He should declare it a crime!" Sir Cador said. He was a tall, raw-boned man, with a mop of red hair and a wild beard. Though he was Duke of Cornwall and a dependable soldier, he was also prone to excitableness. His voice rose as he ranted. "His Holiness should go further... he should excommunicate the main aggressor, and put the whole of New Rome under interdict!"

"He wouldn't dare," Bedivere replied. "Not with Lucius the new buttress of western Christianity."

"That depends," Arthur said. "Pope Simplicius keeps close counsel, but I hear rumours that he hasn't welcomed the emergence of this Imperial rival. Moreover, he may find that he has friends in this matter in Constantinople – Emperor Leo,[11] not to mention the Patriarch. Until recently, the light of the Roman world shone from the East. Will *they* welcome the resurrection of the West?"

"You're not saying the Pope will side with us," Kay said. As often, his tone was sardonic and critical.

"We can't rely on it," Arthur replied. "Not if the Romans raise the issue of British religious observances, as I suspect they will. We have no cardinal in Rome to rebuff any outlandish charges. This also means that we don't know the character of Simplicius as well as we might. Is he an honest churchman, or does he seek material gains? Is he even now putting price-tags on the dioceses of the British Isles?"

Bedivere spoke again. "Most likely, if Rome *does* attack us, the Pope will decry the act, but do no more than that. If he seeks to make a peace and in the process casts both Rome and Camelot as equal transgressors, that will suit New Rome nicely, so long as they have already made gains."

They pondered this. The only sound was the hissing of the fire as it fed on the last of the winter logs. Lucan sat closest to the flames, his chin propped on his fist.

"You're unusually quiet, Sir Lucan," the King said.

Lucan glanced up. "Forgive me, sire."

"You have more important things on your mind?"

Lucan was conscious that all eyes were fixed on him, yet felt strangely unmoved. He *did* have other things on his mind, but he wasn't going to air them here. When he finally addressed the matter at hand it was with simple pragmatism.

"As I see it, my liege, tomorrow we must decide whether we are hawks or doves."

[11]Probably Leo I, "the Thracian," Byzantine Emperor from 457 to 474 CE.

"Indeed?"

Lucan continued. "The Romans have arrived with smiling faces. But that is the way their murderers always arrived. Julius Caesar discovered that."

"And?"

"To avoid a similar fate, we must know exactly what our *own* intentions are." He spoke slowly, thoughtfully. "If we are doves, and conciliate with New Rome... it may be deemed a sign of weakness, and may encourage them to attack."

"It may also confuse them," Cador argued. "It may counter the intelligence their spies have no doubt gleaned that we are a strong island, not to be trifled with."

"That too," Lucan agreed. "It's a thorny issue. Equally so if we are hawks, and threaten resistance. That may frighten them into retreating, or it may provoke them."

"And your recommendation?" Arthur asked.

Lucan sighed. "I wonder if it's even worthwhile playing their silly game. I anticipate that New Rome will make many offers to us tomorrow, none of which we will find acceptable. They will prod us and provoke us, to test our reaction."

"I expect so too," Arthur said.

"Then my recommendation, sire, is that we resist. In no-nonsense fashion. As Lancelot pointed out, Emperor Lucius has backed himself into a corner. He *must* ultimately be prepared to fight. This positioning and re-positioning on the European chessboard is merely a device by which he can gain maximum advantage... militarily, politically, probably both."

"So you advise that we be hawks?" Arthur said.

"It's not something I want, sire. But life in the North has taught me a lesson the Romans learned a long time ago; namely, that it isn't the righteous who take everything, it's the ruthless. We may have right on our side, but that won't be enough. If we don't show a willingness to fight, they will continue with this intimidation, growing ever more belligerent and, presumably, ever stronger."

There was a long, brooding silence, finally broken by Kay.

"Sire, there may be another way. Perhaps we can... *give* something to the Romans?"

Arthur turned to him. "What do you propose?"

Despite being Arthur's sibling, Kay was an odd character. There were times when he appeared to resent being Arthur's inferior, even though he knew he was neither as clever nor as much a warrior. Yet he was a blunt-spoken fellow who was useful to have around for his forthrightness.

"It seems to me that New Rome has engulfed the whole of continental Christendom apart from one parcel of land," he said. "And that is Brittany. Why not offer it as a gift?"

Cador jumped to his feet. "Brittany is our ally."

Kay eyed him warily. "Yes, but to what end? Would Brittany ever come to us in a time of crisis? What could King Hoel ever offer us if we were in need?"

"He helped in our battles before," Cador asserted.

"But now?" Kay persisted. "What could he offer us now that we are strong?"

"We have a treaty with Brittany," Bedivere reminded him.

Kay waved this away. "Treaties are written on paper. They can be torn up or burned."

"There's the not insignificant matter of honour," Lancelot said.

"Is honour more significant than survival?" Kay wondered. "We may beat New Rome in battle. Or we may not. Numerically, their fighting men outnumber ours ten to one."

"You think," Arthur replied, "that if we offer them a free hand in Brittany, they will leave us alone?"

"It's possible that Brittany is all they want, and the entire purpose of their mission here is to investigate our attitude on that matter. It would be geographically convenient for them to incorporate Brittany into their new empire. Britain, on the other hand – well, we are offshore. It would not be an easy fight to take us, regardless of what I've just said. Surely, on that basis, we can hammer out some kind of agreement?"

"To sacrifice an ally would not sit well with the name of the Round Table," Lancelot objected.

"There's no way out of this without paying some kind of price," Kay replied.

The fire crackled as they considered their limited choices.

"Sir Lucan," Arthur said. "You still feel war is inevitable?"

"I do, sire," Lucan replied. "It would be a strange thing if a war between Britain and New Rome were to hinge on as small a state as Brittany. But that could be to our advantage. Would it not suit us if the focal point of the fighting was over there rather than over here?"

"To ensure that, we'd need to send soldiers to Brittany straight away," Bors responded. "In effect, we'd be the cause of the conflict."

Lucan shrugged.

Bors looked amazed. "You actually want to *start* a war with Rome?"

"If Rome is bent on war anyway," Lucan said, "better we fight on our own terms."

"But *we'd* be the aggressors. That would be in complete defiance of the code."[12]

Lucan turned to the King. "Sire, our first duty is not to our reputation as chivalrous knights. It is to the preservation of our people – their homes and their livelihoods. This may be a war of annihilation, and if it were fought *here*, their land and livestock all go up in flames. We should think long and hard on that."

The knights exchanged worried glances.

"Food for thought, Sir Lucan," the King eventually said. "That northern eyrie you call home has set you to thinking in recent times."

"Perhaps, my lord," Lucan said. "Perhaps overmuch."

*   *   *

[12]The Pentecostal Oath, which Arthur made his men swear in Book I of the *Morte*, "and every year... at the high feast of Pentecost." Part of the Oath demands that "no man take no battles in a wrongful quarrel for no law, ne for no world's goods." Starting a war, if not in the defence of others, would presumably qualify.

LATER THAT EVENING, while the rest of the brotherhood retired – either to their bed-chambers, or the drinking hall where Taliesin, Arthur's Welsh bard, regaled them with romances of the elder days – Lucan wandered the higher vaults of the palace.

At last he emerged on one of its high turrets, where the stiff, strong breeze tugged at his tunic and ruffled his black hair. From here he could gaze down on the whole of Camelot, though all he saw in the darkness were sparkling lights: candles behind shutters, lanterns in stable-yards, the braziers of watchmen.

He imagined he was peering from the casement of his chamber window at Craghorn Keep, as a child. An upper valley of the *Hen Ogledd* lay below him, much of it blotted out by pinewoods, other parts filled with scree. A single track carved its way through the middle; it was hard-trodden earth in summer, and in autumn a river of glutinous mud churned by hooves and cartwheels; later in the season it would freeze into ruts and razor-edged ridges. The crooked scarecrow figure lumbering painfully along the track was his mother, as she had been in those final years, embarking each dawn on her barefoot penitential march to the moss-covered Celtic cross in the village of Hexley, some four miles distant. Always veiled and head bowed, prayer beads entwining her fingers; always in the same sackcloth robe, its tattered hem trailing around her blistered, bloodstained feet. Every morning – whatever the month, whatever the weather. And always that same distance. Four miles there, and four miles back. Because no ploughboy or village carter would dare return her in his horse and trap.

Lucan's heart rent itself in his bosom as he recalled that familiar scene.

The tall woman with the flowing crimson locks, statuesque build and noble beauty – reduced over pitiless years to a withered, hobbling shadow; a crone before her time, drenched by rain, bitten by frost, seared by the sun. Every day it took her a little longer to complete the penance. At first she would be back by breakfast. But then, in later years it was mid-morning, and then midday. Eventually, not long after Bedivere had been sent to commence his squiredom, she did not return at all. This time, one of Duke Corneus's vassals *did* bring her home. A woodsman found her lying in a ditch – what remained of her. It was mid-winter and the snow was shin-deep. Possibly she had collapsed before the starving wolves had launched themselves upon her, because enough remained of her legs and feet to show that her blue chilblains had finally turned to purple rot – they could not have supported her for much longer.

And yet still they insisted she'd brought it on herself.

As Lucan wept in the arms of Chaplain Gildas – a genuinely kind man, but one who lived in as much fear of his overlord as everyone else – the old priest advised the boy that Duke Corneus had been just in his ruling. It was no-one's intent that Countess Gundolen should die such a death. But she'd died in the act of penance, which meant that she would now be with the angels – surely a wondrous thing, given that the sin of infidelity was one of the worst a man or woman could commit.

The worst sin a man or woman could commit.

Lucan hadn't believed it then and he didn't believe it now.

Cruelty, anger, bitter and irrational hatred – these were worse offences. Especially when one was drawn to such things through despair at one's own misfortune. To punish the innocent when one should be punishing oneself – that was the worst of all.

There was no proof, he reminded himself, as he moved away from the teetering battlement. To cement the idea, he incanted it aloud, almost like a prayer.

"There was no proof. *Damn you, father, there was no proof!* If you'd lived long enough, I'd have killed you. And so would Bedivere. We both swore it. I've damned you for so many things – for the black banner and devil's sword I inherited from you, for your eluding my wrath when so many others didn't, and most of all for having ever sired me. But tonight... tonight I praise you. For the memory of your actions has taught me a humbling lesson. *There was no proof!*"

When he entered his bed-chamber, Trelawna was asleep. There was a dull glow in the hearth, and the room was dim but warm. He stepped from his clothes and slid under the quilt beside her. She didn't awake, but flung an arm across his chest. Her body was supple and snug. Worries, doubts, evil imaginings – it was easy to put them aside at that moment.

SEVEN

THE FOLLOWING MORNING, the sun rode high in a cloudless sky, but it was still early spring and Camelot's regal banners streamed on an ice-edged breeze.

The conference with the Roman ambassadors was to be the main event of the day, though of course this would not involve the majority of those gathered in the palace, only the King and his senior advisors. Minor nobility would be allowed into the audience gallery, where they were expected to be seen and not heard. Lesser-titled men were not even permitted to wait outside in the lobbies. Not that many would complain about this; most had spent long hours in the saddle to reach this place, and now the delights of Camelot would prove a welcome diversion.

All that morning, rivers of household men and their lackeys poured down the Eagle Road, eager to lose themselves in a day's holiday. Most walked together in chattering bands, while some – suspecting they'd be too drunk by the day's end to think twice about paying an exorbitant fee to have themselves carried back to the palace in a litter – descended on horseback. The mood was merry. Though the stakes would be high in the conference hall, most common men knew these great affairs were beyond their understanding, and did not trouble their heads with it.

Alaric, Malvolio and Benedict walked with the other squires from Penharrow. There was much ribaldry, much ribbing and lampooning of each other, all born from sheer excitement. Camelot was the largest town that most of the lads had ever seen, and thronging with traffic: townsfolk and tradesmen jostled each other as they hurried back and forth, while wagons and carts made even slower progress, and on the narrower roads threw up gouts of liquid mud. There was a riot of noise: steel-shod wheels clashing on paving stones, clog-irons thumping, hammers falling, bells clanging, hucksters and hawkers calling their wares, geese clacking and sheep bleating as they were driven to market. Every status of person was on show, from lords and ladies in curtained carriages, to lepers and cripples begging on corners. Mailed soldiers mingled with vagabonds. Monks and other pilgrims strode in single file, cowled heads bowed. Madmen capered to the jigs of street-musicians.

The back alleys were even more chaotic. Wattle-and-timber buildings leaned towards each other like rows of decrepit old men. Here, the fine townhouses of courtiers and flunkeys gave way to the homes and shops of the town's merchant class, each with its own painted shield hanging over its lintel: cobblers, ironmongers, smiths, glass-painters, carpenters, coopers, saddlers, masons, grocers, haberdashers, poulterers, milliners and locksmiths.

In one square, the lads were mesmerised by a raised stage on which a miracle play was in progress. A pimply-faced youth with straggles of straw in place of blonde locks wore a woman's dress sewn with oak leaves to indicate that he was 'Eve.' 'Adam' was a much older man, balding, with a pendulous strawberry nose and a hanging belly. He wore only a flagellant's loincloth as they fled together from the Garden of Eden, a representation provided by items of flat scenery – illustrated first with vines and fruit, and later with rocks and tangled thorns – which a tireless procession of helpers in hose and sweat-soaked blouses transported across the rear of the stage. Alongside the melodrama, a plump, doughy-looking boy seated on a stool divided his attention between a large currant-bun and a trumpet, on which he blew irregular, discordant blasts – possibly to indicate the mayhem of the world beyond Paradise, or more likely because this was the most his skill with a trumpet amounted to. Despite this, the lesson of the Fall of Man was not lost on the awed crowd, though it was diluted somewhat by other events in the same square, which included juggling, acrobatics and a bear-baiting. The lads inevitably became bored, and soon found their way to the taverns.

There was every kind of tavern in Camelot town, and every kind of bawdy house, though the latter, by Arthur's ordinance, were confined to a low quarter close to the docks, where the tanneries and workshops discharged their effluent direct into the River Itchen. It was no surprise to find that most of the Penharrow retinue, along with many others, had already found their way to this quarter, the knights and men-at-arms in particular having failed to be distracted by the shopping streets or miracle plays. Ale, wine and West Country cider was quaffed in abundance, and saucy girls were on hand to assist the gallant gentlemen in their quest to spend every penny they had.

There was little romance in the air, Alaric thought glumly as he and the others stood crammed in one dingy interior. It reeked of smoke and onions, and the floor was rotted hay, much of which he suspected had fallen from the bedding in the loft, to which a creaking, rickety stairway led an endless procession of lads and lasses. Most of these couples seemed to come down again with almost indecent speed, the lasses promptly discarding their companions and latching onto new customers.

"Why the face?" Malvolio wondered, grinning over his drinking-pot. He and Benedict were already flushed around the gills as the liquor took hold of them.

"I don't have much appetite for this," Alaric said.

Over the last few days, his yearning for Countess Trelawna had become overpowering. He knew better than anyone how ridiculous it was, but could any man control such a floodtide of emotion? He could neither eat nor sleep; he had no patience for raucous company or idle banter. He wondered if this was what was meant by 'love-sickness.' It was a worrying thought. When men were in love they did rash things. He'd held amorous feelings for his mistress for almost as long as he could remember, or so it seemed – at least since he'd begun to find her womanly shape fascinating rather than motherly – but now the flame burned with frightful ferocity. Maybe this ensued from the near-death of her husband. For a very brief time the unobtainable dream had seemed a fraction closer. Earl Lucan was now fit and well again, but the flame could not be quenched.

"We never got to toast your birthday," Malvolio slurred.

"Now's your chance," Alaric replied, making to leave.

Malvolio stopped him. "What ails you, lad?"

"Forgive me." Alaric shouldered his way through the throng. "I need some clean air."

"Alaric!" Malvolio called after him.

"Let him go," Benedict advised, beckoning to a foxy-faced miss with black bangs and witch-green eyes. "It'll take more than clean air to cure *his* disease."

At the tavern door, Alaric was spotted by Turold, who was sprawled on a bench beside the fire, a wench on one knee. On the other knee sat his lute, which he plucked at.

"Too much to drink already, Alaric?" he laughed.

"That's what I'm seeking to avoid, my lord," Alaric replied. "Men say foolish things in their cups."

"And most of the rest of the time, in my experience," Wulfstan observed sagely. He was on the opposite bench, gazing into the flames as he sipped at a pewter tankard.

Alaric departed, and Turold shook his head. "He's turned strange, that one."

"Cusp of manhood," Wulfstan said. "Doesn't know how he's expected to behave yet."

They were distracted by braying laughter, and turned to spot Malvolio struggling in the arms of Benedict and several other squires while a black-haired lass poured a goodly measure of ale behind his codpiece.

"For which there's something to be said," Wulfstan added dourly.

Alaric walked to the basilica, feeling small and inconsequential as he mounted its broad marble steps. It wasn't the first great cathedral he'd visited – he'd darkened the doors at both Durham and York during his travels with Earl Lucan – but St. Stephen's, which, though he'd been to Camelot twice before, he'd never entered, was the stuff of dreams.

As he strode through the vast nave, its white paving stones tinged pink and blue by the towering stained-glass windows, its air heavy with frankincense, he listened to the distant choral chanting of the cathedral chapter and was moved, not so much by the aura of sanctity as by the sense of his own unworthiness. Each stone pillar was painted in beautiful hues of red, green and gold, and carved with passages of scripture in Latin. At the foot of each pillar there was a tomb, and in repose atop each tomb the effigy of some knight who had died in the service of Christ. As Alaric walked up the central aisle, he dwelled on the terrible wars that Arthur and his knights had waged to wrest this land back from heathen powers. The losses had been uncountable, and yet here he was, torturing himself with desire for the wife of one who had stood by Arthur from the beginning, who had served in all five of his most difficult campaigns, receiving one terrible wound after another. It felt as if the weight of his guilt would crush him. And yet Alaric trudged on, trying not to meet the gazes of those supplicants who knelt in the side-chapels or before candle-lit alcoves where saints might grant boons to the pious, for surely he wore his failings the way a condemned man wore his shroud.

Far overhead, the vaulted ceiling was the most vivid depiction of Heaven he could imagine: painted blue, yet spangled with gold and silver stars. Images of angels in flight were etched across it, swan wings spread, battle-horns at their lips, banderoles billowing behind them, bearing more names of fallen heroes.

The main altar itself was the most potent reminder of all that he was a traitor.

The central table was a solid block of Greek gold, liberated by Arthur from the booty of the Saxon horde he had decimated in the desperate battle on the River Duhblas; it was so heavy that it had taken sixteen of his men to carry it. Its sides were engraved with images from the Bible, its top laid with crisp white linens. At either end stood a rose-coloured candle, each as tall and thick as a man's arm. Ten paces behind it, a triptych depicting the life and death of St Stephen arched over the entrance to the choir, which rose in tier upon tier of elaborately carved and polished wooden benches. At the very rear, the basilica's main altarpiece towered fifty feet into the air, a masterpiece of interlocking bas reliefs, each panel – silver inlaid with gold, or gold inlaid with silver – telling a tale from the lives of the martyrs.

Alaric knelt, helpless before this vision of celestial splendour.

Many in Albion had come late in life to the Christian God. Pictish and Saxon incursion after the legions left had sent many Britons back to their hill-forts and their woodland temples, where the faces of pagan spirits were still cut in the bark. Only Arthur's victories had helped reverse this tide. But Alaric was not a recent convert. He had no memory of his real parents, who had been murdered and his home destroyed while he was still a babe in arms. But those who'd abducted him, in one of those strange contradictions that bedeviled Christianity, had seen to it that he was baptised before making him their slave. As such, he had never known any other faith, and had never held with those cynical men who reckoned the weakness of God's servants to be a weakness of God Himself. Prelates might abuse their positions – gluttonous friars might roister with thanes and knaves, priests might steal church-offerings to line their vestment pockets, bishops might seek and wield power like ordinary, avaricious men – but they committed these deeds in *defiance* of Christ, not on His instruction. As such, the Holy Cloth did not protect them. They were as surely bound for Hell as any of those lay-sinners they so roundly condemned in the quest to empower themselves even more.

God was good.

God was kind.

God would forgive.

Though first one had to be contrite. One must seek forgiveness, and seek it honestly – not because one feared punishment, but because one regretted one's offences.

Alaric walked doggedly from the cathedral, leaving by one of its rear doors. He could never seek shrift as things were. Though it was wicked and perverse of him, he loved his overlord's wife. Expressing regret for that would not help – for it would be a lie, and God recognised all lies. Perhaps it was God's little jest, therefore, that the first person he saw on leaving the building was Countess Trelawna. She sat with her ladies in the cathedral garden, in the midst of a manicured lawn with pollarded plum trees to either side.

"Alaric?" she said, noting his peculiar expression.

"My... lady," he stuttered. "I'm surprised to see you here."

"How so, Alaric?"

"I thought... the attractions of the royal palace."

"Ah... the season. To walk on the terraces up yonder would freeze our blood. Down here, the sun's kisses are warmer. I'm equally surprised to see *you*. I thought the city would provide diversions."

"Only brief ones, ma'am." He was surprised she couldn't tell that that his limbs were quaking, his brow flustered. He even resented her for that, so his voice hardened. "I came to the cathedral to find peace."

"Peace, Alaric?"

"And I didn't. In case you were wondering."

"Why do you seek peace? You're a young man. You know no troubles."

Alaric gazed at her long and hard, willing her to understand his torment. She regarded him with all innocence, though several of her ladies were now eyeing him curiously.

"You're right, my lady," he finally said, struggling to fight back tears. "I can't tell you my troubles – they're trifling things. As you say, I'm only a boy."

He turned and left the garden with plodding steps.

Trelawna gazed after him, puzzled. "I meant no insult."

"I don't think he was insulted, mistress," Annette said, averting her eyes.

"I doubt it would be possible for *you* to insult that one," Gerta muttered. She sat several yards away on a stool, working at her embroidery, adding under her breath: "Foolish brat. He'll bring destruction on more than just himself."

EIGHT

THE CONFERENCE CHAMBER in St. Stephen's Deanery was a lengthy hall. There was no central table, but several tiers of benches ranged its facing walls, with ten yards of parquet floor betwixt them. The ceiling was cross-beamed with oak, while high, arched windows sheathed in horn cast shafts of pinkish sunlight across the floor. The Archbishop's Chair, a raised gilded throne, occupied the farthest end. Ordinarily, Archbishop Stigand would hold sway from this lofty position, but today he had surrendered it to King Arthur, as host of the conference.

The two parties faced each other across the chamber, Arthur's knights and barons on his right, and the Roman ambassadors and their aides and advisors on the left. As arms were never to be worn in this place, no weapons were sported, not even ceremonial swords or daggers, and there was certainly no place for plate or mail. As such, the chamber, often the preserve of simple monastic robes – grey, black or brown, with the occasional dash of Episcopal purple – was now a riot of gorgeous colour. Arthur's nobles displayed their heraldic livery: blues, greens, reds, golds, oranges; emblems of every sort from leopards to unicorns, crosses to crowns and chevrons. By contrast, the Romans were in heavier formal garb – gowns trimmed with fur, high velvet collars, sleeveless ermine doublets. Each ambassador displayed an extravagant chain of office.

Archbishop Stigand, clad in a lilac cassock and shoulder-cape, made a curt inspection of the chamber before matters commenced, passing blessings on all those gathered, the priests and deacons with him casting incense from jeweled censers.

By prior arrangement, it fell to Bishop Malconi to eventually open proceedings.

"Your Highness," he said, rising to his feet and addressing the King. "Your beneficence in allowing this hearing cannot be underestimated. That you welcome foreign dignitaries into your great city to voice their concerns is the sign of a truly civilised monarch."

Arthur nodded his gratitude.

"Let us to business," the bishop added. "We have many hard matters to debate. First and foremost, my lord, is Emperor Lucius's frustration with the continued activities of Saxon pirates. They sail across the German sea, through the Channel and along the Gallic coast, raiding our shipping and our coastal towns."

"The Saxons are indeed a troublesome breed," Arthur agreed.

Malconi smiled gently as if he'd expected to be misunderstood. "How shall I put this without causing offence? We have information, King Arthur, that... well, Saxon longships are sailing from British ports."

Sir Cador leapt to his feet. "That is a damned lie!"

The Romans regarded him with bright eyes and blank expressions.

"Sir Cador," Arthur said. "Pray, do not be rude to our honoured guests."

Cador protested. "To suggest such a thing..."

"Do you deny there is a Saxon presence on your eastern shore?" Malconi enquired.

"There are Saxon settlements, yes," Arthur agreed. "But they exist under our auspices. They have no military bases."

"So everything they do, they do with your permission, my lord?"

"Since the battle on the River Duhblas, the Saxons who live in Britain are my subjects," Arthur said, politely but firmly. "They pay taxes to me and obey my laws, which expressly forbid banditry and piracy."

"So unless you are calling our sovereign a liar, and can produce evidence to support such a claim, I suggest you withdraw your comments," Cador said.

"Sir Cador!" Arthur said admonishingly. "This is an open Council. Every man here must feel that he can speak his mind. Only that way may we clear up any misunderstandings."

"It may be a misunderstanding, King Arthur," Malconi said. "I, for one, hope it is. But may I propose another possibility?"

"Please do."

"It is well known that Saxon migration continues into Britain despite your great victories. Is it possible that Saxon forces have set up covert bases along your shore? Perhaps in hidden coves, on isolated islets?"

Arthur pondered this, as did his knights. It was entirely possible that Saxon pirates were operating illicitly from the British coast. The Saxons were an unruly and difficult people, and more and more of them were arriving in Britain.

"This is something we will look into," Arthur said.

"Might I volunteer some assistance?" Malconi replied.

"'Assistance,' your grace?" Bedivere asked.

"Britain is a large and trackless country," Malconi explained. "It must be difficult deploying your forces in times of crisis."

"We already have forces on our east coast," Bedivere replied. "A number of lords, some seated in this hall, hold authority there. Each of our five major ports has its own reeve."

"No doubt. But what of your naval forces in that region? It seems to me that pirates can only really be countered at sea."

"And let me guess," Lancelot said. "The Romans would loan us ships?"

"We would loan you an entire fleet," Malconi said magnanimously. "Not only that... expert crews and captains, with vast knowledge and experience."

"And these captains and crews would need ports, presumably?" Lancelot said. "Roman ports... on British soil."

"That would seem reasonable," Malconi replied.

"Not to us," Arthur said.

"King Arthur, the Saxon incursions into our dominion are becoming intolerable."

"Then fight the Saxons!" Cador said. "If your captains are so experienced, have them navigate along the Rhine, plunder the Saxon towns, burn their woodland groves. Have your Emperor send his legions across the *Odenwald* again... if they dare."

Arthur held up hands for peace. "Gentlemen..."

"King Arthur, we do send patrols north into the German Sea," Malconi replied. "But beyond a certain point, our military vessels are blind. We have few accurate charts of that region. We have no real friends. If our ships suffered damage, which ports could they put into?"

"Why not British ports?" Bishop Proclates said, as if the idea had just occurred to him.

Malconi looked interested by this. "How speak you, your grace?"

Proclates took the floor. "King Arthur, how if we were to make a bargain whereby Roman craft may be moored and repaired in British ports?"

Malconi nodded. "Emperor Lucius would pay a commensurate sum..."

"A nice plan," Kay interjected. "Except that it would arouse the ire of our Saxon subjects."

Malconi frowned. "But King Arthur said the Saxons in Britain are subservient?"

Arthur smiled. "Bishop Malconi, our northern frontier is the most difficult to manage. Beyond it to the northwest lies the warlike kingdom of Rheged, while to the northeast lie even more antagonistic foes – the Picts. The thought of Roman triremes falling into those hands is intolerable. However, the request in itself is not unreasonable." He turned to his own benches. "How speaks the North?"

It was several seconds before Lucan realised that every eye was upon him. "My liege?"

"Earl Lucan, should we avail our northeast ports to Roman military shipping?"

FELIX RUFIO HAD paid scant attention up to now, wondering if, as Trelawna had assured him in the note she'd secretly delivered to his quarters the night before, she would be somewhere in the vicinity. She might even be outside this room. It set his heart pounding. After so many years abstaining – not from sexual congress, obviously, but from *meaningful* sexual congress – she was still the only woman he thought about.

Now, however, his interest in the debate was ignited.

Directly across the chamber, Earl Lucan rose to his feet. Finally Rufio was face to face with his arch-rival, and at first glance was surprised to see, not a barbarian as he'd expected, but a handsomely groomed man. Lucan was tall and well-shaped for battle, and perhaps a little pale of complexion, but he was square-jawed and clean-shaved, with a mop of thick, black hair brushed neatly. He wore a crimson surcoat with a black wolf design on the front. If memory served, Trelawna had once said that her husband was referred to as 'the Black Wolf of the North.' Rufio regarded Lucan with instant dislike. He already felt slighted by the fellow's presence, and at the same time not a little amused. That a man should owe his fearsome nickname to the emblem he wore was unimpressive.

"SIRE, ARE YOU mad?" Lucan said, having risen slowly to his feet. He turned to his fellow Knights of the Round Table. "Are the rest of you mad? What if these Roman dogs plan to arm the Picts? Maybe supply them with skilled troops?"

Immediately one of the Roman ambassadors, a young officer who had been introduced earlier as Tribune Rufio, leapt from his bench. "That is a despicable slur!" he cried. "Our mission is entirely peaceful!"

"Perhaps," Lucan replied coolly. "But for how long?"

Others of the Roman party expressed similar outrage. One who did not, Arthur noticed, was Tribune Maximion, another military man attached to the embassy and – according to Arthur's spies – an older, wiser head than Rufio.

Now, however, Maximion stood as well. "Earl Lucan," he said. "Your words are very disrespectful. Is there some reason why you mistrust New Rome?"

Lucan shrugged. "No more than you would mistrust us were we to contrive an excuse to send our warships along the African coast, where certain Moorish emirs are resisting your rule."

The Roman ambassadors exchanged glances; there was no easy riposte to such a fair point. Maximion took his seat again – which Arthur found interesting. Had the elderly tribune posed his question to offer his hosts a small moral victory?

"Gentlemen," the King said. "As you see, the issue of our northern ports is not a simple one. However, I am not averse to offering assistance should a Roman vessel be found in distress. I shall discuss this matter further, but privately with my advisors."

Malconi nodded obsequiously. Tribune Rufio sat down again, but with poor grace.

"The next matter for today?" Arthur asked.

"The rather grave matter of Brittany," Bishop Proclates replied. "Your friend on the Continent, King Arthur."

"I'm perfectly aware who my friends are, your grace."

"King Hoel regards himself as your military ally?" Consul Rascalon said.

"And?"

"Like the Saxons, he is proving a difficult neighbour."

"Perhaps if your armies weren't gathering beyond his border, he'd be more affable?" Lancelot suggested.

"Let's cut to the chase, my lords," Bedivere said. "New Rome intends to invade Brittany, does it not?"

"Criminal acts must be punished," Bishop Proclates replied.

"What criminal acts would these be?" Cador wondered.

Again, Bishop Malconi rose to his feet. "King Arthur, it gives me no pleasure to report that Brittany's spies stir revolt in our lands."

"Have you evidence of this?" Bedivere asked.

"I'm sure it can be provided," Malconi said.

"I'm sure as well," Arthur said. "But what you really want to know, your grace, is what action Camelot will take if you do invade Brittany. Am I correct?"

Malconi wove his fingers together. "As things are, my lord, Brittany is an anachronistic presence on the Gallic mainland. But we have no aggressive intentions towards her. On the contrary, we seek to help... to modernise."

"By breaking her borders?" Bedivere asked.

"We must consider all options."

"So must we," Arthur rejoined. "But unfortunately it's not possible to form any kind of firm answer on the basis of these vagaries."

"I have a question for their Roman lordships," Cador shouted. Bedivere gave him a warning glance, but Cador was already in full flow. "Does your Emperor still consider Britain to be a Roman province?"

Malconi pursed his lips before replying. "Britain's relationship with the Roman Empire was never formally dissolved."

"Even though the Roman Empire in the West was dissolved in every way possible?"

Again, Arthur interrupted. "Cador, I'm sure our sovereignty over our own realm is not in question." He directed his gaze at Bishop Malconi, who shook his head meekly. "That said, my lord bishop..." Arthur pondered. "That said, while we have the Emperor of New Rome present, in spirit if not body, perhaps we can ratify this state of affairs?"

Malconi looked puzzled. "My lord?"

Arthur's enthusiasm grew. "Let us draw up a document by which Emperor Lucius renounces any claim to the isle of Britain, and more particularly to our kingdom of Albion, and gives his personal guarantee that no such claim will be raised in the future again – for any reason, ever. If your august persons could endorse it as signatories, that would be the basis for a lasting peace between us."

Malconi sounded wary. "I would willingly take such a document back to Rome and ask for the Emperor's approval."

"That sounds like prevarication," Lancelot said.

"Oh, what is this nonsense?" Bishop Proclates retorted in a waspish tone. "None of us could sign such a document. That would be tantamount to making foreign policy in the Emperor's absence."

"But your foreign policy is to have peace with Britain," Bedivere replied. "Or so you say. This would certify it."

Malconi was now all smiles again. "Surely, King Arthur, you can't expect us to close the door forever on military action? Suppose a less amenable monarch than you were to assume power in this island?"

"It would be irrelevant to Roman affairs," Lancelot said. "Britain does not belong to the Roman Empire any more, and never will again."

"I can't disagree with that sentiment," Arthur added.

"Such a document would need the Emperor's signature," Proclates snapped.

"No Roman Emperor can be dictated to in this fashion," Malconi said. "As you must know, sire. As I say, I will consult him on the matter. Perhaps, in the meantime, if we were to know your mind on Brittany, it may sweeten the pill..."

"I have something else that might," Cador said. "How about if, while you are signing a document renouncing all claims to Britain, King Arthur were to sign a document renouncing all claims to New Rome?"

There was a strange, fragile silence.

The Roman ambassadors gazed at Cador with eerie fascination.

Cador's own colleagues, King Arthur included, looked at him askance.

"King Arthur?" Malconi ventured. "You have claims on New Rome?"

"Don't you know your own history?" Cador persisted, though he'd reddened a little in the cheek. "Constantine the Great was proclaimed Emperor of the Romans while here in Britain. In the first instance, this country became his heartland, his power-base, and he was acclaimed by all its inhabitants. In later years, he assumed full control of the Roman Empire. In that respect, a man who was first the ruler of Britain later became the ruler of Rome. Surely you don't deny this?"

"I don't deny it happened," Malconi said. "But I think our interpretation of those events may differ a little."

Cador sensed that he had gone too far, but was determined to stand his ground. "Our claim to the Roman Empire is as good as your claim to Britain."

Malconi turned again to King Arthur. "Sire, we have made no claim to Britain. But your claim to our realm is something we never expected."

"It's possible the position has been misrepresented to you," Arthur said, eyeing Cador coldly.

"Of course," the bishop replied. "Well... today has been interesting, but tiring. We are all wilting a little." It was certainly true that the chamber was becoming stuffy under its horn-shod casements, but it wasn't yet noon. "Might we reconvene on the morrow?"

"The morrow?" Arthur said. "We have an afternoon's session planned."

"We already have much to discuss among ourselves. I would appreciate it if we met again in the morning."

"Very well." Arthur looked frustrated, but nodded. "Gentlemen... take your leisure."

The conference broke up.

"WAS I WRONG?" Cador asked Bedivere quietly.

"You spoke unutterable nonsense," Bedivere replied.

"Well... at least I've given them something to think about."

Bedivere watched the Roman ambassadors as they filed out, deep in conversation. "*That* is undeniable."

Arthur remained on the high seat, his brow furrowed. Once the Romans had gone, Bedivere approached the throne. "You're troubled, my liege?"

Arthur frowned. "I expected them to raise the issue of religion today. That's why I had Stigand waiting in the ante-hall."

"Perhaps they feel it can wait? We have another three days of schedule."

"No, Bedivere... the plan was to raise every major matter today, then spend the next two days debating them, and deliver judgments on the final day. Either they are content there is nothing heretical about our practices, which even if it were true would not suit them, because they desire to present us as heretics to the Pope. Or they no longer need it as a stick to beat us with."

Kay said: "Personally I draw comfort from the absence of a religious quarrel. Archbishop Stigand is a learned father, but Bishop Malconi sets eloquent traps."

"There is no comfort to be drawn when your opponent dispenses with what is clearly his best weapon." Arthur sat up. "Lancelot, send a herald... invite the Roman ambassadors to a feast tonight in the palace. I'd like to speak with them less formally." Lancelot bowed and withdrew as Arthur descended from the chair. "Sir Lucan?"

Lucan glanced up distractedly from his bench. "My liege?"

"You seem preoccupied again."

"Forgive me, sire. I'm still not quite myself."

"You spoke as you said you would last night, sirrah. Those were harsh words for the Romans, but one must respect a fellow who doesn't dissemble."

"I said it before, sire, and I'll say it again. They mean to have a war. The Saxons, the Bretons – invented grievances, designed to provoke us into giving them an excuse they can take to the Holy See. And now, thanks to Cador, they have one – self-defence."

"The Pope would never accept such nonsense," Kay replied.

Lucan shrugged. "He may... if it suits him to."

Kay pulled a face as if it was all too ridiculous. "You're a reassuring presence when there's trouble brewing, Lucan, but sometimes you're too quick to look for a fight. No-one dislikes the Romans more than me, but we need to proceed with caution. No more calling them 'dogs' or making accusations that can't be proved, you understand?"

"Is that the King's wish?" Lucan asked.

"Yes," Arthur said. "Think on it. The rest of you come with me. We have much to discuss."

Lucan watched as Arthur, Kay and Bedivere strode away. He was unconcerned not to have been invited. Arthur had never regarded him as part of the inner circle of the Round Table. Though Lucan had fought long and hard in Arthur's cause, there were many who believed that in his wild, early days he had fought a little too hard. "Like father, like son," they'd whispered. Perhaps that was why he'd been allocated the far north as his personal fief? The northern border was his home and the place he knew best, but Lucan suspected there was a more practical reason: attack dogs were always useful in the face of the enemy, but for the rest of the time it was better to keep them at arm's length.

Again, he was unconcerned. The machinations of the Roman ambassadors, the chattering of courtiers at Camelot – none of those things mattered very much at present.

NINE

THE ROMANS ACCEPTED Arthur's invitation, and early that evening a succession of palanquins ferried them up the Eagle Road to the palace.

The feast was served in the main banquet hall. Normally, the tables in there would be arrayed in a great horseshoe around a blazing central hearth, with King Arthur and Queen Guinevere at its head, Archbishop Stigand to their right, Sir Kay to their left, and all other senior nobility and their consorts seated in descending order of importance down either leg. But now, with the Roman ambassadors and their chief flunkeys present, not to mention sundry other courtiers, barons, churchmen and city burgesses, the hearth had been cleared and additional tables set out.

The gathering was noisy but good-natured. Certain of Arthur's knights, who for various reasons had missed that first day's Council but had now arrived during the course of the evening – Sir Gawaine, for instance, and his brothers, Sir Gareth and Sir Gaheris – had needed to be accommodated on smaller trestle tables, which owing to the numbers elsewhere, were located far from the presence of the King. But such was the etiquette at Camelot that no man took offence on a grand occasion like this, least of all Sir Gawaine, who, being loud, garrulous and a great songster when the drink was on him, was happy to be in any genial company.

The meal was exquisite. The first course consisted of shellfish simmered in garlic, wine and honey, and the main course of roast fowls glazed in sweet, sticky sauce, served with buttered, crusty bread and trenchers of steaming vegetables: cabbages, onions, turnips, carrots and leeks. The procession of servants who brought the repast had to weave their way in and around the jugglers and tumblers who held court in the very centre of the chamber. Rich, sweet wine was poured liberally, or, if the diners preferred, flagons of frothing ale or crisp cider were provided.

From the high gallery surrounding the chamber fluted the sweet voice of Taliesin, accompanied by the harmonious tones of gitterns, dulcimers and reed-pipes.[13] The noise levels rose steadily, shouting and guffawing piercing the smoky air as any cantankerous feeling lingering from the day was smoothed over. Arthur had taken care with his seating arrangements, ensuring that Romans were always interspersed with Britons, who were under strict orders to make cordial conversation. Where possible, the senior Roman ambassadors were placed alongside the most beautiful ladies of court, while potentially recalcitrant elements – such as Cador – were dispatched to the far corners.

Lucan observed the ambassadors with interest.

Consul Rascalon was the most obviously 'Roman' of them, inasmuch as he was portly to the point of being corpulent. His garments were the richest on show, his chain of office the most ornate. He wore a fur-trimmed white satin gown, with sleeves puffed and full from elbow to shoulder, over a lilac jerkin covered with gold embroidery. A blue, flat-brimmed cap decorated with a peacock plume was pulled down over his fluffy white locks. His fat, moist hands were bedecked with gem-encrusted rings, and he made constant fluttering gestures with them as he spoke. All through the banquet he issued curt instructions to the servants, apparently anticipating disrespect and determined to dissuade it by his manner alone. By contrast,

[13]*gittern:* a small early guitar; *dulcimer:* a stringed instrument with a flat sounding-board, played on the lap by plucking or with hammers; *reed-pipe:* an early woodwind instrument.

Bishop Proclates seemed remarkably young for a high-ranking clergyman, and though handsome and virile, there was also something vulpine about him – he had the aura of a hard man, a cold man. Not once had Lucan seen him smile. Though clad in the skullcap and ecclesiastical purple, Proclates's velvet houppeland[14] was high-collared, girdled at the waist and had long, trailing sleeves, which exposed powerful wrists. The cut of his garb accentuated a lean but strong physique.

"I understand you are a fighting man of some note?" came a voice from Lucan's left.

He turned to view the Roman ambassador seated next to him. This fellow was clearly not a churchman. His garb was too simple: a tan leather doublet worn over a white shirt with puffed sleeves laced at the cuffs and collar. His iron-grey hair was cut very short, and he was clean-shaven. He had a refined but angular face which was marked by old scars. His eyes were hazel but of an intense lustre. There was something intelligent but solemn about him. Lucan remembered that they had crossed words during the debate.

"I've fought for Arthur, yes," Lucan said. "I'm Lucan, of the House Corneus."

"You are Steward of the North, I understand?"

"I am. Forgive me...?"

The Roman offered his hand. "Quintus Maximion, Senior Tribune of the Eighth Legion."

"Ah yes," Lucan said. "You've been active in Rome's reconquest of the West."

"I've had some success in the Emperor's name."

"If nothing else, we're both modest men, Lord Maximion."

Maximion half-smiled. "This is a most impressive hall."

He surveyed the chamber appreciatively. Its high roof was of oaken shingles, supported by four great stone arches painted lavish colours and carved with woodland scenes. The walls were hung with weapons and battle-standards, many captured

---

[14]A heavy outer-robe with wide sleeves, worn by both men and women.

from Arthur's enemies. There were also tapestries, sumptuously woven. The floor was of sanded marble, the broad avenue leading into it laid with a crimson carpet.

"It has the rugged grandeur of the wild north," Maximion commented. "Yet there is comfort here, and a sense of artisanship."

"This is Camelot, after all," Lucan said.

"Yes, but many in Rome would be surprised."

"They'd expect a barbarian stronghold?"

"They would expect little more than a palisade, maybe with a few longhouses and cattle-sheds crammed in the middle of it." Maximion glanced at his goblet – it was wrought from silver, ornamented with elves and dragons. "They would expect drinking-horns rather than handsome cups." He assessed his knife and fork – they were of elaborate Italian design. "And a single knife instead of cutlery, maybe the same one used earlier that day to slit an enemy's throat."

"And will they be worried to learn otherwise?" Lucan asked.

"Probably not, is the sad truth."

"The *sad* truth?"

Maximion sipped his wine thoughtfully. "I spoke out of turn, Earl Lucan. I'm only a soldier. I have no personal views regarding our mission here."

"Then why were you sent?"

Maximion shrugged, as if he had already given too many of his feelings away.

"There's no need to answer that question," Lucan said. "I know the answer. And so does King Arthur. You are here to assess our defences, are you not?"

"If that were true, I would be awe-stricken by them. This fortress, I would guess, is impregnable. Should it ever be put under siege, I'd imagine it has stores that could last it many years. During our journey here from Dover, we passed similar castles: Sissinghurst, Scotney and Petersfield,[15] I believe, were some of their names?"

[15]Fourteenth-century castles in Kent and Hampshire, suggesting the route the New Romans took, from the Kentish coast – presumably Dover – to Camelot.

The main meal was now complete, and baskets of fruit and honeyed barley cakes were being passed around by servants. Lucan took a cake and broke a small piece from it. "That would be correct."

"Fine defensive structures, all," Maximion added. "Most disconcerting... for an enemy, I mean. But I fear this is an uncomfortable subject for discussion."

Lucan turned to face him, the elf-grey eyes gleaming in his pale face. "Lord Maximion, you clearly speak with candour. And I would be doing you an injustice if I did not respond in kind. Let me tell you truly... we have no fear of New Rome. An extensive war between us would be ruinous for this kingdom, but we have fought so many wars already. We've all of us in this room buried friends and family. We ourselves have behaved like brute animals when the necessity came. It isn't something any of us particularly want to experience again, but it's something we are used to. You understand?"

"Of course," Maximion replied.

"Every one of Arthur's lords who sits at table tonight can call thousands of men to his banner. And all of them warriors – real soldiers with long experience and good training. Not peasants pressed into service. Not slaves who would rather be anywhere else in the world. But..." Lucan shrugged. "No doubt you have heard this same thing from many others in recent years."

"Perhaps not with the same conviction," Maximion said.

"I apologise if I was impolite."

"No... far from it. In fact, with the exception of the heated exchanges in the Council hall today, which were perfectly understandable, everyone we have met in this land has been most courteous. Your reputation for gallantry is well earned. But let us discuss neutral things. Are you a family man, Earl Lucan?"

"My wife, Trelawna, is here with me..."

Lucan glanced over his shoulder. Trelawna was several seats away, or she was supposed to be – for her place was now vacant. The Roman ambassador, Consul Publius, had been seated alongside her, Arthur's intent being that the countess should charm him with her beauty and wit. Now Publius sat glumly, gnawing on left-over chicken-bones.

Lucan was puzzled. "No doubt she'll return shortly. Are *you* a family man, tribune?"

Maximion nodded. "I have three sons. All serve in the army. My wife, alas, is now departed. The sweating sickness took her five winters ago."

"My condolences."

"Gratefully received."

"I wonder," Lucan said, "does this bereavement mean that you feel you have nothing to go home to?"

"Oh no, Earl Lucan." Maximion gave a thin smile. "I've lived long enough to understand that I still have much to go home to. Would that I could impart this wisdom to others, but ears are sometimes closed at the most inopportune moments."

Lucan frowned. "Some things must be striven for harder than others, my lord. If I were you, I should keep trying."

TRELAWNA MET RUFIO, as their proxies had agreed, in a rose garden, on a balconied terrace accessible only by the West Gallery and a steep stairway.

It had been chosen by Gerta because it was the least likely place where any guests might stray to during the course of the feast, and because it had bowers and trellised screens between which a visitor might walk unseen. Despite this, it was well-lit by oil-lamps, and though only a few casements overlooked it, it could still be seen if a servant chanced past. Hence, the lovers had planned to meet innocently, and offer idle pleasantries as they strolled.

Of course, having seen each other for the first time in so many years whilst entering the feast-hall that evening, and then having to sit for the meal and feign concentration on their food, had been a torturous test, and now that they were alone together at last, their inhibitions broke. They came in sight of each other from either end of a rose-bordered walk, Rufio in his white hose and fitted, blue-and-gold satin cote-hardie,[16] Trelawna in her figure-hugging, flame-red kirtle, her lustrous hair coiled in plaits. It was too much. They flew down the walk into each other's arms. When they finally broke apart, they were breathless, their lips bright.

Rufio shook his head; his deep brown eyes had moistened with emotion. Trelawna felt shudders of girlish joy passing through her; she could barely speak.

"All these... years," he finally stammered. "All these years I've been denied sight of you. I had to rely on memory and imagination – I perfected you in my mind's eye until you were an angel on earth. And now I see that my assessment wasn't even close."

"And you!" she whispered. "You're so much a man now." She touched his cheek. "You even have care-lines."

"We've been at war..."

"They add to you." She luxuriated in the strength of the arms enclosing her. "The fighting has kept you fit."

"There wasn't a battle when the image of your face didn't carry me through, where I didn't picture you waiting for me somewhere... though I confess I didn't know where."

"Here, my love... *here*."

They kissed again. It seemed incredible that the one night of passion they had shared had been six years ago, when they had first met during an identical conference to this one, here in Camelot. Both had been wandering, bored, while the baronage of both nations filled the palace with drunken revelry. True, they had not encountered each other in this very garden, but they might as well have done. Now, in each other's arms, it was impossible to imagine that six years had passed, and not a couple of minutes.

"Good Lord, I've dreamed about this," Rufio said. "Come away with me."

Trelawna was startled. "What?"

"Come away with me, tonight."

---

[16] A buttoned tunic.

"Tonight?"

He nodded vigorously. "There can be no future for us if we separate again."

"But tonight?" She felt a surge of alarm. "I... I cannot."

He clutched her by the hands. "My love... I fear we have no other choice."

"To leave now, on the spur of the moment...?"

"Would it pain you so much?"

Trelawna was torn with indecision, but also mounting excitement. "I think... I think it would pain me more to stay," she breathed.

"So the matter is resolved."

"No." She pulled away from him. "I have..."

"You have nothing... not here. Few friends, no family."

"I have a husband, Felix."

"In name only."

"That doesn't matter. Wherever you took me... I'd be held a sinner, a fallen woman."

He wrapped his arms around her. "I will take you to Rome itself, my love. A word from His Holiness and your marriage is done. We would be free to marry, you and I."

She gazed at him in disbelief. Was it possible? Could it be true?

Again she was beset by whirlwinds of doubt. Surely nothing so wonderful could happen to her? At most this evening she'd expected no more than to steal a few kisses from him, but deep inside her a wellspring of joy was rising. She knew there was nothing that could matter to her as much as a life of love and happiness with Felix Rufio.

"Don't go back to that wilderness in the north, my lady," he pleaded. "Ultimately you will wither there, and die before your time."

"But this is hardly the time," Trelawna said. "With negotiations between our rulers balanced on a knife-edge."

"Bah!" Rufio replied. "We are but cogs in a greater machine. Whatever our private disputes, they have no bearing on these affairs. But even if they did, it would make no difference."

Suddenly he became serious; his face was almost grave. "There's something you should know, my love. The Roman embassy is leaving in the early hours."

Trelawna was shocked. "Leaving?"

"When Arthur and his counsellors are asleep, we will be on the road. Not to Dover but to Southampton, a much nearer port, where a ship even faster than the one that brought us rides at anchor."

"But the negotiations...?"

"They are finished." He kissed her hands. "Don't you understand? My uncle, Bishop Malconi, is a master of this game, and he already has what he came for."

Trelawna's lips puckered. Her brow creased with worry.

"You still have fears?" he asked.

She had few. But some hidden sense told her that, besotted though she was with this man, and though her world would seem empty indeed if he left her now, the course he proposed was wrong.

"My love, there will be no second chances," he urged her.

"You exact a high price, Felix. I'm not British by origin, but this land has become my home. Will I never see it again?"

Rufio smiled sadly. "Britain will shortly be annihilated."

She backed away from him, horrified.

"It is not *my* doing," he added hastily.

"You must explain, Felix."

He nodded. "Understand that in telling you all this, I am breaching an immense confidence – an Imperial confidence."

"I do."

"King Arthur will not surrender to Emperor Lucius. That has been made plain to us, though in truth we already knew it. Therefore he and his minions must be removed. I'm sorry if that seems harsh, but it's the way of New Rome, and you, I promise, will live long enough to see the better world that will result. Of course, both you and I know that Arthur and his nobility will not go quietly. There must be a war – a great and terrible war."

"You think Arthur hasn't fought wars before?"

"He's never fought a war like this one. The arms assembling in Gaul stretch from one horizon to the next. Such a host has never been mustered. Trelawna – you need to know what is coming for this land. Blood and fire, on a colossal scale. My love, if there is anything at all you cherish about Arthur's kingdom, say your farewells to it now, because it will likely be smashed. I'm not seducing you, Trelawna, I'm *saving* you."

Trelawna was so appalled that she could hardly speak. It was too staggering to be true, and yet there was no reason for Rufio to lie – and he was party to all the Romans' secrets. Of course, there was no difference that *she* could now make. Even if she were to betray Rufio and go straight to Arthur, it would not prevent the inevitable. If the Romans were genuinely to leave on the morrow, that was when Arthur would learn the truth. By alerting him now, all she would do was entrap herself in this doomed land.

"When do you plan to leave?" she asked.

"The feast lasts until midnight. For us to make the morning tide, our staff is under orders to make ready for departure by three o'clock at the latest."

"Maybe I can slip from my boudoir," she said, thinking aloud. "Lucan may have drunk so much by then that he won't notice."

Rufio nodded, musing. "I saw him at the Council today," he said. "He seems typical of the equestrian order – confident, arrogant, aggressive."

"How badly you misread him," she replied. "He is none of those things – save aggressive, but only when he has cause to be."

Rufio seemed surprised by that, but shrugged. "He'll have cause soon enough. I beseech you, Trelawna, come with me this night."

"I will try," she said. "I haven't much to give up, but it would help if I knew what I was gaining."

"Allow me to enlighten you." He drew her close, warming his cheek against hers. "I have a many-storied townhouse on the Palatine, overlooking Rome's central forum. The city is not quite the capital it once was, thanks to the Vandal hordes, but, district by district, Emperor Lucius is restoring it – reconstructing its civic buildings, refurbishing its great monuments. There are libraries, public baths, theatres and markets. We have fountains, hot and cold running water. New parks have been opened, and trees planted along the banks of the Tiber to provide shady walks for lovers."

Despite her reservations, Trelawna trembled with joy.

"It is a city of light and sophistication. And in addition, I have a house in the Tuscan hills, where it pleases me to spend the summer months. This is a heavenly place, a rambling country manse built of red stone, filled with Greek and Etruscan artworks, and surrounded by gardens, vineyards and poplar groves. Its peace and tranquillity is never disturbed. *This* will be your home, my love, and when we are married it will be the home of our children. When they finally assume ownership in their own right, the dark north as you knew it will have ceased to exist. Our offspring will never have known it."

If there was anything Rufio could have said that would sway Trelawna to his plan, this was it. She had seen the effects of the northern waste on those forced to endure it – the weathered faces, the foul tempers. Lucan was the ultimate product of that land – an upright man, a sturdy man, but, deep in his heart, a wolf.

"Say yes, please," Rufio begged. "Say you'll come with me."

"Yes, Felix, I'll come."

He caressed her mouth with his, sucking her wine-sweet tongue between his lips, his hands roving her slender contours, clutching her buttocks through her kirtle, reaching down her firm thighs. Her arms enfolded him to a point where he could scarcely breathe. Delight rumbled in his chest as they kissed long and deep.

And this was the state of affairs when Malvolio came upon them.

TEN

WITH NO ROOM at the feast except for delegates and dignitaries, even men of rank among the common soldiery – captains and constables – were forced to find supper elsewhere. It was the same for the squires, though they were deemed at least worthy to be wined and dined in the palace kitchens, which in truth they often preferred. Here there was no emphasis on manners, and though the fare was rough and ready – mutton, bread and leeks in salted butter – there was no shortage of jugged ale and so many kitchen maids and serving wenches that every lad present felt sure he'd have tumbled a lass by morning.

Even Malvolio, normally a bonehead in these circumstances, made good ground with a certain Lotta, whose fiery locks, pouting lips and melon-size breasts promised paradise.

"You squires are too cocky by half," she said after she'd caught him attempting to lift her skirt. "You shouldn't use us so rudely. You're no better than us."

"Quite right, my dear," Malvolio agreed. "Caste and breeding have no role here. We seek only your sympathy."

"Sympathy?" She arched an eyebrow as she poured more ale.

"My dear," he stuttered, to the hilarity of his fellows clustered around the table, many already with lasses on their laps, "we are soon to be knights. Then we will die as one, martyred in the name of King and Christendom. Does such heroism not become us?"

"A fool's coxcomb would become you more," Lotta retorted. Benedict roared.

"Outrageous!" Malvolio declared. "I was born to do good work with a lance."

She shook her head at such effrontery, but though her tray was laden with empty vessels she made no attempt to withdraw.

"Sweet nymph, salve my pain," Malvolio persisted, hiccoughing, which brought another belly-laugh from Benedict. "Let me plant my mouth on those berry-red lips, rest my head on that sturdy bosom."

"It'll take more than flowery bullshit to win these virgin pillows, sir knight-in-waiting." This time Lotta *did* withdraw.

Malvolio feigned hurt. "I still think she likes me."

His companions fell about the table, but Lotta returned with another pot of ale for him.

"Are you really a virgin?" he asked, his words slurring.

"That may be for you to discover, my lord." She walked away again, this time leaving the kitchens entirely.

"I'll return anon," Malvolio announced, standing so abruptly that he toppled backward and fell from his stool. It took three of them to lift him to his feet, insert the freshly filled pot into his hand and propel him in the right direction.

He was so inebriated that once away from the noise and light of the kitchens he found it difficult to navigate. Or possibly the teasing girl had not been teasing after all, but simply wanted to be done with him. Either way, she made herself scarce, and he blundered around the palace corridors, drawing constantly on his ale, which hardly helped because soon he was looking for a latrine as well.

It was by pure chance that he tottered out into the rose garden on the west terrace, unlacing the front of his breeches, and there witnessed something that struck him like a blow between the eyes. Fogged with ale, but not so fogged that he didn't realise what he was seeing, Malvolio turned and tottered back into the palace still with his member on display.

He hurried, gasping, along several passages before confronting someone – fortunately not a lady of court, but Alaric.

"You're a dissolute lad, Mal, we all know," Alaric commented. "But I'd put that away if I were you. It's a little unsubtle."

Malvolio tucked himself out of sight before jabbering what he'd just seen.

At first Alaric thought he'd misheard. He gazed at Malvolio aghast. "You're... you're wrong! You must be!"

Malvolio shook his head. His cheeks had flushed a ruddy hue.

By contrast, the colour drained from Alaric's face. His friend was stone-drunk – he could easily be mistaken. But there was something in Malvolio's demeanour. His eyes, previously clouded, were wide and alert. He panted like a dog. Whatever he'd seen – or thought he'd seen – it had frightened him.

"Where?" Alaric asked.

"I'm not sure..." Malvolio told the way as best he was able.

"Go back to the kitchens, and ask for more ale," Alaric said firmly. "Keep drinking, Mal. Drink until you fall unconscious, do you hear me?"

Malvolio nodded dumbly.

"You say nothing about this, you understand?" Alaric said. "To anyone."

"But Earl Lucan..."

"Especially not to Earl Lucan! Good God in Heaven, don't say *anything* to him!"

Malvolio nodded. He touched a shaking hand to his clammy brow.

"Go on," Alaric urged him. "You're drunk as a mop. Trust me, you'll be mistaken. But if it's some lord sticking it into someone else's lady, and they saw you, this could still be a problem. Let me go and find out."

Malvolio lurched away, and Alaric proceeded along the passage, heart thumping. When he finally found the terrace garden, Countess Trelawna was seated alone on a bench. Apparently, she was taking the evening air.

"Why, Alaric...?" she said, looking surprised.

"My lady..." Alaric felt absurdly self-conscious, as if it was obvious why he'd arrived in this hidden nook of the palace and it would be clumsy to try and deny it. "Malvolio... erm, Malvolio was just here."

"Yes, I saw."

"He's erm... he's very drunk."

"I saw that as well."

Alaric shook his head and smiled. "Forgive me, ma'am. He mistook..."

"He mistook nothing, Alaric. He saw me with my lover, a Roman officer."

Alaric was vaguely aware of hair prickling on his scalp. Torturous seconds seemed to pass, during which they could do nothing but regard each other in mute astonishment.

"Does that surprise you?" she finally asked.

"It... surprises me you would admit it," he stammered.

"Why? Must one go on suffering for love indefinitely and in silence? The way *you* do. Oh, yes, Alaric... I know about your infatuation."

Alaric almost choked. "You... you try to cast me in the same light as...? But my lady, I've never said a word, I've never done anything inappropriate... "

"Of course you haven't. Don't worry, Alaric. I'm not attempting to blackmail you. I'm trying to appeal to you as a friend."

"Your husband is also my friend."

"Just so. But I'm not asking you to lie to him. Merely to keep quiet about what you know until tomorrow, when *I* will break the news to him."

Alaric was still too stunned for rational words. A creeping numbness afflicted his skin.

"Where is your master now?" Trelawna asked.

"In the banquet hall?"

"It won't be too long before they are all drunk and incapable."

"My lady, Earl Lucan doesn't..."

"Oh I know, Alaric. I know my own husband. He doesn't

drink to the point where he falls face-first onto his own gravy-stained platter, but nevertheless he will be drunk. And when he finally returns to our bed, he will sleep like the dead. Is any of this untrue?"

Alaric shook his head dumbly.

"This is why it's best to save the bad news until the morrow. If it reaches him later tonight he will not comprehend it – and it's surely best that he comprehends it absolutely. If it reaches him *now,* he will half-comprehend it – sufficiently to go in search of a sword, and then all Arthur's careful negotiations will be for naught. The choice is yours."

Alaric tried to swallow, but found his mouth was dry. "You will break this terrible news to him yourself, you say?"

Trelawna produced a sealed envelope. "I have written Lucan a letter, which I would be grateful if you would hand to him on the morrow. It will explain everything."

Still barely knowing what he was doing, Alaric took it. "You will not be here?"

"Alas, no. What purpose would that serve?"

"My lady... how could you... how could you do this to us?"

"Alaric, is it true that you love me?"

"More than you could ever imagine."

"Foolish child. What can I have done to enchant you so?"

"Just being who you are."

"In that case, something good will have come from this. You regard me somewhat less idealistically now?"

Alaric shook his head. "My lady, I'm past the stage where I could ever judge you."

"Then you know how I feel? All wisdom and inhibition has left me. I know only that I must be with my love. If you truly feel the same, you will help me."

"I'll give him the letter, ma'am, though I can hardly approve."

She sighed. "Understand that I have misgivings too. But if I'm to live my life I must follow my heart."

"You will break his," Alaric said, his voice thickening. "And mine."

"For you, it was always an impossible dream. I'm sure you understood that?"

Alaric said nothing as hot tears dripped down his cheeks.

Trelawna stood. "I'm for bed. If you feel the urge to betray me, you must obey your conscience. But I beg you to consider the consequences." She turned to leave, but had an afterthought. "Malvolio...?"

"He won't remember a thing. Until the morning, when, of course, it won't matter."

"In the morning, none of this will matter. Goodbye, Alaric."

Alaric made no response, merely stood frozen as she drifted away. It was several minutes before he could take himself into the palace, stopping to dry his tears. He wandered the labyrinthine passages with slow, stumbling footsteps, nauseated by shock. It wasn't just the news that his mistress had imparted to him, though that was possibly the most devastating thing he had heard in his life, it was her manner. It had been cold, almost heartless – but it made it worse that he'd recognised it as a façade. Her lips had trembled; her blue eyes had glazed with moisture. She was clearly torn with sorrow, and yet the promise of her new life must have made this bearable.

Her new life...

It stuck in his craw, banged inside his head like an angry wasp.

Countess Trelawna – *his* Countess Trelawna – was headed for a new life in which neither her husband nor Alaric had any role to play.

He glanced at the letter. Lucan's name had been inscribed on it with Trelawna's usual elegant flourish. When he put it to his nose, he could smell her perfume – juniper and daffodil. Over the years he'd handled so many of these apparently innocent missives. It cut him to the core to wonder how many had been part of this grand deception.

He made his way to the banquet hall by the most meandering path imaginable. Even had he not known where it was, he couldn't have failed to find it thanks to the hubbub of discordant singing. Queen Guinevere and her ladies had withdrawn, as had the Romans. But Arthur's knights and barons were still present, grouped around their King, beating a raucous tattoo with their feet and fists, singing lustily – not the mystical verses of Taliesin, but bawdy fighting songs, tales of battles won and enemies destroyed. Brows were florid, beards soaked with sweat. Flagons slopped ale, wine sprayed from bawling mouths. This might be Camelot, a centre of culture by the standards of the north, but it was still a martial court, and like martial courts all over Europe, except for those now reclaimed by the Roman world – Alaric felt a bubbling resentment – most baronial gatherings ended in this fashion. Roistering – a loutish exhibition of drunkenness and bravado, which Countess Trelawna clearly reviled and yet had been forced to tolerate for so many years. Until now.

Alaric had to fight down more tears. He focused on Earl Lucan in the midst of the throng, Gawaine's arm on his shoulder. He was roaring along with the rest, draining one mug after another; wine, ale or cider – it made no difference to him. It made no difference to any of them. But these weren't just tavern brawlers, they were seasoned warriors; men who'd grown stout of limb and strong of heart through years of turmoil. When this night ended, they'd fall into their bed like sacks of meal, but would be up with the dawn, cool-headed and ready for further debate.

Of course, it was anyone's guess now what tone that debate would take. Or whether those heads would remain cool. One thing was certain, if Alaric handed over the letter now, there would be an eruption. Rivers of blood would run in this palace, rather than rivers of ale. Despite this, an odd perversity almost steered him into the heart of the mayhem, shouting and waving his envelope. But good sense at last forbade it.

ELEVEN

King Arthur was roused from his bedchamber at four o'clock to be given a message from the Watch that the Roman ambassadors were departing the city. If the King was still fuddled from the previous night's carousing, he sobered up quickly enough. But he remained calm and thoughtful. He took a minute to absorb the information, and then issued orders that he was not to be disturbed again until dawn.

"Alaric!" Bedivere called. *"Alaric!"*

Alaric glanced around from the lodge-hall hearth, which he was having trouble lighting as gusts of damp wind kept howling down the chimney, scattering smoke and embers. Most of the other squires, Benedict and Malvolio included, were still snoring beneath their cloaks. Overhead, rain hissed on the thatched eaves.

He stood as Bedivere barged into the hall. The lad was pale-faced from lack of sleep; his eyes were sunken, his hair in stringy ringlets. He'd already made one trip across the courtyard, during which he'd been drenched, and up into the guest-apartments, to slide Countess Trelawna's envelope beneath Earl Lucan's door. That had been two hours ago, when everything was eerily quiet. Now the entire palace was alive with bells and the frantic feet of servants.

"Where is your master?" Bedivere said. "The King summoned the Round Table at first light. Lucan's the only person not to have attended."

"In his apartment, my lord. He won't come out."

"I've just been to his apartment and there was no-one –" Bedivere paused, noting Alaric's wan features. "What's happened?"

The squire stammered out everything. After a night of anguish, during which he'd alternately prayed, wept and tormented himself with dreams of loss and guilt, it now seemed unimportant to conceal that he'd known about the countess's deceit in advance.

Bedivere stood rigid. "You young fool!" he finally whispered. "Why didn't you report this straight away?"

"I thought it a private matter..."

"A private matter!" Bedivere's voice rose to a shout. *"You damn idiot! This could mean death for someone!"*

"I felt that, too. So I thought it best..."

"Best for whom? The miscreants? You thought it best to let them escape?"

Suddenly Alaric's mouth was as dry as paper. This was, of course, the truth, though he could hardly bring himself to admit it – not even to himself.

"Did Trelawna tell you the Roman ambassadors were planning to quit Camelot?"

Alaric shook his head. "She implied that she and her lover were leaving. It shocked me so much I didn't even think about the rest of them."

"That you didn't think is plain as day!" Bedivere looked ready to hit the lad. His lips had tightened so that his teeth were bared. "Get the rest of these oafs on their feet and search the palace. Press any servants you find into helping you."

Alaric did what he could to marshal the rest of the squires, though in an attempt to protect the dignity of his overlord, told them nothing about the night's revelation, which left most of them nonplussed and half-hearted in their quest.

*   *   *

IT WAS ALARIC himself who finally located Lucan. First he checked the apartment and, as Bedivere had said, found it empty and in a state of disarray. Next he looked in the adjoining room which had been used by Countess Trelawna's maid, and found this also empty. Unlike the other room, every drawer and closet in here was closed. There wasn't a thing out of place. All her personal belongings had been carefully removed.

Cursing Trelawna and her staff for a coven of conniving witches, he hurried on his way, at last – thanks to the advice of a royal guardsman descending from one of the high battlements – tracing his master to a pinnacle turret, where he stood between two mossy merlons, his toes on the very brink, the rain sweeping over him.

Alaric sucked a tight breath as he advanced onto the battlement walk.

Lucan wore leather breeches and hunting-boots, but only a loose blouse, which, soaked through by rain, clung to his tightly-muscled torso like a second skin. His long black hair also dripped with rainwater, but his head was bowed as though he was sleeping on his feet. Only his fingers made contact with the rain-slick merlons, providing no real anchor.

Alaric hardly dared to speak – he hardly even dared step forward.

"Did you know, Alaric...?" Lucan said without looking around. His eyes were open, gazing unseeing into the abyss below. "Did you know my father served Uther?"

"I know that, my lord," Alaric replied.

"But did you also know that even by the standards of that most violent king, my father was a particularly violent baron?"

Alaric said nothing. He was wondering if he could dash forward and grab his overlord around the waist without accidentally pitching him to oblivion.

Lucan continued, his voice a dull, dead monotone. "When Arthur acceded to the throne, a handful of those warlords who'd gone before him were subjected to the *Damnatio Memoriae*. And my father was one. Did you know that?"

"I did, my lord."

"That meant his sins were so great, the mere memory of him was outlawed. His name was to be erased from monuments, struck from records..."

"I'm aware..."

"And yet you..." Lucan looked up, taking the rain full in his face. He swayed dangerously. "*You*... who were born so long after he died, know all about him. It can't have been a very effective measure."

"I fear, my lord, you can't kill a memory."

"No." Lucan smiled thinly. "You can't *unsay* a creature like my father. His wickedness will spill down the ages... as I am surely proof."

"My lord, please..."

"We lived on the north-facing flanks of Weardale, above the wooded wilderness of the *Hen Ogledd*, in a jagged tooth of a castle called Craghorn." Lucan's expression remained blank as the rain battered it. "I remember those days so well. Our wild North seems tame by comparison. The local populace was a mix of Brigant-Celts who'd deluded themselves that this entire realm should be theirs because their ancestors once used it as grazing-land, and Picts – painted head-hunters who'd launch murder-raids across the *Brynaich*. But if our enemies were dangerous, our friends were no better – lawless knights and barons, each in his own keep, constantly at feud or rebellion."

"My lord, please come down from..."

"But of course, you know that too. How could you not? Perhaps it's no wonder my father became the man he was, eh? Trying to hold the lid on such a cauldron. He was so wary of treachery and assassination that he became a specialist at both. He made night-assaults on anyone he suspected of disloyalty. Slew them in their beds, trampled their crops, burned their orchards and grain houses."

Alaric felt a rising dread as he watched Lucan's booted feet slide on the wet stonework. "My lord, if you would just..."

"One expedition went badly wrong. Father and a party of his knights were ambushed in the forest of Ewing. Most died in the first flight of arrows. But he and one other fled. They hid in a small chapel, where they tried to claim sanctuary. Their enemies were amused that this man, who had never respected the laws of Christ, should seek to hide behind them himself. So they piled wood around the building, brought oil and set fire to it. Eventually the heat and smoke overcame my father's companion. He died, choking on his own vomit. To escape the flames, father climbed into the steeple, but the intense heat caused the chapel bell to melt. Gobbets of molten iron dripped down upon him; one struck the side of father's face, incinerating it. Still he survived. In the morning, when all that remained of the chapel was a blackened shell, the enemy kicked their way in. My father, now a hideous relic of what he'd once been, was waiting, sword in one hand and mattock in the other. He killed six before they fled, thinking him a demon."

"My lord, this is in the mists of time. Almost no-one recalls..."

"And it wasn't far from the truth, Alaric. Bedivere and I were only boys. We lived in fear of his very shadow as he roamed that gaunt structure, his face a twisted mask. My mother had already ceased to love him – in her eyes he'd been a monster long before he'd come to resemble one."

Again, Lucan hung his head. Again, he swayed dangerously – so much that Alaric took a nervous step forward.

"Though he knew he was a gargoyle, his warped mind invented different reasons for this revulsion," Lucan said. "He became certain that mother was taking lovers..."

"My lord!" Alaric interrupted. "You are not your father!"

"I'm not?" Lucan glanced around. His bloodshot eyes had narrowed to slits in his white, rain-soaked face. "I inherited my father's banner, *his* black wolf-fur... yet they called *me* the Black Wolf of the North, not him."

"A figure of speech..."

"A figure of fear. That's what I am. There's no sense denying it, Alaric. Every slaughter I wrought on Arthur's foes was a nail in my reputation's coffin. The order I brought to the northern frontier was the order of blade and spear. For years the locals lived in terror that my father had somehow returned."

"You are no longer the Black Wolf," Alaric stated flatly. "It's a family emblem, nothing more."

Lucan hunched in the rain and wind. Only with painful slowness did he at last turn, step down onto the battlement walk and sit in the embrasure. "Some of us are just born bad, Alaric."

"My lord?"

"Born of sin."

"My lord, please..."

"Or infected by it, as I was by the serpent's bite."

"My lord, this is nonsense."

Lucan glanced up again. "Where did the Penharrow Worm come from?" He struck his own shoulder. "Why does the injury I received from it no longer hurt me?"

"These things just happen."

"They shouldn't. Not in a world that God has created. This beast came from the mist, from Hell itself... a harbinger of darkness!"

"You slew it!"

"Of course, but it had done its duty. Its call to arms was passed on."

"No, my lord!"

Lucan stood up. "We must all embrace our destinies, Alaric. Do you know what my father did to Fleance, the household knight he suspected of bedding my mother? He hanged him by the feet in the garderobe,[17] so that every man and woman in the castle would shit and piss on him through his death agonies." Lucan strode from the battlements. "Personally, I think he got off easily."

---

[17] A medieval toilet shaft.

*   *   *

LUCAN WAS THE last man to enter the chamber of the Round Table.

King Arthur, crowned and in royal purple, was in his customary place. All other members of the august brotherhood, also in full livery, were seated in their great, carved seats, their personal escutcheons pinned to the wall above their heads. There was a bleak silence as Lucan closed the chamber door behind him. Only the flames sounded on the hearth, and the wind groaned in the chimney.

"Sir Lucan, you have our heartfelt commiserations," the King said.

"Thank you, my liege," Lucan replied, walking around the table to his seat, located between those of Bedivere and his cousin, Griflet. Both men eyed him sympathetically.

"Are you alright?" Bedivere mumbled.

Lucan nodded tersely.

"Sir Lucan, we have discussed matters at length during the course of this morning," Arthur said, "but in short, the situation is as follows. New Rome has picked a fight with us." He raised a parchment written in an elegant hand, along the bottom of which Lucan could see a number of signatures. "They clearly came here looking for a pretext, and Sir Cador unwittingly gave them one."

Across the table, Cador's cheeks burned.

"Not that this matters," Arthur added. "I would have been happy to renounce my so-called claim to ownership of New Rome, but they didn't give me the chance. According to this document, they are disturbed and insulted that we had the temerity to make such a claim of Emperor Lucius, who sent his envoys to our court seeking nothing but good relations. We are not fooled by this charade, and I doubt His Holiness the Pope will be, but this will provide all they'll require to petition for his support. Without this, they'd doubtless have found something else. The main question now is how do we respond? Your suggestion that we launch a pre-emptive strike is thus far finding favour... if for no other reason than to assist our allies in Brittany, who even now, I suspect, can count their days of peace on one hand..."

OUTSIDE IN THE ante-hall, various courtiers and retainers had gathered to listen to the rumble and roar of debate.

By instinct, they stood in household groups. Turold, Wulfstan and the rest of Lucan's *mesnie* were already present when Alaric came and joined them. Archbishop Stigand paced the room with frustration. It baffled him that, despite Merlin having left the realm, taking all lingering pagan influence with him, senior churchmen in Albion were still not accorded the full rights of nobility. Stigand had many times advised Arthur that his Round Table was a dated institution, and that only when his senior abbots and archbishops were allowed to sit in on the greatest matters of state would Albion be granted access to the College of Cardinals in Rome.

"This does not bode well," he muttered, hearing mumbles of consent from the room beyond. "When the King emerges, I shall be in my writing office." He stalked from the hall. "I must consult with my brothers Canterbury and York."

A short time later, the door to the main chamber opened and Arthur's knights emerged, each approaching his own household to issue orders. Through the door, Alaric glimpsed Arthur, Bedivere and Kay still at the table, inscribing various documents.

"Turold!" Lucan said. Turold leapt to attention, as did the rest of Lucan's retainers. "Ride to Penharrow."

"Of course, my lord."

Lucan handed him a bound scroll. "This is a summons for all military forces."

The tempo of Alaric's beating heart rose steadily. On one hand, this was something he'd long been awaiting – a real war in which to test himself. On the other, a war like *this* – with all its terrifying repercussions – was hardly desirable.

"As you see, it bears the Royal Seal," Lucan added, "so it gives us full authority. For the avoidance of doubt, every company of household knights in my personal *demesnes* is to muster, and to bring all squires and pages. Every retainer – every baron, every landed knight, every owner or holder of keep, tower or manor house – is to respond in the same fashion. There is to be no scutage,[18] you hear me? The Castle Guard at Penharrow, Grimhall and Bullwood are also to be drawn upon. Two in every three mounted men-at-arms are to head south with full weapons and equipment, and one in every three foot-soldiers. Every twenty men must be accompanied by at least one officer, to maintain speed and good order on the march."

Though they had anticipated this, his party listened in astonishment. This would be the largest muster any of them had ever seen.

"There is also a summons for all village, town and manorial militia," Lucan added. "One in every three men or lads entitled to bear arms must respond. They will be divided into ordered companies of twenty and must bring full packs and rations. Turold..." The pain Alaric had seen in his master's expression earlier had departed, replaced by a cold severity. "Turold, my entire host must be on the road within two weeks, or you will answer to me. It must be here – at Camelot – within four. Or you will answer to the King." Turold made to leave, but Lucan stopped him again. "For my own household, black livery and black banners."

Alaric felt his neck-hairs stiffen. Only in times of extreme crisis were Earl Lucan's household colours of black and crimson dispensed with for the full black that his father had notoriously worn. It wasn't completely unknown – Lucan and his *mesnie* had worn full black when they'd ridden against the Danes on the River Humber – but there was always something disconcerting about it.

---

[18]A tax, which a vassal could pay in lieu of military service.

"Bring *Heaven's Messenger*," Lucan added.

Turold nodded. *Heaven's Messenger* was the earl's great battle-sword. This, too, had been inherited from his father, though Lucan had ensured the pagan runes with which it was once engraved had been worked out by a smith; and once, in the early days of their marriage, Trelawna had tied a red scarf of hers around its hilt as a favour before a tournament – this was still in place, and softened the sword's appearance a little.

"And bring me the wolf-fur?" Lucan said.

There was brief amazement among his knights, particularly those old enough to remember the bad old days when Lucan waged *all* his wars without mercy. Then, he had always worn the black fur cloak – made out of hides flayed personally by his father from the corpses of the pack held responsible for Countess Gundolen's death. Long before Lucan took ownership, it had been a symbol of brutal savagery. Only in time, at Trelawna's insistence, had he put it away.

Turold nodded and hurried off. Wulfstan arched a bushy grey eyebrow. He was perhaps the only one who would dare voice disapproval. And he did so now.

"Haven't you learned yet, my lord, the trappings of barbarism don't suit you?"

"And this from a man who never in his life has attended to his person," Lucan said. "Who has presented himself to dukes and kings in worsteds and sheepskins."

"True, my lord. On me, the wolf-fur would mean nothing. On you it means too much."

"In due course we'll see if there can ever be such a thing as 'too much.'"[19]

---

[19]It is here that Duke Corneus's letter to his son – at the beginning of this edition – appears in the "Noble Tragedie," but it seemed more fitting to introduce the translation with it, as it informs Lucan's character throughout, and is redundant this late in the story. Narrative styles have changed, since Malory's day; the letter reads as though Malory would have preferred to present it earlier.

TWELVE

As soon as Emperor Lucius's spies brought him news that King Arthur was mobilising his forces, he acted to remove Brittany from the equation. So long as the kingdom of Brittany remained in defiance of New Rome, Arthur would have a safe beachhead on the continent. He could bring his forces ashore whenever he wished, and there were also castles and walled towns there which he could occupy and turn into fortresses.

But still keen not to appear the aggressor, Lucius contrived an incident.

First, he consulted with the Frankish king, Childeric, whose court was in Paris. Childeric, who'd held sway over much of northern France during Rome's absence, was quickly purchased by Lucius. Though formerly a *foederatus* of the Empire, Childeric was not entirely content to return to that status, but part of the bargain he struck with Lucius held that once the whole of the Western Empire was restored, he would be rendered client-sovereign of a much vaster realm than he'd held previously; a realm incorporating all the lands from the Rhine to the Pyrenees, and maybe beyond.

Even so, he resisted any suggestion that his own Frankish subjects might be used to strike at Brittany's borders. Childeric knew full-well that Lucius was involved in a wrangle with Arthur of Britain; two more formidable foes, he could not imagine. Were he to side openly with either, it would go badly for him if the other were triumphant. However, Childeric *did* give permission for his so-called 'free-companies' to participate in the coming fight.

The free-companies were drawn not from the Frankish nobility or their supporters, but mercenary contingents who had been called upon from time to time to shore up Childeric's power in the face of internal challenges. They were a rabble: lawless bands of killers and cutthroats who would fight for anyone prepared to meet their price, and who specialised in looting and burning villages, and capturing women and children who they would sell in the slave-markets of the East. When Childeric's rule was reinforced by the return to central France of the Roman legions, various troublesome elements – bandits and rebels, rogue knights, wolf-heads and other desperadoes – began to join these mercenary ranks, for in the free-companies they could not only follow their natural inclinations and still avoid the noose or the breaking-wheel, but actually be paid for their efforts. As such, they didn't just hail from France, but from all over Christendom. Soon the free-companies had become armies, and yet still were maintained at Childeric's expense, which he found increasingly irksome. Now that he had the legions to hand, he saw no further use for his hired thugs and was only too willing to put them in the service of Lucius, and secretly hope they would be destroyed in the war to follow.

Over time, the free-companies had fallen under the command of an individual named 'Gorlon the Ogre,' a seven-foot-tall fellow so hideous and misshapen that one female captive dropped dead with fright the moment he entered the stable where she was being held. Gorlon was particularly pleased by the thought of a fight with Brittany, for his island stronghold, Mont St. Michel, was located just to the north of their coastal fortress at St. Malo, and Breton shipping was a regular harassment to his comings and goings.

It was said that no man could stand against him. He fought with a double-bladed battle-axe in one hand, a spiked club in the other. It was even rumoured that he was a cannibal.

This was the deranged killer whom Emperor Lucius now planned to unleash on the small kingdom of Brittany.

Gorlon and his free-companies were charged with two tasks. The first was to cross Brittany's borders covertly, but once inside to wreak havoc and murder – which would be made easier for them, as King Hoel would initially think this common banditry, and would continue to hold his main forces in readiness in his castles on the border. The second task was to drive westward towards Brittany's royal city of Rennes, which they were not just to attack, but to despoil. They were literally to do their worst; steal everything they could, massacre its population – anything to lure King Hoel and his men from their secure enclaves on the border; that should not be difficult, as Rennes also housed the Royal Mint and Treasury.

If Gorlon wondered what would happen after this, he did not trouble to ask. All he could see was the booty that would soon be his. The manor houses would provide jewels, tapestries, silver plate, and silken robes. The chapels and roadside shrines could be stripped of their chalices, candlesticks and gem-studded reliquaries. From the monasteries they would take the manuscripts and precious books. Even the ordinary farmsteads would have livestock they could herd away, granaries and storehouses they could plunder. And, of course, there would be a harvest of women and girls to gather – the mere thought of which set his jackals drooling. And if all that wasn't enough, there was still the promise of Rennes itself, and the Royal Treasure.

The Breton border was guarded by four strong castles. In the north lay the bastion of St. Malo, which overlooked Couesnan Bay. Further south stood Fougeres, and south of that Vitre. As the central strong-points in the chain, these two were less than half a day's ride apart, so their garrisons could support each other if needed. Furthest south was the fortress of Nantes. This was more a city than a castle; located on raised ground close to the River Loire and enclosed by many towers and concentric walls, it made the most fearsome obstacle of all. King Hoel had his headquarters here and concentrated the bulk of his forces within its ramparts, for this was the position facing into the region of France along the Loire Valley, where New Rome's closest legions were reported to be massing. However, though all of these castles would need to be taken in the event of a massed invasion of Brittany, they could easily be bypassed if an enemy had other, more specific motives.

On the last night of April that year, Gorlon and his free-companies, who now numbered just short of forty thousand, crossed the border under cover of dark, passing in single file through the wooded region lying betwixt the chateaux of Fougeres and Vitre. Even these undisciplined curs were sufficiently cowed by the ominous presence of Gorlon and his murderous lieutenants to maintain a vigilant silence. Only when they were deep inside Brittany was the order given to maraud.

And this was exactly what they did, bringing orgies of death and misery to every town and village they encountered, but always driving headlong towards their main target at Rennes. Once it became plain that Rennes was in their path, it was Emperor Lucius's expectation that King Hoel would immediately depart the fortress of Nantes, taking the majority of his forces with him – for not only was Rennes the seat of his Treasury, it was held by his beloved niece, the Duchess Miranda. Lucius expected that Hoel would catch up with Gorlon and his free-companies, and that bitter fighting would spill across a landscape now lit by the glare of blazing towns. Reports emerging from the terrorised land would be sketchy, but it would be clear to all that atrocities were being committed on both sides. Emperor Lucius and his forces, seeing the city of Nantes unarmed and Brittany's southern frontier open, would find it a simple thing to intervene as 'peace-makers.' If they, in their turn, were attacked by the army of King Hoel, or any of his allies, they would have no option but to 'defend themselves.'

It seemed a good plan, but the first fly in Emperor Lucius's ointment was Gorlon's efficiency. Lucius had not counted on the mercenary leader reaching Rennes so quickly and striking its walls with a series of devastating assaults. It occurred to Lucius almost too late that, should the freebooting army seize the Treasury of Brittany, Gorlon might be able to set himself up as a new king regardless of New Rome's agenda. So, those legions camped closest to the Breton border were swiftly mobilised. This, in its turn, stopped King Hoel from abandoning the defence of Nantes. Lucius now found himself having to launch a major attack against a strong, well defended fortress.

At Rennes, the defences were less daunting – the walls were high and thick, but the troops guarding them were inexperienced – but Gorlon's first two assaults were unsuccessful. He was not easily deterred – he had many ladders and vast numbers of men who, in his eyes, were little more than coffin-fodder. But after these fellows died en masse, pin-cushioned by arrows, broken by stones, or broiled in cascades of boiling oil and molten lead, he realised that he would need to plan more carefully.

While he did this, the free-companies took vengeance on the surrounding villages, burning every house and hovel, dragging the inhabitants out and butchering them in full view of the city's defenders. If the display was meant to convince the Rennes garrison to surrender, it failed – they saw only the fate that awaited them if they relented. Thus came the second assault, groups of surviving prisoners now herded in front of the free-companies as living shields, though of course when they reached the footing of the walls they had to be discarded. Most were killed on the spot, so yet again a rain of stones, arrows and darts descended. Some hardy attackers scaled the ladders and made it to the battlements, but their numbers were so few that they were slashed to pieces. Again, the assault parties fell back in disorder.

Time was not on Gorlon's side. His next trick was therefore to approach the city walls under a white flag and offer terms. The lives of all citizens would be spared if the gates were opened. This was not a convincing promise, given the flotsam of severed limbs and sundered torsos which was all that remained of his previous captives, and Gorlon resorted to issuing threats again. If the gates were not opened, the citizens of Rennes would not die by sword or spear – they would be burned; bound hand and foot and flung alive onto cremation pyres. The choice was theirs.

Still the town resisted. Duchess Miranda came to the battlements and peered down alongside her captains. There was no doubt that this mad-eyed monstrosity, stalking back and forth among the slain, was speaking the truth on this occasion at least. All in Rennes would die, he howled, women and children too.

More townsmen were pressed into service – merchants, artisans, labourers, servants – given improvised weapons and hustled up onto the walls, which the duchess said must literally bristle with armaments. The ramshackle army outside needed to be persuaded that further threats and aggression were futile. Sadly, Gorlon had already been persuaded of something else. News had reached him that the armies of New Rome, with Emperor Lucius at their head, had laid siege to Nantes. There was no hiding that this was now a full-scale war – and the tides of war could change quickly. Suddenly any outcome was possible.

Thus came the third and final assault upon the city of Rennes.

By this time, the free-companies had constructed siege engines: towers, trebuchet and mangonel. Storms of missiles – boulders and incendiaries – assailed the city wall, and as so many men, a great number of them untrained lummoxes who hadn't the sense even to put iron saucepans over their head, crammed the battlements, there was horrendous carnage. For two days and two nights, the bombardment continued. The battlements were crushed to rubble, the gates pounded to splinters. With frenzied shrieks, the freebooter army again attacked. Now the full weakness of the surviving garrison became apparent. At close-quarter most were cut down with ease, or simply fled.

One supercilious captain – a certain Lord Querco – had his command lay down their weapons at the feet of the advancing horde, and announced that they'd never trusted King Hoel, were glad to have been liberated from his tyranny and were entirely at the victors' disposal. The victors said they also were glad, and this disposal they now undertook. Having already disarmed themselves, Lord Querco and his men were one by one thrown from the highest towers. Querco, shouting until his lips frothed, went last of all.

Rennes was thoroughly ransacked. Its inhabitants were so abused that the narrow cobbled streets soon ran with blood. Duchess Miranda's residence was taken with ease, her bodyguards hacked down as they defended her. While his dogs ravaged the building, Gorlon himself took the beautiful noblewoman upstairs and there, in her own boudoir, raped her with such energy that the bed collapsed, and once he'd sated himself on her, he strangled her to death. The following morning, with Rennes covered by a pall of acrid smoke, Gorlon went in search of the Treasury. He finally located it in a central keep, windowless and accessible only by a single door made from riveted steel and many times reinforced. The door was undefended, but succumbed neither to battering ram nor grappling hook, and was still intact – much to Gorlon's fury – when, later that afternoon, a New Roman cavalry force, some ten thousand strong, arrived under the leadership of Consul Gainus, cousin to Emperor Lucius.

Reluctantly, Gorlon reported to Gainus that he was not yet in possession of the Breton Treasury. There had to be a key somewhere, but though his men had searched high and low, they had not found one. They had seized surviving citizens and put them to long hours of torture, but none had offered the information. Consul Gainus received this news calmly. He informed Gorlon that Emperor Lucius had an entire corps of engineers who would have no trouble dismantling the Treasury door. Meanwhile, the mounted troops he had with him were an elite force which he had raised and trained himself. These would now guard the Treasury and the city walls. The freebooter army must pitch its camp outside and form a bulwark against any counter-attack.

Gorlon was unhappy about this. His men were owed booty, he growled. Gainus replied that they were already laden with sacks of booty. Gorlon said that they wanted gold, not trinkets. Gainus told him that soon there would be more gold than they could spend in their lifetimes. King Arthur was bringing a force to this land containing many of the most prominent knights in Christendom. Any man who seized one could demand a rich ransom for his deliverance. It would be strongly in the free-companies' interest to waylay the British swine as soon as they arrived and teach them the error of their ways.

Gorlon was not a complete fool. He knew King Arthur was a foe to be reckoned with, but he also knew that the legions of Lucius Caesar were close at hand – that would tilt the scales of battle in his favour, though again it might mean the final haul would be unevenly divided. In the light of that, it would be to the free-companies' advantage if they were first into this next battle. So thinking, he ordered his men out of the smouldering city and had them bivouac on the great plain to the north.

News of these disasters finally reached King Hoel in Nantes. Hoel was an active middle-aged monarch, short, squat and bearded, but famous among his subjects for his gay apparel and the liveliness of his manner. Even hawking or riding to hounds, he would wear the most colourful and fashionable garb. His court was a lavish display of pomp, its lords and ladies decked most splendidly. Hoel would positively glow with bonhomie as he received honoured guests in reception chambers clad wall-to-wall with opulent tapestries, and treated them to banquets and entertainments which bordered on being festivals in their own right. But the grandees of his court would be horror-struck if they could see his condition after hearing about the destruction of Rennes: mailed and plated, dabbled with dust and dirt, cut across the brow and the bridge of his nose by flying chips of stone, and on learning that his beloved Miranda was slain, red-eyed with tears.

His knights and men-at-arms insisted their King should flee. There was only one other major concentration of troops in Brittany, and that was on the country's westernmost tip at Brest – its main deep-water harbour. It was essential these men remain at their posts so that Hoel's British allies would have a safe landing, and they were more likely to do this if they had their commander-in-chief with them.

Hoel saw the wisdom in this, and that he could do no more at Nantes. The King and a group of handpicked knights eventually fled through underground tunnels, proceeding for hours along narrow galleries, knee-deep in silty water, passing though endless veils of cobwebs and beneath clusters of bats which hung like fruit on the bough. They emerged into sunlight far beyond the Roman siege-lines, at a woodland stable where horses awaited. Before escaping to the west, Hoel climbed a tree and looked back to Nantes, a broken, smouldering edifice, begirt by the multitudes of New Rome and once again under a barrage of missiles.

As he swung up into his saddle, he muttered darkly: "There'll be a reckoning for this. The Romans are up to their old tricks. They've been here less than a month, and they've sown this land with the blood and bone of honest citizens. They may call themselves 'New Rome,' but when Arthur and his knights arrive, they'll reap the same whirlwind that destroyed the old one."

THIRTEEN

THE ROADS THAT converged on the twin ports of Sandwich and Stonar in Kent were rivers of heraldry as the knights of Albion poured along them. The May sun beat from a depthless sky, reflecting from the sweet grasses of the surrounding meadows, but more so from the multiple colours and devices resplendent on the shields, tabards, banners and surcoats of the many households headed in noisy procession for the kingdom's southeast corner.

Lancelot and his *mesnie* wore their customary white leopards on fields of blue, Gawaine and his people were in their gold pentangles on scarlet, and Bedivere's in their black ravens on orange. Arthur's private forces, his *Familiaris Regis*, were most noticeable of all in snow-white livery decked with the King's shimmering red dragon. Less handsome were the numerous other knights and squires, errant groups and privateers, most with dented arms and ragged, patched-together livery, who were also making the journey. However, though their purses might be empty, their hearts would be stout – for each of these men knew that his performance in the coming war was a possible route to fame and fortune.

No less important were the *fyrd*, the peasant soldiers, who marched or rode depending on their personal wealth. Though clad in improvised harness of studded leather or quilted felt, with the occasional helm and mail-coat among them, and arms amounting to little more than scythes, mallets and hunting-knives, they also drove ox-carts laden with pole-arms, longbows and bundles of freshly-fletched arrows. The enemies of King Arthur were fast learning how dreadful the impact could be of a great cloud of cloth-yard shafts driven by the thews of common men who, by royal order, now practised at the archery butts for three days in every five.

Even the Saxons had provided Arthur with levies. Most – being as mule-headed as it was possible for any men to be – would insist on boarding their ships from the port of Stonar, which they themselves had built and thus regarded as their own, but other Saxons flocking to the coast from the south or the west shared the same roads as Arthur's troops and made a fearsome sight. They were career warriors; battle-hardened *thegns* and their war-bands, their blond heads and scarred, surly faces hidden beneath elaborately carved helms, their barrel bodies slotted into heavy coats of rings, with circular linden-wood shields slung on their backs. They carried broadswords tucked into their belts and long-handled battle-axes at their shoulders; the axes, capped with a steel blade often weighing as much as twenty pounds,[20] were hard to wield in combat, but every man-jack of the Saxons looked as if he was an expert.

"The sight of our yellow-haired friends will enrage the Romans even more," Bedivere said to Arthur, as the King halted at a wayside inn and bade his senior lieutenants share a noon repast.

"Let them rage," Arthur said, selecting a table some distance from the road. "They are making hay over in Brittany. Hoel's official request for help arrived this morning. He'll probably be surprised by the speed of our response, but I fear it won't come soon enough to save the lives of a good many of his subjects."

More of Arthur's knights detached from the main host, trotted up and dismounted. Among them was Sir Gareth,

[20]Battle-axes weighed between three and six pounds, which Malory as a knight would have known; he's apparently presenting the Saxons as almost preternaturally strong, fierce warriors.

whose insignia was a golden eagle on green, Sir Griflet, who wore white chevrons on purple, and Kay, who sported the same colours as the King. Lucan arrived with them, now in his all-black mantle, and despite the fine spring weather, with a huge wolfskin cloak – again black, still with paws attached and fangs glinting in its eyeless skull – thrown over his mailed shoulders. He remained on horseback, but removed his great cylindrical helmet and shook out his dark, sweat-damp locks.

Bedivere glanced up at him with disapproval, but said nothing.

The landlord of the inn served a haunch of venison with stewed figs, and two hot pies stuffed with cabbage, rabbit and chicken. There were also fresh-baked loaves, and a bowl of salad made from greens.

"Our main problem is numbers," Arthur said. "At the most we have forty thousand men, not all of them prime fighting-stock, though everyone will do his job – I'm aware of that. The latest reports from Gaul hold that Lucius has mustered some three hundred thousand."

There was an astonished silence. Many of them had trouble even imagining such a gathering of men.

"What of their experience, sire?" Griflet asked.

"There'll be a limit to it. So many can't *all* have been in the front line during Lucius's recent conquests. But we mustn't assume they are novices. They've won several battles."

"Are the bulk of them volunteers, my lord?" Lucan wondered. "Or conscripts?"

The King glanced up at him, for the first time noticing that one of his guests had not yet dismounted, and frowned. "I suspect the former. All over the Western Empire, men young and old are clamouring for the rights of citizenship. In the tradition of old Rome, service in the armed forces is the most direct method. How now, Sir Lucan, you aren't joining my table?"

"Forgive me, sire," Lucan said. "But I can't for shame participate in a feast when my men are on oatmeal and water."

"There'll be better supplies when we're over the sea," Bedivere replied. "Most of our stores are already loaded onto transports."

Lucan gave a wintry smile as if he had heard such promises before, wheeled Nightshade around and cantered back to the road.

"Your brother's become a testy fellow," Arthur commented.

Bedivere's cheeks reddened. "Apologies, my liege. He's not taking his wife's defection well."

"Let's hope he reserves at least some of his frustration for the battlefield."

"He's donned the black fur again," Lancelot noted.

"He promises me it's for this campaign only," Bedivere replied.

"For my part I'm glad to see it," Gawaine said, cutting a slice of venison. "There's an old saying in the wilds of Ireland – to kill a wolf it takes a wolf."

"Which brings us to our main business," Arthur said, shifting utensils and unfolding a map. "King Hoel and his best men are besieged at Nantes on the Armorican border. But there are still fresh levies to be drawn from other parts of Brittany, not least Brest. But they'll need to be marshalled, and quickly. At present New Rome is having it too easy. I want Emperor Lucius to *know* that he is in a war. To that end, Lancelot, Gawaine... you will sail ahead of the rest. A special squadron of longships has been set aside for you and as many men as they can accommodate. You are to sail directly to Brest, and from there to go inland, rousing the populace. At the very least I want Roman forces harassed, though of course some victories would be appreciated."

"It's occurred to me," Gawaine said, chewing. "We could make the land uninhabitable. Scorch the earth. So there is nothing for the Romans to live off."

"That would be punishing the Breton people unnecessarily," Arthur replied. "This war is not about Brittany, and never has been."

"Let's hope that King Hoel, wherever he is, doesn't learn that," Griflet said.

"On the contrary." Arthur smiled grimly. "Anything that might take Hoel's anger to a new level is to be welcomed."

He glanced at Bedivere. "That's one reason I can't share your concerns about your brother. If he's come here to wage a war within a war, that suits me... as long as it's a war to the same end. Equally, I've no qualms about any methods he may use; within reason of course." Briefly Arthur looked glum. "It pains me to say this, gentlemen, but there'll be precious little chivalry in the days ahead."

IT WAS EARLY evening when Lucan and his household came in sight of the Stour estuary, which was crammed shore to shore with cogs, keels and galleys. All paths leading down to it jostled with soldiers, many now weary and soiled, aggravated to find themselves in long, meandering queues. Arguments broke out, and even fights; Arthur's marshals rode back and forth along the lines, displaying the royal crest and blasting their horns to bring rowdy groups to order. Other bands of men had separated from the main host and built fires out of driftwood. Some were working the river's edge with nets and rods. Tents were appearing, the ornate pavilions of barons interspersed with the simple canvas shelters of the *fyrd*.

Lucan turned in his saddle and regarded his men. All wore black mantles over their mail. In the heat of the day, most had removed their helmets and pulled back their coifs. They were tousled and fatigued, begrimed with the dust of the road.

Looking further afield for a suitable bivouac, he spotted a patch of empty, barren ground. It was dotted with tussock grass, but at least it was dry. He instructed Turold and Wulfstan, and then broke off from the group as they busied themselves. He veered away from the column and cantered to the top of a rise. Beyond this lay more barren, sandy ridges. The estuary glimmered to his left. The crew of the many craft moored there called to each other as they clambered like monkeys through the forest of rigging. They, too, it seemed, were impatient to be off, though many had giving up hope of sailing on the evening tide – they lolled at the gunwales, sipping from wine-cups.

Lucan walked his horse forward until he came to a low defile, through which a stream trickled to the water's edge. The stream was overgrown with sedge and rushes, among which he sighted the tumbledown outer wall of an old chapel. He dismounted and followed a zigzag path through the foliage, splashing across the stream and approaching the chapel doorway, and glanced inside. The small sanctuary was roofless, with a narrow nave and only fragments of stained glass in its arched casements. Ferns and thistles had inundated it. The faint images of saints were still visible on the plaster walls, green with mould. A tall Celtic cross was all that remained of the altar, though it was covered with lichen, and its sacred inscriptions had eroded to a featureless pattern. It would suffice.

Lucan rode back to the encampment. His personal pavilion had now been pitched in the centre, his black banner unfurled on a tall pole. Turold had unfastened his sword-belt and was loosening the collar of his hauberk; he glanced up as his overlord approached.

"The thing I discussed with you earlier," Lucan said quietly. Turold nodded.

"Now is the time. I've found an appropriate place."

FIFTEEN MINUTES LATER, Alaric and the other squires were grooming the horses. Wulfstan had built a corral with pegs and rope, and the animals were stalled inside, their saddles and harnesses removed, their noses buried in a trough of meal. Alaric sensed a presence and turned. The bearlike shape of Sir Gerwin was lurking beyond the rope.

"Alaric, your master wants you," he said. Alaric laid aside his brush and approached. Benedict and Malvolio followed, but Gerwin stopped them with a warning hand. "You *boys* continue with your duties."

They hung back, as Alaric was led away into the gathering dusk.

They walked some distance, crossing several ridges, before

Gerwin halted and faced the lad. Alaric observed for the first time that Gerwin was carrying a leather sack. He also saw that a page was waiting close by, looking nervous.

"My lord," Alaric began, "what is..."

"Take off your mail."

"My mail?"

Gerwin regarded him with a saturnine countenance that brooked no argument. Alaric glanced around. Aside from the page, nobody else was close. Full darkness was falling, but lights were visible on the water. He could hear the shouts of the sailors. The ungainly shapes of three dromonds hove downstream; by the looks of their dim outlines, they rode low in the water, loaded with men and horses.

"Do as I say," Gerwin said brusquely. "Give your sword to me and your clothing to this lad."

Alaric unbuckled his sword-belt and handed it over. He then removed his tabard, unlaced the collar of his mail jerkin and lifted it over his head. He shrugged the straps from his shoulders and stepped out of his mail leggings. Beneath, he wore light felt under-garb, damp with sweat. The page took charge of all these items, folding them neatly before heading in the direction of the camp.

"May I ask why I'm doing this? Alaric said.

"You may not. Follow me."

Gerwin continued along the same path. They crossed more rugged rises, where only clumps of spiky grass grew. Alaric saw that someone else was now waiting for them – a mendicant. Like so many of those vagrant clerics tagging along with the army, hoping to offer salvation in return for succour, his gray sackcloth habit was bound with rope, his face gaunt, his skin yellowed. His hair and beard were unkempt.

"Despite appearances, this man is a true priest," Gerwin said. "He will hear your confession."

"My confession?"

Gerwin viewed him through lidded eyes. "It's for the best, I assure you."

Alaric couldn't reply. For the last minute he'd toyed with a frightening thought that his overlord had discovered his yearning for Countess Trelawna. Could the earl in his cold rage have decided to punish Alaric first, before seeking out the real offender?

"Make your shrift, Alaric," Gerwin said.

Alaric contemplated bounding down the slope and trying to swim the estuary.

Impatiently, Gerwin planted a mailed hand on the squire's head and forced him to his knees, before moving away a respectful distance. Alaric gave his confession, though he hadn't had time to plumb his conscience. Afterwards, Gerwin paid the priest a couple of coins. The priest shuffled away into the darkness. Gerwin now opened his sack. Alaric watched, transfixed, wondering what he would do if a dagger was produced. Instead it was an item of clothing: a scarlet cape.

He gazed at it, baffled – and felt a sudden surge of excitement.

"Up," Gerwin said. Alaric stood with shaking legs. Gerwin placed the cape over his shoulders and fastened it with a hook. "Follow me," he said again.

Alaric followed quickly.

"Ideally you'd be wearing black hose," Gerwin said. "To show you came from dust and that that's where you'll be returning. But we haven't got any. Besides, I reckon your underwear is just about grubby enough."

They splashed through a trickling stream, and approached a gutted ruin, firelight flickering from its arched windows. When they entered, Alaric saw that it was a derelict chapel, but that torches had been set in its sconces and that the narrow nave had been cleared of vegetation. Several of Earl Lucan's most senior knights were ranged down either wall – Turold, Wulfstan, Hubert, Cadelaine and Brione – they all wore their clean cloaks and surcoats. They were helmeted and stood with heads inclined. Each man clasped his longsword in front of him, its point to the earth. There was no movement; it was as if they stood in prayer. From over their shoulders, firelight played on the decayed faces of ancient saints.

Earl Lucan stood beneath a weathered stone cross. He was garbed in black, though he'd removed the wolf-cloak and drawn back his coif. His expression was stern. Alongside him on a slab were several accoutrements; he placed a hand on them as Alaric approached.

"Kneel," Lucan said, when the lad was directly in front of him.

Alaric did as he was bidden, his entire body shivering.

"This scarlet cloak is a memorial to the robe worn by Christ on the road to Golgotha," Lucan said. "As such, it is a symbol of the humility you must always exercise."

Alaric didn't reply. His head was bowed, his hands joined.

"Take these."

Alaric glanced up. Lucan was offering him a pair of leather shoes with a gilded spur attached to each heel. The lad's mouth was dry as wood as he took them.

"Just as gold is the most coveted metal, so gold must be worn on your foot to take away all covetousness from your heart," Lucan said.

Alaric nodded and shod himself.

Gerwin stepped up and handed Alaric's sword to Lucan. It was still in its scabbard, its belt wrapped around it. In turn, Lucan presented it to Alaric.

"This is your sword." He indicated with a nod that Alaric should strap it to his waist. "Just as it has two cutting-edges, so you must keep and maintain right, reason and justice on all sides. Never use it to betray the Christian faith or the right of the Holy Church."

Shudders passed through Alaric's body. The hopes and dreams he'd harboured for so many years still seemed distant, even though he was in the midst of their realisation. He couldn't believe this was actually happening.

Lucan leaned forward and planted his lips on the boy's brow. "Accept this kiss in confirmation of the order I am bestowing on you. As a sign of peace and love and loyalty, which you must always mete wherever you may rightly do so. Also, accept *this*."

The slap to Alaric's left cheek was hard, delivered with a flat hand but stinging force.

"This blow signifies that you must always – for the rest of your days – remember the order of knighthood, which you have now received. And that you must yourself strike blows in that cause, but only those which be valorous and just." Lucan stepped backward. For the first time in several days, his creased brow smoothed and his mouth cracked into that fatherly half-smile of which his squire had once been so fond. "Welcome to our brotherhood," he said. "Rise, *Sir* Alaric."

Alaric rose in a daze, and the next thing he knew hands were clapping his shoulders and the great knights of the household were congratulating him. When they led him outside, his horse had been saddled and brought to the edge of the defile, so he could ride back to the encampment. On arrival there, the rest of the earl's retinue were eagerly awaiting him.

There were cheers as he entered their midst. A fire was blazing and several water-fowl were turning on spits. The earl had also procured several kegs of ale, which the squires joyously broke open. Turold strummed on his lute, and over the next few hours there was much singing. The troops crowding tiredly along the nearby road gazed at them, faces stark and wondering in the firelight.

"Now I suppose we should show deference to you," Malvolio said, burping in Alaric's face.

"They say I'm a knight, but I don't feel like one," Alaric replied. "I haven't got my own raiment. Or a seal."

"Lucan will provide those when the war's over," Wulfstan counselled. "You'll also draw a wage – a proper one, not a few measly coppers to see you by. That should be a new experience. Until you're ready to go off on the quest, of course."

The quest? Alaric eyes widened as he pondered these new possibilities.

"What does it matter?" Malvolio laughed. "We're off to war, so we're all going to die anyway, whether we have commoner blood or knightly blood."

"It matters, you young oaf," Wulfstan said, cuffing his ear, "because knights at least find honourable graves. At the end of the day, that's all it comes down to – ensuring the hole in the ground where they put you is something to be venerated, not pissed on."

The water-fowl were consumed with gusto, and then fish were produced, gutted and prodded into the flames on spears. Ale sloshed freely as the household celebrated long into the evening.

LUCAN OBSERVED THESE events with fondness but no little sense of melancholy. Idealism was the preserve of inexperience. At length, he slid away from the cheery throng, throwing the wolfskin around his shoulders and walking downhill until he stood by the estuary edge, from where he gazed across the sluggish waters.

Trelawna was all he'd had.

Quite literally, she had been the only pleasant thing to ever happen to him.

He had vague, tender memories of his mother, but how terribly that all ended. He valued his closeness to his brother, but how could that compare? When he'd first been inducted into the Round Table it was a great moment, but he'd received that honour because in those grim, turbulent years after the death of Uther Pendragon, he'd happened to side with Arthur, the one destined to win, and the one whose favour he would earn through nothing more than his ferocity in battle. Would God regard that as a good thing? By contrast, Trelawna had brought genuine light into his world, not to mention other virtues – patience, warmth, gentleness, and of course that mystical fairy beauty of hers – all of which had mellowed him in a way the self-important grandeur of Camelot never could. Camelot was a worthy institution, dedicated to the cause of right, but it was built on conquest. Trelawna had embodied something else. She had come to Britain as a victim, as a prisoner, as a frightened rabbit whose innocence and charm had sweetened the dark wolf who'd been her captor.

Lucan didn't weep. He'd done with weeping that first morning on reading her letter of departure. Phrases like "the aching loneliness we both have shared," and "you deserve a better, more loyal love than I," had done nothing to placate him. To counter this, he'd striven to remind himself of the good times they'd had: riding in the sun-dappled forest, boating on mist-begirt lakes, drifting in each other's arms. It was Trelawna who'd completed his education, filling in the gaps in his reading and writing, which the early death of his mother had left behind. He had enjoyed those sessions more than he could say, and so had his wife. True, laughter was often in short supply on the northern border. Yet she had laughed many times in those days, she had smiled, she had kissed him. There had been no falseness there. Oh, he had long known that she didn't love him, but she had always been sweet on him, caring, affectionate, and concerned when he was wounded – as a good, doting wife should. And it was thanks to all these things – and her calm assurance during his long, feverish, hag-ridden nights – that the shadow of his father was nothing more than that: a shadow.

It was impossible to believe that all this goodness was gone from his life, yet as he stood here in the deepening night, the black waters lapping at his feet, streaked with fire from the passing ships – it seemed naught but imagination, something yearned for which had never been. He huddled deeper into the wolf-fur as an unseasonal chill intruded into his bones.

"My lord?" someone said.

Lucan turned and found Alaric alongside him.

"I'm no longer your lord, Alaric. Unless you wish to serve my house as a knight, though in due course the pressure will grow on you to find your own way in this world."

"My lord, I'll gladly serve your house for the remainder of this war."

"That's good to hear."

"On that subject, my lord... to have this honour bestowed on me in a time of strife is a great thing."

"Well, it would have been nice to put you through the normal rigmarole that accompanies these occasions – the cleansing bath, the lying in a bed made of white sheets, the hearing of Mass and so forth – but in the estimation of most men, a battlefield knighting is worth far more."

"It isn't just that, my lord." Alaric sounded awkward, and perhaps a little drunk. "I mean with your personal woe, to think of me at such a time... I can't thank you enough."

"You don't need to thank me, Alaric. You've earned this accolade. Through long, patient years, not to mention the courage you showed in the face of that demon serpent. Had you not acted the way you did, you would not have been knighted today because I would not be here."

Alaric nodded, pensive. Finally he took a breath and said: "Now that we are knights together, may I speak bluntly?"

Lucan glanced around at him. "I always appreciate candour."

"My lord... you are one of Arthur's greatest battle-lords, yet it does you no credit if donning that mantle of fur means what I think it means – that we are here to prosecute this war with vengeance rather than justice."

Lucan looked amused. "In war, many innocents are killed or maimed. Women and children, old men, combatants who have surrendered. Tell me, is that justice?"

"I understand that war is Hell, but..."

"You don't understand, Alaric, because you've never yet seen it. But you soon will." Lucan glanced across the estuary. "And then you'll know the truth of it."

ALARIC WANTED TO continue, but Lucan said they would speak more during the crossing. It was now late, and they were to rise on the cockcrow if they wished to secure a berth before noon. He strode away along the water's edge, his cloak of black fur trailing.

Earlier, Malvolio and Benedict had jokingly chided Alaric for not keeping a night's vigil by the holy altar where he was knighted, as young noblemen had once done.

Now their jest didn't seem so funny.

In fact, when everyone else was snoring, he stumbled back to the ruined chapel. Its interior was smoky and spectral with moonlight; the defaced saints watched him from the shadows. He knelt by the ruined altar, proud to be the newest knight in the world, but nervous that, despite his confession, his soul was already dark with sin thanks to his adulterous love for a married woman.

The lad felt inadequate to phrase the prayer he sought to offer. How did one ask the Almighty to forgive a lust that one was not prepared to suppress? More to the point, how did one ask God for the strength to defend until death a woman who was herself a sinner, especially in the knowledge that to do so might necessitate drawing sword against friend and mentor? The mere thought of siding against Earl Lucan made Alaric sick to the guts. The contradiction of loyalties set his head spinning. But he would not stand by and see violence done, not now that he was a knight. Remembering this, he felt bold enough to voice it: to swear it, to loudly dedicate his moonlit vigil to this purpose.

"I will not allow harm, from *any* source, to come to the woman I love."

Alaric was a knight now.

And he had his quest.

FOURTEEN

WHEN RUFIO AND Trelawna came ashore, they were on the Armorican side of the Loire estuary. To the rear of them, the drifting waters were lost in purple gloom. But ahead of them, the rise of the land was pock-marked with campfires, spreading out in every direction for as far as the eye could see.

Trelawna descended the gangplank with Gerta, the only servant she'd brought. Behind them, two grooms carefully led down the women's horses. Rufio waited at the foot of the plank in company with two of his brother officers from the Fourteenth Legion. They were introduced to Trelawna as Antonius, *Primus Pilus*, and Frederiko, *Hastatus Prior*.[21] They were tall, handsome fellows with olive complexions, dark, curly hair and fresh, innocent faces. Both were off-duty for, despite having ridden from their encampment to meet their commanding officer, they affected casual attire – close-fitting boots, hose and loose blouses decorated with frills around their v-neck collars.

After greeting Trelawna courteously, they conferred with their superior, explaining the current dispositions of the Fourteenth, and where in the line it would be brought to bear.

On the far side of the estuary, Trelawna saw the fire-lit outline of a towering, crenellated rampart – no doubt the

---

[21]Senior officers. The *Primus Pilus* was the senior centurion in a legion, while the *Hastatus Prior* was the centurion in charge of the front battle line.

southern bulwark of the city of Nantes, for though it was already scorched and fissured in many places, innumerable war-machines battered it. The crash and rumble of the impacts could be heard even from this distance. Many of the roofs behind the rampart were burning and several of its towers had collapsed; rubble strewed its footings, alongside piles of huddled corpses.

"There's to be no attempt to storm the city tonight," Rufio said, rejoining her. "Apparently there've been several efforts so far, but all have been repulsed. The Bretons have put up quite a fight. One has to give them that. But they're close to breaking. Our artillery has been degrading their defences for the last two weeks. Anyway, I'm to report to the Emperor straight away. It seems he wishes to congratulate me personally for the mission I've just accomplished."

Trelawna didn't comment, but was fascinated to know the extent to which starting a war could be considered an accomplishment. She supposed that as this had been New Rome's ploy all along, Rufio and the other ambassadors had performed their duty admirably – though it still didn't seem like much to be proud of.

"Would you accompany me, my love?" he asked, taking her hands in his. "Into the Imperial presence?"

"Of course," she replied, feeling strangely unexcited about it. In fact, now that she was here, within earshot of yet another battle, she felt curiously despondent.

The voyage from Britain had not been uncomfortable. With calm seas and a fair wind, they had made good time. As she and Gerta had been allocated the ship's master's commodious quarters, they'd found themselves in proper bunks rather than hammocks, with a private dressing room and latrine, so there had been little to complain about. But for the most part, the other Roman dignitaries who'd shared the voyage had ignored her, the churchmen sniffing in her presence as if affronted by her 'scarlet woman' status, the patricians regarding her as a young man's plaything, a winsome toy that was of no importance. Only two had exchanged pleasantries with her. One of these was Bishop Severin Malconi, Rufio's uncle – a foxy-faced man, but a pleasant one nevertheless, who had expressed remorse that their two nations were at war. The other was Tribune Quintus Maximion – a tall, spare-limbed soldier, with short, iron-gray hair and a noble, if brutalised, face. He had been polite, if a little morose.

Now they had docked, only Maximion and one other military official, Ardeus Vigilano, Duke of Spoleto – who had only spoken to Trelawna curtly during the voyage and showed no interest in speaking to her at all now – came ashore. The ship would soon weigh anchor to catch the ebb-tide, and then proceed south. The rest of the ambassadors intended to remain on board until safe and secure in Roman waters.

"Once again, countess," Maximion said, as a valet helped him mount his horse, "I trust you will find happiness in our new world. Don't be too troubled. The affairs of men are tidal. There is a great storm raging at present. But in due course things will settle, and tranquillity will return."

"That's to be hoped, my lord," she replied.

He saluted her in the Roman fashion, his right hand clasped across his left breast, before riding away into the darkness, his attendant at his heels.

Though she barely knew him, Trelawna couldn't help but feel sorry to see him leave.

A short while later, Rufio, Antonius and Frederiko mounted up, and with Trelawna, Gerta and three packhorses loaded at their rear, embarked from the dock, proceeding along a shoreline path – only to encounter a grisly torch-lit spectacle around the next headland. Forty wooden frames had been erected along the water's edge, and on each one was attached a naked, spread-eagled man. Several companies of Roman infantry, perhaps four hundred in total, stood at rigid attention while torturers beat the prisoners with rods and canes. Their sweat flew as they worked, dealing vicious blows to every part of the hanging, bloodied forms, none of which so much as twitched. There was no sound save the repeated impacts – *thwack – thwack – thwack –*

"Centurion!" Rufio called, sensing Trelawna's silent horror and halting his steed. "What happens here?"

"Tribune Rufio?" The centurion seemed surprised to see him, though not particularly concerned. "Today's attack failed abysmally. His Highness was most displeased. He ordered that the cohorts who failed to take the city wall should draw lots, and the losing cohort be decimated."

"Decimated?" Rufio looked stunned; to Trelawna's eyes, more stunned than she had yet seen from him. He quickly cleared his throat in an effort to regain his commander's dignity. "Decimated, I see. But by flogging?"

"They are to be flogged to death, tribune. Caesar's precise orders."

Trelawna chanced a glance at the prisoners. In most cases their flesh dangled in torn, gory ribbons. Their heads hung low. None moved, because they were almost certainly dead, yet the beating went on as it clearly had done for several hours.

Rufio nodded grimly, feigning approval. But as they rode away, he drew alongside Trelawna and said quietly: "War is a cruel thing. It demands harsh necessities of us all."

"I'd hoped to have left such necessities behind by now," was all she said in response. She neglected to mention that of all the harshness she had witnessed on Britain's northern border, she had never seen Lucan direct any at his own men.

From the scene of the execution, their route took them uphill through the encampments proper. While studying her histories as a girl, and particularly her Latin and Greek, Trelawna had studied the order of the Roman military machine. She had learned how their camps had been arrayed with exact symmetry – their tents all of a similar shape and size, laid out in rows equidistant to each other with roadways in between, almost like towns. But if that had been so in antiquity, it was not the case now. Now, the Roman tents, of many sizes, designs and qualities, were scattered across the hillside haphazardly, with only muddy paths snaking among them. Campfires burned wherever it had taken the legionaries' fancy to light them. The soldiers clustered together in the flickering light, laughing, drinking, and dicing. They seemed vastly different from the Roman legionaries of old. The sentries wore armour of mail coats and leggings, but with heavy, overlapping plates on top, and open-face helmets with steel fins or plumes. They sported modern weapons, from maces and mattocks to pikes, halberds and swords. There were immense numbers of them. With each new rise there was another camp, the glow of whose fires spangled the night.

Emperor Lucius's command tent was located on a central hillock, a huge golden pavilion, its exterior covered with the black images of eagles. It was so large and divided into so many chambers that timbers had been used to support it, and they now swayed in the breeze, the canopied walls flapping and creaking.

Rufio and Trelawna found the Emperor in the central chamber, an airy space laid with a rich carpet and lit brilliantly by rush-lights suspended from bronze chandeliers. Lucius stood at a central desk, surrounded by his prefects and generals, poring over maps. Trelawna wasn't sure what she expected of a man who decimated his own soldiers – a roaring, bestial giant maybe, or a cold figure of cadaverous evil. She was utterly surprised to be confronted by a handsome, genial young fellow with a bright smile and red-gold beard and moustache. He was of average height and stocky build, and clad in a black iron breastplate elaborately cut with Latin characters, black leg-plate of greaves, cops and cuisses,[22] and a cloak and under-pelisse of black and purple silk. His underlings wore similar heavy and flamboyant garb.

"Tribune Rufio," the Emperor said in a delighted tone. "You join us at last."

"Forgive me, Highness," Rufio replied. "I came here with all speed."

---

[22]*greaves, cops and cuisses:* pieces of leg armour, covering the shins, knees and thighs, respectively.

"No matter. Things have moved on apace since your departure from Camelot. But the situation is not out of hand. Far from it..." His expression changed. "And who is this?"

There were quiet murmurs as the Emperor's officials focused their attention on Trelawna. Lucius introduced her as a Gallic countess whom he had liberated from the clutches of one of Arthur's more evil knights, and whom, once New Rome's victory was complete, he would take as his bride. The Emperor's welcoming smile remained in place, but hardened a little as he pondered this. Trelawna couldn't help wondering if Emperor Lucius felt *he* should be the one deciding who his nobles should marry.

"Let's not run before our horse to market, tribune," Lucius intoned, shaking himself back to the matter at hand. "Our situation is this. Thanks to the free-companies, we have the Breton Treasury in our grasp. As you've seen, Nantes is completely embattled and will shortly fall. I have also sent strong detachments to surround the chateaux Fougeres and Vitre. Their garrisons respond to our demands with jeers, but will be less obstinate once their king is in chains. When this particular part of the campaign is complete – and I anticipate that imminently – Brittany will have ceased to exist as an independent power. Thus, when King Arthur arrives, he will be landing in Roman-occupied France. There will be every justification to drive him back into the sea, and once that is done, to pursue him to his own shores, which, given that he will have lost most of his soldiery on this futile mission, we shall storm with ease."

Trelawna listened with fascination, wondering if the Emperor genuinely believed what he was saying or if it was simply bravado. As far as she was aware, so far he had not won any kind of notable victory. Rennes had fallen to a horde of brigands, and Nantes, which faced the full might of New Rome's army, was still holding out.

"Things have turned out better than I could have hoped," Emperor Lucius said, his eyes bright. "Not two hundred miles from where we now stand, Julius Caesar signaled his power to the world with an extraordinary triumph over Vercingetorix at Alesia. Our triumph will be greater still."

Again, Trelawna recalled her histories. Julius Caesar had been in command of a highly professional force, and the ancient Gauls had been disorganised savages. She appraised Lucius as he continued to enthuse about the inevitability of victory. He was clearly a charismatic leader. He seemed young to her, almost boyish, but he was likeable and energetic, and it could not be denied that so far at least, his conquests had run smoothly and to schedule. But she could not help wondering how many of his foes had been cowed by his Imperial name, and the sheer size of his armies, rather than his proficiency on the battlefield. King Arthur and his knights had trod a more difficult path. They had scrapped and schemed and fought and parleyed, in the mud and rain, in the frost and snow, enduring every conceivable hardship. They'd used brawn and brain in equal measure, through one war after another, never knowing defeat. In every way they had earned the power and reputation they enjoyed.

Even as Emperor Lucius drew Rufio to the table where the plans and maps were laid, and even though the other Roman officers, seasoned and well-trained, crowded around in quiet confidence, Trelawna felt her first pang of concern that she might have joined the losing side.

FIFTEEN

Despite Emperor Lucius's soaring confidence about the campaign, New Rome was not to have everything its own way in Brittany.

Serving in Emperor Lucius's army were two North African princes, two bothers – Jalhid and Priamus. Their lands in Cyrenaica had been overrun during New Rome's reconquest, and they and some twelve thousand of their finest warriors had now been compelled to serve on the campaign in Gaul. The brothers had differing views on this matter. Jalhid was the older by twenty years; he knew better than his younger sibling, or so he assumed, the value the Romans placed on their loyal allies, and the riches and power that could be had in the service of the Empire. Priamus saw only that his tribe, who had finally established their own rulership after rising against the Vandals and destroying them, had suddenly been made slaves again. Priamus also did not share his brother's belief that all men were cruel and lustful, and that suffering was the inevitable consequence of Man's quest for power. As such, when Emperor Lucius's spies brought news to Nantes that the first of King Arthur's contingents were landing at Brest, and Priamus was dispatched with his six thousand troops to reinforce Consul Gainus at Rennes, the Moorish prince was appalled to witness the depredations committed by Gorlon and his forces.

All the way to Rennes, they encountered villages laid waste, fields and vineyards reduced to blackened ruins, trees groaning beneath the weight of dangling corpses. The final straw came when Priamus's scouts drew his attention to the remains of a free-company camp abandoned by the roadside. Concealed amid the trees was a fire-pit with a charred pole laid across it, on which were mounted the remains of several children, broached like young birds. Priamus at once convened a meeting with his senior officers, and the decision was reached that they would sooner serve the Devil than pay fealty to any potentate who permitted such atrocities. They thus proceeded west, but now veered away from Rennes, intent upon traversing the whole of Brittany if necessary until they met Arthur's forces, with whom they would hold parley.

News of this mutiny reached Consul Gainus, who, having finally opened the Treasury, had been living in Rennes like a king. Enraged, Gainus called ten squadrons of cavalry from the Roman force now barracked in the city – five thousand men in total – and rode out at their head, determined to capture and punish the transgressors. Twenty miles west of the city, in a barren, rocky region, they were ambushed by Breton irregulars bolstered by forward companies of Arthur's army acting under the joint command of Sir Gawaine and Sir Lancelot. A fierce melee was joined, and for a brief time the numerically superior Romans looked to be getting the better of it, until a third party arrived on the battlefield – Priamus and his Moorish warriors. The Romans had pushed the Britons onto a broad hillock, where they subjected their shield-wall to relentless attacks, but now Priamus charged into Gainus's right flank, causing panic and confusion.

The Roman formation broke, and there was a stampede to escape. The Britons took advantage, mounting up and galloping downhill, overrunning what remained of the Roman camp. Many Roman officers were slain, Gainus among them. The rest of the Roman force fled east towards Rennes, a shredded relic of what they once had been.

On the battlefield, Prince Priamus surrendered his army, explaining that his days of servitude to Rome had ended. The

Moors made a strange sight for the eyes both of Briton and Breton alike, with their dark faces and curled black beards. They wore polished steel corselets over flowing silken garb, and steel helms only the upper spikes of which were visible above their ceremonial turbans. When they fought, they did so with great courage and skill, wielding lances, short, double-curved bows which they could shoot from horseback, and long crescent swords.

Despite the strangeness of such allies, Gawaine – as always, energetic and hearty – congratulated Priamus on this decision, and said that he should join his host with theirs. However, Priamus was reluctant. He knew that his brother, Jalhid, still lived in Rome's favour and would never switch allegiances, which meant that Moor would at some point be fighting against Moor, and Priamus could not be party to that. Lancelot thus proposed a compromise. He suggested that Priamus and his troops should voluntarily become prisoners-of-war. If they laid down their arms, they would be escorted out of Brittany and into the lands held by Childeric – maybe to Paris itself, a neutral capital from where they could watch the rest of the campaign as observers.

Priamus and his men did as requested. They turned over their weapons, and allowed Lancelot and Gawaine, with four hundred knights and men-at-arms and six hundred infantry, to escort them to the kingdom's northeast border.

WHEN NEWS REACHED the garrison at Rennes that Consul Gainus was dead, there was great concern. Second-in-command to Gainus had been Romeus Baldoni, a portly fellow who in civilian life had been a merchant and land-owner, and whose main position in the military was as Staff Prefect. Throughout the many campaigns of Emperor Lucius, he had organised logistics, built camps and served as secretary to the various fighting-men he had served under. He had never himself seen the face of battle.

Baldoni now sent a frantic missive to Nantes to the effect that he and his reduced command were in dire peril. The return mail, signed by Emperor Lucius himself, instructed Baldoni to re-fortify Rennes, and reassured him that fresh forces would soon be en route to relieve him. In the meantime, the traitor Priamus could not be allowed to escape and Baldoni was ordered to send the only mobile force he had left – Gorlon and his free-companies – in pursuit. Relieved on several counts, not least because the free-companies themselves made him nervous, Baldoni passed the orders to the ogre captain, who yet again was given express permission to 'do his worst.'

Gorlon relished his new commission, as it meant that he and his army could head north. This would bring them into the orbit of towns and villages as yet untouched by the war, which he could plunder with impunity – and this he did, delaying often so that he and his followers could thoroughly enjoy these fruits of their labour. This was also wine-growing country, so his army finished most days' work not only replete with theft and rapine, but also drunk and insensible. If his mission in Brittany was becoming a lawless holiday, Gorlon had no great concern. He saw no actual value in taking the Moorish captives his paymasters sought – even if they had wealthy families back home that might trade for them, North Africa was too far away for business to be done – so the pursuit was pressed in leisurely fashion.

Lancelot's scouts continually reported these developments. With a baggage of prisoners who were happy to go quietly, he was able to deploy more and more men in his rearguard until this was virtually the entirety of his force, with only a token handful to perform the escort duty. He finally opted to make his stand at a pass between low hills, filled with dense woodland. Unusually, it had not rained in Brittany for nearly two months, so the wood was tinder-dry. This suited Lancelot even better, as did the market town of Dol, located on its western flank. His first action was to evacuate Dol as the free-companies would soon be arriving, but to leave stores of food and wine there which could easily be found. His own troops were arrayed east of the wood, though first he had parties of sappers hang many skins filled with naphtha[23] from its high boughs.

In late afternoon, Gorlon and his companies entered Dol in their usual fashion, riding pell-mell along the streets, hurling torches. When no-one fled screaming, they dismounted and began to search. They found no living soul to vent their wrath upon, but of course there was a wealth of food and drink. Suspecting the villagers had left these offerings to buy off his ferocity, the ogre captain opted to pitch his camp here for the night. He would still destroy the town, but only in the morning.

Dusk was descending when Lancelot, Gawaine and groups of other mounted knights emerged from the wood, their colours and badges prominently displayed. With much shouting and blowing of horns, they charged the free-company pickets, slaughtering many at their posts, and sending the remainder scampering into the town. Roused from their drunken slumbers, the rest of the freebooters armed themselves. When they learned that vivid crests were borne by those assailing them, their greed was ignited. Arthur's knights were no ordinary knights: they counted dukes, barons and princes in their order; even one or two, made hostage, would be worth a fortune. The freebooters were even more encouraged to attack when they saw that their enemies were few, and now galloping back into the wood as though to escape.

A mad pursuit was launched, the freebooters leaping onto their mounts half-dressed for battle, weaving between thickets and tangled trees, and in the darkest depths of that place, where their numbers became irrelevant, they were met head-on by a furious counter-charge.

Lancelot and Gawaine wrought brutal execution. Swords and axes rose and fell in shimmering, moon-lit patterns as the knights hacked their way in and out of the straggling, disordered horsemen, felling them to every side.

---

[23]A form of petroleum. The Byzantine weapon, "greek fire," very likely contained naphtha.

"This is no trouble at all!" Gawaine laughed, as he and Lancelot passed each other in the noisy gloom.

"They still outnumber us ten to one," Lancelot replied. He stood in his stirrups to peer into the depths of the wood. It was impossible to distinguish friend from foe, but figures were battling back and forth, blundering into one another, cramming every glade with distorted, chaotic forms.

Realising the time was right, he put his hunting horn to his lips, and blew a single, piercing blast. At once, those knights and men-at-arms still locked in combat struggled free and rode away along pre-determined paths, Lancelot and Gawaine among them. They rode hard and recklessly, for they knew they only had seconds before the six hundred archers ranked to the east of the wood poured death into its naphtha-filled branches.

Gorlon wasn't worried about the welfare or even the lives of his fellow freebooters. He'd shed no tears to see their broken bodies hanging from the scaling-ladders at Rennes. He felt no apprehension now as more and more of them galloped furiously into the darkened tangle of trees. After all, the fewer those remaining, the more there was of the final haul to go around. And he wasn't alone in this philosophy. There were several wise heads among the free-companies, most of whom had come to serve as Gorlon's lieutenants.

Pepe la Lieux, real name Ranulf Guiscard, was the son of a Frankish lord who, with no fervour for the law of primogeniture, had murdered two of his three older brothers before being discovered. The free-companies had made a convenient bolt-hole for him, but now, with the unerring instinct for survival that all noblemen possess, he came to share Gorlon's suspicion that a trap was closing.

Darra O'Lug was an itinerant monk who had prowled the leafy byways of Ireland preaching 'redemption through sin.' From village to village he took his perverse gospel, debauching the young girls trusted to his ministry. On being chased out of Ireland, he had arrived among the free-companies, finding like-minded companions. He had particularly enjoyed the daughters of Rennes, but now he, too, could sense that it was time to depart.

Baroni Benevento was a Genoese merchant who had earned himself the soubriquet 'Death-Dealer' for his provision of mercenary forces – plus expert torturers and assassins – to private wars. Only when Roman hegemony was restored over Italy's great merchant cities, and his business rivals filed charges of embezzlement against him, did Benevento take his military market-place on the road, heading north into Gaul, where at the time the jockeying forces of Frank, Saxon and Visigoth still had scores to settle with each other. But first he settled a few of his own, sending his *bravos* to silence those business rivals who had offered evidence against him. Then, as now, it had come to Benevento that it was time to leave.

Sir Turgeis of Coutrances was a knight turned robber, known as the 'Jackal of the Southeast,' whose band had terrorised the highways of Aquitaine for many a year. When he was eventually captured and hanged by the roadside, so thick were the thews in his neck, and so clumsily tied was the hangman's knot, that he survived an entire night on the gibbet and when, in the morning, the local executioner – a village bumpkin of the first order – came to cut him down, he turned the tables on that oafish official, binding him hand and foot and suspending him from the gibbet instead. Whether any of his accomplices who had also been hanged by the roadside had survived the night, he cared too little to check, and made off quickly on the executioner's cart. For Turgeis, self-preservation was an overriding priority.

This was the case where all these men, and others like them in Gorlon's makeshift command, were concerned – so much that they watched in silence as one disorganised company after another rode into the darkling wood, yelling like demons. Long before Lancelot's fire engulfed it, they saw that the days of the freebooter army were over. So thinking, while the battle raged amid the trees, they furtively stuffed whatever spare loot they could find into bolsters, loaded their wagons and packhorses, and vacated the town of Dol to the north.

Lancelot's archers used incendiary arrows, with clumps of tightly-bound pitch-soaked fleece fitted just below the arrowhead, ignited in braziers of hot coals. Their bodkin tips, projected by the powerful, thick-staved longbows favoured by Arthur's infantry, easily penetrated mail and leather coats and continued to burn deep inside their targets' bodies. Of course, in the depth of night, clean shots were impossible – not that they were needed.

A rain of fire slashed down through the tinder-dry foliage of the wood wherein the freebooters milled, covering every quadrant and puncturing the skins of naphtha hanging in the canopy.

The blood-red glare of the exploding skins lit the landscape for dozens of miles. On the crest of a hill just north of Dol, Gorlon glanced back, his misaligned features awed as he gazed on the inferno. By his reckoning, almost the entirety of the free-companies had blundered headlong into the disaster. Even as he and his officers watched, frantic figures could be seen floundering in the white-hot heart of a conflagration which roared from the forest floor to a hundred feet above the tips of the tallest trees.

IT WAS AT first light, when the smog of smoke and morning mist had cleared, and Lancelot, Gawaine and their men-at-arms advanced on horseback through the ash and embers. Scenes of horror greeted them: scores of fallen men, more than they could count, lay huddled together, blackened, twisted, and melted into each other. A fortunate few were riddled with arrows and had probably died swiftly; some had perished on their own blades; others had been incinerated in attitudes of prayer, desperately seeking shrift before plunging into that even more terrible fire. The stench was nauseating, eye-watering.

"We couldn't beat them in a straight fight," Lancelot reminded Gawaine, who nodded grimly, for once every jest knocked out of him. "They were too many. They'd have killed our men as surely as the unarmed villagers they massacred so routinely."

They assessed the town of Dol, to which only minor damage had been done, and rounded up the small groups of freebooters who had either crawled there with burns and arrow wounds, or had simply stayed behind to cower in sheds and stables. It did not take long to establish that those most responsible for the path of destruction had headed north. Gawaine was thus to take the infantry and escort Priamus across the border and northeast to Paris, while Lancelot mounted a pursuit.

By Lancelot's estimation, the freebooters still in harness numbered between six and seven hundred. But they were easy enough to track – by the trail of items they discarded to lighten their load. Some even abandoned their loot.

But not Sir Turgeis of Coutrances.

The Jackal of the Southeast was master of a cavalcade of twenty wagons, each crammed to the brim with sacks of coin and silver plate. He would not release a single spoon, and so he and his party lagged dangerously behind the rest. Perhaps it was no surprise when, around mid-day, an arrow struck him in the back, pierced his habergeon and severed his spine. He fell from his horse, twisted and paralysed. His underlings, who saw this as a double opportunity – both to lighten their load and to enrich themselves – ignored him. He wept and pleaded until a wagon wheel passed across his body, crushing his ribcage.

Baroni Benevento, fearing more for his skin than his ill-accrued wealth, abandoned his haul altogether, and rode east, accompanied only by his most loyal bodyguards: eight raw-boned Danes who had never yet failed him. But like their master, these doughty fellows also had survival instincts. Hoping to curry favour with their pursuers, they tied the disgraced merchant to an alder tree, where they used him for axe-throwing practice. When a band of Lancelot's mounted archers rode up it was all over for Benevento, and his former bodyguard willingly laid down their arms and went into custody.

The others, who had chosen to remain close to Gorlon, made

it as far as the coast. It was believed that Mont St. Michel, the island stronghold, could be made defensible and that, as King Arthur and his army would soon have bigger fish to fry, they might, if they proved defiant enough, be left alone.

Not so.

When Gorlon crested the last rise, he found the strait between the coast of France and his island-home hosting several vessels, including one particularly large galleass, at whose prow and stern the timber castles were draped with flags bearing Arthur's dragon standard. Smoke unfurled from the black barge that normally transported the ogre captain to and from his island, as it burned at its mooring.

Along the beach from both sides, knights and men-at-arms cantered with lances levelled. On the skyline at Gorlon's back, Lancelot appeared with his men.

Close to the water's edge, a royal pavilion had been pitched. Banners and shields hung alongside it. More squadrons of armoured horsemen were mounted to its rear. In front, there was a table at which was seated a man in full mail with burnished steel roundels at his joints and a handsome white and scarlet surcoat belted at his waist. He barely acknowledged Gorlon's arrival as he dined on brisket, sweet-peas, onions and carrots. With his mail aventail pulled back and the sun embossing his light-brown hair, this could only be King Arthur himself. The two knights flanking him – Sir Bedivere and Sir Kay – were less relaxed, with visors down and longswords drawn.

Not that further fighting was in any way likely. With the forces of Albion circling them, the remaining freebooters could do nothing more than disarm themselves, though one – Darra O'Lug – attempted to break for it, galloping at a gap which briefly appeared in the enemy ranks. He made it through, but was pursued and caught easily from behind, a longsword cleaving his tonsured cranium at a single stroke.

At length the King stood and dabbed his mouth with a napkin. He approached Gorlon on foot. "They told us you were coming. We so hoped we hadn't missed you."

Gorlon twisted his tusked mouth into a hideous, sneering smile. He said nothing as he and his men were put in chains and led away.

"Prisoners?" Arthur asked, as Lancelot dismounted.

"A handful slipped through our fingers, but I'd say just short of two thousand."

Arthur stroked his beard.

"Too many to hang," Bedivere observed.

"I agree," Arthur said. "I'll settle for having them all castrated. But not our friend Gorlon. A *real* example must be made of him."

THE DESTRUCTION OF the free-companies was not the end of Arthur's campaign in Brittany.

It was around this time that Emperor Lucius was victorious at Nantes. He finally persuaded the city to yield when, at great cost to himself both in time and money, he ordered the construction of thirty siege-towers, including a one-hundred-and-fifty-foot *helepolis*,[24] each of its four levels armed with three catapults and three arbalest. With their ramparts broken, what remained of the garrison raised a white flag rather than face an onslaught of this magnitude. Emperor Lucius took the surrender in a grand ceremony, only to discover halfway through that King Hoel had escaped weeks earlier and, even now, was raising new forces.

The Emperor was so enraged that he failed to speak for the remainder of that day. Only the following morning had he regained his equilibrium. He emerged from his pavilion and issued orders that one-third of his forces were to advance into Brittany, two army-groups of thirty thousand each to invest the castles of Fougeres and Vitre, the rest to march through the centre of the kingdom, ultimately to attack Brest. All this time, of course, the bulk of King Arthur's forces were coming

---

[24]A wheeled tower equipped with weapons platforms.

ashore, not in Brittany but in France, north of Mont St. Michel, far beyond the range of Roman scouts.

It was therefore even more of a shock for Lucius, still quartered on the Loire, when his breakfast was interrupted by the news that his significantly reduced encampment was being approached – not from the west, as he'd expected, but from the north. When he enquired who by, he was speechless to learn that it was King Arthur and his entire host.

SIXTEEN

BISHOP MALCONI MADE his summer residence in a place that had once been famous for atrocity, a formerly ruined coastal villa called Jovis, which he'd had refurbished with frescoes, marble statues and handsome mosaic floors. It occupied a high point, Mount Tiberio, on the northeast tip of the island of Capri. Bishop Malconi had first purchased the building because he valued his privacy – the local peasants were too wary of its evil reputation to come anywhere near. Some four centuries earlier, Emperor Tiberius, wearied by the cutthroat politics of Rome, had sought refuge here and, according to some, had come to lead a debauched lifestyle, indulging in every kind of sexual perversion and executing any person he took against in elaborately cruel and inventive ways.

Malconi was unconcerned by this grim history. He had his blue sky, his turquoise sea, and below his bedroom window a picturesque view of rolling valleys, their steep slopes clad with cypress, poplar and cork-oaks through which the occasional glimpse of honey-coloured stone revealed the presence of fallen columns and overgrown arches. The restful isolation he found here was broken only by his exclusively male household, who went about their allotted tasks with quiet and unobtrusive efficiency.

However, it was not unknown for Malconi to receive visitors at Villa Jovis.

It was early in July when a heavy carriage of glossy black enamel, covered all over with rich gilded sculptures of tumbling foliage and fabulous beasts, laboured its way up the winding, dusty track to the villa gate. A team of eight straining horses drew it, for the vehicle was truly immense – a party of several men and women could have found comfort inside. The driver was a virtual colossus, swathed in crimson hessian robes with a cowl pulled low. His head, though hidden from view, was huge and square, and he was as broad as an ox.

The gates at Villa Jovis were occupied by a squad of ten security officials, who had been selected from the ranks of New Rome's military for their skill and ruthlessness. Even in the basting mid-summer heat, all wore uniform ensemble of sallet, chain-mail and a leather hauberk studded with steel balls, and were armed with broadswords, which they carried in scabbards on their backs, and any other implement they excelled in, be it flail, mace or war-hammer. Ordinarily, no visitor would pass the villa's wrought-iron gate without enduring a menacing scrutiny from these handpicked guard-dogs, but the sight of the black carriage and its crimson-shrouded driver was enough to bring them scurrying from their posts.

There was a clanking of chains and a creaking of well-oiled steel as the central bolt was withdrawn and padlocks removed. The gate swung open and the carriage was admitted, coming to a halt in a gravelled reception area, where a young groom in a sweat-stained blouse rushed forward to assist with the horses. The crimson-clad driver stepped down – at full height, he was close on eight feet tall – and opened the carriage door. Though a giant and monster in every way, he showed great deference to the passenger who stepped out.

She too was tall – easily the height of a man, but with the perfect proportions of womankind. She was of indeterminate age – anywhere between thirty and fifty – yet there wasn't so much as a crow's foot on her flawless, porcelain-white skin. Her hair was black as bramble-wood and, though bound at the rear in a copper coronet, hung to the small of her back in lustrous, liquid tangles. Her beauty was of the patrician class – fierce and proud, but with more than a hint of feline menace. She had full blood-red lips, high sharp cheekbones and eyes of iridescent green, enhanced by deep slashes of purple-grey shadow. She wore a sleeveless shift of flimsy green cloth, belted at the waist by a slim chain, which did little to conceal the statuesque body beneath. Her fingernails were long and sharp and lacquered emerald, her hands encrusted with jewellery of exotic design, the gold stems of which twined up around her arms as high as her shoulders.

She strode across the reception area and up a paved path between rockeries and spiny cacti, the wooden block-heels of her sandals clopping like hooves. As she approached the villa's heavy ash door, it was opened by a bronzed young man with dark-blond locks over his handsome, boyish face. He was wearing an indecently short toga.

"Duchess?" he said, surprised.

"Is your master at home?" she asked.

"Of course, ma'am. Forgive me, I wasn't expecting..."

"Stand aside."

She strode purposely through the entry hall and a connected succession of apartments. In all of them, young male staff busied themselves with household chores, giving her only passing interest. She crossed the atrium, where a small herb garden was open to the elements. A husky, bearded gardener, again wearing only a sleeveless, short-skirted toga which exposed his brawny, sun-browned limbs, was working with a hoe. Beyond the garden, a narrow avenue between clipped hedges led to an open terrace overlooking the Gulf of Naples. It was usually awash with cooling sea-breezes, but at the height of the day, as now, the sun beat mercilessly on it. At one end lay a small bathing-pool, in which another young man, this one naked, stood thigh-deep, scooping out insects with a net. The duchess briefly regarded his exposed appendage, unimpressed, before continuing along the terrace to its far end, where a canopy had been raised, beneath which Bishop Malconi, wearing only a thin shift, reclined on a divan. There was a damp towel over his face, and to one side a stool bore a bowl of strawberries and clotted cream, and a goblet of iced water. Another young man, wearing a loincloth so flimsy as to be pointless, crouched at the bishop's feet, tending to them with a brush and a pair of delicate nail-scissors.

The duchess hissed at the servant, who stood, bowed and withdrew. Bishop Malconi made no effort to remove the towel, though he clearly knew she was there.

"The steady, sensual gait of a proud, beautiful and domineering woman," he said, his voice muffled. "Zalmyra, my dear sister... what a charming surprise."

"Is it possible you could be unaware of the events in the north?" she wondered coolly.

Malconi removed the towel. Beneath it, his face was flushed and sweaty. "On the contrary, sister. You might even call me their architect."

"In which case I'm somewhat bewildered."

He took a strawberry from the bowl and pushed it into his mouth. "You have *your* areas of expertise, Zalmyra... which are many and nefarious. I have *mine*, which are somewhat simpler. You do what you do, while I merely run the affairs of Europe."

She arched a disdainful eyebrow. "Pray don't mistake me, brother, for someone who can be lulled by your usual hyperbole."

"Zalmyra, your entire world is centred on Castello Malconi. It's a long way from the borders of Brittany. I promise you, there is nothing to worry about."

"My entire world?" She smiled thinly. "Even were I nothing more than a pleb or slave, that would be quite a significant item to dismiss so easily."

Malconi dabbed beads of sweat from his forehead. Cicadas chirped incessantly from the bundles of honeysuckle hanging over the terrace railing. Despite the canopy, the heat of the July day was intense, yet noticeably Duchess Zalmyra remained a figure of marble. Her cold, beautiful face was unflustered. Not a trickle of perspiration snaked down her tall, curved body.

"We know what we are doing," he assured her.

"Is that 'we' as in the royal 'we'?" she wondered. "Or 'we' as in you and Emperor Lucius? Knowing you as I do, I sincerely doubt it's the latter."

"You know exactly what I mean."

"Oh, I see. It's you and that wily old vulture Simplicius."

"God forgive your arrogance. His Holiness is younger than you are."

"He's certainly behaving that way. Only a wet-eared whelp would have allowed this tide of reconquest to run unchecked."

"Bah." Malconi stood and moved to the railing. "You know nothing of what you speak."

"I know a fool when I see one. And any pope who would allow Emperor Lucius to declare war on Arthur of the Britons is worse even than that."

"A fool? When Simplicius has stage-managed this whole affair?" Malconi dabbed more sweat from his brow. "Think about it, Zalmyra – how can he lose? If Lucius defeats Arthur, all is well and good. He will be away from Italy for many months, maybe years, as he tries to settle the seething pot of discontent that will be Britain. The papacy will be left with the free hand in Italy it enjoyed before. But if Arthur wins, that also is good – Emperor Lucius, a rival at the heart of Christendom, will have been removed."

"And Arthur will have taken his place," she said.

"Arthur is not interested in dominating Christendom. He wants only to govern his own kingdom. He might plunder the capital and sever a few heads, but he won't lay hands on His Holiness. In due course he will return north."

"I see... and once again our pontiff will reign unchallenged."

"Of course." Malconi took a sip of water. "All Simplicius needed was an excuse for the war, something that would absolve him of guilt when he gave his permission for the fighting to commence. We were sent to find one, and it was not difficult. Arthur has some hot-headed counsellors at his command."

"And my son is in the midst of this papally-approved hornets' nest."

"He is a soldier. That was his career choice. He's exactly where he should be."

"You must pluck him out."

"He's a *soldier*, Zalmyra. Were we not fighting the Britons, we'd be fighting someone else. We have an entire world to re-civilise."

"Arthur and the Knights of the Round Table are not just 'someone else,' Severin. What of this Black Wolf of the North who I hear my son has particularly antagonised?"

Malconi was surprised that she knew about this, though he supposed he ought not to be. Zalmyra had powers at her beck and call that he didn't like to contemplate.

"Earl Lucan is of a belligerent nature," he admitted. "I've seen that for myself. I also hear that he is a feared warrior."

"A feared warrior? So even in that esteemed company he stands out? It appears that while you've served your two masters, the Pope and the Emperor, with your usual guile, you have failed to discharge your duty as an uncle."

"I advised against it, but Felix is head over heels in love. He's a grown man, Zalmyra – presumably you want him weaned away from your tit at some point."

She slapped his face – with such force that Bishop Malconi was left dazed; he almost toppled over the railing. At the other end of the terrace, male servants whispered together and snickered.

"How... how dare you?" he stammered. "You are in no position to disrespect me."

"I can do more than disrespect you, brother," she snarled. "As well you know."

"You worry unnecessarily... I've told you. A savage war is under way. In a very short time, many of these men you fear will be dead."

"You'd better hope and pray that Felix is not among them."

"I cannot change the tides of politics."

"*You blind imbecile, Severin!* This is not some game! You sun yourself here while black wolves gather at our door?"

"Emperor Lucius will stop them."

Her voice lowered, became scathing. "You may trust everything to that cream-faced boy, but I won't. If nothing else, I'll ensure that what's mine is safe." She turned and strode away.

"Whatever you wish," he called after her. "But I warn you, sister – don't use sorcery. The Church forbids it."

Her laugh was like a whip-crack. "The Church also forbids catamites, yet your house is full of them."

SEVENTEEN

THE MAIN REASON King Arthur chose the Vale of Sessoine as the ground on which he and Emperor Lucius would finally meet in battle was because it was narrow; no more than half a mile in breadth. Its western and eastern slopes were steep, wooded and rocky, and rose to high sharp ridges, so there was no possibility of New Rome's vast army outflanking the smaller British host.

The vale also sloped upward from south to north – only gently, but this meant that whichever army claimed the northern end had a slight advantage. Arthur's scouts had reported this to him less than a week after his capture of Mont St. Michel, and he had sent cavalry contingents riding hard to secure the position. Emperor Lucius was unconcerned when he learned about this; though he had divided his forces, he still had just short of two hundred thousand men at his immediate command, while King Arthur had no more than forty thousand. With such a discrepancy in numbers, Lucius did not expect that an uphill battle would prove troublesome for him.

It was a hot, dry morning in the middle of July when the two armies confronted each other. From the British perspective, the sight of the Romans pouring into the southern end of the vale, multitudinous as ants, was nerve-wracking, and yet only half the enemy was visible, thanks to the veils of dust kicked up by their tramping feet and the hooves of their animals. From the Roman perspective, the sight of the Britons arrayed in tight formation at the northern end, but on much higher ground, caused some of their more experienced officers a twinge of unease.

Many factors contributed to the outcomes of battles. Sheer weight of numbers could easily decide a victory, but there'd been several occasions in the past, well known to the officer corps in New Rome – Alexander at Gaugamala, the Spartans at Plataea – when greater forces had been defeated by the skilled tactics and manoeuvring of the opposition. Granted, in the Vale of Sessoine there was little room for Arthur to manoeuvre, but the British deployment, which was already complete when the armies of New Rome arrived on the field, appeared at first glance to be sound and, with their elevated position, had the air of immovability.

Some of these views were expressed to Emperor Lucius in his command pavilion while he was assigning duties, not least by Tribune Maximion.

The Emperor replied coldly: "You expect me to run away when I outnumber them five to one, simply because we don't like the ground?"

"Caesar will not appreciate this constant doubting of his wisdom," Rufio said as he and Maximion left the tent side by side, having been given their positions in the line.

"The Caesars rarely did," Maximion replied. "Perhaps that's why they aren't with us anymore."

Rufio turned to face him, stiff-shouldered. "That kind of talk is verging on treason."

"Treason? I thought we were discussing history."

"The Caesars are with us now. Embodied in our sovereign lord, Lucius Julio Bizerta."

Maximion pursed his lips. "You idolise him, Rufio?"

"How could I not? One so young and yet so brilliant. One who in such a short time has achieved so much."

"I hate to say this... but it's not impossible that he could lose it all in considerably less time. In a single day, perhaps? Today?"

Rufio's eyebrows arched. Shocking though it was to hear such disloyalty, it was also sobering to suddenly realise that everything they'd achieved in the last few years – all the Emperor's diplomatic offensives, the army's military gains, all the money they'd spent, the treaties they'd agreed, the new governorships they'd set up, the consuls they'd appointed, the roads they'd repaired, the bridges they'd built, the cities they'd walled, the new sense of power and security that had come to run through all their lives – it could all be for naught if this *one day* went against them.

But of course it wouldn't.

Arthur's force was so small that its arms barely glinted through the clouds of dust created by the rivers of Roman troops flowing past him.

"Prudence is important for a commander," Rufio said loftily. "But there is a fine line between prudence and cowardice. Take care yours doesn't vanish altogether, Maximion."

Maximion said nothing.

Rufio took the reins from his groom, climbed into his saddle and cantered away. Before he found his command, he rode up onto a thinly wooded bluff to the east of the vale. Here, the wives and courtesans of the army's senior officers had found a vantage point. Many were seated on stools or at cloth-laid tables, sipping wine and picking at pastries and sweetmeats.

TRELAWNA AND GERTA refrained from such indulgence.

Gerta was seated, and concentrating on her needlework. Trelawna stared down at the tide of men that, slowly and with great noise and confusion, was organising itself into three separate but immense companies. Despite the rising heat, she was scarfed and wrapped in a shawl, and hugged herself as if she was cold.

On first leaving home, she'd thought she'd be able to do without her small entourage of ladies and maids, who'd rarely had more to offer than gossip and flattery. But being alone –

being *really* alone – was a new experience for Trelawna. She didn't know any of the Roman women who dined on the hillside around her; they'd made no effort at friendship, and some even turned their noses away when she entered their presence. She had Gerta of course, but she had always had Gerta – Gerta was at times a comfort, though she also spoke her mind and, as she'd disapproved of this "ill-conceived adventure," as she called it, from the outset, she was now given to waspish comments that Trelawna found tiresome.

It was a relief to hear Rufio's voice as he trotted up the grassy slope. "Trelawna... how goes it?"

"I'm a trifle nervous, as always on occasions like these."

"Have no fear." He jumped from his horse and gathered her in his arms. "That small band at the end of the valley would do well to leave now. I imagine they're already contemplating it." He kissed her forehead. "I promise you, my love, they cannot prevail. Even were numbers more evenly matched, the Emperor *must* win. There is far too much at stake."

"Felix... all that's at stake here is our future. Mine and yours."

"I know, my love, but..."

"But nothing." She disentangled herself from his arms. "I don't know how many battles you've actually fought...?"

Rufio made no response to that, which was not encouraging. In fact, he'd spoken little about his military escapades, and she now wondered with some alarm if he was yet another of these pink young officers who had risen through the ranks of the academy on the basis of his family name rather than through experience.

"*I've* seen war many times," she said. "Never from *this* position, admittedly... as if from the spectators' gallery at a tournament." She tried not to sound as scathing as she felt. "But I've seen enough to know that when swords clash and spears break, only one thing matters – survival."

"We will survive. Our love can survive anything..."

"I'm talking about *you*, Felix. *You!*" She put her hands on the burnished roundels covering his shoulders. "Only one thing matters today... not your Emperor's vainglorious quest to recapture the world, nor the bounty of wealth and harvest of slaves that New Rome will reap. It's *you*, Felix. *You* must survive."

He shrugged. "At the end of the day, I'm a soldier. I must fight."

"Do what you need to, and no more. And then come back to me with all speed." His mood, so buoyant before, seemed a little deflated by her lack of faith. She wondered just how buoyant it had actually been, if it could falter so quickly. "It's not just about surviving, it's about emerging intact," she added. "What good are you to me crippled or blinded?"

"There is such a thing as glory and honour..."

"Bah!" She folded her arms and walked away. "If there was such a thing as glory and honour, Felix, there would be empty chairs all around King Arthur's Round Table, but there aren't. You know why? Because whenever they are emptied they are filled again. By necessity, new men are elevated, and with indecent haste. Those they replace are venerated for maybe a day, and then forgotten. As *you* will be. All men are expendable. That is our fate from the moment we are born."

"This is the way you send me into battle?" Rufio looked as hurt as he was baffled. "With a reminder that I'm nothing but dust? I thought you ladies of Camelot were renowned for the favours you cast upon knights before combat. Am I so inferior that I don't qualify?"

There was earnestness in his face that she hadn't seen before – a plea for kindness. Suddenly he looked so young and, yes, if she was honest, a little nervous. Guilt struck her at having unmanned him in the face of what might be his greatest challenge. She embraced him, holding him to her as tightly as she could, but at the same time lowering her head to the moulded curve of his breastplate. It was important – nay, vital – that he felt he was protecting her rather than the other way around.

"Forgive me, my love," she said. "War is a terrible thing. I'm just frightened."

"I know," he replied with understanding. He stroked her hair. "It's to be expected. But soon you'll be my wife, and the wife of a Roman officer must show fortitude."

"Here is something for you," she said.

As a tribune in the Fourteenth Legion, which almost entirely comprised heavy cavalry, he was well attired, wearing greaves from ankle to knee, a battle-skirt made from strips of thick leather inlaid with iron, his heavy breastplate over a mail jerkin, and vambraces and rerebraces on his arms. For weaponry he carried the *falcata*, a curved sabre specifically designed to be wielded from the saddle, but also a *gladius* – the short stabbing sword so symbolic of old Rome. Trelawna paused to choose, and then the *gladius* rasped as she drew it from its leather scabbard. She lifted the blue silk scarf from her neck and knotted it to the sword's hilt. "A favour for you." She stood on tiptoes to kiss his ruddy lips. "Wear it always in combat and think of me, the sweetheart who waits on your return."

He gave her a smile of such joy that Trelawna's heart almost broke.

"The day will be ours, my love... you'll see!" He leapt back into the saddle and, before riding gallantly away, shouted: "I'll bring you King Arthur's head. And Earl Lucan's. We'll toast them at our own private victory dinner."

She watched in silence as he cantered down the slope, soon enveloped in the dust and confusion of the forming army.

"And how many heads is that you've been promised over the years?" a voice wondered from behind.

"Oh, do shut up, Gerta!"

THE NIGHT BEFORE, Arthur's army had heard Mass. Then they'd returned to their tents and campfires to contemplate the coming day. Few had been able to sleep, so the leading nobles had wandered through their ranks, slapping shoulders and sharing jokes. Arthur had made rousing speeches and led choruses of heroic songs.

The fighting men of Albion had stood together many times. They had great trust in their King and his knights, who'd become talismanic figures on the battlefield. They knew they'd be outnumbered, but strength could be found in comradeship. Uncles, cousins, fathers and brothers now sat alongside each other – so there was much more here than mere familiarity. They knew that many present would die on the morrow, possibly all, but priests and monks were also active in their midst, hearing confessions, giving blessings, assuring everyone that to die in the service of their King and their land would open the gateway to Heaven.

The following day, Arthur deployed his forces at first light. Mist begirt the vale when clarions sounded the assembly. Arthur anticipated that the Romans would attack with their heavy infantry to the fore. It was traditional, and the geography of the vale almost ensured it – there was no room for a sweeping cavalry assault. So thinking, he arrayed his own infantry in a battle-line several ranks deep, stretching from one side of the vale to the other, but shielded in the front by a row of sharpened stakes. At their own insistence, the Saxons occupied the first rank. Behind them, Arthur placed the footmen of his elite *Familiaris Regis*. This would already make a difficult hedge for the Romans to hack their way through – the Saxon housecarls had their battle-axes and iron-bossed linden-wood shields, the *Familiaris* their short, steel-tipped lances – but Arthur was not yet content. Behind them, he drew dismounted men-at-arms from the companies of his retainers who, now that they were on foot, dispensed with their longswords for maces, war-hammers and pole-axes, while the *fyrd* and yeomen made up the rear with their mallets and reaping-hooks.

Arthur's longbows were deployed in two separate phalanxes to the rear of the infantry – on raised ground to the west and east. Behind them were placed the artillery pieces, onagers, mangonels and sling-throwers. Like the archers, they were only to be used at specific moments in the battle, as decided on by Arthur.

All of this had come naturally, dictated by the landscape.

But the problem remained for Arthur to decide what to do with his knights, those men whose names alone were pillars of strength. In the end he decided on a simple ploy. He and his army had gained access to the north end of the vale via two parallel gulleys, to the east and west. These were deep and sheltered, inaccessible to enemy missiles, and could only be approached from a plateau behind Arthur's army, where his stockaded camp was located, so it was impossible for them to be assaulted from behind. He now placed contingents of knights and horsemen in both of these. They were to be his mailed fists; they would not be called upon to enter the fray straight away, but when they were, aisles would clear through the ranks of the infantry and they would charge down and deal a pulverising blow to the enemy.

Not all were pleased – it seemed contrary to the chivalrous code that knights would join the melee behind the common men – but they knew enough of tactics and of the enemy's strength to raise no serious objections.

Thanks to the early start, Arthur's host was in full array when the Romans began to form up. Emperor Lucius organised his force into three main army-groups – solid blocks of infantry composed of symmetrically aligned phalanxes – Flail Cohort marching alongside Mace Cohort, Axe Cohort in support of Mattock Cohort, and so on, each army-group in total some sixty or seventy thousand strong, any one of which was vastly larger than Arthur's entire force. The Roman horse companies were deployed as buffer units between them, so if the first army-group floundered it could draw immediate support from cavalry at its rear. In effect, Lucius intended to drive a titanic battering ram of men and horses along the centre of the valley, straight into the heart of Arthur's deployment. He was still convinced that, if nothing else, he would crush the opposition by sheer strength of numbers.

So confident was Lucius that he and his personal bodyguard mounted up and posted themselves beneath the Imperial purple banner in the centre of the first cavalry company.

Much to Tribune Rufio's chagrin, these units were not drawn from the Fourteenth Legion, but from the Eighth, who were augmented by the Saracen horse-warriors of Prince Jalhid. The squadrons of the Fourteenth were placed between the second and third army-groups, well to the rear, though Rufio grudgingly supposed that at least Trelawna would be pleased.

Arthur chose an equally visible and vulnerable position to the Emperor.

In his case, this was not born of soaring confidence or a greedy desire to claim the spoil when the battle was won, but a choice made of necessity. The King could not afford to hide. If he did, the morale of his men would suffer. As such, Arthur placed his distinctive standard – the red dragon on the white weave – on high rocks to the immediate rear of the infantry line, in the very centre of the field.

Sir Kay, in the blunt language that only an older brother would use, told him that this was rank, mule-headed folly. Arthur could be killed instantly, and then what would happen? Sir Bedivere agreed. The Romans were hauling artillery up field in support of their infantry; they would assail the British with a fierce bombardment before actually engaging. If Arthur were to perish before a blow had been struck it would be the worst disaster in the history of Albion.

Arthur merely laughed. "I need to see what's happening on the field, do I not?" he argued.

"You will see nothing at all my lord, if your eyes are smashed apart by a lead grenade," Bedivere replied.

Arthur laughed all the more. "Your concern is appreciated. But I put my trust in the Lord. God has decided that from this day on, the Roman Empire will be an empire of the soul, not the sword. It is our duty to enforce this transition."

"Amen to that," said Aldemar, the Breton Archbishop of Lorient, who had joined eight hundred of his own knights to "Arthur's crusade," as he called it, and now stood alongside the King, wearing mail under his golden tabard and a pig-snouted helm instead of a mitre.

By eleven o'clock in the morning, the Roman formation was complete, and a group of heralds and officers detached from their ranks and cantered up the vale under a pennant of truce. A similar group detached from Arthur's ranks. They met mid-way.

Ardeus Vigilano, Duke of Spoleto, had command of the Roman party. Kay had command of the Britons. The Duke was a short, portly man, red-faced and with longish ginger locks now running to grey, which, when he shook them loose from his helmet, were already damp with sweat. Spoleto had shown little inclination to be a diplomat during the colloquy at Camelot, and he showed even less now. His terms were simple. Beforehand, the Emperor of New Rome had been prepared to deal with Arthur as a lawful monarch and an equal, but now that Arthur had performed belligerent acts on New Roman territory he must be regarded as a transgressor. The only way he could save himself and the lives of his men would be to surrender all arms forthwith and put himself and his host in the charge of New Rome. The Emperor would then be pleased to enter discussions concerning the easiest and quickest way to hand over power in the former kingdoms of Brittany and Albion.

Kay replied in a casual tone that the battlefield was no place for jest, that they had business to attend to and that they had best get it concluded swiftly.

"However," he added, "King Arthur is not a barbarous man, and is loath to shed the blood of so many. He proposes that we settle this affair in the correct way – a duel to the death between two champions, the winner to take all."

Spoleto looked amused. It had not gone unnoticed by him that one of the knights in the British party wore the white leopard and blue livery of Lancelot du Lac, who it was said no man alive could defeat. "How interesting that you offer such a solution," he said, "when our host outnumbers yours by almost five to one."

Kay shrugged. "A single combat between champions would be the chivalrous option."

A junior officer mounted alongside Spoleto removed his helm, revealing tightly curled white-blond hair and astonishingly youthful features, which now seethed with indignation.

"Hiding behind chivalry, sir knight?" he scoffed. "There wasn't much of that on offer when you captured the free-companies."

"The free-companies, what remained of them, were gelded to reduce their baleful temperament," Kay explained. "Had I had my way, they'd have been branded and blinded as well, and each one forced to carry the stump of his right hand."

"There will be no combat between champions," Spoleto said decisively. "If your king feels he has overreached himself, he must now pay the price of his recklessness."

"Then many men will die today because not a single Roman was brave enough to stand alone."

The young officer spluttered with anger.

Spoleto merely smiled. "The festivities may commence whenever your king is ready."

"How gracious of you. But first we have a debt to repay."

Kay turned in the saddle and signalled. A gap appeared in the front rank of Arthur's army, as men shuffled aside to permit the exit of a four-wheeled cart drawn by a single horse and driven by a single driver, who, rather dramatically, stood with legs astride as he lashed the reins. Those who recognised him would have been surprised to see the luxury-loving King Hoel of Brittany. He now wore full plate armour, but had removed his helmet and drawn back his coif so there would be no mistaking him.

Hoel brought the vehicle to a halt thirty yards to the west of Kay's party, drew a great, two-handed sword from the scabbard on his back and leapt down. In the back of the cart, two men-at-arms wrestled with a burly prisoner – a massive, misshapen brute, a savage animal more than a man, but less terrifying given the manacles that bound his limbs, and the single, bloodstained shift that had replaced his mail and leather.

Hoel stood patiently as the men-at-arms dragged the brute from the cart, and forced him into a kneeling posture.

"Let it be known to all here present that this fellow, Gorlon the Ogre, has been sentenced to death for crimes against the people of Brittany," Kay shouted. "Let it also be known that in order to obtain a swifter demise than was planned, he has spoken in full about the events that brought these outrages to be, and has named the names of those parties who manufactured them. Those parties must rest assured that, once today's matter is resolved, they too will share in Gorlon's punishment."

Far back in the ranks of New Rome's army, Tribune Maximion, who stood among the sturdy legionaries of his Javelin Cohort, glanced to his left, in which direction Emperor Lucius was visible on his snow-white charger. Maximion felt a pang of scorn to see the Emperor's brow glint with sweat. A loud *thunk* drew his attention back to the front, where King Hoel was now using a cloth to wipe blood from the blade of his two-handed sword. Gorlon lay at his feet, his severed head about half a yard from his lifeless trunk. Once he'd re-sheathed his steel, Hoel clambered onto the cart and drove it back towards Arthur's ranks. Sir Kay's party also headed back, but the Duke of Spoleto's group remained where they were, frozen, apparently astounded by the indignity they had just been subjected to. With a strangled cry, one of them galloped forth, lance levelled; the young officer who'd sat alongside the Duke.

On a thinly wooded bluff to the east of the battlefield, Trelawna had watched the entire piece of theatre as though riveted. She had heard about the atrocities in Brittany. On learning about the free-companies' demise, she had known there would only be one outcome for their leader. It was still a shocking thing to witness, but now it seemed there would be worse – for a knight, the very one carrying the lance with the white flag attached, answered the young soldier's challenge, breaking away from Sir Kay's party, wheeling his horse around and charging full-tilt.

A finger of ice touched Trelawna's neck.

Even without that swirling mantle of black fur, that black

livery, that black lance, the dark cylindrical helm with the black ribbon crest, she'd have known who this knight was. The taut, strong body hunched low in the saddle, his black kite shield covering almost the whole of his left-hand side, was unmistakable. The mighty black warhorse, Nightshade, looked even more monstrous than usual in its all-encompassing black trapper. The low trajectory of Lucan's lance – all the better to catapult his opponent from the saddle – bespoke years of combat experience.

By contrast, the New Roman officer sat tall, as if he were on parade. His shield was small and round, and only just guarded his left forearm. He wore a thick iron breastplate over a mail jerkin, and an elaborate burgonet sprouting a plume of blue feathers, which matched the colour of his regimental cloak and the breeches under his knee-length battle-skirt. His visor was down, but beneath that he wore only a leather hood, which fastened under the chin with a strap – so his entire throat was exposed. Even if he managed to raise his shield in time, it was so small and its metal face polished to such a shine that Lucan's steel lance-point would likely careen off and still strike its target.

Trelawna watched breathless as they careered towards each other. When the collision came she wanted to close her eyes, but something bade her keep them open. This young Roman was a stranger; he meant nothing to her, and yet somehow, for a very fleeting second, he had come to represent all the hopes and dreams she'd entertained since absconding with Rufio.

There was a splintering crash as both lances struck their targets.

The Roman made good contact, and Lucan swayed. But there was never any real danger of the knight failing to hold the charge, and besides, his own lance made far better contact – in the lower belly, packing more than enough force to hurl his opponent headfirst into the dust.

The Roman staggered groggily to his feet, his helmet askew so that what little vision his visor allowed was now restricted even more. Lucan steered around him in a circle, wielding a second weapon – a morning star; a snowflake of edged steel on the end of a chain. He spun it in a blur as he bore down. The clatter of steel on helmet was shocking. They heard it on the wooded bluff, where the Roman ladies gasped with horror, many shielding their eyes.

Trelawna did not. She felt she owed it to the young Roman to continue to watch as Lucan swept down blow after blow, each delivered with terrible force. This was the boy's final moment on earth, and he had sought it with courage. His helmet was already battered out of shape, so that even had he not died under the sixth impact, dropping in a heap, blood surging through his buckled visor, they would not have been able to remove it from his head.

Lucan wheeled his horse around again, this time to face the ranks of the Roman army. He removed his own helm, his pale features startling against the blackness of his garb. He held aloft his lance, its fluttering white pennant streaked with crimson.

"Men of Rome!" He stood in his stirrups as his voice echoed across the vale. "Look how your disrespect has sullied a flag of truce? By this action you have set the rules for the day. And you will die by them. *This I swear!*"

As Lucan cantered back to his own lines, to the cheers of his fellow troops, Arthur glanced at Bedivere. "I suppose that's first blood to us."

Bedivere nodded, tight-lipped. "There'll be no quarter offered now."

EIGHTEEN

Magadalena and Alonzo's cottage was located in a low, fertile valley on the Apennine road, just after the point where it turned inland from the Bay of Levante.

The cottage was built from local limestone, its outer wall rendered with stucco, which Alonzo had painted white. Its roof was of dry thatch, there was a small herb garden to the front, a chicken hatch to the side and at the rear a somewhat larger enclosure wherein they grew cabbages, broad beans and asparagus. Beyond that lay their main source of income: an olive grove covering some six hectares, though at present they could only sell their produce in local villages. They would be allowed to sell in larger markets if they had a license of trade, which was the main reason Alonzo was now in pursuit of full Roman citizenship. It carried all kinds of privileges: the right to vote, the right to hold public office and make legal contracts, and of course to operate a trading license.

Alonzo and his wife were already self-sufficient on their tenant farm. But as citizens, they would find full financial security and independence. Maybe then they could buy this land, and perhaps extend it and add more livestock – goats, pigs, even a cow or two. Any future Alonzos or Magdalenas would have a true legacy to call their own.

During the long, lonely days while her husband was away, Magdalena would often stand by front gate, gazing wistfully down the green, V-shaped valley towards the blue Mediterranean, one hand on her flat belly. Alonzo was a young man, but serious-minded. Many times she'd suggested they try for a child before they pursue their goal. But he was adamant that any child of his would be born a freeman with prospects, a citizen of New Rome.

She rose with the cockcrow one bright summer morning, ate a breakfast of bread and beans, and went out to feed the chickens and water the vegetable beds. Alonzo only had another year and a half before his military service was complete. That was the offer Emperor Lucius had made to the serfdom of Italy – five years unblemished service in the Imperial militia, and citizenship was guaranteed. Alonzo had never been a soldier before, but Magdalena had no doubt when he'd first suggested it that he'd make a fine one – he was strong, resourceful and tough from years of working the land. Like so many Ligurian men, he was brawny of build with dark, sun-browned skin. He was also handsome, with flashing eyes and thick black hair. Much as she was, if she was honest, though she doubted she looked her best at present; working the farm alone meant short nights and long, hard days. Today would be especially arduous. The autumn crop was already ripening on the branches, but if the winter crop was to be bountiful some of the trees needed pruning. It was necessary but difficult work, and there would be plenty of it, but – as she kept reminding herself – only a year and half remained, and then Alonzo would be discharged from his legion in France, and their life together could truly commence.

It was mid-morning when Magdalena went up to the olive grove carrying a small ladder. She'd bound her lustrous hair with a hessian scarf and fastened a leather girdle around her waist, from which Alonzo's tools – knives, shears and a small saw – were suspended. She put on her animal-hide shoes, and donned the old skirt she had purposely split to the thigh to allow her to climb among the branches. It was not the kind of attire she hoped Father Pius would see if he passed the plantation on his donkey on the way to say Mass in the village, but work necessitated such things and most of the time she was alone here.

She set about the strenuous task with her usual zeal, clambering lithely, cutting, sawing and snipping away as much dead and excess wood as she could find. In the midday heat, she rested. Under a particularly shady tree at the farthest end of the grove, she took her flask and sipped the clear, fresh water she'd collected from the mountain stream, and then ate salted ham on dry bread and a fresh, green salad which she'd picked in her herb garden. For a brief time, she dozed, lulled by the trilling of the cicadas.

"Magdalena?" came a voice.

She assumed she was dreaming – for it sounded like Alonzo.

"Magdalena, where are you?"

Magdalena's eyes snapped open.

Her brow glistened with sweat, her simple clothing sticking to her body as it so often did in the heat of noon. Had the temperature made her dizzy?

"Magdalena?" the voice said again.

She leapt to her feet, amazed, and peered down the length of the plantation, seeing a figure in trailing red robes coming through the wicket gate at the rear of the allotment.

"Alonzo?" she whispered, hardly daring to believe it. She had not seen him since a year last Christmas. Excitement took hold of her.

"*Alonzo!*" she squealed, lifting her skirts and dashing downhill, weaving between the trees, ducking under their low, spiky boughs. He too began to run, waving both his arms in his eagerness to hold her.

She did not stop to think how this was possible. She could only assume that he had been given unexpected leave. Maybe – horror of horrors – he had been wounded in some way. But if so, he looked fit enough: his long, lean stride drove him up the slope, his heavy red vestments dragging behind him. Her beloved husband was home. She did not know how long for, but did that matter? When he'd first enlisted, they'd thought it would be five years before they saw each other again. If he could manage just one period of leave it would be a boon, but *two*? God was truly with them this day.

And then she realised that it wasn't Alonzo.

They were ten yards apart, in the heart of the grove, when the glamour was lifted.

The thing Magdalena had thought was her husband was indeed wearing a long red habit with a monk's cowl, though it had fallen back as he had clumped uphill towards her, revealing his – or rather *its* – face. It stood eight feet tall. It had brutish, primal features coated in a shaggy down of silver-grey fur. Its feral eyes gleamed yellow under thick bone brows; its ivory fangs were bared like knives. It called her again, only this time it called in its true voice – a guttural, spine-chilling howl.

Magdalena slid to a halt, her mouth locked open. When a scream burst from her, it rose and rose and rose. But it was no good, for the thing already had her, wrapped in its massive arms, pressing her slender form to its barrel chest, crushing the life from her.

It was a mercy that she went unconscious as quickly as she did.

The towering monstrosity tore loose the girdle from which her tools hung, and cast her over its shoulder before turning and striding back through the olive plantation. On the far side of the cottage, a black enamel carriage with a team of eight horses waited patiently.

NINETEEN

The silence in the Vale of Sessoine was eerie. Aside from a single fleecy cloud, the sky was pebble-blue. The midday heat possessed oven-like intensity.

The two armies stood facing each other, motionless. The Romans filled some two-thirds of the great valley, rank upon serried rank, their arms and armour shining like mirrors as they diminished backward into a distant haze. So many were they that from King Arthur's position their farthest end could not be seen. The eagles of each legion, and the flag-poles marking their cohorts, companies and regiments, stood upright in a rigid forest. Arthur's host did not flinch at this prospect, not even from the sight of the papal gonfalon, the black Crossed Keys, billowing in the very middle. So the Pope had declared for New Rome, Arthur had told his men the night before. It was a blow, but popes came and went. The next one would be different.

Arthur gazed along his own battle-front. The Saxons, that fierce northern people whose ancestors had butchered three Roman legions at the battle of the Teutoberg, were still in the foremost rank, unmoved by the merciless heat. The bright colours and demonic imagery with which they'd painted their circular shields – the green eye of Odin swimming in purple mist, the blue serpent Jormangandr woven amid gouts of orange flame, the white head of the horse Sleipnir rising through black twists of branches – were stark against their ring hauberks and the grey metal of their helms. Behind them, the ranks of chivalry waited; Arthur's *Familiaris* infantry and the men-at-arms of his great retainers, their mauls, hammers and pole-axes at the ready. At the rear stood the peasant forces, every improvised weapon one could imagine clutched in their grimy fists. On either flank, Arthur's archers, masked from the Romans, stood in deep phalanx, their great bow-staves not yet strung. They broiled in their steel-studded harness, but listened intently or peered up from beneath their iron caps and brimmed helmets, eyes shielded as they assessed the angle and trajectory of the goose-shafts they would soon be discharging.

And still the silence lingered. The two who had so far died lay prone on the sun-parched grass betwixt the facing armies. The blood glimmered where they had fallen. There would be more of that; everyone knew.

With a shouted command, and a great creaking of cogs and timbers, the Roman artillery – in the first instance, eight great counterweight catapults, located four to either flank – began to discharge, timber arms smacking upright against crossbars, launching hefty payloads of shot. Cast-iron balls, two to three feet in diameter, hurtled forward, bouncing on the open ground in front of Arthur's army, kicking up plumes of dust. The first rounds were range-finders, falling short or ricocheting over the heads of the waiting troops, but the second rounds were more accurate. Again they struck the open field, but further back, coming on apace and crashing into the waiting ranks, smashing shields, crushing helmeted skulls, shattering limbs. Arthur's line held, but from either flank of the Roman army there were echoing *thuds* as the throwing arms snapped upright again. More projectiles were hurled towards his men. With cataclysmic impacts, fresh alleyways were ripped through them, littering the ground with broken, gore-soaked bodies. The gasps and cries of the wounded were soon audible all over the field.

"Quite a pounding," Arthur observed.

"They could maintain this all day," Bedivere replied. The Roman artillery train was organised and efficient. The Roman engineers would have stockpiles of projectiles to hand, with caravans of carts and wagons shipping more up from the rear.

"Have the army lie down," Arthur said.

"Sire!" Bedivere protested. "That will expose *your* position."

"Bedivere, if they are content to waste their munitions in futile efforts to strike a single target, so much the better. Have the men lie down."

The word was passed and, one by one, the infantry companies lay on their faces.

In response to suddenly having nothing clear to shoot at, the Roman artillery crews faltered in their efforts. There was a brief dip in the rate of projectiles. Some direct hits were still made, churning earth and men's bodies alike, but most grenades now skipped harmlessly over the prostrate shapes, embedding themselves in the raised ground to their rear. Shudders passed through Arthur and Bedivere's feet. Dust and fragments of stone sprayed over them.

"Time to take the battle to them," Arthur said.

His heralds raised a green flag with a golden zigzag emblazoned across it. Immediately, several companies of *Familiaris Regis* crossbowmen stood up and dashed forward, only halting when they'd reached a point where the artillery shots were landing behind them. They were perhaps seventy yards in front of the first line of Roman infantry, who watched them bemusedly. The crossbowmen, numbering maybe a thousand, quickly formed themselves into two ranks, covering as broad a field as possible. They each carried six packed quivers, and were equipped with heavy bows capable of releasing bolts over hundreds of yards. Using the iron foot-stirrup at the head of each weapon to gain leverage, they dragged their bowstrings back and loaded bolts into the grooves. Only seconds passed before the front rank had their weapons to their shoulders and had taken aim.

The Roman vanguard was composed of halberdiers. By

necessity, they could not carry shields, but they were heavily armoured. Their sallets had visors attached with narrow v-shaped ports for vision; they wore corselets of overlapping steel plates over a thick mail coat, the sleeves of which extended to their wrists. Articulated steel gauntlets clad their hands, while centrally-ridged greaves covered their legs from ankle to mid-thigh. They had good reason to think they were safe. The first volley of bolts drove into them with *clinks* and *clanks*. Some rocked where they stood. Others were actually injured, the bolts finding chinks in their plating. One man went down screaming, a hand clasped to his visor, blood spurting from the port. The crossbows' rear rank then loosed, the front rank loosed again, and so on in relay. A couple more halberdiers tottered backward. The others plucked at bolts which had lodged in their mail or under their plating.

To THE REAR of them, Emperor Lucius wiped sweat from his brow. "Forward companies to advance," he told his deputies.

"My liege?"

"I'm tired of these foolish games. Arthur is the fly in my ointment and I want him extricated now. *Right now!*"

A trumpet sounded and the Roman catapults ceased. To the steady accompaniment of a lone battle-drum, the halberdiers started forward, tramping slowly and in perfect time, their bladed pole-arms level in front of them.

"Front rank... retreat!" the crossbows' captain shouted.

The front rank, which had just loosed a volley, stepped two paces back – each man passing through gaps in the rear rank – where it halted again and reloaded.

"Rear rank... loose!" the captain cried.

The rear rank raised their weapons and discharged. Another cloud of bolts struck the advancing halberdiers. More *thwacks* and *clinks* sounded as further impacts were made. A few more dropped or reeled backward, clutching at wounds. The rear rank of crossbows retreated two paces and also reloaded.

"Front rank!" the captain shouted. The front rank raised their bows and discharged.

This was the way of it, the crossbows retreating in alternate ranks and maintaining a constant barrage on the advancing infantry. Always the same distance lay between the disparate forces. Behind the crossbowmen, the halberdiers could clearly see the main body of Arthur's army now back on its feet, but if they were making progress in that direction it was painfully slow. Even when the bolts didn't penetrate their armour, they stuck hard, bruising the men, unbalancing them. And it was unrelenting, one volley following another. Whenever men slumped down or staggered backward, others advanced from behind to fill the gaps, but this too became difficult as the bodies of dead and wounded started to clutter the route.

But the Romans' *real* problems only began when a crossbowman fortuitously struck a man in the groin area. The target doubled forward with a keening shriek. The halberdiers' leather and iron battle-skirts were not as sturdy as their plate corselets.

"Upper thigh and bollocks!" the crossbowman shouted. "That's where they're vulnerable!"

His captain took up the cry, and the rest of them adjusted their aim accordingly.

The two ranks of crossbowmen continued to retreat between fusillades, but now were doing visible damage to their opponents, who dropped in threes and fours rather than ones and twos, many curling into balls of agony on the ground.

Arthur glanced along his line. To the east and west, his longbows were in readiness, each archer waiting with bow now strung and at the horizontal, arrows nocked. By Arthur's estimation, the halberdiers would be within range of bowshot in another fifty paces, and then Emperor Lucius would truly see carnage.

The Romans knew about the archers of Albion. They had heard about the British war-bow. A six-foot stave of yew, trimmed precisely so that its thick belly consisted of heartwood and its limbs of narrower sapwood to store tension, and strung with a cord of woven hemp. Its reputed draw-weight of one hundred and fifty pounds could drive their bodkin points, depending on the distance and angle, through plate armour. Some had chosen not to believe this. Others disregarded it simply because the court of King Arthur was admired more for the courage and chivalry of its knights. The archers of Albion could be little more in truth than auxiliaries, peasant soldiers whose job was to mop up the leavings of their lord and betters.

The halberdiers were now about four hundred yards from Arthur's battle-front. It was the point of no return. Arthur passed on his orders. His heralds raised the appropriate flags, and clarions were sounded on both flanks of his army. The King watched as his archers – men honed to incredible strength and toughness through long years of practice – drew their fletched shafts to their ears. They did not aim; there was nothing to see from where they were deployed. But their missiles would fall thick across the entire front in a non-stop shower.

"Loose at will!" was the command.

The sky briefly darkened as the first two flights arched over Arthur's infantry. Their impacts were simultaneous and devastating. There were fewer *clinks* and *clatters*; it was more a succession of *chunks* and gut-thumping *thuds* as the needlepoint arrowheads scythed through plate and mail, plunging deep into the flesh and bone beneath.

The entire Roman advance faltered. Halberdiers dropped their weapons and sagged to their knees, falling backward or sideways, cloth-yard shafts protruding from heads, necks, chests and shoulders. Gasps and wails filled the air, drowning the steady rhythm of the battle-drum. Ruby glisters were visible through the dust. And still the crossbows maintained their own rate of discharge, so that the Romans had to contend with hails of death both from the front and overhead.

There was confusion as the advance came to a halt, and then, as more arrow showers descended, the troops discarded their weapons and began shoving their way backward. Even now they were struck from behind, arrows striking the nape of necks or the middle of backs, transfixing torsos, severing spines.

Emperor Lucius stood in his stirrups to watch, suffused with rage. When he learned that his front line had not even engaged with Arthur's force, he could not contain himself.

"Damn cowards!" he screamed. *"Send the word... cavalry contingents to advance! And cut down any of those bastards they catch retreating!"*

The cadre of mounted officers around him glanced at each other in disbelief.

"Lord Caesar," one of them said. "What we're seeing here is the first shock of action. The men will recover themselves."

"Send the word!" Lucius howled. *"All deserters will die."*

The centurion delivering this message was a hoary old veteran called Marius. He knew that it was lunacy to set Roman forces on their fellow units in the midst of battle. Court-martials could follow later, but such an order while the action was ongoing would create chaos. So he delivered the message exclusively to Prince Jalhid and his Moorish horsemen, whose squadrons, numbering five thousand men in total, were advancing slowly behind the first army-group. He also moderated the order: they were to proceed along the army's western flank, to attack King Arthur's front line and cut their way through to the longbows on that side. Any broken units of Roman infantry they found in their path were to be "encouraged to return to the fray."

Eager to prove his men's worth, and maybe even capture Arthur himself – for what a bargaining counter the monarch of the Britons would be when it came to negotiating Cyrenaica's place and power in the hierarchy of New Rome – Jalhid led his horsemen in a furious charge up the army's west flank, the ground rumbling beneath their hooves. They made a magnificent sight, their chain cuirasses glinting over their ornate silk robes, the steel spires of their helmets catching the sun. Once they had circled around the front of the mangled vanguard they were able to fan out, and ascended the slope in their preferred way, a flying wedge of horsemen, their heroic prince at the point. They had two hundred yards of open ground to cover before they reached the sharpened stakes, but the Moorish warriors valued light arms and swift horses, and they advanced at a fast gallop. Already they were so far forward that the longbow arrows were falling behind them, though the crossbows were still in their path – they loosed two more volleys before throwing their bows over their shoulders and running back to their army.

Jalhid and his warriors reached the stakes almost immediately after them.

Behind this bulwark, the Saxons roared in anticipation, banging axe-hafts on linden-wood frames. The Moors responded with a volley of javelins. The weighted steel heads embedded in countless shields, in some cases passing clean through and striking the bodies behind. In return, the Moors were struck with stones, darts and throwing-axes. They bore through it valiantly, and tried to weave between the stakes, ploughing gory furrows along their horses' flanks. When melee was joined, it was a furious storm of slashing blades, the horsemen hacking down with their scimitars, the Saxon infantry swinging up with their great, heavy axes. The noise was deafening: an ongoing, splintering *crash* of blades striking helms and bucklers, of hafts breaking, ring-coats cloven and bones sundered. Horses shrieked and reared. Men bellowed as they smote at each other, sweat and blood flying.

The Roman halberdiers, emboldened by the cavalry assault, reorganised and attempted to advance again, but their numbers were almost halved and still the arrow-hail was falling, knocking them down like skittles, stitching them to the ground. Many corpses so bristled with shafts they resembled hedgehogs; some were even pinned together. Behind the halberdiers came pikemen, but as they carried no shields either they met a similar fate, dropping like wheat to the sickle.

For long minutes, the Moorish cavalry remained the only Roman troops engaged hand-to-hand, but their ferocity waned as the first wind of battle drained out of them. To inspire his warriors, Prince Jalhid assailed the Saxon shields personally, only for a broad-headed spear to pierce the throat of his steed. Blood gurgled from its nostrils as it collapsed onto its knees, throwing its rider over its head. Jalhid landed in the midst of his foe, one of whom – a great beefy fellow with flaxen hair billowing through rents in his battered helm – grabbed the prince and tried to throttle him, only for a young Moorish officer to ride in and slay the dog with a blow to the throat.

Jalhid was led dazed from the fray, his booted feet tripping on the broken corpses and armour, sliding on blood-soaked grass.

IN THE WEST gully to the rear of Arthur's army, Lucan's *mesnie* waited with many others.

Many had removed their helms and drawn back their coifs or aventails. Sweat beaded every face, for the heat rose between the steep rocky walls as inexorably as the tension. There was scarcely a word spoken as they listened to the din of battle.

At length, Turold could stand it no longer and sent Benedict scrambling up the gully side until he was able to perch on a dead tree overhanging them.

"There's so much dust," Benedict called, shielding his eyes. "I can hardly...."

"Damn it boy, tell us what's happening!" Turold retorted.

"They're concentrating their attack on our right flank, my lord. But from what I can see, we're holding. Further back, they're falling like leaves under our arrow storm."

"So are we winning or losing?"

"It's hard to say..."

"They're falling like leaves, but you can't tell whether we're winning or losing?"

"There are so many of them, my lord..."

"How many remain? Damn it, lad, at least attempt an educated guess!"

"Turold," Lucan said.

Turold glanced at his overlord, who made an oddly detached figure as he leaned over the pommel of his saddle, one gauntleted hand on Nightshade's muscular neck, gently grooming the beast with his fingertips. Lucan was completely clad for war: his black wolf-fur draped across his shoulders, *Heaven's Messenger* buckled to his hip, a spiked mace strapped to his back, a falchion and pole-axe harnessed by his saddle. The black hair hung in sweat-damp hanks to either side of his ash-pale face, and yet he seemed distant, unaffected by events.

"There'll be more than enough for all of us," he said quietly. "Never fear."

Turold nodded and blushed. He resented being cooped up here away from the action. They all felt the same. Their air of anxiety had even infected their great battle-steeds, which were unusually skittish, pawing the stony ground, wafting tails, tossing manes.

"The King himself is in the fray!" Benedict suddenly shouted. Even Lucan glanced up

"Have they broken through?" Turold called.

"No, he's gone forward. Lord Bedivere and Lord Kay are with him."

Lucan absorbed this information, and nodded. Alaric watched his overlord worriedly. He had returned from the parley minus his lance, and word had soon followed that he'd killed one of the Romans. If Lucan sensed that he was being watched, he made no response. He regarded the gully floor with half-lidded eyes, patiently waiting.

THOSE MOORISH HORSEMEN who'd managed to penetrate the rows of sharpened stakes had made no further progress against the hedge of infantry and now, with their leader injured and removed, wheeled about in the confined space, spilling along the front of Arthur's battle-line, still out of longbow-shot but struck again by crossbow bolts and, whenever they tried to make inroads, driven back under volleys of axe and hammer blows.

Many of the *Familiaris* troops were now involved, particularly on the army's west flank where the Saxons had been thinned out. Seeing his own household swapping blows with the enemy, Arthur had felt he had no option but to slam his visor down and descend on foot to participate, much to Bedivere and Kay's consternation. They thrust their way through the ranks alongside him, stepping over the dead.

One particularly ferocious Saracen was on foot directly to the fore of them. He was a beanpole of a fellow, perhaps six foot six inches, but he fought with a scimitar in one hand and a tasselled lance in the other. He had already carved his way through the Saxons and now cut the household men down, slashing them from their feet or impaling them through the body. His cuirass was gashed all over, his silken robes hacked and bloody. A great cut laid open the bridge of his nose, but still he fought. Arthur engaged him directly, parrying a couple of blows and then swinging *Excalibur* through his neck with such force that his head was entirely severed.

"Sire, this is madness!" Bedivere shouted, fending off blows himself.

"This is like the Romans, is it not?" Arthur replied as he felled another. "To get some other party to fight their battle for them!"

A Moor rode up and struck at the King with his scimitar. Kay parried the blow, driving the curved steel deep into the rider's thigh. The rider tried to rein backward, but Kay grabbed a javelin and flung it into his chest.

Bedivere stepped backward through the dust and blood to glance beyond the attacking horsemen. The Moors were relatively few in number and now considerably fewer than earlier. Any companies advancing uphill to join them had to run the gauntlet of the longbow deluge. Those caught in it, infantry and cavalry alike, were taking massive losses, but still coming on in numbers – the pikemen and halberdiers were now too few to form Alexandrian phalanxes, so they discarded their pole-arms and produced swords. Despite this damage, the entire Roman infantry line was shortly to engage.

Bedivere summoned a herald and sent a message that the archers were to continue their current rate of discharge for as long as they could. He also sent word that Arthur's war-machines were to be readied. By his reckoning, the infantry line could withstand an assault so long as the Romans were not able to put their entire weight into it.

Both battle-fronts now joined in full, beating frenziedly on each other. Bedivere fought his way back to stand beside Arthur and Kay. The stench was revolting: a mix of blood, sweat, rent bellies and shattered bones. There were scenes of horror on all sides: the wounded lying paralysed and broken, blood bubbling from their mouths; mangled corpses of every description – torsos without heads, lopped limbs, opened bowels. But still the assailants raged at each other. Frantic blows hewed through wood, iron and flesh. Shields exploded, throats gargled as steel sheared windpipes. On Arthur's side, it wasn't just the Saxons and the men-at-arms now in combat. The peasants and yeomen drove through the gaps with threshes and pitchforks, reaching between mailed legs to stab Roman feet with hunting knives, to slice Roman hamstrings and, when they fell to the ground, to slit their throats or hammer the brains from their helmets. But ever more Roman companies were joining the fray. Many of the newcomers had hoisted shields above their heads, affording themselves protection from the arrow-showers.

"We need the rest of our host!" Bedivere cried as he sensed the line weakening.

"Not yet!" Arthur replied, stepping back to gain his breath. "We've still no more than bloodied their nose. We neither commit our reserve nor move from this position of strength until we are absolutely ready."

But the 'position of strength' was failing them.

The sheer numbers of the Roman infantry pushed them steadily backward. No matter how many were chopped down, more legionaries stepped into the gaps, their sturdy hide and timber shields filled with broken arrows, their blades of their axes or *gladii* or the spiked and knobbed heads of their maces smeared with a sludge of brains and blood as they cut and hacked and smashed.

"Sire, we can't hold them!" a ventenar[25] screamed, blinded by a gash on his brow.

Arthur fought back gamely, *Excalibur* flashing as he smote arms, shoulders and necks, sundering all in ruby fountains, and yet he knew he could not ignore the pleas of his men. Bedivere's sword and shield had broken, so he grabbed the pole-axe strapped to his back. He thrust its spear-point into the groins of the Romans, slammed its hammerhead down on their skulls, reversed the weapon and clove to them to the teeth with its axe-blade. But still the enemy poured forth like a flood-tide.

"*Sire!*" the wounded ventenar shrieked.

"My liege, he's right!" Bedivere cried.

Arthur again stepped backward, spattered with ordure. "In that case," he shouted, "*unleash the fire!*"

The first projectiles Arthur's war-machines launched were earthenware pots, each containing a hundred gallons of naphtha, their vents crammed with burning rags. They sailed over the top of the battle-front, spinning, travelling deep into the guts of the Roman force, where they blasted apart, spraying liquid fire in every direction, immolating dozens of legionaries at a time.

Men watched aghast as their own hands blazed in front of their scorched faces, the flesh and muscle melting away, leaving bare bones. They screamed like banshees as they tore off their cloaks, their surcoats, even their corselets and hauberks, but always the unquenchable flame ate its way through. Seared and hysterical, cavalry horses stampeded regardless of their riders' efforts, trampling over dead and wounded alike, breaking ribs and crushing faces. After the naphtha came tubs of quicklime and sulphur, spreading in corrosive plumes amid the packed, panicking troops, blinding and choking them. Barrels of pitch

---

[25]A low-grade officer in charge of twenty men; a sergeant.

and bubbling oil followed, scalding and blistering those caught in their deluge, igniting furiously.

"I see King Arthur likes to use fire," Emperor Lucius screamed. Strands of froth hung from his lips. His eyes rolled like jade baubles in a face grey and running with sweat. "As he likes fire so much, fire will be his future. *Write this, scribe!*" he screeched, though there was no scribe near enough to take his words down. "All prisoners of war taken this day are condemned to death, the prescribed method to be cremation on the griddle, and in the case of the King himself..." Lucius gave a shriek of deranged laughter. "The King will be fried in a great pan, which will first have been greased with tallow drawn from the burnt husks of his knights!"

But fire was not the only weapon Arthur's artillery now turned on the Romans still vastly outnumbering him. After the boiling oil, Arthur's ballistae discharged fresh clouds of arrows, while his onagers hurled linen sacks, loosely tied, each containing ten thousand lead balls. As their bindings broke in mid-air, they spread out and rained across a wide area. Men and horses dropped side by side, struck hundreds of times over.

Inevitably, the Romans' frontal assault began to wane; Arthur and his infantry felt the force pitched against them weakening. He and his men were no longer retreating but advancing, stepping over the heaps of newly slain. Bedivere broke his pole-axe when he clove a centurion from the crown of his head to the tip of his chin, and in so doing gained a clearer picture of the field beyond. The Romans still had overwhelming numbers, and continued to flow forward, though now their formations were riven apart and they were advancing loosely and in disorder.

"Now, sire!" Bedivere called. "Now must be the time!"

"Aye," Arthur agreed. "Now is the time."

TWENTY

THERE HAD NEVER been any such person as Saint Belladonna, which ought to have suggested, to the few Ligurian peasants who knew about the Convent of St. Belladonna, that it wasn't actually a convent at all, even if it did utilise a genuine old convent building located in a high, secluded valley.

More than likely the few rustics who worked in the convent grounds, minding the sheep and goats, tending the vegetable gardens and keeping the paths clear, were well aware that the nuns of St. Belladonna's were somewhat younger and comelier than was the norm. They must have thought it inappropriate that the sisters wore habits which were more like sleeveless, knee-length togas, revealing much indecent jewelry, and kept their long, lustrous hair bound beneath dainty head-scarves rather than veils or wimples. But as the regular procession of male callers at St. Belladonna's included priests, bishops and even cardinals, as well as the usual dukes, barons and merchants, who were the gardeners to complain?

On a warm afternoon in early summer, one particular new arrival set an elderly shepherd called Marcus hurrying from the outer pastures and along the valley road. Marcus was a tough, wiry man, brown-skinned, with long, grey hair and a long, grey beard. And though, at eighty, he didn't generally hurry anywhere, the sight of the black enamel coach with the eight sleek horses drawing it provoked in him an almost unnatural degree of energy. For all his sprightliness he entered the convent by the tradesman's door only a minute before the black coach, with its gilded sculptures and its colossal red-cowled driver, halted at the front entrance.

As Duchess Zalmyra stepped onto the forecourt, the convent door swung open, and the 'Mother-Superior' emerged. Her name was Esmerelda. She too had once been a comely lass, though now her slender form had turned buxom and her golden hair had wizened to grey. As such, the garb she wore was perhaps more in keeping with her title. Her robe was cinched at the waist with a simple leather belt, and fell to her sandalled feet. Her head-scarf was more demurely tied, so that not a lock or even a wisp of hair escaped to hang fetchingly over her handsome young-old face.

"Ma'am?" she said, hands clasped.

"You received my message?" Zalmyra asked brusquely.

"I did, ma'am. I have a girl who I think will please you."

"Let me see."

ZARA WAS NOT yet seventeen, but pretty as a Mediterranean flower: lightly tanned, with hazel eyes and lush ripples of dark brown hair. She had only been at St. Belladonna's six weeks, but had already serviced many illustrious clients, including some who had been back to see her again and again. She had thus learned quickly, and already had a pouch of personal gold stored in a knapsack in her boudoir.

She stood upright as she waited in the antechamber, hands behind her back. She possessed an air of confidence, for she knew that she filled her knee-length toga to perfection. But she also affected humility, for some of those who came here were not always happy unless they felt they were depraving an innocent.

When Esmerelda showed in Duchess Zalmyra, Zara did not blink. She had entertained wealthy women before – it was not unusual, and this one had the regal air of an aristocrat. By her flimsy attire and the fine naked form beneath, she was also, quite evidently, a sensualist.

Esmerelda stood primly to one side while Zalmyra circled the patiently waiting 'sister,' who smiled meekly.

Zalmyra finally spoke. "You will come with me, girl. To my home."

For the first time, Zara was surprised. This had never happened before. She glanced at Esmerelda, who nodded.

"Bring all your belongings," Zalmyra added.

Again, Zara was surprised. Again, she glanced at her mistress.

"This will be a lengthy assignment," Esmerelda explained.

Zara shrugged. She supposed it was all in a day's work for her. Or a week's. Or even a month's. It made no real difference in the end, except that on this occasion maybe she would be even more lavishly treated than usual. Bowing to Zalmyra, she withdrew from the room. When the door was closed, Zalmyra turned to Esmerelda.

"There is no-one who will miss her?"

"No-one, ma'am. She came to us a foundling."

"But she has made close friends in the order, no doubt?"

"All my sisters know that some must move on. Not all vocations are strong."

"And none of them will seek her out?"

"They haven't sought any of those others who've left with you."

Zalmyra smiled coldly. "When she comes down again, escort her to my carriage personally. It may put her at ease."

TWENTY-ONE

"THE SIGNAL!" BENEDICT cried from above. *"The signal!"*

The knights and men-at-arms glanced up, alerted. They too heard it – the three-note clarion call they had been waiting for.

"Mount up!" Lucan called to his *mesnie*.

With hurried shouts and a neighing of nervous steeds, men leapt into the saddle. Lucan turned to Turold, who hefted the black banner. They nodded at each other. Lucan glanced at Alaric – the lad's face was bright with sweat, but he, too, nodded.

"Remember, this is not a tourney," Lucan instructed him gravely. "These Romans have come here to kill you. To kill all of us. And when we are gone, to enslave and despoil our families. There's only one penalty for that... they must die."

Alaric mopped the spittle from his lips, and lowered his visor.

THE WEST GULLY wherein Lucan and his household had been waiting contained the retinues of a many other illustrious names: Bors, Cador, Lanval, Bellangere, Daniel, Sagramore, Agravain, Galezzin, Tor and the two sons of the late King Pellinore, Lamorak and Aglovale – some six thousand men in total, all skilled and seasoned to battle.

They thundered down the gully at a canter, their horses picking up speed as the narrow passage widened out, finally emerging on the hillside to the rear of Arthur's infantry. Briefly, Alaric lifted his visor to survey the scene. To their right, the longbow men were at rest – they didn't want to strike their own men, and at any rate were surrounded by empty carts and wagons which earlier in the day had been piled with sheaves of arrows. Directly ahead, the infantry broke apart to create an aisle maybe fifty yards in width. Beyond that lay the open field, and a monstrous clutter of the dead, dying and maimed, stretching as far as the eye could see.

But the Romans were not yet at bay. Immense numbers were still to the fore. Their foot-companies clashed with Arthur's infantry, and to the rear of those, more cavalry cohorts were advancing, although there were broad gaps between them.

As Arthur's cavalry drove down through the carnage, their canter accelerated to a gallop, the rumble of their hooves amplifying to a thunderous roar. Alaric glanced left. There was no sign yet of the knights from the east gully.

At the point of the charge Lucan rode like the wind, his pace never flagging as the two forces meshed. One Roman horseman came against him after another, many armed with lances. He bore past them all, *Heaven's Messenger* striking flesh and bone like a spear of flame. If they weren't in his path, he veered towards them, his wolf-fur billowing. They drew blades and mattocks against him, but his sword always struck true, colossal strokes dispatching legionaries from this world as wind blows flies from a carcass. Even when he found himself amid a cluster of them, *Heaven's Messenger* spun in a blur, smiting skulls, chopping necks. These were the men of the Eighth Legion, distinctive in their maroon livery. Expert horsemen by all accounts, masters of the sabre. But Lucan slew all he came to. He barely felt their retaliatory blows, barely noticed that his shield was soon broken or his mail rent and leaking blood. He slew and slew like a thing possessed, striking the blades from their hands, shearing through their corselets and helms.

Alaric could barely keep up. He too engaged with the Romans. He found their resistance strong, a genuine challenge;

the savagery of this fight was a far cry from the practised skills and gallant courtesies of the tournament. He dispatched a couple, but in many places he only just managed to evade their slashing blades. A stinging blow from a chain-mace tore his visor away and almost knocked him senseless. He struck back, but his attention was divided between the honour of combat and the pursuit of his master, who he felt sure was now ranging the field like a spectre of death with but one target in mind.

Lucan was already halfway down the vale, much of the Roman horse having fallen back under the first onslaught of Arthur's knights, when Alaric galloped up to him, pink-faced and sweating, blood dribbling from his broken nose. Lucan whipped around, fleetingly mistaking the lad for an enemy. Alaric reined back, but Lucan saw him in time and restrained his blow. Before they could speak, Alaric saw something else which distracted him. He pointed past Lucan's shoulder, eyes wide. Lucan glanced around, and then removed his helmet. His sweat-soaked hair was streaked across his ghost-like features, and his steel-grey eyes gleamed like dagger-tips as they focused on the immense construction which had emerged from the Roman ranks and was now advancing ponderously towards them. It resembled a wheeled fortress, some forty yards across and maybe fourteen feet tall. It was built from solid timber and hung with shields, and had a battlemented upper rim. Even from this distance the earth seemed seemed to shake to its progress.

"My God!" Alaric stammered. "What... what is *that*?"

"A Hell-Breather," Lucan replied grimly.

"A Hell-Breather?"

"I've heard about these things, but never actually seen one."

"How does it move?"

"Inside it there'll be maybe a hundred oxen yoked together, and their drivers. And elite troops, of course, waiting to burst out once it breaches our defences."

The approaching monstrosity's upper deck supported ballistae, onagers and packs of archers, who moved freely from one parapet to the other and were already busy picking off those of Arthur's horsemen who'd been reckless enough to ride into range. However, its lower deck was even more heavily armed. From the front and on either side of it, great fire-tubes – cast-iron cylinders, their muzzles carved like dragons' mouths – protruded from horizontal ports. Smoke poured out of them; inside the belly of the beast they'd be attached to cauldrons filled with bubbling, flaming mixtures of sulfur and pitch, constantly heated by glowing-hot coals, and immense pairs of bellows, which teams of sweating engineers would work frenziedly. The result was plumes of jetting fire, which could engulf any opponent venturing within thirty yards.

Alaric watched, aghast, as gouts of liquid death blazed out, men and their chargers tearing away shrieking as they turned into living torches. Those who evaded the flames were simply shot from their saddles by the archers on the roof. One fellow – Lucan recognised him as Crispin Roncesvalles, the messenger who had first brought news of the crisis – was struck by maybe six shafts at once. He'd have dropped to the ground had he not been sewn to his own saddle. His corpse hung limply, flopping back and forth, as his terrified animal bolted away.

OTHERS OF LUCAN'S *mesnie* now rode up: Wulfstan, Turold, Gerwin, Brione, and Benedict. All were begrimed and bloodied.

"God's bread," Turold said. "Is that a Hell-Breather?"

The great machine was now about seventy yards away. They could hear the heavy trundle of its wheels and iron under-carriage, the creak and groan of its timber bulwarks.

"These machines are not invulnerable and have slow impetus," Lucan said. "But if it reaches our line, the King's position is compromised."

"Lure it within range of our catapults," Alaric suggested.

Lucan shook his head. "No. It would have won the Romans too much ground by then. Look what's coming behind it."

Large numbers of Romans, mostly those who had fallen back under the British cavalry charge, were re-forming to its rear. "No," he added. "We need to stop it *here*."

He licked his lips as he studied the contraption, assessing it for any weakness. On campaign, Lucan always carried a rope and a grappling-hook; even now it hung in a coil alongside his saddle. But on this occasion that would make him too easy a target. He spied another way to gain entrance. The Hell-Breather's front hoardings cleared the ground by about a foot and a half, to allow it to progress over a field littered with corpses; more than enough for Lucan's purpose.

"Turold. Take any men you can gather and attack it from the west."

"My lord?" Turold looked baffled and not a little frightened.

"Draw its archers' attention away from the front. You hear me?"

Turold nodded and slammed down his visor.

"Alaric, go with him." Lucan handed his reins over and dismounted. "And take Nightshade."

Alaric looked startled. "You're not taking that thing on alone, my lord? You could be killed!"

"We're in the middle of a battle, Alaric. We could *all* be killed."

"Everyone, follow me," Turold shouted. He wheeled his animal around and commenced a wide, circling gallop westward of the vast machine. The others followed, including Alaric, now leading the riderless Nightshade. Arrows slanted towards them as they entered range; one of the gallopers at the rear – a straggler from another formation – was hit in the armpit and slumped sideways from his saddle.

The Hell-Breather, meanwhile, was drawing steadily closer.

Lucan replaced his helmet and lay down flat in its path, hoping to conceal himself among the many other sprawled, broken bodies. As furtively as he could, he slid *Heaven's Messenger* from its scabbard and placed it by his side, one hand clasping its hilt. With a noise like the breaking of the heavens, the mechanism was now maybe twenty yards away from him. The ground quaked to the clanging of its undercarriage, to the squeal of its wheels, to the lowing and grunting of the animals inside.

Its front fire-tube was angled directly down at him. Lucan eyed it through his helm, and lay perfectly still, blinking away a sweat of terror. All it would take was one intense, prolonged blast of flame, and he would be liquefied inside his own armour. But no such order was issued. The only thing belching from the dragon-muzzle was smoke.

Its black shadow fell across Lucan. His body froze. He sensed the wooden skirting sliding across him, and suddenly he was inside it – where it was all darkness and seething heat, and a mingled stench of sweat, manure and sawdust. The hooves of lowing beasts hacked into the ground only inches from his body. He leapt up, sword brandished. His eyes were not attuned to the dimness, but navigating by the tiny chinks of light penetrating the hoardings, he could just distinguish the heavy forms of oxen, arrayed in rows on all sides and harnessed to an overhead framework of ropes and timbers. Two-handed, he swept his sword down onto the spine of the brute to his left and it dropped to its knees, bellowing in agony. His second blow fell in the same place on the ox to his right. This too stumbled and collapsed. He stepped over its carcass to strike the next one, and had dropped maybe six in a row before the oxen behind began to struggle and the great machine came to a shuddering halt. A Roman drover wearing only leather breeks clambered across the rigging to see what the problem was. Lucan sprang up and thrust *Heaven's Messenger* into his belly, ripping the blade sideways so the drover's entrails gushed out, before hauling him down.

Lucan clambered upward himself, ascending via a trapdoor.

The first deck was divided into compartments, each enclosed with timber partitions but crammed with a scaffold of joists and supports to support its own fire-tube. In the first one he entered, loincloth-clad engineers were too busy to notice him, adding fresh ingredients to the mix bubbling in the great cauldron or hanging on the bellows. Above them, an officer swung in his harness, peering down the length of the tube. They were eight men in total, and four had died before they knew what was happening, dispatched with single sword strokes to their skulls and necks.

One of the remainder cast a ladle of scalding pitch in Lucan's direction, spattering him and sizzling in his wolf-fur. Lucan cut the fellow's legs from beneath him, and disembowelled him as he lay screaming. Another charged with a firebrand. Lucan severed the offending hand at the wrist with his sword, and drove his dagger into the fellow's gullet. When he turned again the others had fled, including the operator. They would be seeking help, and it would be close at hand. In fact, at the rear of the compartment, a ladder led down to sunlight, and with much gruff shouting, an armoured legionary was already climbing, with another behind him, and a third behind that. With two blows of his sword, Lucan severed the ladder's mooring, sending it crashing down amid the lowing, stamping oxen, the troopers falling with it.

Another ladder led up, and Lucan climbed it swiftly, emerging onto the upper deck. Its broad wooden surface was covered with a gluey resin, so that men could move about without sliding or falling as the engine rocked. Runnels had been cut in the deck, and filled with large stones and rocks to be used as missiles. There were also stockpiles of arrows, tied in bundles. On all sides, catapult and ballista crews – three men to each mechanism – worked feverishly, spokes banging and oily gears ratcheting as they loaded and shot repeatedly. Aside from these, there were fifteen archers, each armed with a double-curved composite bow. Thanks to Turold and his party, riding back and forth to the west as if seeking a way to approach, they had concentrated on that battlement, but Lucan wouldn't have long.

The nearest machine was an arbalest – a great crossbow designed to discharge twelve cloth-yard bolts at the same time

– and it had just been reloaded. Its crew remained unaware of Lucan even as he struck them, sheathing his dagger behind one's ear, cleaving the nape of another's neck, and tipping the third one over the parapet. The other Romans on the deck now discovered him, but not before he knocked loose the pivot-peg holding the arbalest in place, swung it around, took aim and unleashed all twelve bolts at the perfectly aligned row of archers, every one striking a target.

The remaining engineers came at Lucan with mauls and mattocks, but only a couple wore mail shirts or corselets, and none wore helmets. He hewed his way among them, lopping necks, slicing limbs. When *Heaven's Messenger* was briefly knocked from his grasp, he snatched the mace from over his shoulder and dealt out skull-crushing impacts. Only two survived his onslaught; they fled down to the lower deck, yelling.

Lucan moved to the western battlement. He signalled to Turold, who, marshalling the rest of his men, charged courageously. Directly below Lucan, another fire-tube raised itself to meet them. He looked to his right, where an onager rested on a heavy frame. It was so bulky that most normal men would have trouble moving it on their own, let alone lifting it. But such minor issues had no place on a day like today. Throwing away his mace and sliding *Heaven's Messenger* back into its scabbard, Lucan took the onager by its windlass, and with much scraping of wood and groaning of iron, dragged it out of position and shoved it against the west battlement. With every inch of strength in his body, he levered it up, bending his legs, straightening his back, the muscles in his arms, chest and shoulders screaming in agony, until he'd angled it fully upright. And then he pushed it.

It fell heavily, rolling, and struck the barrel of the fire-tube with a resounding *clang*, buckling it and bending it double – just as a massive gout of flame was about to be expelled at Turold. With an explosive *whoosh*, the white-hot payload back-drafted through the blocked tube, engulfing its entire crew, blazing up around the officer in his command chair, blooming through the entire interior of the Hell-Breather – accompanied by the shrieks of men and beasts.

Coughing on scorching smoke, the deck smouldering under his feet, Lucan vaulted over the battlement and hung full length by his fingers. It was still a drop of seven feet. The landing was difficult, the wind driven from Lucan's body, but he had the strength to roll away. The next thing he was on his feet, tottering in the direction of his *mesnie*, who had reined up and were watching in astonishment as this machine, by which the Romans had many a time cleared paths through hordes of foes, ground to a standstill, flames blossoming from every aperture.

Lucan swung up into his saddle and noticed the wide spaces around them. It was almost as if there'd been a lull in the fighting. Stragglers from both sides staggered back and forth, some disoriented and battle-shocked, others dazed by the pain of wounds. But the majority of Arthur's cavalry contingents appeared to be falling back en masse. Not so the Romans. There were still fragmented groups of them on the higher ground, but these were the remnants of larger companies, and now, cut off by the cavalry charge, had been unable to retreat. Some were still fighting, but most were marooned in no man's land, awaiting the next Roman advance, which, given that Arthur's cavalry had recoiled, looked imminent. In fact, javelins began to fall close by, and Lucan's *mesnie* turned to see fresh cohorts of Romans marching towards them, men who had not yet been in the fight coming rank upon rank.

It seemed incredible to Alaric that they could have killed so many, and that such an uncountable number could remain, footmen and cavalry. Their arms and armour glinted, undimmed by dust or blood.

"No wonder everyone else has retreated," Benedict said in a voice of woe.

"Don't be fooled," Wulfstan replied. "No-one's retreated. This is merely a feint. A ploy to pull them forward, drag them onto the spearhead of our reserve."

Lucan took a last look at the Hell-Breather, now a blackened, blazing framework, then he wheeled Nightshade around and headed back to the lines, calling his men to follow.

WHEN EMPEROR LUCIUS saw Arthur's cavalry withdrawing, he announced that he would personally lead the pursuit. His senior officers advised against this, but though Lucius knew full well that he had had suffered catastrophic losses, he only needed to look around to see that he still had more than enough warriors in harness to inundate the Britons' position. He thus ordered the trumpets to sound, clanged his visor down, levelled his lance and galloped forward at such a tilt that it was all his officers could do to stay abreast. Company by company, the units of the Eighth and Fourteenth Legions fell in alongside him, creating a broad battle-line which bristled with lances and drawn sabres.

"Protect the Emperor!" went the cry to his rear.

The Roman infantry regiments, including those beaten back and exhausted, some with less than a third of their number remaining, were thus goaded to charge again – this time at double-speed, running rather than walking, despite their weight of arms and armour. But they were advancing behind their own cavalry screen, so their view of the vale's north end was concealed – and they did not see the infantry ranks on Arthur's east flank shuffle aside, creating an open passage from which a fresh stream of horsemen issued.

This was the other half of Arthur's chivalrous host: the mounted portion of the *Familiaris Regis*, King Hoel and his Breton knights, and those other Knights of the Round Table who had not yet entered the fray: Tristan, Hector, Dornar, Caradoc, Udain, Ider, Palomides, Urre, Lavain, Gareth and Griflet – another six thousand combatants, and at their head the fearsome forms of Lancelot du Lac and his *mesnie*, distinctive for their leopard badges and their blue and white livery. At the same time, the cavalry force that had retreated, which if Emperor Lucius had only looked he would see was still largely intact, wheeled around and came back pell-mell into the action.

Arthur, Kay and Bedivere, anchoring the centre of the infantry line, also mounted up. Arthur raised his royal banner so that it streamed in the hot, gusting wind, and blew a single blast on his battle-horn. He lowered his standard and charged, and the infantry line went with him. Howling like a barbarian horde of old, the whole army of the Britons surged down the slope of the Vale of Sessoine.

Their mounted companies engaged first, Lancelot projecting himself into battle at the spear-point. With his first contact, he impaled a Roman general through the breast with his lance. In the same motion he drew his sword, slicing throats in all directions. Roman horsemen fell around him without even realising who or what had slain them.

Lucan, on the other flank, was the next into battle, careering through the enemy cavalry with abandon, laying to his left and right, *Heaven's Messenger* soon slathered with gore not just the length of its blade, but up and over its hilt. He now engaged with Roman horsemen wearing orange livery. They showed skill and courage, but his rage grew inexorably. *Heaven's Messenger* twirled about his head as he struck and parried and fended and butchered, carving his way through line after line of these handsome fellows, oblivious to their counter-blows, feeling only the ache in his sword-arm.

So furious was his charge, and the charge of all those others like him, that even the fresher Roman ranks dissolved into complete disorder, horsemen falling back among their infantry, orders being issued to no-one, which made it even easier for Arthur's men, who, by comparison, were so well organised for war that their horses were trained to fight alongside their masters. Nightshade was in the thick of the combat; the noble brute reared at a clutch of Roman footmen who came at it with pikes, its iron-shod hooves ploughing into their helms, smashing their face-plates, pulverising the features beneath.

In the heat of battle the Knights of the Round Table knew

no retreat. Forward, ever forward, was their motto – so, though the Romans ranked in front of them grew denser and denser, still they chopped their way among them. Lucan had his entire pack at his heels: Turold, Wulfstan, Guthlac, Gerwin, Cadelaine, Brione, Alaric and many others, flailing on the enemy with their blades and mattocks. Blood flowed in torrents as mailed and plated bodies fell on top of each other. Riderless steeds shrieked insanely, rampaging back and forth, causing more mayhem.

In the midst of this chaos, Lucan came upon a Roman horseman he recognised: a short, portly fellow encased in gilded armour cut with elaborate patterns – though, separated from his followers, he had now reined his steed and thrown down his weapons. He lifted his visor to reveal a plump, purple face and strands of long, red-grey hair: Ardeus Vigilano, Duke of Spoleto. His charger was in a dreadful state, broken arrow husks protruding from its sides, its head hung low, blood gushing from its nostrils. Spoleto himself could only raise one arm in surrender, for the other was punctured through the elbow by an arrow.

"I'm your prisoner!" the duke pleaded. "Whoever you are, brave knight of Albion, I throw myself on your mercy. My family will pay you a king's ransom for my safe return. They will make you the wealthiest man in the whole of Christendom."

Lucan hesitated only a second before ramming *Heaven's Messenger* into Spoleto's gargling mouth, and twisting it so that teeth and bone shattered.[26] "All I ever had or wanted you people took from me!" snarled a bestial voice that Lucan himself barely recognised. "You can *never* repay it... except with your souls."

The slaughtered nobleman fell to the ground, and Lucan dug his spurs into Nightshade's flanks, driving the animal on.

[26]The conflict between the ideals of chivalry and the brutality of war is one of the themes of the "Noble Tragedie."

*　　*　　*

"MY GOD!" TUROLD shouted, lifting his visor. He, too, was gashed and scarred, his mail rent, blood streaking his black mantle. Alaric reined alongside him in a similar state. Turold indicated Spoleto's corpse. "That suit of armour alone could pay the household wages for an entire year."

"We can collect the bounty later," Alaric said, standing in his stirrups to locate their lord, once again fearful that *Heaven's Messenger* might now fall on a gentler head.

Turold laughed. "Aye... unless some camp-following scullion's beaten us to it. Can't you sense it, lad? We're winning."

He slammed his visor closed and urged his mount forward. Alaric followed.

IN FACT, THE army of Albion was *not* winning the battle – not yet.

Numerically, they were still outmatched, though they had the momentum thanks to the downhill charge. The morale of New Rome's finest was strained by the prolonged fight and by the sight of so many comrades-in-arms lying drowned in gore and filth. But the real turn of the tide only came fifteen minutes later, when King Arthur spotted the banner of Imperial Rome just ahead of him. Seated on his horse, fully armoured, but with visor open and mouth agape as he witnessed the slow destruction of all his dreams, was Emperor Lucius Julio Bizerta. An entire phalanx of mounted bodyguards had drawn up around him, clad toe to crown in the black enamel plate of the old Praetorian Guard, maces and falchions in their fists.

Arthur glanced to his right. Kay was still close, and Lancelot was ranging towards them. His horse, much bloodied, had to pick its way through the piles of mangled corpses. Arthur signalled to both and indicated the Imperial bodyguard. They nodded and, hunching forward, entered into a full gallop, in the midst of which Arthur and Tristan joined them.

The two small companies clashed with explosive force,

sparks flashing, splinters flying from shattered lances. The Emperor's bodyguards fought valiantly, but compared with Arthur and his knights were little more than human shields. The first shock of impact saw two of them eliminated, one skewered through the groin, the other with his left arm cloven at the shoulder. The remainder rained blows on their assailants, but for every contact they made, Arthur's men made two or three, and very quickly the last few Praetorians fell from their saddles, blood spouting from joints in their armour.

Emperor Lucius was alone, fists tight on the reins of his terrified horse, his pale face lathered with sweat, his green eyes bulging as they fixed on the ferocious horseman confronting him – a horseman who could only be the King of the Britons.

"Your time has come, hell hound!" Arthur said, snapping up his visor.

"You crazed, barbarian beast!" the Emperor shrieked. "It was my *destiny* to rule."

"And it was mine to draw a sword from a stone, and now to plant it in another."

Arthur plunged Excalibur forward. Lucius attempted to deflect it, but Arthur's aim was the stronger and surer. The Emperor's sabre broke, and the longsword pierced his breastplate and the breastbone beneath it, and the beating heart beneath that. Lucius's head hinged backward in a silent shriek, a crimson font arcing from his lips.

An age might have passed as he hung there, and then the mightiest man in the world toppled slowly from his saddle. When he struck the ground he was cold clay.

Tristan seized the Imperial banner and held it aloft, howling in triumph.

THE WORD SPREAD through the Romans' tattered ranks like a wildfire.

Some refused to accept it, and strove on, slashing in all directions, still taking lives, but ultimately being dragged from their saddles or cut from their feet. The rest – the vast majority – turned and fled in a gargantuan, chaotic mob, causing more pain and destruction en route, horses maddened with fear driving through clumps of hapless infantry, bounding across the carpet of wounded and dying, their hooves impacting in flesh and bone as though it were soft mulch. So pressed together was the staggering horde, that it would only take one arrow to bring a man down, and maybe fifty others would trip over the top of him, to be trampled in the panic. Even men of rank fell victim to this pandemonium. One such was the wounded Prince Jalhid, whose bier was overturned in the stampede; before his bodyguards could reach him, feet, the hooves of horses and even the wheels of carriages had furrowed his body.

Arthur's knights cantered among the fleeing droves, hacking and spearing. His infantry followed, swarming across the mounds of wounded, finishing them off with blades and clubs. They would continue in this fashion until the order was given to cease, though orders did not traverse easily over so chaotic a field. For maybe an hour after Arthur sent the word that only those Romans still armed were to be offered no quarter, the massacre continued. The British archers, who had now replenished their ammunition, also gave chase, loosing shafts willy-nilly, bringing down one man after another; it was almost sport for them – they laughed and joked.

Ironically, it was mainly those Romans who had advanced far up-field who were spared. Broken up, now, into small groups and isolated from each other in the sea of corpses, they knew they could never reach safety, and so downed their arms and offered surrender. Most of these were wounded anyway, or their weapons were blunted, so they simply sat and put their hands behind their heads. Some gibbered and wept; others knelt in prayer as Arthur's cavalry encircled them.

NOT EVERYONE WAS ready to end the fight. Lucan rode hither and thither, chopping down any Roman he encountered who, by accident or design, still held weapons. "Rufio!" he bellowed, tearing off his helmet. "Felix Rufio, where are you?"

No-one answered this challenge, but still, here and there, he had cause to vent his wrath. A party of six legionaries – filthied and bloodied – knelt up and asked for mercy as Bedivere and other knights dismounted to take their surrender. One legionary, whose entire front was blistered by naphtha, begged for water. As Bedivere handed over a bottle, the fellow produced a *gladius* and slashed out, lopping the knight's left hand off at the wrist.

Bedivere fell backward, gasping, and his squire, Percival, wove a cloak over the stump, but the rest of his retainers raised spears and swords, to shrieks and moans from the six Romans. "Enough!" Bedivere called hoarsely. "Enough... these men have surrendered. It's battle-madness, nothing more."

"Indeed," replied Lucan, who had witnessed the incident and leapt from his saddle. He hefted *Heaven's Messenger*. "'Twould be madness to leave it at that!" With six brutal blows, he split each captive to the teeth.

Bedivere, white-faced and shuddering, could only fix his brother with a baleful stare. "Do you feel better now?"

"I'll feel better when we've made raven-food of them all," Lucan replied. He glanced at Percival, a handsome Welsh lad. "That wound needs cauterising, or he'll bleed to death before you get him to surgeon Tud. Take fire to it, or hot metal. And don't stint."

The squire nodded and supervised the carrying-away of his now insensible master.

Lucan re-mounted Nightshade and rode back across the field, calling for Rufio.

"I can tell you where Rufio is, Earl Lucan!" sounded a feeble voice.

Lucan turned in his saddle, and saw another bunch of prisoners seated nearby. These were of a less unruly order, and were in the charge of Arthur's *Familiaris*. They, too, were bedraggled and bloodied; their arms and armour had been stripped from them and now they were roped together. Lucan dismounted again, but this time his sword remained sheathed. The Roman who had called was recognisable, though at first Lucan was unsure why – and then he remembered. It was Quintus Maximion, the tribune he had spoken to during the feast at Camelot. The once dignified commander was now a sorry sight, one eye swollen like a plum, the bridge of his nose cut to the cartilage, his right forearm deeply slashed. He wore only his maroon breeches, his sandals, and a ragged vest covered with grime and sweat.

Lucan surveyed him grimly. "I believe I warned you this could happen."

Maximion nodded. "That is so."

He seemed less devastated by the disaster than his comrades. He gave an air of frank, weary acceptance.

"You say you know where I can find Felix Rufio?"

"I've a good idea."

"Now would be the time to tell me."

"I had no love for Felix Rufio before, and I have even less now. But I have a price. The whipped dogs you see around me are the sole remnant of my command. These men have fought hard. In the cause of an arrogant madman, I agree, but nevertheless, they showed loyalty and courage. They do not deserve the fate they fear will befall them."

Lucan cast his eye over the clutch of prisoners. They remained seated, heads bowed. None could meet his gaze. It was possible they'd seen him wreak his gruesome execution on the small band who had assaulted Bedivere, but more probably they had been fed propaganda by their Emperor about the doom facing any who fell into Arthur's grasp.

"If their surrender is genuine," Lucan said, "if they make no effort to escape or resist, they have nothing to fear. They will be held as prisoners. Once the war is over, the common men will be released. Those of rank and title may be held for ransom, but they'll not be mistreated. That is not the way in Camelot."

Maximion nodded. "Such things I have heard. But can you give your guarantee?"

Lucan turned to the centenar whose platoon stood guard over the group. "These are your prisoners, captain?"

The centenar nodded warily. "That's correct, my lord."

"I need a firm guarantee that none of these men will be harmed."

"That's the rule across the entire army, my lord."

"I need *your* guarantee regarding this particular group."

"Of course."

"If any of them are hurt, you and your men will answer to me. Is that understood?"

The centenar looked a little disconcerted. There were few in the royal household who had not heard about the Black Wolf of the North. "As I say, my lord... of course."

"This one" – Lucan pointed at Maximion – "is now my prisoner. Cut him loose."

"As you wish, my lord."

Lucan strolled away, leading Nightshade by the bridle. Maximion limped after him, rubbing at the weals on his wrists.

"What of your three sons?" Lucan asked.

"Only one was present today. I know not where he is, but I fear the worst."

"Where is Felix Rufio?"

"He fled the battle early."

"How early?"

"During your second charge. His cohorts were demolished by it. I think he also took one look at you... scything through his ranks like a black whirlwind, and his nerve broke."

"He fled the field alone?"

"Some of his men went with him. Maybe thirty. His closest companions."

"And where will Rufio and these thirty companions have fled to?"

Maximion shrugged. "Wherever he is, it won't be long

before he learns that Emperor Lucius is dead and the dream that was New Rome in ashes."

Lucan was surprised. "Surely you'll rally to fight us again? You still have forces in Brittany."

Maximion shook his head. "Most of the Senate and the High Command – those beyond the Emperor's select band of flatterers – were questioning this reconquest long ago. The sheer cost of maintaining it, even had Albion surrendered, would have been prodigious. It won't take much to persuade those who are left to go home in peace."

"And where is home for Felix Rufio?"

"He owns two houses, to my knowledge. One is in Rome, one in Tuscany. You'll easily locate both, and he knows that. Hence there's only one refuge left for him now – his ancestral home, Castello Malconi in the mountains north of Italy."

"He has a castle as well?"

"His family are the Dukes of Orobi. His mother, Zalmyra, currently holds the title. She presides over Castello Malconi, which guards one of the highest passes."

"So he abandoned his troops to the slaughter... and ran home to his mother?" Lucan looked genuinely perplexed. "And this is the creature my wife abandoned me for?"

"Be warned, Earl Lucan. Zalmyra is no ordinary mother. She has many cruel arts at her command."

"No matter," Lucan replied. "So do I."

TWENTY-TWO

KING ARTHUR PITCHED his main camp at the south end of the Vale of Sessoine, and for several days after the battle his army scoured the surrounding woods and valleys for Roman survivors. They also located the main Roman baggage train, which had simply been abandoned. Arthur was able to replenish his material losses several times over – not just weapons, munitions and other armaments, but also medicines, foodstuffs, and sacks of pay in gold and silver.

His men spent dismal hours working on the battlefield, extricating those too badly wounded to stand or walk, and taking them to the hospital tents, though these were already overloaded with groaning, bandaged forms and thick with a miasma of sweat, blood and despair. Chief physician Morgan Tud and his staff worked tirelessly, repairing what damage they could. Where possible – usually in cases where mangled limbs must be amputated – they offered the patients cheap wine laced with gall. This was so bitter that many at first refused it.

"If it was good enough for Christ on the cross..."[27] the grey-bearded doctor would sternly say, insisting they take a draught.

"It wasn't," the patient would whimper. "Our Lord refused."

"Because he was man enough to endure his pain," the doctor would reply. "That option is also open to you."

[27]Matthew 27:34.

The matter of the deceased was even less easily resolved. Large companies of troops were employed sorting out the corpses, laying their own dead in long rows which priests could say Masses over before burial. The Romans, they piled in mountains for cremation though they too, at Arthur's insistence, received holy rites first.

The holding of prisoners was also a tricky issue. Captured Roman grandees were installed in the separate camps of the British lords and captains who had taken them, and were given comfortable quarters, including private tents, changes of clothes, good food and clean water, though in nearly every case they were also put in leg-irons – a state of war still existed. The ordinary prisoners were herded into special pens made with the hafts of their own pikes, roped into fences. They were fed from great cauldrons with thin soup or gruel, which had been taken from the Romans' own baggage train and which Arthur suspected was all they had been fed on before.

The only hostage in Earl Lucan's camp was Tribune Maximion, who washed and shaved and allowed the gash on his arm to be stitched, but insisted on wearing his own clothes, soiled rags though they were. He cut an isolated figure, his ankles manacled together, watching without seeing as the knights and men-at-arms went about their duties. On the second day, he was summoned to Earl Lucan's pavilion.

LUCAN WAS SEATED in a blackthorn chair which his men had pilfered from the baggage train. He'd dispensed with full armour, and now wore a mail shirt over leather breeches, and cross-strapped riding boots. Maximion was given a stool, and sat. Two of Lucan's knights stood in attendance, Turold and Gerwin – they too were stripped to shirts and breeches, but leaned on their ungirt longswords.

"The accommodation is to your satisfaction?" Lucan asked.

"It's certainly more than I expected," the Roman replied.

"Enjoy it while you can."

"I wouldn't say I was enjoying it, my lord."

Lucan gave a wintry smile. "Compared to what may lie ahead, this camp is the lap of luxury."

"I see."

"When we last spoke about Felix Rufio, you gave an impression that you held little admiration for him."

Maximion shrugged. "I never admire folly. Not even the folly of a child."

"How well do you know the Malconi family?"

"I only personally know Rufio and his uncle, Bishop Malconi. But they are all cut from the same cloth – they are vain, ambitious and treacherous."

"In short, typical of the Roman gentry."

"How well you think you know us."

"I'll be blunt, tribune... my war with New Rome has now become personal."

Maximion looked surprised. "It wasn't from the beginning?"

Lucan ignored the remark. "At the first opportunity I intend to divert from this army, and pay a visit to Castello Malconi and this fearsome woman, Duchess Zalmyra."

"You won't get near the place."

Lucan's eyebrows lifted. "Is it so hard to find?"

"It won't be easy for one who doesn't know that region. And, as I've already told you, she is a mistress of dark lore. Not only that, it's now late July, and in high Liguria the autumn comes early."

"The weather does not concern me. Nor does my ignorance of the region... because you, Lord Maximion, will be showing me the way."

Maximion looked surprised. "You wish me to accompany you?"

"As my prisoner, you must earn your keep. And acting as a guide in your own country will hardly be taxing for you."

"I won't do it if I'm to be chained like an animal."

"The chain can be removed if you give your word as a Roman officer that you will not try to escape."

Maximion pondered. "I'll give you my word. There's no shame in that. Thus far, you've been a fair captor."

"I'm always fair with those who serve me," Lucan replied. "But to those who oppose me I am the perfect opposite."

"I don't know when you plan to embark, but before we do, I'd like permission to leave your camp and search this bloody field for my son."

Lucan nodded. "You may search tomorrow. But listen, tribune... you have given your word, so now I will give mine. If you fail to return to my camp at dusk, I will hunt you down and kill you. They call me the Black Wolf of the North. Have you heard this?"

"I have."

Lucan's steely eyes gleamed. "When I have killed you, I will hunt your son in Brittany and I will kill him as well. And then I will hunt your other son, wherever he is in your disintegrating empire, and he too will perish. Do you believe this?"

"Yes," Maximion replied, earnestly.

"Good luck on the morrow. I'll have your shackles removed at first light, and you'll be issued with a ticket of leave so that none other may lay hands on you."

ALL THROUGH THAT night, bands of unarmed Roman soldiers approached Arthur's camp, waving improvised white flags. Many who were wounded had become feverish with infection, while others – after a couple of nights in the surrounding mountains, wet, cold and hungry, with wolves howling and no sign in the vale below of the mass hangings and decapitations they'd been led to expect – were only too willing to be put in custody.

At mid-morning the next day, Lucan was summoned to the royal pavilion, where a Council of the Round Table was to convene. His mail and mantle had been cleaned, as had his wolf-fur. Most of the rest of the senior knights were in attendance, mailed and in their finest livery.

King Arthur received them with Kay and Bedivere seated to either side of him. Bedivere was still ashen-faced; the stump of his left hand was bound with bandages and covered by a leather glove. Many others bore lesser wounds. None of their brotherhood had died in the battle, though they had lost many retainers; Lucan's own household of sixty knights was down to fifty, with only forty fit for duty. Griflet had lost all of his, and had begged absence from the Council to mourn.

"Gentlemen, your attention," Arthur said, presenting a parchment. "I have here an estimated tally of casualties. In total, we have eight thousand dead, and sixteen thousand wounded, many of whom may still expire. Several hundred are still unaccounted for.

"The army of New Rome, however, suffered an even more grievous loss." He glanced up, grave-faced. "Gentlemen... to the best of our knowledge, some fifty thousand Romans lie slaughtered."

There were subtle gasps. The battle at Castle Terrabil, when the insurgent forces of King Rience of North Wales and eleven Irish princes were crushed, had long been thought Arthur's bloodiest battle, and yet only forty thousand perished that day, and that between both armies.

Arthur continued: "Among the butcher's bill we must include over three hundred men of very senior rank. Emperor Lucius Julio Bizerta, Duke Ardeus Vigilano of Spoleto and Prince Jalhid Yusuf ibn Ayyub of Cyrenaica are the foremost of these, along with some nine hundred men of middling title."

"God help us," Lancelot said slowly. "We've depopulated the Roman nobility."

"Not entirely," Arthur replied. "They still have several legions in central Brittany. Breton irregulars attack them relentlessly and they have sent negotiators to seek terms. King Hoel and his deputies have ridden to meet them. But they are still a cohesive and well-armed host. In addition, there are numbers of legionaries still on the loose here in France. We cannot assume they will surrender until they actually do. Therefore we

remain in arms, here, until such time as the threat is removed...
whereupon we will break camp and march south."

"We're not going home, sire?" Bors asked.

"We're going to Rome," Arthur said, simply. A tense silence
followed. "Gentlemen... let us be under no illusions. The aim
of New Rome's mission in France was to lure the kingdom of
Albion into war. They sought, unprovoked, to destroy us utterly.
The architects of that scheme are still alive, wallowing in their
ill-deserved wealth while so many better men, of their nation as
well as ours, are wallowing in their own guts. This cannot – nay,
will not – be tolerated. We shall camp outside the city of Rome
and I will demand the miscreants be handed over."

"And if they refuse, sire?" Bors wondered.

"We'll put the city under siege. I doubt they'll be equipped
to withstand one, while we – thanks to the generously donated
cargo train of the late Emperor Lucius – have fodder and water
for years."

"Sire... by 'miscreants,' I take it you mean the ambassadors
who deceived us at Camelot," Sir Gareth asked.

"That's correct. I'll have a gallows prepared for each of them."

"But three of them were churchmen. The Holy Father
will never countenance the punishment of clerics by lay
authorities."

Arthur smiled as if he had anticipated this. "The Holy Father,
I'm sure, will respond to reason. I understand he has concerns
about the Moorish influence along the North African coast.
How could he not? The Moors are pagans, and their presence
in that region grows daily. However, as we speak, Sir Gawaine
is at the Court of the Franks in Paris, where he entertains King
Childeric and his nobles with drinking contests and tales of his
bawdy adventures."

There were snickers among the knights. This was all too
believable.

"My latest information," Arthur added, "is that Gawaine
has befriended his prisoner, Prince Priamus, brother to the late
Jalhid. Prince Priamus now has sole rulership of Cyrenaica, for

which he is most grateful. When he returns, if we wish it, he will be a moderating influence among the Moorish emirs, of whom our Holy Father is so nervous."

"'If *we* wish it,'" Bedivere reiterated. "Those are the important words."

"And the cost to the papacy of this moderating influence?" Lancelot wondered.

Arthur smiled again. "The defrocking of those two-faced scoundrels, Bishop Severin Malconi of Ravenna, Bishop Proclates of Palermo and Bishop Pelagius of Tuscany. The lay-ambassadors, I suspect, will be handed over for much less."

There was a long silence as they absorbed the plan. No-one relished the prospect of remaining in arms for a long siege in Italy, but most, like the King, suspected that it would not be for especially long.

"If that is all, gentlemen," Arthur said, "return to your posts."

They left the royal presence with a general clatter and noise, muttering together as they walked away, leaving only Lucan behind.

"Sir Lucan?" Arthur asked.

"Sire," Lucan said, "you have everything well in hand."

"Your approval is most welcome."

Lucan shuffled his feet. "As it appears there'll be no more hard fighting, might I suggest that my usefulness is past?"

"You may suggest it. I won't necessarily agree."

"My lord," Bedivere interrupted. "I strongly advise that our... *comrade* be kept in harness. We do not know the fighting is over."

Lucan glared at his brother, but said nothing.

"I take it, Lucan, you have a private matter you'd like to resolve?" the King said.

"That is so, sire."

"You wish to detach from the army and go your own way?"

"Now would be the ideal time. While the trail is still warm."

"I object to this most strongly," Bedivere said.

"On what grounds?" Lucan demanded.

Bedivere levered himself to his feet. "You know what grounds, Lucan. Revenge has no place at the Round Table. You'll sully yourself, and all the rest of us."

Lucan turned to Arthur. "My liege, I have the right to seek satisfaction."

"You didn't get enough satisfaction on the battlefield?" Bedivere asked. "That foul sword of yours must have drunk ten gallons of blood."

"I must take the matter under consideration, Lucan," Arthur said. "I'm not sure we can spare you yet." But Lucan didn't immediately withdraw. "Is there something else?"

"There's nothing else, my lord," Lucan replied tautly. "Nothing at all as important to me as this. If you could see your way to making a judgment *now*?"

"*Now*, sirrah?"

"In a year's time, it won't matter either way."

"Excellent," Bedivere said. "Then in a year's time we'll give you our decision."

"Enough, Bedivere," Arthur interjected. Bedivere sat back, gripping his butchered arm with a grimace. Again, Arthur pondered, watching Lucan from under kneaded brows. "Wait outside," he finally said. "Until I summon you."

Lucan bowed curtly and strode from the pavilion.

Outside in the sunlight, the royal enclosure operated with its normal efficiency. Servants ran errands, squires polished armour, cooks cut vegetables and stirred broth. Alaric was seated nearby on a barrel, but jumped to his feet as Lucan approached. Lucan clasped hands behind his back and paced. He sought to look firm and resolute, but saw how he must have looked to his former squire: lost, worried, his future beyond his control.

"I'm sorry all this has happened, my lord," the lad said. "No-one deserves this less than you."

"Everything happens for a reason, Alaric. All we mortals

can do is search until we find that reason. If the search takes us to perilous places, so be it."

"Nothing I can say will convince you to return home to Penharrow?"

Lucan glanced at him, and briefly it seemed as if he was contemplating it. "No, lad. Penharrow no longer exists, as far as I'm concerned."

Alaric's shoulders sagged, but he tried not to show it. "Wherever your search takes you, I'll be there too. Every step of the way."

Lucan gave a forced smile as he paced, his thoughts already elsewhere.

"ALL THINGS CONSIDERED," Kay said, sipping wine, "I see no problem. He *does* have the right."

"Right to what?" Bedivere asked. "To murder his wife?"

Arthur was surprised. "You think he'll kill her?"

"Don't you, sire?"

Arthur seemed unsure. "Has he done such a thing before?"

"No," Bedivere admitted. "But he's never been slighted like this before."

"This is ridiculous," Kay said. "Lucan is a savage on the battlefield, but there've been no complaints about his governorship of the March."

"Not recently," Bedivere countered.

"Besides," Kay said to Arthur, "this Tribune Rufio is another of those Roman bastards on your death-list, isn't he? He was at Camelot. He did his bit for the Emperor. How better than to send Lucan after him?"

Arthur turned to Bedivere. "What is the basis of your concern?"

Bedivere had no obvious answer prepared. "Well... he's still wearing that damn wolf-fur. The battle's over. What's the purpose of it?"

"It's his insignia," Kay replied.

"His insignia!" Bedivere scoffed. "He inherited that mantle from his father, a monster by any standards. I've long feared he's inherited more than that."

"Haven't you yourself argued that he's mellowed in recent times?"

"Yes, but more recently still, Lucan was bitten by the Penharrow Worm," Bedivere said. "Who knows what kind of effect it's had? I mean, he even *looks* different."

"Looks can be deceptive," Arthur replied.

"I hope you're right, sire."

"What this boils down to, Bedivere," Kay sneered, "is concern for your family's reputation."

"And concern that my brother's soul will be lost," Bedivere said.

"Well," Arthur rejoined. "As his *earthly* overlord, I can't legislate for something he *might* do. He's a knight of the realm – I can't restrict his movements because he *may* commit a crime. Answer me this, Bedivere... if I were to refuse Lucan leave to go, would he not just go anyway?"

Bedivere rubbed tiredly at his brow. "I fear he may, sire."

"Even though his lands, castles and titles would be forfeit for disobeying me?"

"You may make such a ruling," Bedivere said. "But the Northern March would beg to differ."

"Exactly my thoughts," Arthur agreed. "I've just lost a sizeable part of my armed forces. I can ill-afford a civil war. Your brother's been dishonoured and he needs to clean his name. Let him find his wife and kill the wretch who stole her."

"And if he causes havoc in the process, sire?"

Arthur chuckled grimly as he poured himself a goblet of wine. "Beyond this tent, there are sixty thousand unburied corpses. Could your brother do worse than that?"

LUCAN WAS SUMMONED back and informed of the King's decision.

"Of course," Arthur added, "you may not take the entire

northern host. That would denude my army too much. This war isn't over yet."

Lucan nodded. "That's as I expected, my liege."

"So how many men do you propose to take?" Arthur asked.

"Thirty should be sufficient. All will come from my personal household."

"You have volunteers?"

"I will have. I'll make sure of it."

"Very well." The King nodded and waved Lucan away. Lucan withdrew, but glanced back when the King called after him: "Sir Lucan... I've given you leave to undertake this quest, but I want you to remember that you are a knight of the Round Table. You carry our status with you. It will not please me if it comes back tarnished."

Lucan regarded them coldly before bowing and leaving.

When he got back to his own camp, Alaric had got there ahead of him, and was busy at the hewing block with his longsword.

"Has Maximion returned?" Lucan asked.

"He has, my lord. It seems he found his son slain in front of the stakes we used as baulks on the infantry line. He made a pyre from broken pikestaffs."

Lucan found Maximion sitting, hollow-eyed, on an upturned bucket.

"At least you've returned," Lucan said, "which means that your other sons will live."

Maximion nodded vaguely. "Now we've *both* lost someone close to us."

"You have the consolation that he was lost to a valorous deed."

"I'll try to remind myself of that whenever I picture my youngest boy with his face cloven, his limbs dismembered, his chest laid open to the heart and ribs..."

"You're not devoid of guilt in this matter," Lucan advised him. "You were happy enough to serve Rome when the conquests were easy. Presumably your sons were following your example?"

Maximion glanced up at him. "And what part, I wonder, did *you* play, Earl Lucan, in your loss? Perhaps you're not devoid of guilt yourself."

"Perhaps not." It was easy to admit that now, Lucan reflected – to his own surprise. "In any case, if your son's heroism is no consolation, you must find something that is – because duty calls. We depart for Castello Malconi first thing tomorrow."

Maximion rose to his feet. "Good."

"That pleases you?"

"Most certainly. You think I wish to linger in this blighted place?"

TWENTY-THREE

CASTELLO MALCONI SAT atop a pinnacle crag overlooking a deep, trackless valley; a great cleft through the Ligurian mountains filled with a rubble of fallen rocks.

There was no access to it except from the north, via a passage wide enough for a coach and horses to pass along, which snaked for several miles between walls of rugged granite. Heavy iron portcullises were located along the passage at regular intervals, with guard posts on top of them. The passage ended at the edge of a cliff, and admittance could only be gained to the castle by a drawbridge spanning a terrifying crevasse. The entire structure was surrounded by an outer rampart built from massive slabs, crenellated and reinforced every hundred yards by turreted barbicans and raised timber platforms on which arbalest and ballistae were placed. The loftiest portion of Castello Malconi was the central spire, from which streamed the family emblem – a black boar with a burning eye. From outside, Castello Malconi was faceless and sheer with no apertures or windows, scarcely even an arrow-loop. Inside, it was similarly soulless, its jumbled inner buildings forming a horseshoe around the deep inner courtyard. Cold stone was the order of the day, much of it black with age and mildew.

But there was much more to the castle than met the eye.

Back in the days of the first Caesars, when the Malconi family had constructed their stronghold as a bastion against the Germanic tribes beyond the Alps, they had mined deep into the virgin rock on which it was perched, creating subterranean barracks in which hundreds of soldiers could be billeted. A tunnel spiralled down to an extensive undercroft, where horses could be stabled and armour and weapons stored. Deeper still lay a suite of work-rooms and laboratories, wherein Malconi alchemists produced potions, poisons, gases and other mysterious, quasi-magical weapons for use against the insurgent tribesmen.

In those days, Castello Malconi had echoed to the sounds of a Roman fort: trumpet calls, hobnailed sandals crashing as squads were called to attention, the clink of hammers, the grinding of whetstones. Now it stood in silence; at night, barely a candle-flame flickered from its parapets. As ruler of these lands, Duchess Zalmyra had baronial duties and a military obligation, but these responsibilities had been rendered null and void by the same Imperial decree that had stripped her battlements of their personnel and marched them off to war in the service of Lucius Julio Bizerta.

There was only a handful of domestic servants; exclusively cripples, mutes and hunchbacks – the sort of unfortunates who could find employment nowhere else – with the one exception of Duchess Zalmyra's monstrous personal bodyguard and valet, Urgol.

Even now, as the hot July night brought thunderclaps and gushing rain, Urgol was hard at work in the bowels of the grim fortress. Here, at the deepest point, there was a place called the 'Pit of Souls,' a brick well of origins unknown, though from the sulfurous smoke constantly drifting up it, it surely descended to the mouth of Hell.

The well was girded around its rim by a wooden walkway, little more than a ledge, with only a single rail to prevent one falling into it. Sconces had been carved into the encircling rock walls, green chemical fires writhing in each one, casting liquid patterns of light far down into the shaft and far above it, where cobwebs clustered as thick as dusty fabric, and spiders the size of dogs hung motionless in the shadows.

The walkway was accessible from a single arched passage, which connected with Duchess Zalmyra's work-chambers. Beside this entrance, a steel-grilled platform jutted out several feet over the Pit of Souls. Urgol was on top of it, his furry shape clad only in a leather loincloth. He had erected timber saltires – diagonal crosses – at either end of the platform, facing each other. When firmly in place, he checked the manacles at the tops and bottoms of their crossed beams, to ensure they were screwed in tightly. Behind him, from the arched passage, echoed the voice of his mistress.

"*Reged anthraloggabar... more-ud uvusona anaxus... torrodona laggo-tyburr...*"

It was a language he had never understood, though he had heard it many times. Even now it sent chills down his spine. On completion of his task, he ducked down the passage. At its far end, a fiery glow marked the entrance to the duchess's chambers, somewhere he never entered unless he was specifically bidden.

"*Pegfal vus ga ravalax... stevros thralanto paiador...*" the duchess incanted, her voice rising to a shriek. "*More-ud uvusona anaxus!*"

He turned right and passed along another gallery, to the dungeons. Most were empty, their bars rusting. But in two of them were captives. The first was a woman in her mid-twenties, once a handsome creature but now naked and brutalised, covered with welts and grime, filthied by her own soil.

Despite her piercing screams, Urgol entered the cell, took the woman under his arm and lumbered back towards the Pit of Souls. There he bound her to the first of the two saltires, her arms and legs spread-eagled. She wept and wailed piteously, jabbering that her name was Magdalena, that she was a good Christian and that she had a husband in the service of the Empire. They were simple folk, who had never done anyone wrong.

It meant nothing to Urgol. His mistress's commands were all.

The second captive was a younger woman – little more than a girl, in truth – but of hardier stock. She too was naked and brutalised, but she fought him as he dragged her from her cell, spitting on him, calling him an "inbred freak." She only began to weep again as he shackled her to the other cross.

The two captives faced each other, only two yards between them. They were bathed in green light and dimly aware of the yawning shaft beneath their feet. Duchess Zalmyra emerged from the passage, her tall figure clad in a simple sleeveless robe of black cotton, belted at the waist. Her hair hung in loose, tar-black ravels. In the eerie light, her pale flesh was almost luminous. Urgol stood back as she surveyed the two prisoners. Briefly, they ceased their caterwauling; their tear-swollen eyes fixed on the beautiful, severe figure who would be the agent of their doom.

Zalmyra produced a long, crooked knife, razor-sharp and glinting, and the two prisoners set up a new wailing and gibbering. Magdalena interspersed her floods of tears with stammered prayers.

Duchess Zalmyra also prayed. *"Pegfal vus ga ravalax... stevros thralanto paiador!"* She joined her hands, the crooked blade pointed upward. *"More-ud uvusona anaxus... BABI!"*

She swept out with the weapon, slicing Magdalena's throat without a sound. The woman's eyes goggled, and her head tilted backward as a frothing red tide cascaded down the front of her naked body, pouring through the grille and into the blackness below.

Zara bit down on her tears and she too tried to pray. She had not lived a good life, short though it was. She had pleasured many men and women, and had imbibed foul and forbidden substances. She had cut purses and taken the Lord's name in vain, but now, if there was time, she would implore His...

The blade slit her windpipe as surely, swiftly and silently as it had Magdalena's.

"More-ud uvusona anaxus... STYMPHALIUS!" Zalmyra cried. Her eyes closed in ecstasy as the hot blood sprayed over her.

Urgol watched from the green-tinted shadow as the sorceress hacked the two bodies open down their fronts, at last prying the ribcages apart and rending out pulsing hunks of crimson muscle. She slid the knife into her belt, and stood by the edge of the platform, a heart clutched in each hand, blood and steam jetting out of them. "*Pegfal vus ga ravalax!*" she called shrilly, dropping her gory offerings.

A sudden shocking silence followed, lasting an age, the echoes of her exultation fading as she gazed down the shaft. An intense cold enveloped them, and Urgol stirred uneasily.

"What ails you, my friend?" Zalmyra asked, not looking at him.

"It is nothing, mistress," he replied in his guttural voice.

"Don't lie to me, Urgol."

"I told you my fear before." Even though she had specifically asked him, it was often difficult to gauge her mood, and the truth was not always appreciated. "These women might be missed. I've heard that Emperor Lucius is a pious prince, and that he will seek out the perpetrators of heinous acts..."

Zalmyra smiled. Blood patterned her neck and face, and her emerald eyes shone with fanatical zeal, yet she was calm. There was no rage in her voice when she replied: "There is nothing heinous about what we have done. The strong take everything. That is the only law in times of strife."

"The Empire is strong too..."

"The Empire has died, Urgol. This last week. Emperor Lucius is slain, and he took his empire with him."

Urgol did not ask how she knew this. His mistress had many complex devices: scrying-stones, crystal orbs, mirrors filled with swirling mist which gave glimpses of the future. But this was troubling news to him.

Duchess Zalmyra held that she lived outside the laws of men, but it had long been a benefit to her family that they were grandees of the Roman Empire. He personally had no love of Rome. In the old days it had persecuted his people, chaining them to the oars of galleys or forcing them to fight to the death in the Great Circus. When the Christians came to prominence they had halted such cruelty, only to try and force his tribe to convert, driving those who refused into the hills, to live as wild men. But despite all this, a strong Rome was a useful ally in times of crisis.

"Not that it would have stopped me, anyway," Zalmyra said. "We Malconis have always forged our own path. I had no need for the Emperor's approval. And no human life which is not of our lineage is worth any more to me than its sale-price."

An eerie, ululating howl rose from the depths of the well.

"Speaking of which," she said, "it seems the transaction is complete."

A chorus of inhuman squawking and shrieking carried up from the pit.

"Step back, Urgol, into the far corner," Zalmyra instructed. "Lest you share the same hideous fate I have arranged for the Black Wolf and his cohort."

TWENTY-FOUR

EARL LUCAN'S PARTY made their departure from Arthur's encampment without fanfare.

They were thirty in total, including himself and his scout, Maximion. The rest were his household knights and their squires, and a handful of longbowmen originally recruited from the Penharrow *demesnes*. Dawn mist still flooded the land as they rode out.

The only person to see them off was Bedivere. He stood by the stockade gate, wrapped in a heavy cloak. Lucan reined up alongside him and dismounted.

"Let her go, brother," Bedivere advised quietly. "Haven't you been tortured enough? You can't force her to love you by violence."

Lucan pondered. "It's not about love anymore."

"So what *is* it about... hate?"

"You don't understand, Bedivere. Because..."

"Because what?" Bedivere interjected. "Because I've never suffered?" He held up his bandaged stump. "I'm a lesser man now than I was before."

Lucan half-smiled. "You'll never be less a man to me." They put their arms around each other and hugged fiercely – as they often did, for they never knew when, or *if*, they would see each other again. "I should have given her children, Bedivere." Lucan's voice thickened with emotion. "What kind of husband are you if you can't give your wife a child?"

"I'm sure it wasn't for lack of trying," Bedivere replied, and faltered. "What I mean is... these things are God's decision, not Man's."

Lucan climbed back into his saddle. "Well, if it is God's decision that my line will end with me, He needs to be aware... it won't end easily."

With a solemn smile and a wave goodbye, he rode away alongside his men.

The troop was fully mailed and heavily armed. They took laden pack-horses, but had also crammed their bolsters with sausages, salt pork and biscuit-bread, for it was uncertain how long they would be on the road, especially if the weather turned before they reached the high country. Most of the men were glad to be away from Sessoine. Much wasted flesh had yet to be interred, and was now putrefying. And the cremation pyres were little better.

IN TRUTH, ONLY Malvolio found difficulty in leaving. He had not taken well to life in the military camp, nor to badly preserved food, or water from animal skins.

"Gods, my bowels are set to break again," he moaned.

"And you with your mail leggings on," Benedict chuckled. Over the last few days, he'd grown used to seeing Malvolio walking gingerly around the camp wearing naught but a long-tailed shirt and a pair of socks. "There'll be no quick evacuations this time."

"This is a curse, and now we're away from the physic."

"You never saw the physic before."

"I hoped it would pass," Malvolio said, grimacing as their horses jogged along.

"You'd had it three weeks before we even engaged the enemy, had you not?" Benedict shook his head. "A cynical man might say you hoped it would pass, but not until *after* the battle."

"I was on the field with the rest of you!"

"Aye, but late... because you had, as I recall, an evacuation."

Malvolio scowled, but clamped a hand to his stomach as his innards grumbled. Benedict chuckled again. It was true; Malvolio had made it onto the battlefield eventually, but mainly to encourage the men from behind. No-one was annoyed by this – Malvolio was Malvolio, and this was no less than they'd expected from him. Benedict, for his part, felt rather proud. He had fought well, and hoary old warriors had commended him for it. The gash on his left cheek, neatly stitched but "a lifelong blemish on otherwise pretty features" as the surgeon who'd applied the needle declared, didn't worry him. It was a badge of courage. Such badges made a pretty fellow prettier still.

IT WAS MID-MORNING by the time they reached fresher climes. The sun had risen, the mist had burned away, and they found themselves proceeding through open grassland. Maximion, who at last had accepted fresh clothing – riding boots, leather breeches and a loose linen shirt with Celtic embroidering at its cuffs and collar – was riding at the point, on a fine roan charger whose master would never have need of it again.

He found himself alongside a rather serious-looking knight whose plate and mail were gashed and dented, and yet who was fresh-faced, almost a babe.

"You are called Sir Alaric, are you not?" Maximion asked.

Alaric seemed surprised to be spoken to. "That is so."

"Forgive me, but you seem a little young to be a fully-fledged knight."

"The situation was forced on us by the war. Mine was a battlefield commission."

"Aah... the honourable way to win one's spurs."

Alaric regarded him suspiciously. "Why are you helping Earl Lucan?"

"Why are *you* helping him?"

"He's my lord."

Maximion chuckled. "My reason is more practical."

"How so?"

"I seek to stay alive."

"You're our prisoner. Earl Lucan will not murder you."

"Are you so sure?" Maximion gave him a sidelong glance, noting the young knight's tension-taut posture. "I suspect you are not."

Alaric tried not to show how troubled he felt. "This is a dark quest we embark upon."

"Well... you serve a dark master."

Alaric looked stung by that comment, but elected not to respond.

"Do I detect a divided loyalty?" Maximion wondered.

"He's not as dark as men say."

Maximion glanced behind them. The cavalcade stretched backward over maybe a hundred yards. Turold, Lucan's *banneret*, was closest but out of earshot, the black standard angled over his shoulder. Behind him rode a clutch of squires. Lucan himself rode alongside the squires, but twenty yards to the west – alone.

"On the surface, I would agree," Maximion said. "But... the 'Black Wolf of the North'? How did he earn such a soubriquet?"

"Did you not see him in the battle?"

"He fights like a *bare-sark*. It's a frightening sight, but that does not make him unique."

Alaric looked thoughtful. "I think it's also to do with who his father was."

"His father was a villain?"

"Of the first order. But... Earl Lucan was never that. He reviles his father's memory, though there were incidents when he too showed a crueller side." The lad paused to get his memories in order. "When I was very young – just a child really – I was kept as a slave at Tower Rock Keep, which was held by Baelgron, a robber baron of the Northern March. He used me as a climbing-boy for his chimneys. He and his knights lived by pillage, but they weren't so foolish as to pillage in Arthur's lands. They raided across the border into Rheged, where their depredations were merciless. Many complaints were made by King Owain of Rheged. At length, Arthur ordered Earl Lucan, as Steward of the North, to censure the miscreant. Lucan did as required. He assembled his host and invested Tower Rock Keep. Baelgron was happy to surrender, for he had committed no crime in Albion. But when Lucan announced his intent to extradite the criminals across the border to Rheged, there was an outcry; Archbishop Valiance of York threatened dire consequences if Christians were handed to pagans for justice.

"Earl Lucan thus sent a message to King Owain, who assembled his court on the northwest side of the border. Then Earl Lucan took his prisoners, Baron Baelgron included, to the southeast side – and beheaded them. Thirty men in total. Because his vassals feared excommunication, Earl Lucan wielded the blade himself. He used his own battle-sword – *Heaven's Messenger*. Satisfied, King Owain and his entourage went home again."

Maximion's eyebrows rose. "That was an extreme resolution."

"That wasn't the end of it," Alaric said. "Earl Lucan tore down Tower Rock Keep, stone by stone. Any wealth he found was sent across the border in reparation. Baelgron's family were turned out and lived the rest of their days as vagabonds. Archbishop Valiance denounced the earl from his pulpit, but took no further action. Even King Arthur was said to have been shocked by the fierceness of Lucan's response, but he himself had sent many a brigand to the hangman, and war on the northern frontier had been averted, so he was content merely to voice disapproval."

"It sounds as if the ultimate outcome was a good one?"

Alaric shrugged, as if this was a harsh lesson that many had been forced to learn. "The northern border was long a lawless realm. Robbers and reivers infested every corner. When Duke Corneus, Earl Lucan's father, commanded there, he was part of the problem – he was the *worst* of them. At least Earl Lucan introduced a rule of law."

"Surely he should be praised?"

"He is, but Arthur's courtiers temper their praise with fear. In time, Camelot became a place of culture and breeding. The *Cult d'Amor* found a home there. Those who espouse such virtues find Earl Lucan discomfiting, for they know his ancestry and capabilities."

Maximion shrugged. "Clearly he has inspired *some* loyalty. You and these others are mostly here as volunteers."

"I came on this mission as part of an oath," Alaric said, though he refrained from elaborating on this – which the Roman noted.

"Do you admire your master?"

Alaric nodded. "I was the only inhabitant of Tower Rock Keep to benefit from its destruction. After the castle was demolished, he saw me wandering, a barefoot orphan with nowhere to go. He took me in and raised me almost as his own. I would lay my life down for him in all circumstances... except one."

"Indeed? And what might that be?"

"Apologies, my lord, but you ask too many questions. You are still our captive."

Maximion smiled to himself. "We are all captives, young Alaric – you and your master are the captives of strange, knightly conventions. Our Roman view of the world is less romantic, but more practical."

"It didn't save you."

"No... no more, I suspect, than yours will save you."

As EVENING APPROACHED, they left the open countryside and entered a region of forest.

The trail was clear enough, winding between leafy dells filled with lengthening purple shadows. The thickets were not dense, and Lucan did not anticipate an attack. There were brigands on all the roads of Europe, though many of the more dangerous bands had been drawn to the banner of the free-companies, and now were no more. Lone malefactors lurked in the deeper woods who might pose a threat – ettins, trolls and the like – but Lucan had no fear of such beings. To die in battle with Godless forces would be a guaranteed plenary indulgence,[28] something he suspected his soul was in dire need of.

But no-one and nothing assailed them, and within a couple of hours the woodland opened into a natural clearing occupied by a rambling stone manse, with cheery firelight shining from its windows. Over the front door hung a sign bearing the image of a red gauntlet. Better, on the sward to one side of the inn, several ox-carts had been drawn up, laden with wine kegs. Two leather clad *bravos* stood guard over them with crossbows. They became visibly tense when Lucan and his men rode into the clearing, but their master, the wine-merchant, was also present: a portly individual in a blue girdled houppeland trimmed with white fox-fur, and a mustard-yellow chaperon. He was in heated debate with the apron-wearing landlord, who was a typical Frank: big and beefy, with crisp blond locks and thick blond moustaches.

"Eight crowns is outrageous, master vintner," the landlord expostulated. "I'll give you six crowns a keg and no more."

"This is the best vintage I have. It comes from my vineyards in Provence," the wine-merchant replied. "You'd be getting it cheap at double the price."

"Six crowns a keg is my final offer," the landlord said. "Perhaps you think there is someone else around here who will pay more?"

"There is," Lucan interrupted. "You... wine-merchant! I'll take your entire stock."

Hoots and cheers sounded from his men, who had been thirstily eyeing the laden carts. The wine-merchant looked startled. Perhaps he didn't believe that these travel-stained ragamuffins – mercenaries, he presumed, for they wore no colours save the Penharrow black – could afford such a price.

[28] A cancellation of the "temporal punishment" owed by a soul in Purgatory before he may be admitted to Heaven.

But then Lucan threw a sack of Roman gold at his feet, and the merchant sank his hands into it greedily.

The landlord was naturally disgruntled, but Lucan turned to him next.

"Innkeeper, my men have earned themselves a feast. Several days ago we won a great victory and have had no chance to celebrate. Can you provide for our needs?"

"Our dining room is only small, my lord..."

"No matter. We will pitch camp. But there's more gold where that came from, if your food is good."

"My wife bakes a splendid game-pie, my lord. It's as large as a table..."

That will do. Bring us six such pies."

"Six?"

"You also have suckling pigs?"

"Erm, yes my lord, we have suckling pigs."

"Fowl, salmon from the Loire?"

"We have all these things..."

"Bring us suckling pig, salmon and fowl. And bring bread as well. In short, bring us everything your kitchen can provide."

"I will, my lord, yes." The landlord stumbled away. He turned back, almost giddy. "Uh... thank you."

"Don't thank me, just serve me."

"Fattening them up for the slaughter, my lord?" Maximion wondered.

"Better they be crammed with food, tribune, than with lies," Lucan replied.

"You must join us, tribune," Turold laughed. "I'll wager your Emperor never promised you fare like this."

"No," Maximion agreed. "In that respect at least, my expectations were low."

THE MEN ATE and drank with gusto.

It was a warm night, but the entire company gathered around the large bonfire they had built, while the landlord and his serving wenches came in constant procession. One after another, the wine kegs were axed and their contents poured, foaming, into cups, chalices and horns. Turold strummed on his lute and the men regaled each other with bawdy tales. Malvolio expressed a desire to be in Rome, where the brothel keepers would shortly be making Arthur's army very welcome.

"I'd have liked to see Rome," Wulfstan mused. "The Vandals made a mess of it, or so they say, but there are holy shrines there where even such as I might find shrift."

"It is still a city of bells and steeples," Maximion put in. "The Vandals did damage, but Emperor Lucius commissioned many public works. The defaced buildings were cleansed, the broken columns replaced, the sanctuaries where Gaiseric and his chieftains stabled their horses were re-sanctified."

"And how did Emperor Lucius pay for all this?" someone wondered. "By draining the coffers of foreign lands?"

Maximion shrugged. "The citizens of New Rome paid for the capital's restoration."

"How many slaves did he use?" someone else asked.

"None. The workforce was voluntary – masons and labourers came from all over the West, and were well-paid for their skills and efforts."

"And while these well-paid volunteers worked, the ghosts of a million martyrs looked on," came a voice from the beyond the firelight.

It was the first thing Lucan had said for a couple of hours. For a moment, he was a gaunt outline in the dancing shadows, his black garb rendering him almost invisible. Only his pale features were visible beneath his anthracite mane.

No-one responded, least of all Maximion, who watched his captor warily.

"Have you all forgotten what Rome once stood for?" Lucan said. "Blood on the sand. Bodies flayed by scourges, boiled in oil, hanged on crosses with their legs broken. Old Rome, New Rome... why should a different name wipe clean the sins of the past?" He wiped his mouth with the back of his hand, his metal-grey eyes roving from face to face. "I think it's time we showed the sons of Romulus and Remus[29] that the world has done with them once and for all. If I had my way, we'd put a fire under every last one."

A moment passed, during which no-one dared respond.

Lucan tossed his wine-cup away. "I'm for bed. The rest of you should follow. We rise with the sun."

The men stood up, yawning, throwing the dregs of their wine into the fire.

"A rare sign of weakness from your *seigneur*," Maximion mumbled to Alaric. "In drink, he crosses completely to the other side."

"But in the morning, he'll be sober," Alaric retorted, rising to his feet. "And yet you will still be our prisoner, and your army will still have been destroyed and your Emperor slain, and still there'll be no-one to protect those who have offended my lord when his wrath falls upon them."

"Believe that last part at your peril, Sir Alaric," Maximion said.

THAT NIGHT, AS he slept, Earl Lucan had a visitor.

The first he was aware of her, she was standing just inside the entrance to his pavilion, silhouetted against the moonlight. He stirred in his bed-roll, attempting to focus on the shapely form through eyes glazed with drink and fatigue. She walked towards him, confident and sensual, her hourglass figure swaying from side to side.

"Trelawna?" he murmured.

"If you wish," came a breathy whisper.

When she was close, he saw that she was wearing a diaphanous green gown, which was laced up the front, though its lacing now hung open, exposing breasts like lush, heavy fruits, their nipples dark and distended, a flat milk-white belly, and below that, a dense tuft of pubic fur.

---

[29]The legendary founders of Rome.

"Trelawna..." He tried to reach to her, though his limbs were so leaden that he could barely lift them. A constricting paralysis seemed to have clamped his entire body.

She knelt alongside him. "As you say, my love." Her cool hand fluttered on his bare thigh. It was the gentlest of touches, but it swiftly aroused him. "Oh... *my!*" she said, noting his immediate reaction.

With gentle shrug of her shoulders, her garb slid from her body so that she now knelt before him, entirely naked. As she shifted position, a shaft of moonlight caught her, and the beauty of her shape almost stopped the heart in his chest. And yet, as she teasingly lowered her mouth to his loins, it struck him that the glossy tresses spiralling over her porcelain back and shoulders were not of honeyed gold, but were black as raven feathers.

Only with a supreme effort, did he manage to reach down and grip that hair.

With a hiss that would have done justice to the Penharrow Worm, she spun around and flung herself on top of him, full-length. Again, he was so enfeebled that he could hardly react. The beautiful visage poised an inch above his own was savage and catlike; the eyes bored into him with iridescent, emerald flames.

"My brave warrior," she cooed. Her breath was sweet as wine, and yet there an underlying taint – something like blood. "My brave warrior... embarked on your path of destruction. But don't mistake yourself for one of the righteous."

"Who... are you?" he stammered.

"The question here is, who are you?" she replied. "Following your unfaithful wife with a hangman's zeal and yet even now, at the point of my womanhood, I can feel you rising to the same error of judgment. My goodness, brave warrior, how long has it been?" She gave a purring chuckle. "I need only adjust my hips... move them an inch... and you will penetrate to my core."

"Succubus..."

"If only that were true. Your imminent infidelity could be excused. No, Earl Lucan, Knight of the Round Table, Black Wolf of the North... you are very much awake, very much the master of your own flesh, which even now belies your piety..."

"My lord!" Turold shouted, entering the tent with a sword and a fire-brand.

Lucan sat upright abruptly, bathed in sweat but also shivering. He moved quickly to adjust his loincloth, and surveyed the otherwise empty interior. Turold's torch revealed nothing amiss, save perhaps a few traces of dissipating mist.

"You were crying out in your sleep," Turold said. "Are you ill?" Lucan got shakily to his feet. Turold eyed him with alarm. "A dream, perhaps?" he suggested.

"No dream," Lucan replied.

"Maybe your wound...?"

"Those weren't cries of pain, Turold."

Turold looked puzzled.

"I've just received a warning to turn around," Lucan explained. "It seems that not only might our flesh and bones be in peril, but our souls as well."

Alaric also entered, with sword drawn.

Lucan glanced at him. "Has anyone else been disturbed?"

"No-one, my lord," Alaric said.

"Then return to your beds, both of you. Say nothing of this."

Turold withdrew, but Alaric remained.

"Well?" Lucan asked.

"You look shaken, my lord."

"And?"

"My lord... you no longer have a squire, but if you need assistance..."

"I have no squire, Alaric, because what I do now would teach nothing to a young man seeking his way in the world."

Alaric knew that it was not his place to speak out. His cheeks burned as he tried to give a discreet voice to his feelings. "My lord, this mission... I honestly don't think..."

"Do you know what faces us, lad? I'll tell you. The Ligurian mountains. Towering peaks with only scant passes and wild valleys between them. In some parts thickly wooded, in others parched and desolate. This would offer concern enough, without even considering what kind of strength the Malconis might hold in reserve. I hope the men have enjoyed tonight. Things will get much harder from here."

"That was your purpose in wining and dining them?"

"I wined and dined them because they deserved it. But you're right to think me a tyrant, Alaric. It's a very cruel fate I'm dragging them to."

"You haven't dragged anyone. We all volunteered."

"Ultimately, that won't count for much."

TWENTY-FIVE

THE JOURNEY ACROSS France was an ordeal Trelawna would never forget.

When crossing Britain with Lucan, they would travel in stately procession without haste, regularly stopping at the castles and manors of friends, family and loyal retainers, easing the boredom of a long journey with comfort and conviviality. But this was a headlong flight, following twisting, torturous tracks into the Ligurian mountains with no rest-breaks save at night, and it was physically and emotionally draining.

The battle had been every inch the atrocity she had anticipated.

At home in Penharrow she had nursed many who had returned from war. She had seen first-hand the dreadful impact of weapons and hatred. Even so, the horrors at the Vale of Sessoine had been a thousand times worse. It had been much the same for the Roman women, who had wept, wailed and even vomited at the scene of carnage. One elegant lady was transfixed by the sight of her young husband dragging behind his horse, an arrow lodged in his throat. Her screams of despair drew even Trelawna to her side, at which point the woman whirled around, calling her a "heretic bitch," demanding she keep away.

"Heretic?" Trelawna said to Gerta, stunned. "She called me a heretic... without knowing my beliefs."

"Of course," Gerta whispered. "To their mind, we are

inferior. And when one is inferior, proof of sin is not required. My lady, you will never be accepted by these people. Return to your husband now, before it's too late."

"I've made my choice, Gerta. If you wish to return, do; you have my permission."

Shortly afterwards Rufio joined her on the low rise. He was filthy and bloodied, his handsome orange livery in rags, his armour dented and spattered with gore.

"We must leave," he panted.

He was accompanied, for the most part, by comrades from the officer corps of the Fourteenth, though neither Antonius nor Frederiko were there, as both apparently had been slain. Trelawna did not consider this a desertion of duty, even though the conflict was still raging. She concluded that Rufio at last had shown good sense. Though such a commodity was in short supply over the next few hours, as they headed away from Sessoine with no apparent plan or direction, having gathered few supplies save those already packed in their saddle-bags. Many of the men were wounded and only crudely bandaged. A number of the horses limped.

They had now been travelling for a week, heading roughly southeast, and Trelawna was bone-weary and agonised from the saddle. She was also famished; the scraps they had brought for rations had served for only a couple of days. Rufio continued to give orders as if he were in charge, and to some extent he was, though Trelawna suspected this was because everyone else was too demoralised to argue with him. Those few occasions when he managed to speak to her privately – for they had no tent and at night slept beside a campfire among the others – he barely mentioned the battle, except to say: "We should have used artillery to bring them down from that high position," or "blast Lucius and his ego... he sent men to certain death under those hails of arrows."

Rufio never touched on his own role in the fray, if he'd had one. He was dirty and bloody enough when he'd returned, but Trelawna had not seen him during the actual fight and, on cleansing himself in a stream two days into the escape, she'd noted that his own wounds were few and light. The swaggering, handsome devil she had fallen in love with now looked a shadow of his former self. He shuddered and gnawed upon a knuckle to calm himself. He'd also become ill-tempered, castigating those around him in the foulest language, and when Frankish peasants, having identified their soiled standards as Roman, showered them with stones and dung, he rode among them with sword drawn, ordering their homes burned and livestock slaughtered.

But word had spread that New Rome was beaten, and much to Rufio's chagrin, the inhospitality continued across the Sequana border in Burgundy, the northern quarter of which they had hoped to traverse en route to the Ligurian foothills.

Duke Draco of Burgundy had remained an independent power during New Rome's reconquest. He had thirty thousand men at his command, and many well-maintained castles. He had never objected in principle to the return of Roman hegemony, and at one stage had sent ambassadors to Emperor Lucius's court to name his price for full compliance, but so high had it been that even Emperor Lucius had found it ridiculous. At length terms had been reached to obtain Burgundy's neutrality. Of course, once Arthur had been defeated, Lucius would have returned to Burgundy with his legions, having found a problem with these terms, at which point Duke Draco would have grandly consented to Roman wishes. It was all a game, in the spirit of which – when Rufio and his party found that they were also being stoned on the outskirts of Burgundian villages – Duke Draco had clearly, yet again, changed his allegiance.

"Gallic bastard!" Rufio spat, feeling this betrayal more than any of the others.

Certain of his lieutenants had mentioned the possibility of their seeking sanctuary in Draco's ducal palace at Lyon. It was closer than Castello Malconi, but Rufio had judged that Arthur would probably pay Draco more for them than even his mother could afford, and had thus refused. Despite this, it was disconcerting to have any bolt-hole, even an unreliable one, so unceremoniously closed to them.

His anger and frustration finally boiled over after several days climbing into the ever-steepening foothills. They halted to rest on a broad slope where rock-slides had shattered the pine trees, but where dark regions of shadow-filled woodland still beckoned on either side. The sole centurion Rufio had in his company was the veteran, Marius, who, on his own initiative, had posted watchmen at the rear to detect any pursuit. One of these now caught up with the party, shouting that they were in grave danger.

The watchman, a junior officer of the Fourteenth Legion, leapt from his horse and sank to his haunches, gasping. His animal was lathered with sweat. The party circled him, unnerved. Rufio dismounted, handing his reins to a valet.

"Speak, fellow!" he said. "What danger?"

"My lord..." The watchman straightened up, rubbing his aching backside. "I dallied to the rear, in an effort to gather intelligence..."

"Yes, yes," Rufio said impatiently. "What have you learned?"

"Does anyone have water?"

A water skin was thrown to him. He took several deep draughts before continuing. "I lingered at an inn called the *Red Gauntlet*. You remember it, my lord?"

"I do. It was some way back, as I recall, but a pleasant enough distraction. Little wonder you chose *that* as your sentry-point."

"My lord, I chose it because it's a popular haunt. I fancied anyone on our tail would call there to refresh themselves. Well... someone did. A knight in black wolf-fur, and a pack of cutthroats. All veterans of the fight at Sessoine – I know this much because they paid for their food and drink in pillaged Roman gold."

Rufio said nothing. The rest of his band listened intently.

"I managed to sidle close while they were in their cups. It was a risky policy. Had they noticed, it would have been the worse for me..."

"Enough with your heroics!" Rufio snapped. "Get on with it!"

"In short, my lord... they loathe and detest us. Their leader wishes to kill us all."

"Did they tarry there?" another officer asked, hopefully. "Drinking, making merry?"

"They made merry for one night, sir, but were on the road again by dawn. I had to ride at full gallop to get ahead of them. They are making better time than us; they have brought fit horses, plus water and fodder."

"We can feed and water our own nags when they get us to Castello Malconi," Rufio said distractedly.

The watchman looked surprised. "Castello Malconi? But that's days from here, along terrible roads... and your enemies are closing. Tribune, we'd be better cutting southwest from this point, seeking shelter with Draco of Burgundy."

"We've already had this discussion," Rufio retorted. "Draco would betray us."

"Betray us...?"

"Too much jibber-jabber! Mount up. We can't delay."

But the watchman did not mount up. Possibly he had been expecting more than this – if not congratulations for his good work, at least some food and rest. When neither of these was forthcoming, and he was presented instead with the reality of ever-harder mountain trails, something inside him snapped.

"Why should Duke Draco betray *us*?" he asked loudly. "It's *you* they want. You're the one who dishonoured one of their greatest lords." He turned to the others. "Why should the rest of us suffer for what *he* did?"

"Hold your tongue!" Centurion Marius hissed.

"And what kind of refuge will we find at Castello Malconi?" the watchman cried. "It's a pile of rock in a forsaken waste! His mother worships dark gods. She'll more likely kill us than give us succour..."

"*You plebian bastard!*" Rufio shrieked, striking hard and unexpectedly with his sabre. The first blow clove the watchman to the teeth. The second struck the joint between his neck and collar-bone, plunging to such depth that it could not be retrieved.

The corpse toppled stiffly over, Rufio's blade still wedged in place.

"*Vermin-ridden scum!*" Rufio screamed at the rest of them. "Are you so quick to forget that you are Roman soldiers? This war is not over because we lost one battle. Arthur knows that too. That's why he hunts us. You wish to go to the Duke of Burgundy, who will do away with you, one way or the other, if for no other reason than to avoid housing and feeding you... then be my guest! *Craven-hearted knaves!* You would abandon your commander just because times are hard?"

"No-one agreed with him, my lord," Centurion Marius ventured.

Sputum slathered Rufio's chin. He pointed at them with shaking finger. "From this moment, if one jackanapes among you utters a single word in defiance of my orders, he dies." He clambered into his saddle. "We ride on... do you hear me? We ride on until I say we stop! There are two more hours before nightfall, valuable time which we cannot afford to waste."

The party moved wearily on, Rufio riding at the front. Alongside him was Trelawna. Her honey hair hung in unwashed strands. Her fine clothes were torn and travel-stained. But she was still beautiful. She sat upright in the saddle, staring directly ahead.

"I suppose you think I acted too harshly?" he said tightly.

"At least you improved on your master's example," she replied. "You only killed one, instead of one in every ten."

"You should say a prayer that those who are following us will restrict themselves to killing one in every ten. Somehow I suspect they won't."

"There is one solution, Felix. That you continue to your family refuge, and I return to my husband."

Rufio looked amazed. "You're suggesting I give you up?"

"It's the best chance your family has of extracting itself from this tragedy."

"You think my family needs such a chance? Do you know who we are, my lovely baroness? We are the Dukes Malconi, the embodiment of Roman nobility, in the cleft of whose noble arse your husband and his vagabond retinue are little more than an itch." Suspecting this latest idea had come from Gerta, he glowered over his shoulder. The elderly servant rode several yards behind them. She returned his gaze severely. "Perhaps we should send your prattling wet-nurse back," he said. "So she can leave them in no uncertainty about the danger they face?"

"Threats will not dissuade them," Trelawna said. "They are sworn to the quest."

"The quest! Always I hear about this! What is this quest of which your country bumpkin knights are so fond?"

"With each knight it is different. They pursue the chivalrous ideal."

"What is that supposed to mean? They dedicate themselves to good deeds?"

"To the knightly virtues – courage, honour and so forth."

"And how do they square that with slaughter and pillage?"

"Arthur has rules against such indiscretions."

"Nevertheless, your knights indulge."

"There are rotten apples in every barrel. The ideal remains untainted."

They rode in silence, before Rufio asked: "What of Sir Lucan? Is he a rotten apple?"

"No... but he is tainted, in his way. As a youth he suffered much."

Rufio recollected the dark spectre he'd almost been confronted with in the midst of the battle. There'd been no mistaking the black mantle, the cloak of black wolf-fur – the longsword swirling as the demonic shape hacked his way though Roman horsemen, their sundered corpses crashing to earth, gore pulsing through broken helms and pierced breastplates.

It hadn't been difficult to turn tail and flee.

That was something Rufio didn't like to admit, not even to himself, but there was no doubt, when he'd seen his opponent delivering death on all sides like the Reaper, working his way ever closer... it had been a barely conscious decision to quit the field.

"I wonder why Arthur would use such a man," Rufio said, thinking aloud.

"Lucan only ever slays Arthur's foes."

"In grotesque numbers."

"Men like Lucan made the kingdom safe."

"And freed it of political rivals."

She glanced around at him. "What do you mean?"

"One man's rebel is another man's freedom fighter. Your great King Arthur is just another tyrant. You know he now marches on Rome itself?"

"Rome attacked Arthur's allies first."

"Tit-for-tat massacres. How chivalrous."

"You can hardly talk, Felix. Your Emperor despoiled an innocent land with mercenaries."

"In whose company Earl Lucan would feel very cozy."

"Does he terrify you so much, soldier of Rome?"

Rufio spun around in the saddle, the back of his gauntleted fist catching her a stinging blow in the middle of the face.

Behind them, Gerta squawked with outrage. Trelawna hunched forward, one hand clamped to her nose, which streamed blood. Rufio reined up, wild-eyed and red-cheeked, looking as if he was about to strike her again. The rest of the company laboured past, uninterested. Most probably thought the heretic bitch had got exactly what she deserved.

Only slowly did Rufio's anger seem to abate. "Forgive me," he said at last, when all the others had gone, though he didn't sound particularly contrite.

Gerta glared fiercely at him as she wrapped her arms around her mistress.

"It seems my full anger is being horse-drawn from me today," he added.

"Aye," Gerta retorted. "Onto the helpless."

"What did you say, servant?"

"Gerta, ride on," Trelawna instructed.

Very reluctantly, Gerta spurred her horse forward.

"That crone needs to learn some respect," Rufio snapped.

Trelawna put a crumpled wad of linen to her nose. "In all my years in that brute land you despise so much, no man laid a finger on me."

"Well, what do you expect?" he shouted. "You accused me of being frightened, but why wouldn't I be? All our dreams are laid waste. New Rome, which took twenty years of political and military craftsmanship to reconstruct, is gone in an instant."

"Much like the freedoms of those many lands New Rome reacquired."

"I love this new-found reaffirmation of your loyalty to Arthur's realm, Trelawna... now that his man is hot on our heels."

"If only he *were* coming as Arthur's man. There'd be a possibility he might show some restraint."

"Oh, dear Christ, alarm me no further!" Rufio wheeled his horse around to continue uphill. "Your barbarian friends are nothing but ignoramuses! They may win the odd battle, but there are other powers in this world! *Powers they cannot imagine!*"

TWENTY-SIX

Bishop Malconi reasoned that the smaller his party, the less chance there was of it being noticed. Thus, aside from his travel-coach – a solid wooden box plated with steel, once overlaid with fabric bearing the red and gold lions of Ravenna, but now clad in simple rustic brown – he journeyed north with only his ten bodyguards, who wore their hauberks under cloth and were armed unobtrusively.

Such anonymity served its purpose as he passed through the dusty villages and rural towns of Lombardy, but when he left lowland Italy behind and entered the Ligurian foothills, he became afraid that he now wasn't protected enough. The bleaker and wilder the terrain, the more the bishop travelled with his coach shutters bolted, his bright eyes glued to a viewing slot too narrow for even a broad-headed arrow to penetrate.

Even in late summer, with the meadows still green and only tinges of red in the trees, this was a desolate region. The few people they saw were illiterate shepherds who lived in turf huts, the only livestock sheep and goats. The higher they rose into the great Alpine massifs, the more this meadowland fell behind them, until soon they were following narrow ways amid misty crags, or winding through dense pinewoods. The road was increasingly difficult, churned to porridge by rain and hardened again by the summer sun so that it was all ruts and divots.

Night was a particular challenge – for that was when they heard things. After dark, Malconi would not even venture out of his carriage. He now wore mail himself and sat rigid inside, his face beaded with sweat. Outside, his *bravos* – not quite as afraid as he, but still on edge – slept around their fire, two of them always standing guard, listening to the encircling woods and to the cries and gibbers of unnatural creatures.

On the final day of the journey, high above the world, they toiled onto an undulating ridge, a narrow spine of rock along which the final leg of the road was laid. The vast gulfs to either side were a test of a man's steel; one needed only to stray a yard from the road and he would plunge to his doom. With early afternoon came rain, heavy and teeming, and after the rain a miasmal gloom. By late afternoon, they were relieved to find bluffs approaching, and soon they were following a narrow passage between sheer walls of granite.

"Make haste!" the bishop called through the roof of his coach. "We are almost there."

The driver did not make haste, for the alley was so tight that he could barely advance without the carriage's wheel hubs scraping on rock. Several times the way was blocked by iron portcullises, now rusty and thick with moss. Far overhead, on the stone lintels of these gateways, were walled and roofed guard-posts, but no guards were on duty. In each case it took two of the bishop's men to scale these great iron frameworks and work the crank-handles, slowly lifting the obstructions out of the way.

At last, with dusk falling, they came to a point where the passage ended, and a bottomless chasm lay before them. On the far side sat the arched entrance to Castello Malconi, although at present the drawbridge was raised and out of reach. Wearily, the bedraggled party gazed up.

"Sister!" Malconi cried. "Sister, we seek admittance!"

After what seemed an age, a lone figure appeared on the black battlements: Duchess Zalmyra. She wore a fleece shawl; her long, tar-black hair was bound in a scarf.

"Zalmyra… your passage gates are unmanned!" Malconi called up to her. "How can this happen in a time of trouble?"

"It has happened," she called back, "because, thanks to your master, there are no men to operate them."

"If by 'my master' you mean Emperor Lucius, you'll be shocked to know that he is dead."

"Hardly shocked, brother." She still made no effort to have the drawbridge lowered.

"For God's sake, Zalmyra! Arthur's army is on the move. It heads southward through France, sacking every Roman-held castle or town."

"You seemed unconcerned by this possibility a few weeks ago."

"That was before I knew Arthur had put a price on my head."

Her voice crackled with scorn. "How little foresight you princes of the Church show."

"Open the gates, I beg you!"

She shrugged and turned away.

With much squealing and grinding of cogs, the drawbridge was lowered. Malconi almost ran across it, his guards and coach following at a more sedate pace.

His sister met him in the courtyard. Malconi could only regard the deserted parapets with mouth agape. "You have no household guard?"

"Most died at the Vale of Sessoine," she replied.

"Then we are in very serious trouble."

"You have your Praetorians. Will they not suffice?"

"Against the whole of Arthur's army, which grows stronger by the day? Now, I hear, the Franks have joined him; they call it 'liberation,' the insolent curs. Everything Childeric has he owes to Rome, yet now he accuses us of tyranny and says his people are glad to be free."

"And who wouldn't?" Zalmyra chuckled. "Emperor Lucius called the Franks his servants. King Arthur had the wisdom to call them friends."

"This is madness, complete madness."

"If so, it's a madness cooked up by your beloved Simplicius."

"He may save me yet. I can't believe he'd cut off his strong right hand without resistance."

Zalmyra laughed again. "He sacrificed fifty thousand men at Sessoine. Why would he not sacrifice you?"

Malconi's voice became desperate. "Proclates of Palermo and Pelagius of Tuscany have been named as well. Warrants for our arrests have been issued. But surely Arthur won't make good on this threat? We are men of the Church."

"Arthur may consider that you have betrayed the Church," she said.

"Betrayed...?"

"Not the Church of Simplicius, that tottering palace of wealth and intrigue. But the people of Christendom, the ocean of innocent souls entrusted to you and your kind by Jesus Christ, and abused and neglected ever since."

"But that isn't true."

"Hah! Tell the people of Brittany."

Malconi felt butterflies in the pit of his belly as he recalled the stories he'd heard about the war-crimes committed in Brittany. Neither he, nor any other churchman, had ordered such depredations, but neither had they sought to stop them. "Say you'll give me refuge. Zalmyra, I beg you..."

"Don't beg, Severin," she said disparagingly. "In the name of your carpenter God, don't lower yourself to that. I'll give you refuge. Of course I will."

"And you'll find new men, new soldiers with which to fight?"

"I need no soldiers. When the Vandals came against our bastion... half a million of them died in the valley below, and they landed not a single blow on us."

"But Arthur won't attack from the front. He's too clever..."

"Arthur won't attack at all, you fool. He is otherwise engaged. But there *will* be a challenge... in due course."

"You think you can meet it?"

"I already have. He's a flesh and blood man. Very human. But strong. I got close enough to sense that much." She smiled strangely. "No matter. The agents of our defence are abroad on the slopes of these mountains even as we speak."

Malconi remembered the cries and gibbers in the benighted vales below. "Don't tell me you've unleashed demons?"

"Ask me no questions, brother, and your prissy Christian conscience can remain clear."

TWENTY-SEVEN

WULFSTAN BRACED HIS foot against the corpse and tugged on the sword-hilt. With a grating of bone, he freed the weapon.

"Roman *falcata*," he said, holding the bloody blade aloft. "Seems our friends are falling out among themselves."

"How long?" Lucan asked.

"Well... this fellow was killed about a day and a half ago."

"We're gaining on them," Turold commented.

Wulfstan nodded. Before they departed *The Red Gauntlet,* its landlord had informed them that, just short of a week earlier, a party of New Rome's soldiers had passed by in the company of two women, one young and fair, the other matronly.

Lucan glanced across the rock-strewn hillside. The encircling pinewoods were deep, filled with impenetrable shadow. It was easy to imagine someone observing them, though everything he'd learned about his quarry so far suggested he was in headlong flight, not thinking rationally enough to launch an ambush.

Less than half a day later, they encountered a village.

It was located at the lower end of a narrow defile. The first they saw of it was a stockade made from pine-logs, the gate partly open. Roofs of houses, thatched with sticks and firs, were visible beyond. There was no sound, and no sign of movement on the village rampart. Lucan and his men reined in about sixty yards away. They were within bowshot, but still nothing happened.

"I have a bad feeling about this," Malvolio said tightly.

For once Benedict didn't dispute with him.

"Disperse," Lucan said quietly.

The horsemen fanned out into a broad skirmish-line. Steel clanked as visors were snapped shut. With shields raised and spears lowered, they advanced. For several moments the only noise was the snuffling of horses and the clumping of hooves.

Still nobody appeared on the village stockade.

They halted again, about thirty yards short.

"That open gate is a clear invitation," Wulfstan said, voicing a suspicion Lucan shared, "but it isn't a risk I'd take if I was them. My lord... I don't think there's anybody here."

"Everyone, hold your ground," Lucan said, climbing from the saddle. He glanced to his archers, who were mounted nearby, arrows nocked. He made eye contact with them, and they nodded their understanding.

He put his helmet on, brandished his shield and, drawing *Heaven's Messenger* from the scabbard hung over his wolf-fur, continued on foot. The village gate remained ajar, although the narrow gap afforded no glimpse of what might wait on the other side.

The gate swung open easily when Lucan pushed it.

Immediately beyond there was a large weapon which the Romans called a 'Scorpion': a wheeled crossbow with a pivotal base, two thick bundles of sinew rope twisted down the centre of its rectangular frame, adding immense torsion power. Eighteen four-foot bolts currently rested in its grooves, its hempen string at full stretch. But there was nobody there to aim it, or to release the missiles. The village's main street, which was narrow and stony, was also deserted. Lucan ventured through and stepped around the war-machine. To his left a ladder led up to the guard-walk on the stockade, which was also unmanned. He looked further afield. The houses were simple affairs, log-built and of varying shapes and sizes. In the centre of the road lay a stone trough filled with water.

Everything he saw told him that this settlement had been

abandoned; doors stood open, windows were half shuttered, but he knew that something was wrong. And then he began to spot clues: red-spotted feathers scattered in one of the animal pens; a wood-axe lying on the road with its handle broken. Some of the window shutters, he realised, were hanging from twisted hinges. Open doors had been smashed in, their timber frames splintered.

He turned back to his men and signalled. They advanced on foot, leading their steeds.

"This place was sacked," he said, as they joined him.

Wulfstan lifted his visor. "By our Roman friends? I didn't think they'd have the wherewithal."

"I'm not sure." Lucan forbade them from watering their horses at the trough, and ordered them to search the village, and to be cautious. Now that he looked more closely, he saw what appeared to be claw marks on some of the smashed doors. Blood was daubed in many places. And yet there were no bodies.

"Whoever attacked, they didn't come through the front gate," Wulfstan noted. "This Scorpion hasn't even been discharged."

"How did they get hold of such a weapon?" Turold asked.

Maximion dismounted alongside them. "Some of the men probably did military service. They may have looted it from a battlefield, or perhaps been granted it as a boon for good work... something to protect their village."

"So where are they?" Turold asked.

"My lord... *my lord!*" came a shrill voice. Benedict, at the far end of the main street, Malvolio beside him. They stood in front of a barn, the door to which they had just opened, but they now stood back, grim-faced. Alaric reached them first. He half-entered the barn, only to back out with a grimace. The rest of the men converged. Lucan shouldered his way through last, waving away a cloud of droning flies.

The villagers were heaped inside.

Or what remained of them was, a great tangled mass of torn flesh and contorted limbs. It was not just the men; there were women and children too, even small babies, all steeped in thickening blood. Their skulls had been crushed and their throats ripped out. Belly cavities gaped, and coils of glistening intestine were strewn about like strings of sausages. Bizarrely, their animals lay beside them: dogs, chickens and goats, even a shaggy highland cow, all rent and mangled in a frenzied, bestial attack.

"Our Roman foe did *this*?" Turold said, aghast.

"No," Lucan replied. "This is something else."

"These bodies are practically fresh," Wulfstan said. "My lord, these people have only recently been slain."

"And they were dumped in here because the sight of them would have alerted us before we entered the village," Turold added.

Lucan spun around, shouting: "Prepare for attack... quickly!"

They clumped together in the main street, weapons drawn, watching over the rims of their shields. The village remained deserted.

There was a prolonged silence. A slight breeze whipped up eddies of dust. Down at the far end, near the entry gate, the horses grew skittish, pawing the ground and tugging at their tethers.

And then there was a chilling, ululating cry, and a huge object came whistling through the air. At first Lucan thought it a boulder, but when it struck full on Benedict's helmet, crumpling it like tin, he realised it was the anvil from the smithy.

On all sides, figures scuttled into view – on the roofs of the houses, at the ends of alleyways. They crouched, simian-fashion, their thick, muscular forms covered with dark, greenish-grey fur, their faces and elongated snouts striped blue and scarlet.

"Apes!" someone shouted. "In *these* mountains?"

"No ordinary apes!" Maximion replied, equally astonished. "The Berbers call them baboons! These beasts dwell in Africa!"

"Do they normally carry weapons?" someone else said, stunned to see that many of the creatures carried stones or lengths of timber.

More and more of the baboons now appeared, hemming in the small party of warriors. Though squatting or crouching, they were the size of men. They snarled, roared and screamed, their fang-filled mouths gaping horribly.

At the far end of the street the horses panicked, ripping their tethers and bolting this way and that. One ape, a grotesquely vast specimen, had smashed its way in through the gate. It must have been concealed somewhere down the valley, following the men in to spring the trap, closing off their only avenue of escape. With a deafening howl, it grappled with one of the packhorses, lifting it bodily and bouncing it down across its knee, shattering its spine.

This was the signal for attack.

With a chorus of demonic screams, the simian tribe hurled their missiles and surged forward, leaping and scrambling over each other, two or three to every man. The *mesnie* fought back with a courage born of desperation. Gerwin buried his pole-axe in a baboon's skull. With a single stroke of *Heaven's Messenger*, Lucan cut clean through one simian neck and shore deeply into another. But the assailants were stronger, faster and fiercer than their human opponents. They shrieked like damned souls as they battered and tore and bit, dragging their hapless targets to the ground. Brione of Bullwood had his faceplate rent away, and his eyes clawed out by jagged, dirty fingernails.

Alaric fended them off with his shield, before it was yanked from his grasp. He drove his sword through the belly of one baboon, only to be struck on his sallet with a heavy stone, which knocked him senseless. He toppled to the ground behind Lucan. Lucan spun around, distracted by that and by Wulfstan, who he saw face-down in the dirt as two of the beasts pounded him with rocks.

Lucan lunged, his blurred steel striking in lightning flashes, shredding flesh, fur and muscle. On all sides, his men were beaten with clubs and mauled by claws and teeth in a frenzy of speed and savagery. Hundreds of the apes flooded the compound, and now their gigantic leader, having killed three horses, lumbered forth. It grabbed two men up, one in either hand, and slammed them on the ground, like a washerwoman drying rags. Its third victim was Malvolio, who, having fortuitously impaled one of its smaller cousins in the breastbone, was snatched into the air before he could even shout. The abomination glared at him face-to-face, and then flung him, cart-wheeling, over the heads of his comrades.

Maximion had grabbed up a spear, and tried to hold them off with its barbed point as he backed towards the nearest longhouse. "Earl Lucan!" he cried. *"Earl Lucan!"*

Lucan glanced around. Maximion was pointing into the building. It would be easier to resist this ravening horde in an enclosed space than out in the open. Two more baboons came at him, leaping, howling. He smashed the iron boss of his shield into the face of one, and smote the other in the groin, dragging *Heaven's Messenger* sideways, ripping the brute in half, its blood and intestines exploding.

Another beast barrelled into him from behind, jumping onto his back, wrapping its black, crooked claws around his helmet and yanking it off. Lucan dipped his shoulder, flipping it over his head, and the monster dragged him down on top of it. Its gnashing, froth-slathered fangs were less than an inch from his throat; its fetid breath spilled over him, making him gag. This close, *Heaven's Messenger* was useless, so Lucan dropped it, freed his dagger from his belt and plunged the blade to its hilt in the creature's left eye-socket. Another baboon leapt at him, landing both feet in his chest, and Lucan hurtled backward. But when he rose to his feet he had a falchion in hand. The baboon charged at full speed, head down. Lucan side-stepped and caught it a slashing blow to the back of the skull, laying its brains bare.

"The building!" he bellowed, retrieving *Heaven's Messenger*. *"All of you, inside!"*

Alaric and Wulfstan still lay nearby, showing signs of consciousness. Lucan grabbed them by their chain aventails and, one by one, hauled them to their feet. Blood was trickling across Alaric's face and Wulfstan was still in a daze.

"Into the house!" Lucan shouted, pushing them stumbling in that direction.

A few yards away Turold was having less luck with Benedict. He attempted to haul his squire to his feet, but the lad's helm was so crushed out of shape, red-grey sludge leaking though its many apertures, that Benedict must have been dead.

"Turold, leave him!" Lucan shouted.

"My lord, he's not..."

"He's gone, damn it! Now leave him!"

In ones and twos, the brutalised knights and men-at-arms tottered towards the open door. One of the archers had already got there, and now stood guard. Another had emerged in one of the upstairs windows. Both were stringing arrows and letting fly with speed and precision, feathered shafts thudding into any apes that came close. But this did not stop the assault. No sooner had the men still on their feet staggered inside the building, battening doors and hatches, than the tribe swarmed all over the exterior, hammering the shutters with claws and fists, even digging through the thatch of the roof. Inside it was chaos: packed, noisy, dark, rank with the stench of sweat and blood. When daylight suddenly shafted in, it was blinding; a shutter had splintered from its hinges and a squire standing in front of it was dragged bodily out. Before anyone could try to retrieve him, two feral forms came scrambling through the aperture. The first went down under a flurry of axe and mace blows, while the second was skewered to the wall by Lucan, with Maximion's spear.

Outside, those who hadn't made it into the refuge screamed as the apes beat their heads and ribs with stones, or flung them back and forth, ripping off what remained of their armour, chewing through their limbs, gouging their eyes, breaking their backs, rending their bellies open and hauling out ropes of guts and pulsing organs. The gigantic baboon upended one poor fellow, rent him asunder by yanking his legs apart, and hung him high to drink his innards as they gurgled out. Still not sated, the giant cast the corpse aside, wiping gore and faecal matter across its brutal mouth, and hurled itself at the house, the entire wood-and-daub structure shuddering from floor to roof. The archer above fell from the window with the impact. The apes caught him and carried him away, froth spurting from his mouth as he shrieked.

Inside, Maximion cornered Lucan. "There's something you must see..."

Another crashing impact shook the building. Another shutter was punched inward as the giant struck it. More baboons attempted to force entry, only to die under storms of blades and mattocks. Lucan followed Maximion up a twisting timber stair to an upper floor, where the windows, out of reach of the crazed simians, had not yet been shuttered.

Maximion led him to a window at the rear. "Our only chance is to find a place to hold out. I suggest up there." He pointed beyond the stockade, which lay some ten yards behind the house. Maybe a hundred feet above the valley floor on a rising hillside of stony rubble, a dark niche was visible. It looked like a cave entrance. "Even if it's only a cubby-hole, we'll be defended on three sides and only need face them from the front. You understand the strategy – you employed it at Sessoine."

Lucan glanced down. "We'll need to clear the stockade first."

Maximion indicated a joist in the ceiling overhead, a squared-off pine log perhaps twenty feet in length. "Hack that loose and we can make a bridge down to the top of the stockade. The men can escape over it..." As Maximion spoke, there was another mighty jolt downstairs, timbers *crunching* as they broke.

"Axes!" Lucan hollered down to the ground floor. "Bring axes."

Only three of the remaining men had axes. They brought them up and set to work on the overhead bream. Wood-chips flew as the gleaming blades swung and swung until, with a cracking and tearing, the oaken shaft collapsed under its own weight, dragging bundles of thatch with it, sunlight blazing through behind it. With grunts and shouts, the rest of the men now manhandled it to the window and thrust it out. It dropped to the top of the stockade, forming a fragile bridge.

"Down!" Lucan shouted. "All of you!"

One by one, his warriors clambered down. The narrow alley between the house and the stockade was still empty. At least two fell into it – both landing heavily and awkwardly, but they wasted no time staggering to their feet and scaling the stockade.

Lucan moved again to the top of the stair. "Anyone else left down there?"

Only the gibbering of the baboon tribe greeted him, their feet and claws pounding the treads as they came. He turned. Alaric was the last other man in the room; he had removed his dented helm, his face bright with sweat, his locks matted with blood.

"Go," Lucan said. "I'll hold them off. Climb to the cave."

"My lord, I..."

"*GO!*" Lucan thundered.

Alaric clambered into the window-frame, just as a clutch of monstrosities entered from the stair. Lucan fell on them in a tumult, his longsword and falchion windmilling, parting flesh and bone as a flame melts butter. Blood and brains splattered as he slashed and clove. The apes fell before him like corn to the scythe, tumbling back down the stairs.

Alaric watched from the window, astounded, never having dreamed a man could show such ferocity. The falchion split one brute to the tip of its snout and lodged fast, but it mattered not to Earl Lucan. *Heaven's Messenger* sang its song, and as it shore through them he grabbed up a battle-axe and laid it on skull, limb, neck.

"*My lord!*" Alaric screamed.

"Go, lad!" Lucan shouted back. "I'll follow you."

Alaric clambered frantically down the joist, while Lucan turned again on his tormentors, though now at last they were quailing before him. So many carcasses were piled around him, so many cluttered the stair, so much blood and hair streaked the walls of the stairwell that for a brief time even these demented horrors thought better of attacking. But ultimately, even through his fury, Lucan knew the collapse of the house would be the death of him. It shook and shuddered under the blows of the giant outside, until the roof came down in a torrent of twigs and dust, more apes leaping down and cavorting around him. Lucan butchered his way through them as he stumbled towards the window. The room was now tilting, the floor up-ending, there was a drawn-out whine of twisting timbers. One last baboon grappled with him. Lucan stove its cranium with the pommel of his sword, and as it slumped, drove the battle-axe blade deep into its spine. Then the window-frame, already warping out of shape before him, was suddenly clear – and he leapt through it and tumbled head over heels down the joist, just before it dislodged and fell to the ground.

As the house imploded, splinters and dust gusting out in all directions, Lucan swung his body over the sharpened tips of the log palisade, hung with both hands and dropped. He hobbled up the rocky slope in pursuit of his comrades while the monster ape and its minions leapt and howled in the wreckage behind him.

Higher up, wounded and exhausted men clung to the boulders like survivors of a shipwreck. They regarded Lucan with white, haggard faces as he clambered among them. It was difficult to count how many were left – no more than twelve, certainly. Turold was one of them. His sword, still slathered with blood and ape-hair, was tight in his fist, but he had thrown off his helmet. His fair hair was a sweat-soaked mop, his tear-soaked features livid with rage.

"Up there!" Lucan shouted, pointing towards the cave.

Turold nodded tautly. Lucan continued up, encouraging the rest of the men to climb. They obeyed, although when Lucan reached the cave a wild shout from Alaric drew his attention back down the slope. Turold remained below, shrieking as he tottered towards the advancing baboons.

"Benedict!" he screamed. *"This is for you, lad!"*

One of them bounded forward and he felled it with a

massive back-stroke. But another took its place, and when this was dispatched, another, and in short order they had swamped Turold and were dragging him down, burying him beneath fur and muscle.

Lucan watched from the cave mouth, helpless.

The giant baboon now thrust its way through the smaller ones, clutching a sharpened pole from the stockade. When Turold reappeared, the apes had ripped off his mail and woollen under-garb, and now they forced him face-down, yanking back his head by the hair and spreading his legs apart. The larger one, ululating with evil, positioned the sharpened pole point-first to his rear end.

Turold glanced to Davy Lug, the last remaining archer. "How many arrows do you have left?" he asked.

Lug produced a single shaft. "Just this, my lord."

"Make it quick and clean, and half my lands and titles are yours."

Lug nocked his final missile, drew its feathers to his ear and – as Turold's distant shrieks took on a new, more piercing note – drove it down the slope. The arrow flew straight and true, striking Turold's open mouth and plunging clear down his throat into the vital organs below.

The captured knight fell dead – long before his impalement was completed.

"You're a rich man when we get home, Davy Lug," Lucan said, grimly.

"Half your estate for killing a comrade-in-arms?" The archer sneered and spat. "Only a man vain enough and mad enough to have brought us to this fate in the first place could think I'd agree to such terms. You keep your blood-soaked lands and titles, my lord."

Lucan glanced after him, but was distracted by a fresh outburst from below. The apes screamed and gibbered with rage, as their leader seized Turold's body in both hands and flung him down on the rocks, again and again, until every bone in his corpse must be smashed to fragments. When the creature gazed up the slope to the cave, drool frothed from its maw – but an immediate attack did not follow.

Tense minutes unfolded as the tribe roared and howled and gestured, but made no advance. The men watched them tensely, drenched with sweat.

Lucan, trying not to think about the fate of his friend – the fates of other friends were still his responsibility – turned and stared up past the cave entrance. The rocky slope soon became sheer; there was no possibility they could climb further. He entered the cave. It narrowed quickly, so that no more than a handful could find shelter in it for long. It was not a cul-de-sac, but a passage formed naturally between fallen boulders. Though it tightened until it was barely passable, it appeared to wind on and on into the hillside, a darkened chink which might afford salvation to someone.

"No way through," Maximion said, appearing alongside him with a firebrand.

"Not for all of us," Lucan agreed, taking the flame and peering through the gap as far as he could. He turned again. "What's happening here, tribune? This is Italy, is it not? A civilised land. And yet we're overrun by a tribe of killer apes?"

"Elementary devilry for a sorceress of Zalmyra's skill."

"This is her work? Even though it destroyed one of her own villages?"

Maximion knuckled the sweat from his eye. "The Malconi care nothing for anyone but themselves. She'd think nothing of unleashing demonic forces, no matter what destruction they wreaked."

"And which demon is this? The great ape?"

Maximion, so indifferent to pain or fear up until this point, looked haggard as he shrugged. "I heard tell of a story once. After Queen Cleopatra and her Roman lover, Mark Anthony, committed suicide, Caesarion, Cleopatra's son by Julius Caesar, was forced to flee Alexandria. A group of Praetorians were sent in pursuit, but they never reported back. At length, they were tracked along the Nile delta to an abandoned citadel, where their remains were found. Each man had been disembowelled alive. It seemed they had been lured to this place by Egyptian patriots. It was once sacred to Babi, a desert demon who appeared as a hulking, ferocious baboon with an insatiable craving for man-guts. The stories hold that he could summon endless forces of cannibal apes."

"My lord!" came a cry from outside. "They're coming again!"

Lucan moved back into the light. Further down the slope, the baboons were venturing upward in a slow, cautious wave. The giant one – Babi, if that was indeed its name – was in their midst rather than leading them, which seemed to Lucan a cunning strategy; a simple animal would charge frenziedly, but a thinking creature would have self-preservation in mind.

"We can stand in this entrance two at a time," Lucan said. "While two fight, the others rest. We change over when we can."

Grey-faced with fear, the remainder of his *mesnie* nodded and hefted their weapons.

"Not you, Alaric," Lucan added.

Alaric looked startled. "My lord..."

"Take your armour off, go to the back of the cave and worm your way through – find out where it leads. I ask because you're the leanest."

Alaric glanced towards the cleft in the cave's rear wall. Blackness skulked beyond, but what his overlord said was true – no-one else could insinuate himself through it. Reluctantly, he began to strip off his mail.

During the baboons' first attack on the cave, Gerwin fell.

The best fighter in the whole of Earl Lucan's retinue, save the earl himself, he had volunteered to stand alongside Lucan for the first guard, but almost immediately was hauled from the entrance by three or four of them, dragged to the ground and hammered around the bare head with rocks and stones. Lucan fell upon them, but the gigantic one – Babi – lurched forward, and Lucan was forced back into the shelter.

Babi's attack was the signal for a full-on second onslaught, the beasts cramming into the narrow arch. Lucan, now with Wulfstan by his side, let fly with a torrent of flashing steel. Monkey limbs fell; monkey faces were split from brow to chin. But the two knights were bitten and rent even through their mail. Hands strong as vices clamped around Wulfstan's throat and started choking the life from him. He gasped, wheezed, and slid down the cave wall. Another of the brutes sidled past and infiltrated the cave proper – it took Davy Lug's dagger to rip its belly open and spill its entrails. Lucan dispatched his two opponents and rounded on the one throttling Wulfstan, shearing through the nape of its neck.

Baboon corpses now filled the entrance, and this was enough to impede the third onslaught. Lucan stood back, leaning on the pommel of his sword, panting, sweating in rivers. Others took his and Wulfstan's places, yet more baboons soon vaulted over the barricade of dead flesh. Swords, axes and mallets rang on bone and sinew in that dark recess, now foul with blood and the stink of dying breath.

HAD ALARIC BEEN able to grease his naked form with pig-fat, he'd have found his passage through the twisting labyrinth easier. As it was, he was scraped and gouged, but almost as soon as he wormed his way into that torturous defile, a chink of light became visible. When he reached it, he found that it was nothing more than a reflection on a rock face; the true source was far overhead. The passage had become a chimney, though no chimney ever contorted as this one did. Even so, the lad snaked his way up, sweat stinging his eyes, his blood running freely. A speck of sky was visible, but it was still far above. Gasping with pain and effort, grunting incoherent prayers, he barked his shins and elbows, and cracked his head on jutting granite. The sounds of battle diminished to a distant, tinny clamour. Soon all he could hear was his own breath. But he was almost there. The air seemed fresher. The blot of sky now seemed the size of a table, but there was still some distance to go yet.

DOWN IN THE CAVE, two more fighters had been dragged to their deaths. Lucan had been forced back to the front simply because he was the closest. Davy Lug stood alongside him, wielding a flail. He threshed on the apes as though mad, but then Babi's massive claw raked across his face, ploughing flesh and bone, popping an eye from its socket. The archer tottered backward, screaming, and another knight, already wounded, took his place. A smaller ape came at this one and he skewered it, but so deeply did the blade of his sword bite and so slippery with blood was its hilt that it slipped from his grasp. The disarmed knight was taken by the legs, and dragged into their midst, where a hundred rocks rained on him.

For a moment Lucan stood alone.

His eyes locked on the yellow pinpoints under Babi's bony brow. The brute stretched open its massive maw, crouching and coiling its misshapen form as though ready to spring. The other baboons, of which there were still too many to count, also coiled. They would force their way inside through sheer weight of numbers. And then, suddenly, there was a thunderous grating and crashing from overhead – as though an avalanche of stone was descending.

What happened next was hidden from the men in the cave by a choking cloud of dust, filling their eyes and noses, coating them in fine white-grey powder. The noise was ongoing and cacophonous, yet grew louder and louder, forcing them to clamp hands to ears...

ALARIC HAD NOT intended to bring half the mountainside down.

On emerging far above the milling baboons, he had seen one boulder – an immense egg-shaped stone – perched precariously on the cliff edge. Jammed beneath it, at an angle which might provide leverage, was the broken bole of a tree. The naked boy put himself behind it and heaved. A first it seemed an impossible task, his muscles straining in his wounded flesh, sweat springing from his brow. But in that isolated moment there was surely no weight in the world that Alaric – the lives of whose friends depended on him – could not shift.

With a splintering of wood and grating of stone, the mighty rock slowly moved, and then, in an instant, dropped over the precipice. It struck one ledge after another before striking the apes, and in the process took down vast numbers of other boulders, which descended on the gibbering tribe in a colossal deluge of rubble and scree.

So much of the cliff-face disappeared that, as the dust settled, Alaric found he was able to walk down the rubble, picking an easy route.

One by one, his comrades emerged from the recess, coughing in the dust. If at any stage it had occurred to him that his rash act might have buried them alive, it had proved unfounded.

The baboon tribe had enjoyed less luck.

With the echoes of the landslide still ringing in their ears, Lucan and his handful of survivors descended. The terrain in front of them had changed beyond recognition. It was little more now than a vast apron of jumbled moraine – spreading not just down the hillside, but through the stockade and far into the village. Of the baboons, only the occasional crushed face or twisted, twitching limb poked above the surface.

Babi himself was more easily found; buried to mid-way up his shattered torso, his hide thick with dust and dirt. His left arm had broken off at the elbow, only a glinting white spear jutting through the gluey pulp. His jaw had smashed sideways, and both his eyes had gone. But he was still groping feebly about, a soft gurgling rising from deep inside him. Lucan watched dispassionately. When he pressed the tip of *Heaven's Messenger* against the monster's throat, and leaned slowly forward, it was not an act of mercy.

One or two baboons had survived on the peripheries of

the slide, and now bounced around on all fours, gibbering – though more with fear and confusion than anger. When Lucan brandished his sword at them and gave a battle howl, they fled.

"Did God supply you with a thunderbolt?" Maximion asked Alaric.

"I pray it was Him and not some other," Alaric replied.

He eyed Lucan, who turned and caught his gaze. This time, for once, the emboldened ex-squire did not look away.

TWENTY-EIGHT

As THEY ROSE higher into the Ligurian massifs, Trelawna wondered what kind of world her lover was taking her to. Rags of mist blew across a dismal, sloping landscape; a place of rocks, chasms and black, stunted trees. Each night, more soldiers slipped away under cover of dark. The tiny handful soon remaining was cold, tired and desperately hungry. Their mounts plodded listlessly, some lame, others simply exhausted.

"What is this place?" Trelawna asked. "This country, I mean?"

"Italy," Rufio replied. "You are now in Italy's far north."

She smiled wryly. "Every country has a north."

"Even my most loyal companions are abandoning me," Rufio complained. "They owe everything they have to my beneficence. I gave many their commissions. I promoted some from the ranks..."

"They don't want to die," she said simply.

"Which shows what a milk-livered bunch they are. We are a day's ride from Castello Malconi... one day, that's all, and the danger will be past."

"Tribune!" came a voice from behind.

They turned, to see a scout who had been posted at the rear galloping towards them. He was red-faced and sweating. Steam rose from his horse's flanks.

"Well?" Rufio demanded.

"It's Earl Lucan, sir. He's less than a day behind us."

Rufio placed a fist to his knotted brow. His eyes screwed shut.

"You can keep running, Felix, and hope we make it to Castello Malconi in time," Trelawna advised him. "Or I can do what I said... return to my husband and beg his forgiveness. If he kills me, he kills me... but at least the affair will be over."

"And how do I live with my conscience?" he replied. "If I send you to your death while I run for safety?"

"Your conscience hasn't troubled you much until now," Gerta muttered.

"Silence, you hag!" he screamed, pointing with trembling finger. "Trelawna, I swear... if your servant misspeaks herself one more time, I'll..."

"Gerta, you're not helping," Trelawna said tiredly.

Gerta returned Rufio's fierce glare. "Take it out on me if you wish, Roman lord... though you should be taking it out on your real enemy. Were you a knight of Albion you'd know there's only one solution to this problem. You would ride down there yourself and challenge Earl Lucan to single combat." She turned to her mistress. "But I'll hold my tongue from now on. I know how painful the truth can be."

She turned her animal around and rode slowly away.

Rufio watched her balefully, saying nothing, and gradually his expression slackened. "Single combat? Against the Black Wolf of the North..."

"Only a fool would consider such an option," Trelawna said.

"Maybe I'd rather be a fool than a coward."

"Felix...you're not actually considering this? You won't stand a chance."

Rufio reached to his waist and, still missing his sabre, drew instead his *gladius*. He glanced around, surveying the rock-strewn plateau on which they had halted. "This looks as good a place as any. Who knows... maybe God will guide my blade to his heart? If He doesn't, I'd like to know why. I'm a Roman officer and a gentleman, after all. I did my part to spread Christian civilisation."

"You can ask Him why personally," Trelawna retorted.

"Less than one minute after you've entered the field."

"If you've so little faith in my ability, Trelawna, at least have respect for my courage. That all-licensed wet-nurse of yours for once speaks true... I should have done this days ago. In any case, needs must. When that husband of yours catches up with us, who else will save me?"

"Gentlemen!" Trelawna cried, turning to the only two officers remaining, Centurion Marius, and a sub-tribune, Cohortis Bartolo. "Tell him he's throwing his life away!"

Both remained grim-faced. "Sometimes we must take hard decisions, ma'am," Marius said. "Value life too highly, and it ceases to be worth living."

Rufio turned back to the scout. "Ride down to that wretched little band and issue my challenge. In the meantime, Marius, you are charged with continuing the journey. Take my lady and her maid to Castello Malconi."

"At the very least, I should stay with you!" Trelawna cried.

But Rufio was resolute – he already regretted his decision, but he could not reverse it. She protested further, but Marius was only too glad to take her reins and lead her away.

"You hellish old cat!" she hissed at Gerta. "You've consigned my love to his grave!"

Gerta stared doggedly ahead. "He risked the same when he took arms against King Arthur."

"But he survived that. And now you've pitched him into the same fight again. Your vindictiveness has taken away my one chance of happiness. How dare you!"

"How dare *you*, mistress," Gerta retorted, her wizened cheeks reddening. "It's your girlish folly that brought us here, not mine."

Trelawna was too stunned to reply, so Gerta ranted on.

"When you were first taken as Earl Lucan's prize, I feared for you. I dreaded your fate in the hands of that dark, solemn warrior, and yet at no stage did I have the premonition of disaster that beset me when you made the ridiculous decision to run away with a milksop boy whose world was hanging by a slimmer thread than he could ever imagine."

"Hold your tongue!" Trelawna stuttered. "Who do you think you are addressing?"

"At present, mistress, I am addressing no-one. A once great lady who is now a chattel... a pawn in a game between warlords."

Trelawna could make no immediate response. She seethed with anger, but also with hurt. The truth of Gerta's tirade tore her insides, yet she could not bring herself to admit it. Everything she had once been – honoured noblewoman, adored beauty of King Arthur's court – was now gone, leaving a yawning gap in her life, to be replaced by Heaven knew what.

"And I've known you too long be fooled by this charade of anger," Gerta added. "You want this thing to end, just as I do."

"You think I want to see Felix die?" Trelawna said in disbelief.

"Perhaps not that, though it hardly matters. We're being sent to this fearsome fortress regardless, are we not?" Gerta's voice became hoarse with emotion. "So now we get the worst of both worlds."

FOR EARL LUCAN'S party, there'd been little time to recover.

Only eight now remained: Lucan himself, Alaric, Wulfstan, Maximion, Hubert, Guthlac, and Davy Lug. And, surprisingly, Malvolio.

They were back in what remained of the village when the chubby squire showed himself, emerging pale and cut across the brow from a dilapidated house. When the monster ape had hurled him, he'd smashed through a pair of shutters and into a heap of furniture. He'd lain there senseless through the entire fight – at least, this was the story he gave, though none of them had the energy to dispute with him. In fact, Alaric had been amused.

The burials followed with indecent haste. There was no time to swathe the broken forms in linen. A pit was dug and the dead were laid out. With no priest to sing a eulogy, Lucan spoke himself, his mailed hands clamped on the pommel of his longsword.

"Hail to those who gave their lives in service to overlord and King!" he cried. "Those of us remaining will honour their names and the memories of their deeds. We lay them now in soft earth to ease the passing of their ghosts, but to render it easier still we pledge a sacrifice of those who slew them. These sleeping sons of Albion will not have died for naught; peace will be theirs when all wrongs are righted, and blood for blood stains this black Roman earth."

"That invocation sounded pagan," Malvolio whispered afterwards.

"He's taking us beyond the scope of God's love," Alaric replied dully.

When the soil had been laid and a single wooden cross erected, they searched for their horses. A few mounts had survived, found scattered around the village or beyond the stockade. Many were bleeding, or lathered with sweat, but they were adequate for the survivors' needs. Nightshade was among them, which Lucan was grateful for. There was a single packhorse upon which they loaded the few stocks of food and drink they'd been able to preserve. The men were in an equally poor state – all hurt to some degree or other. A cloth bound the head of Davy Lug, concealing his torn eye-socket; it was already thick with clotted blood.

Before leaving, Lucan had them hitch the Scorpion to the tail of Malvolio's mount.

"That's a cumbersome cargo," Wulfstan observed. "It will slow us down."

"We need something with which to strike the Malconi ramparts," Lucan replied.

Wulfstan seemed dissatisfied with this. "My lord... might I appeal to your good sense?" Lucan regarded him stonily. "This machine is useful, but it will not replace those good men we have lost. The odds are increasingly stacked against us. No man would think the less of you for turning back now."

"If I cared what men thought of me, I wouldn't have come to begin with."

Again they followed the trail left by the fugitives, though this time Wulfstan had trouble thanks to the churned ground left by the baboon tribe. They only knew for sure they were on the right path a day later; they were ascending a steep trail through brakes of tangled, leafless thorns when they rounded a bend and found a horseman awaiting them.

"Greetings, Earl Lucan," he said, one hand raised.

"Who are you?" Lucan replied.

"Roberto Giolitti, outrider of the Fourteenth Legion."

Lucan regarded him skeptically. "Say your piece."

Giolitti nodded curtly, and issued Tribune Rufio's official challenge. At first Lucan thought he'd misheard. So did the rest of his men. They swapped wondering glances.

"Your master would fight *me*?" Lucan said.

"That's his desire. Too many others have died, he says."

"When and where?"

"There is a plateau an hour's ride to the east of here. He awaits your pleasure."

"Go ahead," Lucan replied. "We will follow."

The Roman wheeled his animal around and ascended the path. Lucan turned to his men. They still regarded him with wonder, though many wore hopeful smiles. Could their ordeal now be at an end? Was it possible that as soon as this evening they would be heading home again? Alaric looked unsure, and Wulfstan, by his frown, felt the same.

"This may be a trap," he said. "I wouldn't put it past them. They've used sorcery against us once already."

"They'll pay for that," Lucan replied. "When Felix Rufio lies dead on the field, the rest will hang." He caught Alaric regarding him with distaste. "Look at me that way if you wish, sirrah. But it's Arthur's law, not mine. Arthur rules these lands now... as the Malconi are about to learn."

TWENTY-NINE

THEY FOUND THE plateau, an exposed spot, very drear and rocky, with a belt of dark fir trees at its far side. Midway across, Giolitti had joined two other Roman soldiers, all on horseback. They wore the orange leggings and cloaks of the Fourteenth, but by their ornamented breastplates, roundels and greaves, and the plumes on their helms, the other two were high-ranking officers. One in particular, though he bore the same dents and abrasions of his comrades, had polished his plate so that it shone in the afternoon sun. His visor was drawn down, covering his face. Even from a distance Lucan could see that he was taut with fear.

As the new arrivals reined up, Giolitti approached them. "My master requests that you fight on foot," he said.

"On foot?" Lucan replied. "He's a cavalry officer, is he not?"

"His horse is lame."

"As you wish." Lucan and his men dismounted, Wulfstan signalling to Malvolio to take charge of the horses.

"There are some formalities first..." Giolitti began.

"There are no formalities," Lucan interrupted. "Let's get on with it."

He put on his helmet, drew *Heaven's Messenger* and was handed one of their few remaining shields, kite-shaped and painted jet-black. He advanced warily but confidently, the sword-blade angled on his right shoulder. By contrast, the visored Roman almost stumbled as he came forward. He'd drawn his *gladius* and hefted his round cavalry shield, which, though bossed and rimmed with iron, was far too small for hand-to-hand combat on foot.

The combatants halted when they were a couple of yards apart. In the intensity of the moment, it was probably understandable that neither noticed the favours bound to each other's hilts – a red scarf for Lucan, a blue scarf for Rufio.

Though well concealed beneath polished plate, the Roman's limbs were visibly shaking. In some ways this made it the more impressive that he had come here voluntarily. He must have known Lucan's reputation, and Trelawna would certainly have made an effort to stop him. Assuming, of course, that this actually *was* Felix Rufio.

Lucan removed his own helm and said: "Let me see your face."

The Roman lifted his visor. Only half the visage beneath was visible, but it was bathed with a sweat of fear. The eyes – bright, glassy baubles – had fixed on Lucan's pale, scarred features as though mesmerised. Lucan immediately recognised the man who had verbally jousted with him at Camelot. He briefly wondered, that this twitching, thin-whiskered thing, clearly so terrified of him, could really be the source of all his woe.

"Felix Rufio." Lucan's voice dripped ice. "Welcome to the end of your days."

"Wait!" Alaric cried. "Where is Countess Trelawna?"

Lucan glanced around, briefly puzzled. He'd expected Trelawna to be here, and it was a surprise to him that he had not noticed she wasn't. What that said about the fight and his reasons for it, he didn't like to ponder. He raised an eyebrow at Felix Rufio.

"In a place of safety," the Roman said.

"A place of safety?" Alaric replied. "What does that mean, exactly?"

"It means nothing," Lucan decided, pulling on his helmet. "Because from me, no such place exists. *En garde, Rufio!*"

Lucan lunged straight into the duel with a smashing overhead blow.

Rufio just had time to fend with his shield, which was cloven almost in two. He tottered backward. Lucan threw his own shield down; ostensibly a chivalrous measure, but now he took *Heaven's Messenger* in both hands. Those who knew him of old had witnessed the power of his double-handed blows. Rufio backed away, *gladius* still hefted, but the black-clad avenger stalked him like a panther. The longsword swept around again. Rufio deflected it with a ringing clash, but so fierce was the impact that it numbed him to the shoulder. Again he staggered away. Lucan pursued, the slanted eye-slots giving him a demonic appearance. He launched a third blow, now from overhead. Again Rufio parried; again he was jolted to the breastbone. He staggered, the sweat inside his helmet blinding him. Saliva bubbled from his lips as he tried to stop himself from whimpering in fear.

"Are you going to fight or keep running?" Lucan growled.

Rufio could barely think straight. Suddenly his entire world, his whole experience of life had condensed to this handful of seconds; his survival through each one was all that mattered. But the next blow came with such devastating power that the *gladius* was swept from his grasp and sent spinning across the ground.

Lucan lowered *Heaven's Messenger* and regarded the abject, cowering figure. Slowly, he removed his helmet and pulled back his coif. "Do you intend to die fighting like a man, or butchered like a hog?" he said. *"Pick that sword up!"*

Rufio tripped as he went after his weapon. He scrambled towards it on hands and knees, his Roman seconds watching in despair. When he grabbed the *gladius*, he stumbled back to his feet and waved it ineffectually.

"I've come all this way for such as you?" Lucan said. "I wouldn't normally sully my steel. But too many good men are groaning in the darkness, waiting for justice."

He drew *Heaven's Messenger* back for the final stroke – and it was taken from him.

Snatched from his hand.

By something that had descended from above.

Some *thing*.

It was essentially female, in that it had a head with long, streaming hair, and arms, legs and breasts, but in place of hands and feet were eagle's talons, and in place of skin it had a hard rind of greenish scales. It was immense in size; twice the height of a normal man, its bat-like wings spanning maybe fifteen feet. Its face was its most repellent aspect: a grotesque visage with bunches of bone sprouting from its brows and cheeks, a jutting chin and nose, and jagged spades for teeth. With an ululating shriek, it lofted skyward with its prize, a mane as wild and green as seaweed billowing around it.

At first the men could only gape, Briton and Roman alike.

Maximion, incredulous, shouted: *"Stymphalianus!"*[30]

The monster clutched *Heaven's Messenger* triumphantly as it hovered, wielding it by the hilt. Lucan could barely comprehend what he was seeing, although one reality stung him quickly: *Heaven's Messenger* – the sword his father had told him could never know defeat – was now, suddenly, to be turned against him.

The monster dropped with furious speed, and Lucan evaded the blade by inches, diving and rolling on the ground. Hubert, next in line, drew his own sword and parried the blow, but the winged monstrosity lashed out with its other claw and caught him by the harness, carrying him kicking and shouting into the air. It rose inexorably to ninety feet or more – and released him.

Hubert plummeted to earth in silence, landing with a ghastly *crunch* of bones.

In the midst of this mayhem, with men ducking for cover, Malvolio was unable to handle the horses. They tore free in their terror and bolted. Meanwhile, Rufio's Roman seconds dashed forward, hauled him to his feet and hustled him from the field.

---

[30]The *Stymphalides*, or Stymphalian birds (for Lake Stymphalia, where they roosted), were fierce man-eating birds in Greek myth. Heracles's sixth Labour was to destroy them, which he did by startling them into the air with a rattle and then shooting them down with a bow.

The winged horror swooped again on Lucan's scattering force. It cut Guthlac down with a blow across his shoulders, which cut through his leather hauberk and shore deep into the muscle and tendons beneath. The man-at-arms staggered forward and dropped, sliding to a halt on his knees – only for the beast to catch him with its feet and wing its way skyward again. His blood rained across the others as it tore and slashed him apart in mid-air, before hurling him in a tumbling arc.

Then the first arrow struck it.

Davy Lug – less the archer than he once was, having lost an eye – had still managed to retrieve several feathered shafts from the dead baboons in the village, and now launched them one after another. The fourth was the first to make real impact, transfixing the monster's right foot. The next caught it a glancing blow to its jutting, bony forehead, but sixth struck it clean in the right eye, burying itself in the soft pulp.

Squawking in rage, its wings beating frenziedly, the horror flitted back and forth overhead, clawing at the wound and smearing green blood across its miscreated face. It snapped the arrow shaft, leaving the iron barb in place. Lug drove another arrow at it; this one sunk half its length into the monster's left thigh. Its screams rose in pitch, becoming agonised as it soared upward and away. When maybe a hundred yards distant, it spun in the air to howl and gesticulate at them, before continuing to retreat, streamers of emerald blood trailing behind it.

Davy Lug dropped to one knee, exhausted. Wulfstan crawled on all fours towards Hubert, who was the closest casualty, but his body was utterly broken, beyond any help. Alaric's sword was drawn, but he stood rigid, eyes locked on the distant creature. Lucan turned to face the Romans, seeing two of them – including Tribune Rufio – back in the saddle, wheeling their horses around to escape.

He leapt to his feet, but neither Nightshade nor any of their other mounts were near at hand. The horses bounded back and forth in their terror, Malvolio staggering helplessly after them. Lucan glared at the squire, and then ran after the Romans on foot. Giolitti, who was still dismounted, stepped into his path, drawing his sabre. Lucan drew his dagger and struck out; the blow was parried, but packed such force that it knocked Giolitti off his feet. Lucan continued past him, although Rufio and his surviving second were now far across the rocky plain. Lucan hadn't even covered half the distance when the tail-end of their two horses vanished into the fir-wood. He slowed to a halt, breathing hard, sweating fiercely – and almost as an afterthought glanced over his shoulder, expecting Giolitti to have run up behind him. But the Roman had now been engaged by Alaric, sparks flying as their blades clashed.

Looking back around, Lucan spotted the two riders one final time, much higher up the treed slope, disappearing beyond a rise.

When he returned to the others, Giolitti's blade lay in the dust and he stood with hands raised, Alaric's sword-point at his throat. Wulfstan had also come over, leading his own horse by the reins. Malvolio stood some distance away, looking nervous, the other horses back under control. Lucan approached the prisoner, picking up the discarded sword and examining the curved blade as he did. It was about two-thirds the length of a normal sabre, but well-made – manufactured from strong steel and yet surprisingly light. Its edge, though scored from battle, was still very keen.

"Legionary Giolitti?" Lucan said.

Giolitti nodded tensely.

"You served under Felix Rufio on his campaigns?"

"I did, my lord."

"Did he inspire loyalty? He must have done, to encourage you to die in his place."

"My lord," Alaric said, "he has surrendered."

Lucan regarded his former squire with interest. "And what do you suggest, Alaric? Make *him* a captive too? When only five of us remain, one a snivelling loon... with scarce enough horses to carry our own supplies?"

"He's been disarmed. We could simply release him."

"There is a pack of Romans ahead of us on this mountain. You want to put one behind us as well?"

"My lord, look at this man. As soon as we release him, he'll run like a rabbit."

"To where, Alaric? He's closer to his master's refuge than he is to anywhere else."

Legionary Giolitti shook his head. "That's no refuge for me. I never wanted to go there in the first place. Hellish things are said to happen in Castello Malconi."

"Hellish things which you apparently embrace," Lucan said. "Luring us to this open space so your demon could attack us?"

Giolitti tried to swallow his fear. "No demon of mine, my lord."

"Nevertheless, it's your misfortune to have supplied the lure."

"That was unintentional. I had no idea the demon would attack."

"I'm afraid the deaths of our friends must be answered..."

"My lord, please," Alaric said.

"I've never been a willing servant of Tribune Rufio," Giolitti pleaded.

"Yet you came with him this far."

"When there was a whole company of us, and military rules applied. But like you, we've suffered losses. Only a handful remains."

"Your party was attacked as well?"

"Not attacked, but... men slunk away in the darkness."

Lucan pondered this. "So other Romans are already loose on these slopes? Maybe among these rocks? They could be stringing arrows on us right now."

"My lord, please," Alaric said again.

"Enough talk." Lucan hefted the sabre. "Make your peace with God, legionary, and I'll make your journey to Him a swift one."

"*NO, MY LORD!*" Alaric bellowed, swinging around and pointing his longsword at his master's chest. "I... I won't allow it."

There was a brief, ear-pummeling silence.

For the first time in as long as any could remember, Earl Lucan seemed surprised. His lips tightened; his grey eyes narrowed imperceptibly.

"This is not the way of the Round Table," Alaric stammered.

Lucan said nothing. His gaze burned into the defiant youth.

"My lord... you are not thinking clearly. The serpent venom has damaged your mind. Your hatred for these people has gone beyond reason. And your soul will pay the price."

"Put up your sword," Lucan said quietly. "Or, so help me, I'll cross it with mine."

"I'm prepared to take that chance."

"All our men are dead because of these murderers..."

"No, my lord! Not because of *them*. Because of *you*." Alaric could hardly believe what he was saying; he almost choked on the words, but they flowed from him anyway. "Forgive me, but it's time for the truth. Your pride condemned your *mesnie* to death, as surely as Emperor Lucius's pride condemned his army. There's nothing any of us can do now that will bring them back, but I'm damned if I'm going to stand by and let more blood be shed for no good reason."

Giolitti glanced from one to the other, beaded with sweat. Malvolio watched with a kind of fascinated horror. Slowly, Wulfstan came to his master's side.

"Kill Alaric, my lord, and you reduce our fighting potential by a fifth. As things are, I'm not sure how we'll take Castello Malconi, but to weaken us further would be unwise."

"I'm only trying to do what's right," Alaric added. "In a better time, you would do the same, my lord. I know you would."

"Foolish whelp," Lucan whispered. "You realise I can never trust you after this?"

"With all respect... I don't think there will be an 'after this.'"

Lucan lowered the Roman sword. "If there is, be assured... we'll discuss this incident, at some length."

Alaric nodded and lowered his own weapon. He mopped the

sweat from his brow, and glanced around – to see Maximion watching from several yards away. He'd expected to find approval in the elderly officer's face, but now saw only fear. It so distracted Alaric that he didn't notice Earl Lucan kick the side of Giolitti's knee. Sinew cracked and the soldier gasped. His leg buckled and he dropped to all fours. The sabre flashed, and his head fell.

Alaric spun around again, horror-struck.

Lucan faced him coldly. "I won't let prepubescent folly endanger this quest. If you wish to level your steel again, be my guest... but it will serve no purpose now."

Alaric's sword was still clasped in his hand, but he could only gape at the decapitated form on the ground. Lucan turned his back and walked away, approaching Maximion.

"When that monster first attacked, you gave it a name?" he said.

Maximion initially found it difficult to respond. He stared fixedly at Giolitti's truncated corpse. "Stym... Stymphalianus."

"Another demon of the ancient world?"

"According to the folklore of the Greeks, there was a whole flock of them – winged monstrosities from the swamps of Arcadia. They were reared by the god Ares..."

"And how many such horrors can this sorceress summon?"

Maximion shook his head. "I must guess that she can't do it indefinitely... else she'd be ruler of the Empire herself, with a host of abominations at her bidding."

"My lord!" Wulfstan interrupted. "If this she-devil has such powers..."

"The Round Table did not make its reputation by fleeing in the face of evil," Lucan replied.

"Nor did it by throwing away the lives of its men in futile quests for vengeance," Maximion said.

Lucan gave a wintry smile. "In due course, we'll see how futile this quest is."

"Might I remind you, my lord," Wulfstan said, "that of all gathered here, only *you* are a Knight of the Round Table!"

Lucan regarded him carefully. The older knight's face was ingrained with dirt, cut with runnels of sweat. Though an outdoorsman by training, he looked so haggard and bedraggled that it was difficult to imagine he could keep on going.

"I see," Lucan said. "You wish me to proceed alone?"

"Your words, not mine," Wulfstan replied. "But if any scribe ever makes a record of this expedition, I'd like it noted that I proceeded from this point under duress."

"Dissent on all sides, Earl Lucan," Maximion said.

"And the Stymphalianus somewhere overhead," Lucan growled, glancing skyward. The others also looked up. "That's right, gentlemen. The Stymphalianus still lives, and will attack us again. That is its sole purpose in visiting this mortal realm. Any one of you is now free to leave. But I'd imagine its purpose is to hunt and kill us all. So good luck on your solo travels. Alas, Tribune Maximion, you may *not* leave – you are still my prisoner and have a duty to perform. However, in that respect you are fortunate, because I will protect you. No harm must befall you before you've guided me to Castello Malconi."

"And after that?" Maximion wondered.

Lucan shrugged. "After that I'll have no use for you."

THIRTY

THE LAST LEG of Trelawna's journey was the most arduous she had ever known.

They followed a narrow, uneven road, along an undulating spine of rock, on either side of which lay appalling chasms. Strong winds buffeted them; icy rain drenched them. All three – Trelawna, Gerta and their sole escort, Centurion Marius – were weary to the point of collapse. Their horses walked slowly, stumbling constantly. When they finally left the exposed ridge, they entered a deep cleft, a tight passage between sheer granite walls. For several hours they followed this torturous route, passing beneath rusted portcullises which were raised and unguarded.

The journey's end came as dusk was falling. They left the narrow way and found themselves on the lip of a crevasse, crossed by a wooden drawbridge, on the far side of which an arched, black tunnel led into the belly of a colossal stone fortress. In the middle of the bridge, a figure waited for them. He stood eight feet in height, his gargantuan form draped in crimson robes and cowl. When he glanced up to appraise them, a truly monstrous face was exposed – brutish and bestial, covered with silver-grey fur.

Fingers of ice touched Trelawna's heart. She still remembered the haunting dream she'd suffered on the night she'd thought Lucan was dying – the pursuit through the thorn-wood by something more terrible than she could ever imagine. The very *thing* that now seemed to be blocking their path to the castle.

Centurion Marius dismounted and led his animal onto the drawbridge.

"I am Leobert Marius, *Centurion Primus* of the Fourteenth Legion," he said. "I come here under license of Tribune Felix Rufio, charged with escorting his bride-to-be and her servant-woman. We have travelled long and hard, and would appreciate admittance."

The bestial face glowered at him with indifference. Only after an age did the powerful figure turn away and walk towards the entrance passage. Marius indicated the two women should follow. They dismounted and led their animals forward, glancing fearfully into the lightless depths below.

The entrance tunnel was built from bare, echoing rock and black with grime. In the courtyard, more bare brickwork soared on all sides. There were interior windows, but most were arrow-loops. The only light came from a single candle, now carried down a steep stair by a servant dressed in sackcloth. He was hideously disfigured, with a crooked back and lumpen feet, but behind him descended someone who simply had to be Duchess Zalmyra. The noblewoman was tall and swathed tightly in a brown woollen wrap, which left her arms and shoulders bare but accentuated her statuesque proportions. Her slick black hair was braided into a single rope and hung over her left shoulder. Her beauty was intense but severe – the sort men would die for, and in many cases probably had. She approached the new arrivals with a slow, elegant tread, and circled around them. When she finally halted, she touched Trelawna's hair, which had become stringy and straw-like.

"Well, you're a pretty enough little thing," the duchess commented. "You'd fetch a good price in a whorehouse."

"Fie!" Gerta cried. She'd been quiet and pale in the cheek for the tail-end of the journey, but now her old spirit returned. "This is the Countess of Penharrow! How dare you address her so!"

"This harridan's tongue offends me," Zalmyra said to her servant. "Take it from her."

Urgol grabbed Gerta's throat in a single paw and lifted from her feet. The maid squawked in terror. Trelawna screamed and tried to intervene, while Marius stood by, helpless. But then another voice was heard.

"Mother... desist!"

Rufio and his last officer had emerged on horseback from the entry passage. Both men and animals looked utterly drained, and were caked with dirt.

Zalmyra raised a hand, and Urgol released Gerta, who collapsed, gagging, into the arms of her mistress. Trelawna was at first too astonished that Rufio was alive to even speak. After lowering Gerta onto her haunches, she hurried over.

"Mother... this is the woman I love," Rufio stammered. "What's more, she and her party have come here as our guests."

"Guests show invitations and bring gifts," Zalmyra said coldly. "These, I suspect, have brought only trouble."

"I brought the trouble," he retorted, taking Trelawna in his arms – as much to support himself as to show affection. "If you want to reckon with someone, reckon with me."

"Don't tempt me, Felix," the duchess said, turning on her heel and leaving the courtyard, Urgol and her candle-bearer trailing after her.

"We rode hard to catch up with you," Rufio gasped.

"I felt sure you'd be dead," Trelawna replied, tears glazing her eyes.

"I may as well be." He extracted himself from her embrace. "It was none of my doing."

"Does that mean Lucan is alive, too?"

"You sound as if you hope he is," he said. Trelawna was surprised by that – more so because it was true. If Rufio suspected it, he seemed too exhausted to care. "I can only tell you that he was still alive when I left him."

He went on to explain about the aerial monstrosity that had attacked mid-way through their duel, and how he had seen it tear at least one of her husband's followers to bloody rags. But there was no joy in his face as he recalled the horror.

"He gave me a chance... can you believe that?" He chuckled with bewilderment. "Your husband. He bade me pick up my sword after he knocked it from my hand. But I don't think it was out of kindness. I think he just found it impossible to imagine that a man like me had walked away with his prize possession. At the very least he wanted to see a warrior in me." Rufio's face twisted in self-loathing. "I'd rather he'd run me through."

Trelawna tried to take him in her arms again, but he pushed her off.

"Lucan is an expert fighter," she said. "That is why Arthur rewards him with lands and titles. There's no shame in being defeated by him. At least you're alive..."

"I've not been defeated yet!" Rufio snarled. "If Lucan's still alive, things will only get worse for him the closer he comes to Castello Malconi. Nearly all his men are dead. He himself is a battle-scarred relic. But mother won't stop there. No-one challenges our family and lives. Which reminds me... keep out of mother's way. I don't think she sees any value in our relationship."

Unsure how she should respond to that, Trelawna tried to take his hand, but he waved her away and strode towards the nearest door. Apparently, he was too tired for further conversation.

"Welcome to your new home," Gerta said wearily.

THIRTY-ONE

Lucan's party ascended doggedly over ever steeper, more rugged terrain, and through drifting palls of mist. There were terrible sounds from the high places around them: screeching and what sounded like multiple roaring voices echoing down the great, rocky gullies.

In due course, their road led up onto a narrow ridge with sheer slopes dropping into bottomless voids. They traversed it in single file: Lucan at the front, Wulfstan behind him, then Maximion, Davy Lug, Alaric and, last of all, Malvolio, whose horse drew the archery machine at its tail, the great mechanism groaning and creaking. The ridge road rose and fell through troughs and peaks, and its surface was rutted and uneven. The going was slow and difficult. At last, Malvolio's beast, which was the most encumbered, halted in its tracks and no amount of spurring and whipping would urge it forward.

"My lord," Malvolio called weakly. "This animal cannot continue. The arbalest is too much for her."

Lucan glanced back along the line. Malvolio's horse's head drooped. Froth seethed from its quivering nostrils. "Cut it loose," he shouted. "Let the animal follow at its own pace. You walk."

More crestfallen than he had been at any stage so far, Malvolio turned in the saddle, seeking to unfasten the tether connecting it with the archery machine.

And with a searing screech, the Stymphalianus swooped.

Its target was the man who had hurt it so grievously.

Davy Lug had turned in the saddle, when the great, leathery body flashed past him, a single talon slicing his throat from ear to ear. He sagged sideways from his mount, eyes wide, clawing at the gaping wound from which a crimson torrent already spouted. Still screeching, the Stymphalianus wheeled and surged back down, wielding *Heaven's Messenger* like a lance, aiming directly at Lucan's heart. He parried the first stroke with the Roman sabre – with such force that the longsword was knocked free and thudded point-first into the ground – yet at the same time the monster caught a clump of his hair, hauling him out of his saddle. Lugged ten feet in the air, Lucan slashed upward, cutting cleanly through his own black locks. He landed back on the ridge road, the wind crushed out of him.

The Stymphalianus swooped again, its massive wings beating like battle-drums. Anyone who looked closely – and the men did, still mesmerised by the speed of the attack – would have seen that its wounded eye-socket was now a yawning crater, glutted with green gore, where it had yanked the arrowhead loose, taking bone and flesh with it. A broken shaft still protruded from its thigh. Alaric launched a javelin, but it glanced from the monster's scaly hide. Its ravaged, demonic face twisted with glee as it struck down at him. He hefted his shield, stopping the beast's claws, but was hurled from his saddle.

The winged horror now launched itself towards Maximion, who ducked frantically. Its claws raked across the back of his scalp and neck, drawing gouts of blood. Wulfstan was next in its path, although he had wheeled his horse around and was facing it with broadsword drawn. It halted directly above him, snatching and slashing as he hacked at it. With a *chunk*, his blade made contact with its left foot, and two of its clawed toes were severed. Howling, it veered away and bore down on Malvolio, who still sat goggle-eyed.

Lucan, who had got back to his feet, flung the sabre. It spun past Wulfstan and struck the monster on the wing, slicing the taut green membrane. The beast veered leftward, squawking in pain, but grabbed at Malvolio's shoulder with its uninjured foot, fishhook claws sinking through mail and into flesh, and then hoisted him kicking and shrieking into the air – except that, thanks to its wounded wing, it no longer had the strength to soar away.

It was an advantage Wulfstan could not ignore.

He dropped his sword, stood in his stirrups and, using his saddle as a springboard, hurled himself upward, grabbing for his squire's feet, but missing those and instead catching the strip of bloody skin hanging from the monster's wing.

The Stymphalianus swerved from the ridge, the ground plunging steeply away beneath it, the two men still dangling, but it again failed to gain height – in fact, it was slowly dropping. Its screeches of rage became squeals of pain as a great portion of its wing was gradually torn from the bone. Wulfstan knew that he was finished; the fleshy flap he clung to was only attached by a thread of tissue. Just before it broke, he caught a last despairing glimpse of Malvolio's face, bloodless and terrified.

"Hang on!" Wulfstan bellowed. *"Just hang on!"*

And then he was gone, turning over and over, his limbs flailing as he tumbled into the abyss. Malvolio had no time to scream. The claw fixed into his shoulder seemed to be weakening, so he took a firm grip on it, both hands locking around the ankle-joint. The Stymphalianus was falling ever faster; they began to spiral downward. The creature's squawks became choked gurgles. Malvolio could barely catch his breath. From his perspective, the world was cavorting end over end – rocks and sky, rocks and sky.

It was pure fortune that when they struck solid ground, the creature was beneath him. Even so, Malvolio received a massive jolt. He rolled away, agonised, each breath rasping through his chest like the blade of a saw, but knowing that his peril was not passed. Whimpering, he managed to lever himself up into a crouch. He was on a steep hillside comprised mainly of rocks and spiky grass. He was unsure how many hundreds of feet down from the ridge he'd fallen, but close by him the slope ended in a precipice, and he could see clouds passing below.

He turned again – and saw the Stymphalianus, prone and senseless, tangled in the tatters of its own wings, one of them a mangled wreck. One of its legs had folded beneath it at a gruesome angle. It glanced up at him, but its one remaining eyelid fluttered as though barely conscious. Gasping, Malvolio grabbed up the nearest stone, a heavy disk of granite, and heaved it towards the monster, which gave a thin, keening wail. He raised the stone high and brought it down on the fiendish skull, not once, but three, four, five times – brutal, bone-crunching blows, which systematically flattened it to a pulp.

When he'd finished, he sank to his haunches again, his chest heaving and aching. A few minutes later, his sobs of pain became sobs of grief – twenty yards higher up the slope, he'd just spied the body of Wulfstan. The old knight lay jack-knifed backward over a tooth of rock. His mouth had frozen open, and his eyes were lifeless.

THIRTY-TWO

Despite their fatigue, Trelawna and Gerta did not sleep well in their first night at Castello Malconi.

The guest-chambers they had been allocated were austere but not uncomfortable, comprising a small privy and a sleeping area, its walls hung with woven cloths, its floor covered by a carpet. It contained a double-sized bed and two armchairs, facing each other across a bearskin rug laid in front of a hearth that was already crackling. The narrow window, which looked down over the courtyard, sat at the end of a deep embrasure, behind a tapestry depicting naked nymphs at play in a spring, with satyrs peeking slyly from the surrounding foliage.

On first seeing this, Trelawna was briefly reminded of her imagined home in the sun-drenched south – troubadours, poetry and the *Cult d'Amor*. But then the night came, and their fire and candles winked out, and a deeper darkness than they'd ever known fell over Castello Malconi.

They had seen neither hide nor hair of Felix Rufio or Centurion Marius since first being led up here by another of the duchess's hunchbacked servants, this one female and very ancient, with abhorrent, lopsided features. Though she had told them that a bathroom could be found at the end of the passage, they only dared venture that way once, and it was so dark that they soon scurried back. The entire fortress now droned to the mountain wind. From unseen regions, above and below, they fancied they heard voices – groans of pain alternating with malicious, tittering laughter. Once there came a whispering at their keyhole. Whatever it was, it spoke in an unknown tongue, though they felt certain the message it imparted was obscene. Trelawna attempted to re-light the candles, but unseen breaths blew their flames out. The two women, neither of whom had ever felt this vulnerable or alone, could do naught but huddle beneath the quilt and embrace each other, shivering with fear.

After what seemed an eternity, Trelawna slept, only for a knock at the door to suddenly rouse her. On the pillow next to her, Gerta remained deeply asleep.

A voice sounded. "Countess? It is I, Marius."

When Trelawna opened the door, she could have cried for joy at the sight of the soldier waiting beyond, even though she barely knew him.

Centurion Marius was of the yeoman class, but he possessed a simple courage and honesty, which appealed to her greatly since her world had fallen into such turmoil. He was middle-aged, of squat build and heavily muscled; his complexion was beef-red from long hours spent outdoors, and his face disfigured by many old cuts. But by simply attending to her needs during the journey here, he had won her over. He was now stripped of his arms and armour, wearing only his maroon breeks and a coarse woollen under-tunic. But it was all she could do not to throw herself into his arms.

"Forgive my absence last night," he said. "I would have stood guard, but I was shown to a barrack-room and once darkness fell I didn't know my way around."

"That's quite understandable," she replied. "We couldn't find our way around, either. We didn't even get the chance to bathe."

"There's a bathing area not too far from here. Would you like me to escort you?"

"What time is it, Marius?"

"Almost eight of the clock, ma'am. The sun is up, though there's heavy cloud cover and I can hear distant thunder."

Trelawna was unconcerned about the weather. The fact that daylight was spilling along the passage was enough for her. She gathered the towels. "If you could show me to the bathroom, Marius, I'd appreciate it."

DUCHESS ZALMYRA HAD risen early that morning to observe her scrying-orbs.

Nothing she saw pleased her, so she ascended to Castello Malconi's main reception hall. This was octagonal in shape, its black marble floor carved with astrological symbols, its pillars cut with the heads of esoteric figures. There she waited impatiently until the two guests she had summoned attended her. They were her son, Tribune Felix Rufio and her brother, Bishop Severin Malconi. Both were tousled by sleep and only partly dressed. She had ensured, before their arrival, that their apartments would contain none of the luxuries they were used to.

She regarded them from a raised, high-backed seat. Over her normal garments, she wore a trailing house-robe stitched together from the tawny hides of lions, their manes lying thick and lush across her shoulders.

"Zalmyra!" Bishop Malconi cried. "My quarters are infested with cockroaches!"

She arched an eyebrow. "I hoped it would remind you of your house on Capri."

"And my room is the last word in asceticism!" Rufio complained. "It has nothing in it save a truckle-bed!"

"A reminder of the life you perhaps *should* have had."

The bishop was still spluttering with indignation. "But why? What is..."

"Enough gabble!" she said sharply. "This Knight of the Round Table you have managed to offend is apparently quite dauntless. He comes on apace. I forecast he will be at our gates in the next few hours."

Both men looked dumbfounded.

"Destroy him!" the bishop finally said.

"No qualms now about my summoning the things of darkness, brother?"

"This man seeks to do murder. He must pay whatever price is deemed fit."

She pondered. "He and his band have already dispatched two powerful guardians. It now falls on me to call something far more terrible. But these are complex rituals and will require time and sacrifice. All your Praetorians are positioned in the gatehouse?"

Malconi nodded. "All of them."

"Send a message. When Earl Lucan arrives, they are to fight him to the last man."

"How many does he have with him?"

"One."

"*One!*" Malconi looked even more startled, though not disagreeably so. He'd been expecting Lucan to have an army.

"But he and his companions have thus far displayed exceptional courage," she added.

The bishop shrugged. "My men fear no-one. And rightly so. They are easily the most vicious..."

"Enough bragging, Severin! You are partly to blame for this disaster."

"Me?"

She leaned forward. "This house cannot fall just because the Roman Empire has fallen. If *you* had not failed to curtail the lusts of that hot-blooded fool next to you, the war would now be centred on the capital. Our fastness would remain unmolested."

"Zalmyra..." Malconi tried to laugh it off. "Entire barbarian hordes have perished attacking this fortress. Do you expect two men to...?"

"*Do you not hear what I say?*" she thundered, her face a livid scarlet.

He drew back, abashed.

"They have come this far, haven't they?" she shouted. "And they have beaten every obstacle I've put in their path. Now stand your men in readiness, Severin... and advise them that any who run will die in my dungeons over decades! *Go!*"

The bishop headed glumly for the exit, closing the door behind him.

Zalmyra rounded next on her son. "And *you!*"

"Never fear," he said. "I will fight too..."

"You will do no such thing. I observed your first pathetic attempt to stop this man."

"I'll do better next time," he said, determinedly.

"Next time he will kill you. It was only my intervention that saved you before."

"Things will be different now we have nowhere else to run. Mother, Trelawna means more to me than I can say. Whatever happens, I won't let him take her..."

"There is more here at stake than your golden-haired strumpet!"

Like his uncle, Rufio hung his head.

"*You* are the House Malconi," she added. "The last male heir. We can ill afford to throw your life away in a futile gesture. So when our enemies arrive, you will hide."

He glanced up at her, astonished.

"Where is that fellow who came with you?" she asked.

"Bartolo? Sleeping... in a proper bed at long last, which is less than he deserves. He's the only one to remain loyal to me."

"Wake him and send him to the gatehouse."

"While I hang back from the fight? How will that look?"

"I care not. This is my house and these are my rules. If he doesn't like them he can take his chances outside. Now wake him, Felix, or I will send him such dreams as to make his journey through our mountains seem like a year in Elysium."[31]

---

[31]"Elisionne," per Malory. Elysium is the Classical Roman name for Paradise. As a pagan, Zalmyra would presumably not speak of the Christian Heaven.

THIRTY-THREE

AFTER SHE HAD bathed and dressed in a fresh gown and kirtle, Trelawna ascended to the high battlements, Marius keeping her company. She combed out her tresses as she strolled to the parapet and was faced by a nightmarish vista of barren peaks, deep ravines and razor-topped crags.

"The magnificence that was Rome," she mused. "It doesn't look like much of an Empire from here, does it?"

"This isn't the Empire, ma'am," Marius answered. "Just an outpost of it. Though I doubt, when your King Arthur is finished, there'll be much else left."

"*My* King Arthur? I think you'll find, centurion, that in my homeland I'm now as much an enemy of the state as you are."

"I can't believe that in a chivalrous land a damsel like you will be punished."

"Oh, in our chivalrous land, damsels like me – who plot against their husbands – are *severely* punished."

A moment passed before Marius asked: "Did you plot?"

"It could be construed that way," she said. "I consorted with the enemy."

"*How* will they punish you?"

"We call it petty-treason, and the penalty is to be burned at the stake."

Marius looked genuinely shocked. "King Arthur imposes such a barbarous law?"

"He hasn't, thus far. But King Uther did many times. And the law still exists."

"Forgive me for saying so, my lady, but you seem fearless in the face of this threat."

She continued to comb her damp locks. "I suspect my husband will not permit it."

"Even though *he* is the one who seeks to return you to face justice?"

Trelawna's mouth curled into a half-smile. "He doesn't seek to return me, Marius. Neither to face justice, nor anything else."

"Is he truly so vengeful?"

"At one time I'd have said 'no.'" She looked thoughtful. "There was always a darkness inside him – his father was a devil in human guise. But things had changed. Lucan had mellowed. And then I did what I did, and now everything has changed back."

"Don't concern yourself." Marius straightened up. "I will protect you."

"You are a brave and honourable man," she replied. Under her breath, she added, "But who, my gallant Roman, will protect *you*?"

Louder, she said: "Where do you come from, Marius? Surely you have a wife and children?"

"I do, my lady. They are at home now –" His words were cut off sharply, with a heavy *thud*.

Trelawna spun around.

Centurion Marius fell at her feet, blood streaming down his face; what looked like a hand-axe was buried in the top of his skull. Behind him stood Duchess Zalmyra's giant servant, the one called Urgol, now wearing only a leather loincloth. "You must come with me, countess," he growled.

Horror-struck, Trelawna backed against the battlements.

"No... no..." Marius stammered. Eyes rolling, delirious with pain, he tried to get back to his feet, snatching at Urgol, seizing handfuls of silver-grey fur. "I won't let..."

Urgol took Marius in both hands and tossed him over the parapet.

Trelawna leaned through an embrasure, watching in horror as the body cart-wheeled down the cliff-face, somersaulting as it bounced from obstructions. A massive paw caught her shoulder; she attempted to pivot away, screaming, only for a second paw to clamp over her mouth. The monstrous figure regarded her.

"Even to eyes like mine, you are well-made for bedding," he growled. "But now you have a *real* purpose."

She bit hard into the thick leathery pad of Urgol's palm, and he yanked it away.

"Murdering brute!" she spat. "You are a disgrace to your nation."

Urgol showed ivory teeth. "What do you know of my nation, little white ewe?"

"You are a woodwose.[32] Your people were once the princes of Europe."

"And then the Romans came. And they drove us to near extinction."

"My people suffered the same fate."

He grabbed hold of her, and threw her over his shoulder. "You are all Romans to me..."

Trelawna wailed and kicked, drumming her fists on his broad back, but he ignored her, descending from the battlements via a dark switchback stair. For minutes on end they forged downward, until, at the bottom, deep in the castle's bowels, they came to a colossal oaken door studded with nail heads. Urgol drew a key from his belt and unlocked it. Sensing that only horror lay beyond this portal, Trelawna renewed her struggle, finally catching Urgol a blow in the middle of his nobbled spine. He grunted, and slapped her on the buttocks. She cried out with pain, and his Herculean shoulders shook, a guttural rumble sounding from his belly as he laughed at her.

[32]Middle English. The "wild man of the wood," which appears widely in heraldic images and in carvings in English churches, much like the Green Man.

He slapped her again, and again, laughing louder and louder.

Though there was no light down there, Urgol strode with confidence, making each turn readily. Trelawna clung to the apelike fur in terror as they descended another steep stair, this one made from iron and dropping through open space. It was dizzying; she felt that if she fell now, she would never stop falling. They entered another enclosed corridor, passing rooms filled with eerily coloured lights. Bare chambers glimmered blood-red; book-lined workshops shimmered in aqua-blue. Other passages meandered away, some indigo, others ochre-yellow. And always the darkness was present – clotted oily blackness filling every niche. She passed a wall of bars on her left, behind which the firelight illuminated three rotted corpses; little more than bones and gristle, suspended against the far wall by high wrist-shackles. To her disbelief, they looked up, their desiccated skulls turning to watch as she was carried past.

"Countess Trelawna!" a sepulchral voice called after her, from one of the corpses. "Your treachery has found you out... just as ours did!"

Too numbed to reply, Trelawna craned her neck around to see where she was being taken to. Through the colour-streaked darkness a chilling figure was coming towards them: vast of height and girth, with a visage that was a cross between a devil-mask and a demented ape. She spotted the pale oval of her own face peering over its shoulder, and realised it was a mirror; but when they reached it, her reflection in the mirror grinned and pointed at her.

"She who is fairest of them all will not be so for much longer," it cackled.

The next door they came to was almost rusted into place – so stiff that even Urgol had to force it with his shoulder. And this was the moment Trelawna had been awaiting. Feeling him relax his grip, she threw herself sideways and was free. She alighted on the passage floor and ran blindly, ducking through the rainbow-hued labyrinth, sobs of terror caught in her throat, eyes streaming tears – and running hard into a tall figure blocking her path.

She fell backward, gasping – and found herself gazing up into the coldly beautiful features of Duchess Zalmyra. The tall noblewoman wore a sleeveless gown of semi-translucent black silk, held at the shoulder with a dragon clasp and cinched at the waist with a slender gold chain. Her hair still hung in a single glossy braid. But this time she was smiling gently.

"Countess?" She put a hand on Trelawna's shoulder. "Something distresses you?"

"That creature..." Trelawna stammered. "The woodwose... he tried to abduct me."

Zalmyra frowned. "How dare he? You are my guest."

"And he killed Centurion Marius."

"Marius?"

"My bodyguard. The one posted by your son. Urgol killed him with an axe, and threw his body from the battlements."

"So as well as giving up his life to protect your honour, that brave soldier of Rome also gave up any chance of a Christian burial?" But now there was something in the duchess's tone which seemed a little mocking. "No matter on that score, countess. The carrion birds of this valley have become very used to our table-leavings."

Trelawna sensed the gigantic figure approach from behind. He clamped her arms with his hairy paws, and she closed her eyes in revulsion as Zalmyra ran cold fingers across her cheek.

"I'm so glad you came to this place of your own volition, my dear. A *willing* sacrifice is much more acceptable to the dark powers."

Trelawna tried to struggle again, but Urgol held her firmly.

"Your infernal husband," Zalmyra added, "and I used that description advisedly, has destroyed everything I've sent against him. It has cost him dear – both in friends and in the ultimate salvation of his soul. But that doesn't seem to have troubled him. Hence, I must provide an opponent that will *really* stretch his abilities. *Take her!*"

Urgol carried Trelawna through to a place more hideous than anything she had yet seen: a brick well lit by greenish fire, from the depths of which a cloying, sulfurous fog slowly rose.

"Welcome to my Pit of Souls," Zalmyra said as Urgol tore off Trelawna's clothing.

When she was completely naked, he spread her against one of two wooden saltires, which faced each other across a steel grille overhanging the well, and shackled her. Trelawna's feet slid in a slimy detritus, which she felt certain was blood. She tilted her chin proudly as Zalmyra came close.

"My dear Countess Trelawna... I trust you are a God-fearing woman?"

"Certainly I am! And you will never take that from me, you witch!"

Zalmyra smiled. "I wouldn't dream of it. A martyr is a rare commodity these days."

Trelawna bit on her lip, trying not to show the terror the word 'martyr' instilled in her.

"Mind, I don't mean to put *you* on that high pedestal," Zalmyra said. "What would Jesus Christ think... a common adulteress? But deep down, I believe you are essentially a good, kind person. Virtues which are saintly enough. And you were born of noble blood." Zalmyra's smile curved like a sickle. She produced a long, crooked blade. "The pumping hearts of peasant girls and harlots are useful to a degree, but the heart of a Christian noblewoman? Well, you can imagine the price I'll command."

Trelawna was determined to remain bold. No matter what torment they inflicted on her, she would beg nothing from these degenerate vermin, and yet she knew they were entirely serious. This was not just some pantomime to frighten her.

"*Pegfal vus ga ravalax!*" Zalmyra cried, raising her knife on high.

"Be warned, witch!" Trelawna stated defiantly. "Your son loves me."

"So I've heard..."

"Kill me and he'll despise you."

"He already does. It's something I've learned to live with. *Stevros thralanto paiador! More-ud uvusona anaxus...* "

"Can you live with the knowledge that you'll have killed your grandchild?"

Zalmyra ceased her chanting. She lowered the blade. Urgol stepped forward from the shadows. The vile twosome exchanged curious glances.

"It's true, Duchess," Trelawna said quickly, almost breathless. "I carry the Malconi heir in my womb."

"Felix never mentioned this."

"Felix doesn't know."

"Why doesn't he know?"

"No-one knows. I didn't mention it for fear the story would endanger my annulment."

Zalmyra smiled cruelly. "You are lying, countess. I can see it in your face."

"What you see in my face is the fear of a mother who may never see her child. Just as I see the fear in your face that you may never see your grandchild."

There was a long, intense silence, before Zalmyra sheathed her blade. "It may be that you are more useful to us alive after all. Urgol, release her."

The woodwose unshackled Trelawna from the saltire and thrust the ragged bundle, which was all that remained of her clothes, into her arms, before hustling her along the nearby passage. When he returned to the Pit of Souls a short time later, his mistress was as he'd left her, gazing pensively down the fume-filled shaft.

"We promised the dark gods a grand gift," she said, "and we must give them one. But if a Christian noblewoman is unavailable, maybe a Christian nobleman will do instead. Where are my brother's soldiers?"

"In the gatehouse, ma'am."

"And where is my brother?"

"In his room. Bemoaning his fate."

"As well he may. Bring him to me."

"Your brother, ma'am?" Urgol sounded incredulous.

"Bring him! For the first time in his life, Severin has value to me."

"MOTHER DID THAT to *you*?" Rufio said.

Trelawna had found him in an upper gallery in the central keep. He was fully armoured and pacing, stopping every so often to peep agitatedly through one of the four arrow-loops that looked down towards the gatehouse. He was so preoccupied that at first he'd barely noticed the state she was in: bruised, tousled, streaked with tears and naked, apart from the dirtied rags with which she'd wrapped herself.

He remained distracted. "Well... I warned you to stay out of her way."

"*What?*" Trelawna thought she'd misheard. She'd tried to keep her voice level as she'd explained to him what had just happened, but almost inevitably her eyes had overflowed, and her tone had risen until she was almost hysterical. And *this* was how he responded! "*Felix... she was going to kill me!*"

He began pacing again. "If she was going to kill you, you'd be dead. She was probably just trying to frighten you."

Trelawna was lost for words – but she could not afford to blurt out that she'd only saved her own life by lying about being pregnant. She'd lain with Rufio once only – all those years ago during the first Council at Camelot. Since then, she'd been determined not to make love with him again until they were lawfully married. Besides, though it was unknown to both the men in her life, she had once subjected herself to examination by a village midwife, and had been told that it was never her destiny to be a mother.

"And this is all you've got to say about it?"

"What would you have me do, Trelawna? She's our last refuge."

"Oh, well... I suppose... nothing." Trelawna flopped onto a

stool, trying not to show how devastated she felt. In fact there genuinely was *nothing* she wanted him to do. She certainly did not want him to confront the witch – he was so weak that the truth would doubtless come out about their relations.

"I thought you'd be happy that someone so strong is protecting us," he said.

"With a protector like your mother, who needs a foe like Lucan?"

Rufio looked disappointed – as if she was being ungrateful. She could have shrieked at him, but if that was the way Rufio was, perhaps she ought to be getting used to it? It was understandable that he was nervous, though it wasn't endearing. She'd often told herself that men did not enamour her purely for their courage and daring, but increasingly she was having trouble with this. As she watched Rufio glance through another arrow-loop, she was reminded that he'd already stood up to Lucan once, and had survived without a blemish. Suddenly that seemed typical of him – when so many others had failed to survive at all. And yet, this unsatisfactory fellow, who wrote passionate letters seemingly at the expense of any other useful talent, was the only thing she had left in the world. And she *did* have feelings for him; she willed herself to believe that, as she crossed the gallery towards him.

"Felix... let's just leave this place."

"What?"

"Let's just sneak away. Lucan won't follow us forever. If we leave no trail, if we travel in disguise, he can't possibly know where we are."

"Give up everything, you mean? Our titles, our wealth?"

"None of that really matters..."

"Of course it matters. There's no point having a life if it's not worth living. Besides, it's too late. He's virtually at our door."

"And let me guess," she said, "this place is a cul-de-sac. There's no other way out."

"Rather like our affair," he grunted, which floored her, given everything she'd surrendered for him.

Before she could muster a reply, there were voices in the adjoining passage. Bishop Malconi appeared in company with Urgol, both apparently en route to the lower levels. Trelawna shrank back at the sight of the woodwose, who waited in the doorway as Malconi addressed his nephew.

"It seems your mother is finally in need of *my* advice," he sneered. "How the world turns. This time, at the very least, I shall exact the price of a better bedroom." His gaze shifted to Trelawna, but now there was no warmth or pleasantness there. "Well, well... if it isn't the little whore who has caused all our woes. My, what a beauty. Daughter, you are the very reincarnation of Eve. And thanks to your predatory cunning, good men who otherwise would not have strayed will once again face the fury of God."

And he was gone in a flurry of Episcopal purple, Urgol lumbering behind him.

Rufio stood to one side, lost in thought. When Trelawna finally spoke, it was with trembling voice. After everything that had happened in this hellish place, it was only now that she almost crumbled. "Could you... could you not have said something on my behalf? Not even *then*?"

"What's that?" Again Rufio seemed distracted, and then he became wildly angry. *"Good Christ, woman!"* He stormed from the room. *"Very shortly I may die for you!"*

THIRTY-FOUR

"WE PROCEED," LUCAN said, after they'd stood for several minutes on the wind-blasted ridge, perched above the abyss where their friends had disappeared.

"We should at least stay and say a prayer for them," Alaric protested.

"Why? Will it bring them back?"

"My lord, there are only two of us left... and one prisoner who is badly wounded."

The deep lacerations across the back of Maximion's neck and skull still wept bloody tears. As they'd used up all their medicinal supplies, there'd been little Alaric could do to patch them adequately. Despite this, Maximion glared at the lad, eyes fierce in his grizzled face. "Don't cry on my account, little paladin. I've been wounded many times. There's nothing your dark lord or his enemies can throw at me that I can't recover from."

"There you have it," Lucan said. "We proceed."

But they didn't proceed much farther that day. As they were now almost out of food and water, the spare horses were cut loose and left behind, along with the archery machine. But still the narrow track was difficult; they only just made it off the ridge-way before darkness fell, at which point they were confronted by a narrow cleft, which meandered through towering crags. According to Maximion, this cleft was miles long, but it led directly to Castello Malconi. As night was now falling, Lucan opted to camp, which they did on a ledge beneath an overhang, on the edge of a terrifying precipice. There was nothing on which to tether the horses, so they needed to take it in turns, one man sleeping while the other stood watch. Maximion, for his part, was simply happy to lie on bare rock and fall into a deep, exhausted slumber.

With no fuel to make a fire, and the temperature dropping below freezing, all Lucan and Alaric could do was pull up their coifs, put on their helms and huddle inside their cloaks. The overhang would have provided shelter against rain, though none came – instead, there was mist: thick and probing, filled with twisting eddies which looked like incorporeal forms standing far over the gulf, mocking and beckoning to them. They heard screams from high places: perhaps the wind shrilling through nooks, perhaps something more ominous. If the Stymphalianus was still alive, they would be easy meat for it. All kinds of horrors plucked at their minds during those long, torturous hours.

At first light, Maximion was surprised to be woken, not by Lucan, but by Alaric – very haggard and sallow-faced. He put a finger to his lips and gestured for the prisoner to leave the shelter of the overhang and move into the cleft, where the horses were now waiting. Maximion rose stiffly, cramped with hunger and fatigue, and a deep chill which set his joints aching. As he went, he saw that Lucan still slept in his bed-roll.

"You should leave now," Alaric said, once they were out of earshot of the camp. "Before Earl Lucan wakes." He had already re-saddled Maximion's horse, and offered him the reins. "You've discharged your duty."

"And that's it?" Maximion said dully. "After everything that's happened, you point your finger and say all is now well, I can go?"

"Short of summoning a Persian carpet, I'm not sure what else I can do for you."

"It's hundreds of miles back to civilisation. I have no weapons, no supplies and only the clothes I'm standing in."

"If you say here, Earl Lucan will kill you."

"And you, who have been so insolent with him?"

Alaric adopted a philosophical air. "I will die when we try to take Castello Malconi. Probably alongside my lord, which will be the best outcome possible."

"You think he came all this way to die, young knight?"

"Either way, it makes no sense you waiting here to find out." There was a distant rumble of approaching thunder. "If you go now, you can be down past that exposed ridge before the storm breaks."

Maximion saw no sense in arguing further. With the lad's help he swung up into the saddle, turned the animal around and set it walking. Alaric watched as the mounted figure, still wrapped in his bloodstained cloak, headed off along the ridgeway road.

When Lucan woke, Alaric had prepared breakfast. A few strips of salt bacon from their last knapsack, berries and nuts that he'd gathered en route, and a salad of bitter greens collected from chinks in the rock; it was barely sufficient for two men, but was better than nothing. He'd also located a fissure from which a natural spring flowed, so at least he'd been able to refill their water-skins.

Lucan grunted his thanks as he sat and ate.

"The meat is cold," Alaric said, "but I didn't want to risk a fire."

"They already know we're here," Lucan replied. "They may even be wondering where our friend Maximion has gone."

"I released him. With your best wishes."

"Indeed?"

"His job is done, my lord. You said he had no role to play when we arrived here."

"I gave no order for his release."

Alaric scraped his plate. "I know. You would have released him into the afterlife, and I can't allow that."

"This is the second time you have defied me in almost as many days, Alaric."

The lad glanced up. "I fear it won't be the last. If we manage to enter Castello Malconi, I will prevent your anger falling on Countess Trelawna. Even if it costs my life."

"How noble that would be." Lucan eyed the lad, briefly intrigued, and slowly a light of understanding dawned in his eyes. "Or would it? What exactly do I see here? A stranger... who was never content with the bangtails and doxies, because he was too busy stropping his goskin over the chatelaine of his house? Is that the truth?"

Alaric didn't flinch from the metal-grey gaze. "It's cruder than I would have put it."

"So you're another who's in love with my wife?"

"You don't sound surprised."

"Surprised?" Lucan stood up and adjusted the saddle on Nightshade's back. "Every man who meets her loves her. I've borne that curse since the day I took her to the altar. But you've been wasting your energy, lad – as this episode surely proves. When Trelawna chooses a man, all the others can die and rot in their own filth."

"That's no excuse to kill her."

Lucan regarded him with icy amusement. "You tragic young fool. You came all this way... and for what? An impossible love. Oh, they'll write ballads and *chansons* about you, Alaric. The boy who wanted to be a suitor but settled for being a traitor."

"I never betrayed you."

Lucan mounted up. "It hardly matters. At least I understand your surliness these last few days. It's to your credit that you made no attempt to sabotage this mission. My reward is to let you leave this place on your own two feet, with two eyes in your head, a tongue in your mouth, a hairless cock between your legs and your little heart still pumping in your sunken chest. Now hurry along; you might still catch up with your friend the Roman."

Alaric clambered onto his own horse. Lucan was already headed along the canyon road. Alaric rode to catch up. "I've sworn that I will prevent you harming Countess Trelawna. And I will."

"Words are easy, lad. Deeds are not."

They followed the narrow route for an hour, saying naught to each other. Alaric scanned the high parapets nervously, but no voice called down. The only sounds were the clumping of their hooves, the jingle of harness and the ever-closer rumbling of thunder. The sky, a crooked strip overhead, was grey as a stone lid.

At length, Lucan girded himself. He slid *Heaven's Messenger* into the scabbard on his back, and slotted a pole-axe in place alongside it. He checked that he had his dagger at one hip, and buckled a falchion in place on the other. He pulled up his coif. Alaric also began to arm, ensuring that he had his longsword, and that he too carried a dagger.

When they rounded the next bend, Castello Malconi lay before them – the vast, bleak fortress built from cyclopean stone, but at first seen only through the narrow gap at the end of the passage.

Lucan reined up and dismounted. Alaric did the same, but when they walked forward, the former squire was stunned by the bottomless gulf lying between themselves and the castle entrance. Naturally, the drawbridge had been raised.

"Care to go first?" Lucan asked.

Alaric's hair stood on end as he peered over the precipice. It was maybe twenty yards to the other side. "This is impossible."

"I thought as much," Lucan went back to his horse, took the rope and grapple, and returned. "This is a one-way trip, Alaric. For one man only."

He hurled the grapple across the chasm. An iron grille rose alongside the drawbridge, to allow archers to shoot at attackers opposite. The grapple caught on this the first time. Alaric watched in disbelief as Lucan, pausing only to pull on his helmet and wrap the rope around himself, jumped from the edge and swung down and across.

He struck the stonework some fifteen feet below the raised

drawbridge, with enough force to expel the breath from him. At first, he dangled, looking as if he was ready to fall, but then he recovered, and, planting both feet on the flat surface, walked slowly up the cliff, pulling himself hand-over-hand.

Alaric was stunned – despite all they'd seen on this terrible journey, only now did he have his first inkling of what was actually required of a man to become a Knight of the Round Table. Then he was distracted by movement on the battlements overhead – a figure had appeared there. There was a wild shout, and the next thing a boulder had been dropped down at Lucan. A second figure appeared, and a spear followed. Neither aim was accurate, and now Lucan had reached the gateway itself, which was set into a recess. He was able to clamber onto a shelf alongside the timber drawbridge, and to use the iron grille as a ladder. Sheltered from the defenders, he made it swiftly to the top, where he flattened his body along the drawbridge's upper rim, slid through the narrow gap and dropped down into the entryway on the other side.

Alaric felt worse than helpless. The rope dangled down the far side of the crevasse – there was no possible way that he could reach it. Another shout called his attention back to the parapet, and to a black object flashing towards him. He just had time to hop aside as a javelin bounced past. Now there were cries from *inside* the gatehouse. The defenders on the battlements withdrew from sight.

THE FIRST PERSON Lucan met in the entry tunnel was armed with an impressive crossbow. It had two stocks, one fastened atop the other, and two bow-staves primed and drawn.

The bowman wore a studded leather hauberk and carried a flail in his belt, but he still looked astonished to see Lucan. Doubtless, he'd never imagined that anyone would come in through the front door. Before he could raise his crossbow, Lucan had swung the pole-axe, cloven his sallet and split his cranium. The fellow dropped lifeless beneath a shower of his own blood. Lucan snatched up the crossbow, dived and rolled out of the way as two more *bravos* emerged from the door to the upper gatehouse. The first missed him entirely, running along the passage towards his fallen compatriot – only to be shot in the middle of the back. The second died in the doorway as Lucan spun to face him and shot again, punching the missile deep into his belly.

Lucan threw the bow down, grabbed his pole-axe and hurried along the arched passage. Before he entered the courtyard, three more *bravos* appeared in front of him. One carried a javelin, the second a pick, the third a war-hammer and a *gladius*.

The first threw his javelin. Lucan danced aside, pelted forward and leapt into their midst, bowling all three men over. He rolled past them and jumped back to his feet. The pick-man scrambled to face him, but the steel spike on the pole-axe plunged through his left eye, ripping into his brain. The *bravo* who'd thrown the javelin grabbed a dagger and slashed at Lucan's stomach, but the knight jumped backward and smashed the pole-axe down, clouting the back of the guard's skull with the hammerhead.

The remaining *bravo* was a rugged-looking customer. His sallet had fallen off to reveal a shaven head and scarred face, but he backed into the courtyard as Lucan stalked him. "Lay your weapons down," Lucan said. "You can ride from here unharmed."

"We don't get paid as much for running," the *bravo* replied, though the sweat gleaming on his bare pate belied his brave words.

"You won't get paid at all when those who employ you are dead."

The *bravo* spotted the remaining four members of his squad emerging from the gatehouse behind Lucan, and he smiled, showing rotted teeth, before lunging forward, his arms windmilling. Lucan retreated a couple of steps, parrying every blow, and then retorted, ramming the pole-axe haft into the *bravo's* ribs and driving the steel spike down through his foot. The bravo gave a croaking gasp and turned ash-grey. In the same fluid movement, Lucan released the pole-axe, drew *Heaven's Messenger* and swept it round in a glinting arc, which finished with the shaven head rolling across the blood-spattered flagstones.

THIRTY-FIVE

TRELAWNA STAGGERED INTO her bedroom, only to find Gerta still in bed. She tried to rouse her, but the maid was pale of complexion and could only mumble. When her eyes cracked open, they were rheumy and unfocused. Her brow burned to the touch.

She brought the old woman some water, but Gerta only managed a few choking sips. The countess wept as she stepped back, even as she realised this had perhaps been inevitable, with their recent horrors and hardships. She felt as if all companionship had finally abandoned her. She couldn't even pray. What was it Zalmyra had called her – a common adulteress? And it was true. She had sinned so much that God must have turned His back on her by now, and for what? For the vanity of believing that she deserved better than her severe but comfortable life in Albion's dark North. She surveyed the small room in which she'd been ensconced. It was the only place in this awful fortress where she felt even close to being safe, and yet it was little more than a prison cell.

A familiar sound distracted her – breathless cries and the ringing of steel on steel.

Trelawna hurried down stairs and along passages until she entered the gallery where last she had spoken to Rufio. He was present again, leaning by an arrow-loop, chewing his bottom lip as he watched the events outside. Trelawna moved to the next loop; down in the courtyard, a mailed, helmeted figure with black wolf-fur swirling around him did battle with four men-at-arms.

Even as she watched, another figure joined the fray. It was Cohortis Bartolo, attacking with *gladius* in hand. Lucan dispatched his opponent just in time to meet the fresh assault. Like Rufio, Bartolo was from the officer caste. He'd trained in the gymnasium and on the parade square, and was very experienced when it came to issuing commands, but in hand-to-hand combat he was closer to a novice than an expert.

With two strokes, Lucan sent him stumbling backward. Bartolo fended desperately, but only the intervention of another of Bishop Malconi's *bravos* saved him. This one, a thickset sergeant called Brutus, ran at Lucan with a morningstar. By fluke, its chain wrapped around the blade of *Heaven's Messenger*, and the sword was half-torn from Lucan's grasp. He released it, but grabbed Brutus by his mail buckler. Falling backward, Lucan stuck a foot into his opponent's belly and tossed him head over heels. Winded by his fall, Brutus scrabbled for the dagger at his belt, but Lucan was already up and facing him, falchion in hand. A single thrust split Brutus's nose to the cartilage and shattered the teeth underneath.

The remaining *bravos*, three including Bartolo, circled Lucan warily.

Bartolo hove in for the next strike, and Lucan deflected the *gladius* with the falchion, and punched the Roman on the point of his chin, which again sent him staggering. Another *bravo* lunged, only for Lucan to catch him in the midriff with the point of his blade, ripping through leather and muscle. The *bravo* sank to his knees, gargling blood.

From the high gallery, Rufio watched with a blanched face, focusing intently on Lucan – his nemesis. Never had he seen such speed, such precision and strength in blows. He felt at his hip, where his own *gladius* was buckled, and gripped its pommel so tightly that tendons gleamed in his knuckles.

In the courtyard, the one remaining *bravo* – the youngest –

had had enough. He cast down his weapons and fled along the entrance tunnel, halting only to enter a side-chamber where the drawbridge wheels and chains were connected, kick loose the peg, and continue on his way. The timber drawbridge creaked noisily down in front of him. He was halfway across it when a mailed and mounted figure came thundering from the other side.

ALARIC NEVER SAW the footman until it was too late. They collided at full speed, the horse barely breaking stride as the minuscule figure went screaming into the depths. Alaric entered Castello Malconi, and charged along the tunnel, the echoes of his hoofbeats clattering in his ears.

The first thing he saw in the courtyard was the carnage: slaughtered men lay everywhere. The next thing was Lucan, engaged by one final opponent – a lone Roman officer wearing the apparel of the Fourteenth Legion. The officer retreated under the hail of blows Lucan was raining on him with both falchion and *Heaven's Messenger*.

Alaric reined in his beast, its steel-shod hooves skidding across the flagstones. He leapt from the saddle just as *Heaven's Messenger* struck Cohortis Bartolo beneath the breastbone, tearing clean through his breastplate with a metallic screech.

IN THE UPPER gallery, Rufio bit through his bottom lip completely. Bloody froth sprayed from his mouth as he clamped down on a scream of anguish.

"Bartolo!" he hissed. "Bartolo..."

Down in the yard, Bartolo toppled away from Lucan, sword lowered. Blood flowed down his battle-skirt. He tried to keep his feet, but swayed and dropped to one knee.

"Another one falls for me," Rufio whined. He tore at his hair. *"Another falls while I cower!"* With a rasp of steel, he drew his *gladius*. "I'll finish him! This has to end now!"

"Wait, you damn fool!" came a harsh voice.

Zalmyra and Urgol blocked the gallery door. The translucent black gown was plastered to the duchess's statuesque form with human gore. Her beautiful face was also spattered; ruby droplets dabbled her glossy black hair. Trelawna stared at her, aghast.

"Stay exactly where you are!" Zalmyra said, moving to one of the arrow-loops.

Below, Bartolo crawled away on his belly, smearing a crimson trail behind him. From overhead came a cacophonous rumble of thunder. Lucan glanced up, before turning to face Alaric, who was approaching warily, one hand on his sword-hilt. But before the lad could issue the inevitable challenge, he spotted something to the rear of his lord. Lucan turned: from a nearby door, which had opened behind him, a figure had emerged.

To both their amazement, it was Trelawna – looking dazzlingly beautiful in a fitted gown and kirtle of virginal white. Her joined hands were woven with rosary beads as she prayed and regarded her husband with a look of deep sorrow and remorse.

At first, Lucan could not move. Alaric responded more quickly.

He dashed forward, passing his overlord, drawing his sword in the process. Before he reached the countess, he turned, but continued to back towards her. "Enough is enough, my lord! Your honour must surely be satisfied by now."

Lucan briefly admired the courage in the youngster he had reared and trained, but then reminded himself that he still had a purpose here. His fist tightened on *Heaven's Messenger's* hilt as he slowly advanced.

"Another step, my lord, and we fight," Alaric shouted. "I swore an oath."

Alaric stood directly in front of the countess. If nothing else, he told himself – even if his weapons broke – he would shield her flesh with his own.

That was when she grabbed his neck with a pair of eagle talons – and dragged him back through the door into the darkness beyond.

In the same instant, lightening seared the sky. Thunder reverberated, and the rain followed in cataracts, whipped by a wind that came howling out of nowhere. Lucan stood rigid in the heart of it, eyes riveted on the empty doorway, unable to comprehend what he'd just witnessed. Slowly, astounded, he removed his helmet.

IN THE HIGH gallery, Rufio was equally dumbfounded, though Trelawna had sensed that something horrible was about to occur when she'd seen her doppelganger first emerge.

"Azdalah," Zalmyra said with cold satisfaction. "Better known as the 'Old One'... one of the most feared demons of Babylonian myth. It emerged from my Pit of Souls like some colossal sea-monster. Hundreds of its tentacles now wind their way up through this castle, each one capable of producing at its tip a facsimile by which it can lure its prey." Her face cracked into a malevolent smile. "Once they are snared, there is no escape. They are dragged down into the very depths of the world, where unimaginable suffering awaits them."

DOWN IN THE yard, rain swept over Lucan in drenching sheets. A dozen yards away, Cohortis Bartolo still slithered on his mangled belly. He knew that he was dying, but he had one last purpose – because a figure he recognised had appeared in a doorway ahead of him. His young wife, Rosa – dressed as though for a summer day in a long toga and sandals, her dark curls filled with blossoms. She beckoned him to crawl out of the rain and nestle in her arms as he breathed his last.

"Rosa..." he gasped, the strength fading in his limbs – though there was still enough left for him to cover those final few yards, at which point Rosa snatched him up, broke his back across her knee with a sound like a splintering branch, and dragged his corpse backward into the darkness.

"THERE IS NO way to fight this abhorrence," Zalmyra chuckled, looking down through the arrow-loop. "Or even control it. It will infest the entire fortress, and from here will depredate the surrounding countryside. But it will be worth it." She turned a venom-green eye on Trelawna. "Just as it was worth it to shed my own brother's blood to invoke this horror of horrors. The Black Wolf of the North, my dear, has finally met his match."

THIRTY-SIX

BEYOND THE DOORWAY wherein Alaric had disappeared lay a downward stair.

"Alaric!" Lucan shouted, hurrying down into a depthless maze of darkened passages. There was a stench like spoiled meat, and as his eyes attuned to the half-light, ghastly objects emerged on all sides – glistening, gelatinous tentacles snaking forward. Each one was padded along its underside with saucer-shaped suckers, and yet at its tip had sprouted an even more horrible appendage; a curled foetal ball which, even as Lucan watched, would slowly unknot itself, straighten up and assume the proportion of a full-grown man. Lucan could only gape in disbelief as, one by one, these figures strode forward. Despite the pulsing root to which each one was still attached, their crude, half-made features swiftly transformed into recognisable humanity. They were even wearing clothes, in some cases mail, and they bore weapons.

"Bedivere..." he whispered, as the closest stepped into the half-light.

And yet he knew immediately that this was not his brother. Bedivere's patrician features and chestnut curls were unmistakable, but there was no emotion in that bland visage – no love, no frustration, no annoyance. And that was not the way of Bedivere.

Lucan struck at the apparition with his sword. A gout of black

341

ichor sprayed over him. But the thing did not collapse – it grabbed at his arm with one claw-like hand, and with the other attempted to draw its own weapon. Lucan hacked at it in a desperate fury, closing his eyes as *Heaven's Messenger* clove his beloved brother's skull, severed his shoulder, bit deep into his torso. More black foulness erupted over him, but at last the ghoulish facsimile was down, and Lucan spun around to face more enemies. Two of these, Lancelot and Gawaine – he could scarcely believe he was facing such opponents – had already drawn their swords, and by their glint, these were made of real steel.

Sparks flew as the blades clashed. Neither of the two monsters boasted the skill of the knights they imitated, but their blows were relentless and brutal. It was all Lucan could do to fend them off. He found himself backtracking – only for a faint cry to remind him that Alaric was in the grasp of these devils. He lunged forth in earnest, slicing the throat of the Lancelot facsimile and lopping off its left arm at the elbow. The other he disarmed with a backhand slash, before driving his dagger to the hilt in its chest. Undaunted, it reached for his throat with both hands. He struck them off at the wrists, and cut its legs from under it. And yet, as the monstrosities floundered in gore and filth, they began to reform.

The Bedivere facsimile was already reconstructed, though in horrible, disjointed fashion. As it rose to its feet, it was crooked and mangled – the way a battlefield casualty would really be had he been patched together by a butcher rather than a surgeon. Lucan cut the thing down again, striking its cranium with both hands, splitting it to the breastbone. On all sides, more gleaming tentacles slithered forth, familiar shapes blossoming like grotesque flowers on their tips. Lucan barged his way through them, reaching the top of another stair and descending.

At the bottom, the figure that greeted him stopped him in his tracks.

It was tall and slender, its youthful looks offset by its bald pate and long beard. It wore a loose robe belted at the waist, and carried a knotty staff.

"Merlin..." Lucan breathed. For near-fatal seconds, he was transfixed.

Merlin: the sage, druid and foremost counsellor of Arthur's court. When Lucan had first arrived at Camelot, it was Merlin who had taken him aside and advised that evil was not to be found in a man's heart as though implanted like a seed, but in his mind – where he had planted it himself, and from whence, if he had the will, he could draw it again like a weed.

"Merlin, I..."

With a corpse-like rictus, the facsimile raised its heavy staff in both hands – and Lucan glimpsed the pulsating tentacle to the rear of it. So he struck first, *Heaven's Messenger* slicing the throat and neck and, with a grating crunch, the spine. Merlin's head toppled, but the blinded abhorrence struck this way and that until Lucan skewered it through the midriff. As it dropped, quivering, into its own black innards, Lucan stepped over it to chop at the tentacle. It comprised thick scale and sinew, but Lucan cut and cut like a madman, and at last it came apart in glutinous strands. The Merlin horror, already attempting to reconstitute itself, immediately transformed into a puddle of oily slime.

There was another hoarse, and this time agonised, cry – much closer to hand.

Lucan found Alaric on the next level down, still in the grasp of the false Trelawna, though the alluring figure had melted back into something only half human. On his arrival, it sprang upright from where it was crouched over the lad, and Lucan saw that Alaric's throat was torn open and gouting blood.

With a roar, he charged.

The half-formed horror, its face a lumpen mass, raised both hands, which again were giant talons, and a maw appeared where its mouth should be, broken snags of teeth framed on seething corruption – but Alaric, choking and gasping as his life throbbed out from him, still had the strength to draw his dagger and jam it upward into his captor's groin. The monster was distracted in time for *Heaven's Messenger* to also strike it, shearing the cords between its neck and shoulders, plunging into its festering innards.

It collapsed in a heap, and yet it again attached itself to Alaric, clawing at him, tearing at him. Lucan stepped over it to attack the tentacle. With three heavy blows, it was cloven, and the Trelawna-thing dissolved into a foul, fish-smelling unguent.

"My lord..." Alaric choked, as Lucan tried to aid him. He bled profusely; the ragged hole in his throat had exposed his windpipe.

Lucan cursed as he searched for something with which to staunch the flow. The only thing in reach was Trelawna's scarf – still knotted around the hilt of *Heaven's Messenger*. It was little more now than a rag, thick with gluey filth, though there was sufficient of it to tie around Alaric's neck. Lucan ripped it loose, using his teeth when his gloved fingers failed him.

"Keep your hand on that," he said, when he'd fixed it in place.

Alaric mumbled something in response. He'd turned white and his eyelids were fluttering – but he still had the strength to point at something behind Lucan's back.

Lucan spun around. Turold was standing there, rent and torn as he had been after the baboons had finished with him. He produced a war-axe and raised it on high. Lucan catapulted himself forward, barreling headlong into the figure, knocking it backward over its own muscular tentacle. Lucan smote at this first, laying it open, then turned his sword on Turold, catching him with such a blow that he was severed in two.

Lucan spun back to Alaric, picked him up and threw him over his shoulder.

The journey to the surface was even more terrible than the journey down. Tentacles swarmed after them. From every side, familiar figures offered challenge: Bors, Kay, Lancelot again. Even Wulfstan. Lucan held back, mesmerised by the sight of his old scout, but when the thing shrieked like a bird of prey and jabbed out with a steel-headed lance, he retaliated in kind, driving his blade through the aged, once-trustworthy face, ripping it downward so that the abomination's entire lower jaw fell off.

Lucan panted and sweated as he twisted and turned, seeking a route up to the light and yet constantly having to battle his way through the imitations of friends. Bors struck his face with a spiked club, knocking him dizzy. Benedict attempted to snatch Alaric from him. Both went down beneath Lucan's frenzied blows, yet always it seemed the mutilated husks he reduced them to rose back to their feet, reshaping before his eyes into nightmarish parodies of what they once had been.

"Whoresons!" Lucan roared. "Hell spawn!"

The face of Sir Gareth swam into his vision. He smote it. Bedivere stepped into its place again. "They took my hand, Lucan!" he howled, holding up his gory stump.

But in the other hand he held a dagger, and he thrust it at Lucan's eyes. Lucan shoulder-charged the figure, toppling it down a stairwell.

Now at last there was a doorway through which daylight vented. Lucan stumbled towards it, only for another figure to step into his path. This one wore a white surcoat bearing a red dragon, and a golden crown on his helm. He had a neat beard and moustache, and a sunny-brown, square-cut mane.

It was Arthur himself.

He held a shield in one hand, and in the other a battle-axe, but Lucan could not bring himself to run steel through his lord and King. Perhaps he was too exhausted to think straight. Sweat stung his eyes. Saliva and blood drooled from his mouth. He turned away as their hands reached for him, as their swords struck at him – and he spied another door, only a short distance away. He hobbled drunkenly towards it, Alaric a dead weight. But beyond the second door was a stair, which spiralled upward.

Lucan halted and looked back.

There were so many of them that they stumbled and tripped over the mass of slippery, fleshy tentacles lying back and forth across the floor. The closest was Sir Griflet; Lucan parried his blow and sundered his breastbone. The next was Wulfstan, still missing his lower jaw, what remained of his human features collapsing inward like melting wax, though he now lashed at Lucan with a morningstar. Lucan caught the chain around his forearm, and cut his friend down again, tearing him open from gullet to crotch. But always more of them stepped into the gaps, hedging the room thick with moaning, gibbering, blood- and ichor-spattered abominations. There was only one option. He commenced the arduous ascent, his back bowing beneath the burden of his unconscious friend.

STREAKS OF LIGHTNING split the sky. Thunder bellowed through the mountains. The rain lashed incessantly, rivers gushing from every roof and gutter. It was no weather to be travelling, but Duchess Zalmyra had made up her mind.

"Be warned," she said. "Stay close to me as we descend to the undercroft."

She had produced a wand made from rowan wood, a jade orb fixed at one end, from which an emerald light burned; she held it aloft as they hurried down the switchback stair. Zalmyra walked at the front, and Urgol brought up the rear, a huge, iron-headed club at his shoulder. In between, Trelawna and Rufio struggled with Gerta, who they had managed to rouse, but only with difficulty. They reached ground level, where a narrow door opened into the courtyard. Trelawna glanced through as the sky again flashed with celestial fire. Cacophonous thunder rolled. The deluge intensified.

"Not that way," Rufio said. He indicated an internal door, and a stair descending beyond it; Zalmyra's green light was already receding into the regions below.

Trelawna adjusted Gerta at her shoulder and was about to follow, when movement caught her eye on the far side of the castle. She looked once, and then again.

It was Lucan. He'd emerged on an upper gantry, maybe thirty feet above the courtyard. He had a body draped over one shoulder – to Trelawna's horror, it looked like Alaric – and was now backing along the battlement, using one hand to fend

off a horde of slowly pursuing figures. Though he wielded
Heaven's Messenger with his usual might, cutting them down
like chaff, they always rose to their feet again and continued.
He had perhaps another five yards in which he could retreat
and then, aside from a single flagpole flying the Boar's Head
pennon, he'd be at a dead-end.

Rufio reappeared at her shoulder. "What are you doing?
Mother's patience is..."

"Your mother can rot in Hell!" Trelawna snapped. "Look!"

Rufio gazed across the courtyard – in time to see a fleshy
tentacle grope from a cellar window and slide serpent-like up
the wall towards Lucan, a humanoid figure riding on its tip.

"That looks like Arthur," Trelawna said with disbelief.

THE KING ALIGHTED on the battlements.

Lucan had now retreated as far as he could, and laid Alaric
down next to the flagpole. Once again, he was confronted by
his lord and sovereign. Arthur's visor was raised, but the face
below it was solemn. "You are a great warrior, Lucan," he said
softly, "but evil is rooted in your soul. It's a burden you were
born with, but even so, everyone at Camelot hates and fears
you in equal measure."

"You're lying!" Lucan shouted, his throat sore with gasping.

"I tolerate you, Lucan, because you direct your wrath at my
foes. But one day my foes will be dead, and your usefulness
will be done. Hell will be grateful to receive you!"

"You're not my King!" Lucan roared, but still, when he
struck at the figure, it was with the pommel of his sword
rather than its point.

The first blow dented the King's shield. The King retaliated
with a stroke of his axe. Lucan parried, severing the axe-haft.
More by instinct than design, he followed this through with
a lethal backstroke, which ripped through the King's aventail
and sliced his throat. The figure staggered back, arterial black
gore spurting outward.

"You are not my King!" Lucan wept. He kicked the wounded figure in the chest, toppling it through the embrasure.

With renewed howls, the others launched themselves forward. Lucan hewed an alleyway through them. Benedict went down with face cloven, Bors with neck sheared, Griflet with lungs and heart exposed.

Gagging for breath, Lucan fell back again. He had bought himself but a fleeting respite. He glanced over his shoulder and saw Alaric's lifeless form. If he could just get the lad away from this place... but there was no time. Lancelot ghosted towards him with a maul in one hand and a mattock in the other. Lucan blocked both blows, and chopped Lancelot's legs from under him, and the horde of horrors was held in brief abeyance as the corpses in front melded themselves back together. Lucan swung around and cut the flagpole rope.

FROM THE OTHER side of the castle yard, it seemed a futile, almost pathetic gesture – the Malconi pennon collapsing in the rain. But then Trelawna saw Lucan pull down the rope and vanish below the battlements – she wondered if he was attempting to escape, before realising the truth. The lifeless figure he'd been carrying – Alaric, definitely Alaric – was now propped upright in an embrasure, the rope looped around his body. As quickly as he could, Lucan lowered him down towards the courtyard. But there was no movement from the lad; he would land heavily and awkwardly. Trelawna laid Gerta against the door-jamb, and rushed outside.

"Trelawna!" Rufio shouted. "Don't be a fool..."

"She's chosen which side she's on," Zalmyra said, returning to his side.

"But she's... she's..."

"There's nothing to be done about it. Come. Urgol is preparing the carriage."

Rufio shook his head. "You go..."

"She has chosen *death* before you, Felix! I'd have thought

even a moon-calf of your sort would find that sufficient reason to move on. But as always..." Zalmyra backed away. "The decision is yours."

She descended the lower stair again. Rufio delayed, torn with indecision. Gerta watched him through weak, watering eyes.

"My mistress is a woman of judgment after all," she said hoarsely.

Rufio glared down at her. "You old crone! We could have had a good life together!"

"She already had a good life. She just needed to realise it."

"The Devil take the pair of you!" Rufio said. "And he *will!*"

He dashed down the stair. On the next level stood a junction of vaulted passages, where he found his mother, her path blocked – astoundingly – by Emperor Lucius. Clad once again in his polished black plate with its silver enamel workings, the Emperor's visor was drawn up, and his eyes ablaze with indignation. He wore a *gladius* at his hip, but was making no move towards them; Zalmyra held him back with her wand, the jade orb burning with intense radiance.

Rufio could scarcely believe what he was seeing. Slowly, he turned. From the adjoining passages, more tentacles slithered into view, forming equally recognisable figures. He was dumbfounded to see his Uncle Severin, naked and pallid, his throat slit and chest rent open. The bishop held out a pleading hand. Yet when Rufio looked closely, that hand was curved like an animal's claw, with long, yellow fingernails. Rufio drew his *gladius* and slashed at it, severing the hand at its wrist. Black ichor spurted, and the abomination leapt at him. In its other hand it clasped a crooked-bladed dagger. It was not a weapon Rufio had seen before, though of course he'd never been party to the sacrifices in his mother's Pit of Souls. Even now it flashed too quickly for him to visualise, penetrating his battle-skirt, plunging to half its length in the right side of his groin. Rufio gave a gasping screech. The facsimile withdrew the blade and raised it high, grinning dementedly – only for Zalmyra to poke its chest with her green orb. There was a crackle of discharging energy, and the ghastly figure folded up on itself, curling into a blackened, smoldering ball. The tentacle to which it was attached withdrew from view. But there were others circling around them.

"Mother!" Rufio choked, his voice shrill. He doubled up beside her, but she kept hold of his collar to prevent him falling, and began to incant in an ancient tongue.

The Lucius apparition advanced with its own *gladius* drawn. Again Zalmyra held up her green light to ward it off. But this time there was no need. A mighty blow struck the figure from behind, delivered with a colossal iron-headed club, crushing it with such force that its body burst out on all sides in a porridge of black bile and putrid, half-made organs.

Urgol stepped into view, and kicked the butchered tentacle into a recess to their left. "Mistress... your carriage awaits!"

Zalmyra hurried past, allowing him to shield her with his vast, hairy body. She dragged Rufio, though he could only stagger, one hand clasped to his wound.

LUCAN USED HIS last ounce of strength to lower Alaric. He tried to ignore the blows raining on his back, although steel now bit through his fur and mail. If he could just get Alaric to the courtyard without dropping him...

A hand gripped Lucan's coif and yanked. He resisted, but then felt the rope slacken. The lad must have touched the ground, if sooner than Lucan had anticipated. He released the rope and swept around, swinging *Heaven's Messenger* in a great, butchering arc. Limbs fell this way and that. Caradoc lost both arms from the elbows down, black juice jetting from his stumps. Gawaine had lost one arm, but still aimed a pick-axe with the other. Lucan deflected it and drove his steel at the facsimile's face, only to see it parried.

He was exhausted.

The embrasure stood immediately to his rear. It would be a quicker death, surely, falling thirty feet onto flagstones, than being torn apart by these horrors? Though the outcome would be the same. Suicide meant certain damnation – as if his soul wasn't already damned enough. Spurred by that thought, he struck at them again. An upward thrust eviscerated Gawaine; a swift backhand sheared through Bedivere's neck, the head dropping backward on strands of tissue. More black filth exploded over Lucan, but still they pressed against him, now trying to take hold of him rather than inflict wounds. And then he heard a terrible wailing: *"Alaric! Alaaaric!"*

He managed to turn and peer down through the embrasure. Alaric's soft landing in the courtyard was explained.

The ragged, rain-soaked figure of Trelawna's maid staggered, as though drunk, across the courtyard. But closer, at the foot of the battlements, was Trelawna herself. She was seated on the floor, holding Alaric in her arms, crying out his name, sobbing.

It was a brief, harrowing moment, though Lucan knew that he should not be surprised. No-one could have survived such a wound for long. And there was certainly no time to lament it – not when those responsible were still within sword's length.

His strength revived by hatred, Lucan spun around and launched himself into the horde of abominations. His steel sang as it smote them, laying twitching, limbless forms on all sides. Those struggling to rise were sundered again. Those not yet stricken were impaled, or beheaded, or butchered where they stood.

"Come one, come all!" Lucan roared. "I summon all monsters to their doom!"

At first he thought they were falling back because his onslaught was too much for them, but then he realised they were not falling back, but clearing a passage through their mewling ranks – a passage along which, with slow, purposeful steps, a new figure was now approaching.

In all ways it was larger than Lucan – taller, stouter of limb, broader at chest and shoulder. Yet it wore the same dark mail and black livery, and the same cloak of black fur was draped down its back. Like Lucan, the newcomer had removed its helmet and pulled back its coif to shake out oil-black locks. It might at one time have been as wolfishly handsome as he was, though now those features had been obliterated by a mask of hideous scar tissue. Its eyes were tarnished sapphires, glinting through holes in parchment. The mouth was a lipless tear, the nose a scorched and flattened patch.

Lucan's sword almost fell from his hand as the vision glided towards him.

A gleaming tentacle oozed behind it. Like all the rest, it was the construct of a demonic mind, and yet there was no mistaking it. Even after so many years of tumult, Lucan recollected every detail of the human dragon monster that had once been Duke Corneus, his father. With slow deliberation, the imitation drew its own version of *Heaven's Messenger* from its back; this one still bore the unholy runes along its blade. Lucan failed to move, failed to respond in any way. He was mesmerised by the distorted form that had haunted so many of his worst nightmares.

"Still... a weakling... boy?" it rasped, in that voice of twisting, tortured wood. "Still... a milksop? No guts... no spine... couldn't even... father a child..."

"Murderer," Lucan whispered.

"Were going... to kill me... were you not?" The atrocious mouth laughed its terrible, heartless laugh – a laugh Lucan had heard down the decades, echoing from those many places where, without any writ from the King, Duke Corneus's foes had been hanged, or garroted, or drawn apart by horses, or nailed to the doors of their own castles.

"Words... boy?" The imitation duke lofted the imitation sword to his massive shoulder. "Only... words? Well... if not battle... prepare for... slaughter. Unless... you beg. Like that weak-spirited... mother of yours. Begging... pleading.... each morn... before her penance..."

"*Murderer!*" Lucan shouted, raising his own sword.

With the speed of a viper, Duke Corneus lunged.

THIRTY-SEVEN

Rufio had lost so much blood that Urgol had to lift him into the black enamel coach, where Zalmyra laid a cloak over him. She closed and bolted the shutters, and sat facing her son through the dimness, while the woodwose climbed to the driving-bench. With a crack of his whip, the powerful team of horses surged out of the undercroft, trundling up the spiralling ramp, running down any figures that blundered into their path, severing tentacles with steel-rimmed wheels. At the top, the two foremost stallions reared, their hooves smashing the doors off their hinges.

The team crashed out into the courtyard. As they rattled towards the entry tunnel, Zalmyra opened her shutter just once to look out. Amid the carnage strewing the courtyard, she spotted the distinctive golden hair of Countess Trelawna, though it was now plastered across her shoulders and breasts as she sat cross-legged in the rain, cradling the form of a fallen knight. Another figure, the countess's old nurse, crawled through the flood-waters.

"What's happening?" Rufio gasped, too weak to open his own shutter.

"Nothing," she said, closing out the light. But she seemed distracted. They rumbled into the entry tunnel; ahead, the drawbridge was already down. Abruptly, the duchess rapped on the ceiling. "Urgol! Stop!"

The vehicle slid to a halt, and shuddered as Urgol climbed from the bench. He opened the duchess's door. "Mistress?"

"Go back," she said. "Bring Countess Trelawna. She's coming with us."

Urgol nodded and clambered back to the roof to retrieve his iron-headed club.

Rufio looked up with an expression of almost absurd hopefulness.

"Don't mistake me for a caring mother-in-law," Zalmyra said. "I've no interest in your pretty little courtesan. It's the brat she carries in her belly. Even if we didn't need heirs, no grandchild of mine will be fed to the Old One."

Rufio's expression changed. "Grandchild?"

She sneered. "Somehow, your lack of knowledge makes you even more pathetic. You know why she never told you? Because she didn't trust you to keep it secret. Her annulment is too precious to her."

Rufio peered at her, baffled. And then, to her surprise, he cackled – as if genuinely amused. "Trelawna's annulment is the *only* precious thing to her," he finally said. "There's no grandchild. She wouldn't let me lie with her until we were lawfully married."

"*What?*"

Now it was Rufio's turn to sneer, though he also cringed with pain. "We lay together once, but many years ago." His cackle became a full-throated laugh.

Outside, Urgol leapt down from the roof, club at his shoulder, and set off along the tunnel. At first, Zalmyra said nothing, although the look on her face was so terrifying that Rufio, had he not been sure he was dying, would have cowered from her.

"*Urgoool!*" she shrieked. The woodwose rushed back to her door. When she spoke again, her marble-white face had blanched to an even more bloodless hue. "Urgol... I've changed my mind. Go back there... *and destroy the little slut who brought this destruction on us!*"

Urgol nodded and strode away.

"No!" Rufio cried.

"Don't be foolish," his mother said as he tried to climb out. "She's as good as dead anyway."

"You vindictive bitch!" He gagged with pain as the cloak fell away, revealing a body drenched with gore. Slowly, fumbling, he managed to open the door.

"Then go and die," Zalmyra said. "Those who defy the Malconi have earned their fate."

"And the Malconi haven't?" He grimaced as he put his feet on solid ground. "You who stand for nothing good?"

"Don't be an imbecile. This is a minor setback. We will rise again."

Rufio heaved himself to the ground. "I couldn't... couldn't wish for anything less."

He stumbled away, and Zalmyra remained alone in the coach, absorbed in the bauble on her wand. The emerald fires inside it blazed. "In which case, my dear son, we must rise without you!"

HIGH OVERHEAD, THE thunder still raged and the lightning flashed. Below that, with no less savagery, Lucan fought with the facsimile of his father.

They smote at each other two-handed, dancing back and forth along the battlemented walk, a host of other ghouls watching in silence. Sparks flew as the hate-filled blades bickered, but Lucan was tired to his core. The ferocity of his father's blows was more than he could endure. Even when, fleetingly, he spied an open guard, and drove through it, embedding his blade to eight inches in Duke Corneus's chest, the fight continued. Black blood cascaded from the wound, but the demon was neither hurt nor weakened. Lucan tottered backward, and the monster laughed as it came on.

"Weakling!" it grated, showing long pegs of green teeth which even the real Corneus had never possessed. "You are ailing... I can... feel it. You are not fit... to unfurl... my black banner..."

"Once this is over, I will never unfurl it again," Lucan retorted, counter-striking, slashing hard under his father's guard, chopping through mail and flesh – so deeply that his blade lodged. Lucan tried to yank it loose but it would not shift. Still the duke was unhurt, and Lucan had to draw back unarmed.

Behind him now was nothing but a drop of thirty feet. More chill rain swept over him. Thunder drummed. Even if, by some miracle, he could dispose of this arch-abomination, another would follow, and another. There were more up here than he could count, and still more tentacles writhed along the battlements and groped up the outer wall, balls of clenched, foetal flesh unravelling at their tips.

Cruel laughter distracted him back to the vision of his father, slowly levering *Heaven's Messenger* from his shoulder. With a scrape of bone and fresh gouts of black gore, he worked it loose – and examined it, seemingly amused that the pagan runes with which the blade had once been inscribed were scored away.

"And which god..." he wondered, "will save you now? The one you... defile each day... by your very... existence?"

Lucan backed to the battlements. The drop was perilous. He could not hope to survive it without at least shattering his limbs.

The apparition cast away its own sword, hefting Lucan's instead. Rain slashed over the burned features, as the green teeth bared in a rictus grin. "Let me... test your faith... with... a Christian blade..."

It raised *Heaven's Messenger* above its head. Lucan leapt forward, but the facsimile had been waiting for this, and greeted him with a forearm smash in the throat, knocking Lucan flat on his back. He lay stunned, helpless. Towering over him, the living ghost raised the blade on high for one mighty, butchering blow that would split him from cranium to crotch. Lucan tried to pray, but he no longer knew how. The apparition laughed again, and prepared to strike.

But the lightning struck first.

The jagged bolt tore down from the firmament in a blaze of blinding blue flame, finding the long steel blade held aloft. There was a detonation like the bursting of Heaven's vault, and a glaring flash...

THE POUNDING RAIN had washed Alaric's lifeless body so clean that there was barely a drop of blood or speck of dirt left on him. As he lay in Trelawna's arms, he looked as though he was merely sleeping. And now, almost as quickly as the downpour had begun, it started to abate.

Slowly, in a daze, the countess looked up.

A pearlescent blue sky was breaking through the ragged clouds. The hiss of falling rain slowly ceased, to be replaced by a trickling in the gutters and a dripping from the eaves – and by the approaching stump of heavy feet.

Trelawna saw Urgol advancing across the courtyard on foot.

His thick, hairy hide was wet and matted. For some reason it made him look less like an ape and more like a man, though still a gargantuan, brutish form. His fierce yellow eyes were locked on her; his sharp teeth showed through his snarling lips. When ten yards short, he produced his iron-headed club from behind his back.

"Lay your head on the paving stone, countess," he grunted. "This can be so quick you won't even know it has happened."

Trelawna gazed mutely up at him, paralysed. Urgol shrugged, and in two strides was alongside her, his bludgeon raised.

And with a shriek, Gerta leapt onto him.

The old woman had little strength left in her frail body, but she summoned everything she had, clinging to his wet fur with one hand, attempting to claw out his eyes with the other. Urgol shrugged her off the way he would an irritating insect. Almost as an afterthought, he swatted at her with the club, catching her full in the ribs, hurling her at least ten feet, a thing of rags and sticks, tumbling end over end.

Trelawna screamed as much in outrage as in fear, and

attempted to get to her feet, but was still hampered by Alaric's corpse. Urgol turned back to face her – and felt a stinging pain across his left forearm.

He spun around, and found Rufio rocking back and forth, his lower body drenched crimson, a *gladius* quaking in his fist. Urgol tried to push him away, but Rufio slashed at him again. Urgol whipped his arm back, snarling. Rufio gritted his teeth in an effort to show that he was unafraid, but it gave him an even more cadaverous aspect.

"Do what you must, Urgol," came a sibilant voice, travelling on the wind. His mistress, still enclosed in her carriage, speaking from afar. "Ignore his name, his lineage. Obey my will…"

Urgol swung his club back, and swept it down, striking Rufio's legs sideways, smashing them like shards of charcoal. Rufio dropped, only beginning to squeal as he lay in the wreckage of his own body.

Urgol turned back to find Trelawna. She had got to her feet and tried to retreat, only to slip in a puddle and fall onto her side. But someone else now blocked the creature's path to her.

Lucan.

The filth of battle had washed off him in the rain, but he looked bedraggled and weary, and confused.

THE THUNDERBOLT THAT had blown the facsimile of his father to jellified fragments had seared every one of the facsimiles, all over Castello Malconi. Simultaneously, they'd collapsed on themselves, the writhing tentacles blistering and bursting; the shredded, smouldering remnants whipping in a frenzy, hissing and half-melted as they withdrew to the depths of the fortress, from which a stench too foul to breathe now rose.

Lucan had seen it. As he'd descended to the courtyard, he'd trudged through the smoking, semi-liquefied husks, among fragments of burned tentacles which could do no more now than twitch feebly.

He understood how this had happened. But *why?*

Urgol's scornful voice brought him out of his reverie. "Well... if it isn't another warrior of Christ. Here to collect souls for his master." The woodwose bared his fangs. "I go one better... I collect souls for myself!"

His club crashed down, and Lucan had to duck aside. He hefted *Heaven's Messenger,* but it was nothing more now than a cindered cross-hilt. He threw it away, casting around for another weapon. The pole-axe stood in the foot of the shaven-headed *bravo* he'd slain earlier; he yanked it free and dodged as another massive club-stroke was aimed at him.

Trelawna watched the combat, terrified.

Urgol struck again. Lucan parried, the impact jolting his body with nauseating force.

"Not yourself, sir knight?" the woodwose rumbled. "What would the Lord say?"

Lucan responded by kicking at the club to try and dislodge it, and slamming the pole-axe haft down on Urgol's naked foot. Urgol took a step backward, but then lurched in with another overhead buffet, which again almost knocked Lucan from his feet. They circled each other warily. The only sound in the castle yard was the heavy rasp of their breath, the scuffing of their feet, the crash of steel on timber.

Lucan still had the deadlier weapon, but the extra weight of Urgol's club, with his mammoth strength, was telling. When the woodwose set about him in a flurry, it was all he could do to fend off three blows, before taking the fourth – a huge thrust – in the chest, hurling him off balance. He slashed back with the axe-head, but the woodwose smashed it aside and threw a ham-fisted punch. It caught Lucan square on the cheekbone and rang his skull like a bell.

Lucan hit the ground hard, but retained just enough of his faculties to roll away. The woodwose followed, club raised, so he kept on rolling, blow after blow striking clanking concussions from the flagstones. And then a corpse – another of Lucan's victims from earlier – barred his way, and Urgol caught up and stood astride him. This final blow would have pulverised Lucan's face, had he not heaved the pole-axe to the horizontal, fists gripping its haft one to either end.

With a massive *CRACK*, the axe-haft shattered, but the blow was absorbed. Lucan kicked upward, couching his mailed foot in the leather-clad sack between the woodwose's thighs. Urgol doubled over and staggered back, and Lucan again rolled away. The beast swung around in pursuit. Lucan tried to stand but slid in a puddle; again he rolled. Urgol followed sluggishly. Even should the knight get to his feet in time, he had no weapon – there was nothing with which to fight back.

"Lucan!" came a desperate voice. *"Lucan!"*.

Lucan glanced to his left. Though Rufio lay prone, his face the colour of slate, both legs twisted at awful angles, there was something in his outstretched palm – a *gladius*.

"Take it…" he gasped.

Lucan scuttled forward, snatched the blade and veered to one side as the mighty club sailed down after him. It hit Rufio full on the forehead, crushing his entire skull to mulch. But the knight was now, at last, on his feet; he twirled, *gladius* in hand.

Urgol came with a roar. The club descended in a blur, but Lucan spun from its path. As he did, he cut down, carving deep into the woodwose's thigh.

Its bellow of rage became a howl of anguish.

Lucan continued to spin around the beast, and then he was fast on its back, his arm locked around its brawny neck. With a single thrust, he drove the *gladius* deep to the left of its spine, twisting it to a chorus of cracking vertebrae.

Urgol's eyes rolled white, and a spume of blood burst from his mouth.

"My Lord would say," Lucan hissed into his ear, "consider yourself collected!"

The woodwose gave a faint mewling sound as it crumpled into a lifeless heap. Seconds passed as Lucan stood over it, every muscle taut, his body rank with the stench of sweat and blood, and yet so doused by rainwater that steam rose off him. Slowly, stiffly, he looked around him. No-one else in the castle yard was alive except Trelawna, who sat where he'd last seen her, head slumped to her breast.

When he finally limped towards her, she glanced up and regarded him with a strange indifference. Though still a beauty, her eyes were bleak holes in a face made haggard. Her expression didn't change when she glanced down at his drawn *gladius* – not until he tucked it into this belt, and she spotted the ragged scarf knotted around its hilt, and a strange mirthless smile came to her lips.

DUCHESS ZALMYRA WATCHED these events from the driving-bench of her coach, every terrible incident playing out in the green scrying-orb. Now it was over, and she was impassive. The death of her son, Rufio, meant no more to her than the death of her servant, Urgol; in fact, it probably meant less. Rufio had been a failure, a weakling – like his father before him, unfit to head the Malconi clan. His fate had been the same, and was equally deserved.

Zalmyra touched her belly before taking up the reins. She was still ripe enough to produce more sons. All she needed do was entice a strapping young man, and she had never had a problem with that before.

She lashed the team of horses away.

LUCAN KNELT BESIDE Alaric's splayed corpse, and after straightening his limbs and planting a kiss on the young man's alabaster brow, laid the sodden wolfskin over him. At the same time, Trelawna crawled to the broken form of Gerta. The old nursemaid was pale, but at least unmarked. Like Alaric, she looked as if she was sleeping.

Very softly, Trelawna wept. Minutes passed, in which the autumn chill leached into their bones.

"Quite a refuge you chose," Lucan finally said, "the Malconi clan."

Trelawna wiped away her tears. "Gerta said the same. If only I'd listened..."

"Gerta was your voice of wisdom. Alaric was mine. We both chose to ignore them."

"Then we both should have died."

Lucan glanced towards the high parapet, which was still wreathed in acrid smoke from the lightning strike. Again, he felt only fear and confusion. "For some reason... it was God's decision that we shouldn't."

Trelawna wept again, and at last he moved across and joined her, placing an awkward hand on her shoulder, which he was grateful that she didn't shrug away.

"So what now?" she sniffled. "We go home... we realise we love each other after all... and these many deaths are forgotten?"

"No," he said. "We just go home."

EPILOGUE

DUCHESS ZALMYRA MADE good speed along the canyon road, her tawny furs billowing as she drove the black coach at full force, her whip cracking on the horses' flanks. Not far to the east, another thunderhead was rolling over the jagged mountaintops. She must clear the ridge-way before the next storm struck. Not that this had prevented her halting briefly in the canyon to apply her green-orbed wand to the skull of the black warhorse tethered there, causing such pain inside its head that it shrieked and bucked and hurled itself against the canyon walls until it had smashed its own bones and torn its flesh to unrecognisable pulp.

Once on the exposed ridge, her own horses became skittish. She whipped them all the harder. Though it would have been more prudent to walk along the knife-edge track, they all but galloped. The carriage jolted and bounced. The duchess cut her tawny robe loose, and freed her hair to blow behind her in a rippling, blue-black plume. She struck and struck at the horses' foaming, bloody flanks, screaming curses. And then, to her astonishment and dismay, she spotted an obstacle ahead, and was forced to rein the frantic brutes in. It took her fifty yards to stop, the horses puffing and sweating.

Zalmyra rose to her feet in disbelief.

A great crossbow, laid across a horizontal frame, blocked her escape. A bedraggled, mailed figure was hunched behind it, clearly taking shelter, but with one hand clamped on the release-lever. Maybe twenty extra-large bolts were loaded into the machine; a ray of sunlight broke from the gathering cloud and embossed their needle-tips.

Zalmyra pondered her position very carefully.

The archery machine was forty yards in front of her; already she and her team were in range. There was nowhere else she could go; the warrior didn't even need to take aim. If she drove at him hard, she wouldn't get within ten yards before her horses were bristling with shafts. The only possible alternative was to retreat, but she could not turn the carriage around. She would have to walk, which would make her easy prey for the Black Wolf of the North.

It was strange that the mailed figure had not triggered the device already, though perhaps he was unsure of her intentions. Might she charm him – as she had charmed so many men in the past before killing them? By his aspect, he was frightened. He had likely been through agonies and despair just to get this far. Not just frightened therefore, but maybe *mad* with fear.

Zalmyra was coldly furious to have been thwarted in this way. How could a simple man-at-arms with a brutish weapon like this put paid to all her plans?

She took the wand from the chain at her waist. Its orb began to glow with an intense aquamarine lustre; she still had credit with the dark powers. In her mind she incanted, and as she did she stood, spread her arms and closed her eyes. The air swirled around her in a vortex. She felt her body tightening and contracting: her skull, her ribcage. Her inner organs were squeezed, as her joints contorted out of shape. The pain was horrific, but she bore through it.

DESPITE HIS TERROR of the unholy adversary he was facing, Malvolio rose slowly to his feet. His hand slipped free of the Scorpion's release-lever, his weariness from the long, arduous climb back to this high ridge forgotten. The tall woman on the driving-bench no longer looked so tall. In fact she no longer looked like a woman. The thin black gown she was wearing suddenly seemed to consist of black feathers, and her outstretched arms had become tapering, bony appendages, sprouting yet more feathers. She was shortening, shrinking inward, while her neck was extending to impossible length. Where once she'd had a nose and mouth, he saw the glint of an orange bill.

"A swan, by damn!" he whispered.

Whoever this woman was, she had changed her form into that of a large, black swan. Almost lazily, the great fowl took wing, lofting its way along the path towards him.

Malvolio grabbed hold of the release-lever again. But the swan veered away to the west, allowing the breeze to carry it. Its wingspan covered maybe six feet or more. It was beautiful, framed on the clouds behind. A voice inside Malvolio told him that he still must shoot at it; that this gorgeous thing was a façade, and inside it beat the heart of a devil. But it was already out of the Scorpion's sights. The weapon's undercarriage was steel and timber, and far too heavy for him to shift on his own. In any case, the swan rose upward, soaring into the sky, so even if he could have turned the machine around, he could not discharge his missiles at such an angle. He tried anyway, grunting, feeling like a dumb ox who had just squandered a great opportunity.

"Loosen the pivot!" a voice said.

Malvolio spun around, astonished to see Tribune Maximion alongside him.

The Roman was ragged and grimy, but had approached from behind him, as if he had journeyed some distance along the ridge-way road while Malvolio was down on the lower slopes and now, for some reason, had returned.

"Loosen the pivot!" Maximion said again, reaching to a nut located low in the weapon's frame, and turning it.

There was a mechanical *clunk*, and suddenly the upper section of the machine swung freely on its base.

"*Here*, you fool!" Maximion said. "Do they teach you nothing useful in the ranks of chivalry?" He rotated a crank-handle, and a shining steel screw ascended, raising the bow by several inches. Malvolio could now swivel or pivot the weapon in any direction, and up and down as well.

Malvolio swung the mechanism to the west and levered it upward. The black swan still rode the wind, maybe thirty yards away, soaring steadily and gracefully. He struck the trigger, unleashing a hail of bolts which rattled away like a flock of metallic hawks, flying straight and sure.

There was an explosion of feathers, but no sound.

The swan dropped from the sky, turning over and over.

As it tumbled, it reassumed the dimensions of a human female, the rags of its black garb trailing behind it. Its only feathers now were those of the many shafts, maybe ten or twelve in total, transfixing its head and body. Malvolio leaned dangerously out to track its progress. Far below, maybe four hundred feet or more, the grisly figure struck the boulders, rolled a few yards and then lay, mangled and motionless. He watched it long and hard to ensure it remained still. When he eventually turned back, Maximion was leaning tiredly against the Scorpion.

Before Malvolio could say anything, they heard a hoofbeat.

A small party had arrived on the far side of the black coach: Earl Lucan, pushing a two-wheeled handcart, three forms shrouded in black fur lying atop it. Countess Trelawna was behind him, seated on Alaric's horse and wrapped in a shawl, her head hung low.

Lucan, looking more than a little puzzled, sidled around the stationary coach and proceeded along the road to the Scorpion, where Malvolio and Maximion awaited him. The squire pointed down into the gulf. Lucan focused on the inert form at the bottom.

"You?" he finally asked.

Malvolio nodded warily.

Lucan turned to Maximion, a querying look on his face.

"My horse died on me," the Roman explained. "I managed to climb off before its carcass fell down the south face of the ridge."

Lucan's brow furrowed, as if he was debating some complex issue with himself. Finally he said: "Climb aboard the coach. You too, Malvolio. But... first, help me place these bodies on top." He led them around to where the handcart awaited. "I'm sorry to say this, Malvolio, but one of them is Alaric."

The squire merely nodded again, and wiped his runny nose. His eyes remained dry; as he would later tell folk, he had no more tears to shed. One by one they moved the fur-wrapped bundles, and bound them in place on top of the coach. The other two were Gerta and Felix Rufio. Lucan said that all three deserved better than slow corruption in the now derelict Castello Malconi.

"*Vae victus*," Maximion replied with a shrug.

Lucan glanced at him. "None of them perished the way you suspect."

"Does it matter?" Maximion wondered.

"Perhaps... if you count chivalry a virtue."

Maximion smiled to himself. "Your way of life is so much simpler than ours, Earl Lucan. And there are doubtless benefits in that. But don't make the mistake of thinking it will last forever."

"What way of life is this?"

"Honesty and straight-talking, instead of intrigue and treachery. Powerful lords who exactly match the image they present to the world, with no attempt at pretence. All the powers under Heaven compressed into the hands of a few, and all the rest complying like sheep... or dying. It's an efficient way, if not a kind one, but ultimately it will fail. You may have an enlightened king now, and great knights to enforce his rule with impossible feats of courage. But that won't always be the case, and in due course, as your world crumbles, you will look to the Roman way."

Lucan's lip curled. "You think, in destroying Emperor Lucius, we missed a chance to improve our world?"

"You missed a chance to learn from the mistakes of others, my lord. And I fear that you, and more like you, will miss that opportunity again and again... until the end of your days." Maximion sighed. "Though I concede that time will not come along soon." Fresh thunder rumbled overhead; once again rain began to fall. "Bah! More wretched precipitation! I take it you wish me to ride on top with the dead men?"

"No," Lucan said. "I will ride on top."

Maximion looked surprised, and even a little grateful.

"Don't get me wrong, tribune... it's merely that I doubt your foppish Roman constitution can endure much more, and you're the only item of value I'm taking home."

If Trelawna heard this, she didn't glance up. She didn't even flinch as the icy droplets struck her uncovered head.

While Maximion climbed inside the coach, Lucan took hold of her bridle.

Her empty eyes raked over him. "If I'm no longer your prize, why not leave me here?"

"Don't be foolish," he said. "There's a place for you inside the coach."

The rain hardened, sweeping over them. The wind strengthened.

"Erm... my lord?" Malvolio wondered. "Am I to ride inside the coach too?"

"Don't be absurd, boy."

"No, no. Of course not." Malvolio smiled at his own foolishness as he climbed up to the bench, ensuring to leave a place from which his master could take the reins. He pulled up his coif, though it did nothing to stop the rain. "How, erm, how far are we going?"

"Home to Penharrow," Lucan replied. He glanced back at Trelawna, who had now climbed from her horse. "Though in *your* case," he told her, "home to Camelot."

She didn't react, so he took her by the hand, and led her to the open coach door.

"You can live in the comfort of the palace," he muttered.

"It's the best I can do for you. Though many would die for such an honour."

"Oh, my love," she said as she climbed aboard, "so many have."

Here endeth the Noble Tragedie of

Lucan and Trelawna...

ABOUT THE TRANSLATOR

PAUL FINCH is a former cop and journalist, now turned full time writer. He first cut his literary teeth penning episodes of the British TV crime drama, *The Bill*, and has written extensively in the field of children's animation. However, he is probably best known for his work in horror.

To date, he's had ten books and nearly 300 stories and novellas published on both sides of the Atlantic. His first collection, *Aftershocks*, won the British Fantasy Award in 2002, while he won the award again in 2007 for his novella, *Kid*. Later in 2007, he won the International Horror Guild Award for his mid-length story, *The Old North Road*. Most recently, he has written three *Doctor Who* audio dramas for Big Finish.

Paul lives in Wigan, Lancashire, with his wife Cathy and his children, Eleanor and Harry.

APPENDIX I

The Salisbury Manuscript

UNCOVERED IN JUNE 2006 in the vestry of the nine-hundred-year-old parish church of St. Barbara and St. Christopher in Salisbury, the Salisbury Manuscript (British Library MS Add. 1138) – the only known copy of the *The Second Book of King Arthur and His Noble Knights* – remains one of the most controversial documents in current medieval scholarship.

Debate as to Malory's supposed authorship of the text has reached fever pitch, forming three camps: the Maloreans, who argue that Malory wrote the work himself, as claimed on the title page; the Caxtonians, who argue that the London printer, William Caxton, or one of his clerks wrote the manuscript to "cash in" on the *Morte*'s success; and the Herefordians, who attribute the manuscript to a third person, "Pseudo-Malory," who may have written in Hereford in the fourteenth or fifteenth century, possibly in Welsh.

"There's the notorious textual links to the Hereford, of course," says Dr James Newton (Queen Mary, London), a leading Herefordian, speaking of last year's discovery of common narrative elements in the Salisbury and *The Children of Camelot*, also known as the Hereford Fragment; see *Savage Knight* by Paul Finch for more on this. "Written as they are in different languages and at different times, there must have been some sort of translation or transmission of the story, but there's still a strong argument for a connection. And Pseudo-Malory occasionally references Celtic mythic elements and a clash between the Christian faith and an older British religion, where Malory sees British Christianity at odds with Saxon paganism. And, of course, many of the stories are set on or near the Welsh border."

A similarly geographic argument supports the Malorean camp. "More than half the stories in the *Second Book* are set in the north of England," says Dr Kayleigh Whybrow (Huddersfield). "Although the *Morte D'Arthur* was apparently written in London, Malory – according to some sources – may have been born and raised in the North. And several of the tales in the *Second Book* involve conflict with the Scots or with Reivers, which were pressing concerns during Malory's time."

But Newton's answer to this is simple enough. "Pseudo-Malory moved," he explains. "The Cambridge scholars in the early nineteenth century dismissed the writer of the Hereford Fragment as the wife of an English nobleman, practicing her written Welsh. What if her husband lived in the north of England? Maybe there's even a family connection with Malory – Pseudo-Malory could have been Malory's mother or grandmother – and that explains some of the textual connections between the two books. Pseudo-Malory wasn't writing a sequel to Malory; it was one of Malory's sources."

Newton's book, *Pseudo-Malory: A Wife in Camelot*, is due to be published in 2012.

The Landsdowne Connection

SPECULATION CONTINUES AS to the mysterious "Mr. Wm. Landsdowne," who is named on the first, newer title page in the Salisbury Manuscript as having donated the Manuscript to "the Library."

While most of the 504 paper sheets of the Manuscript date to late fifteenth-century France, the additional title page was written on mid-nineteenth century paper stock from Liverpool. The added page reads "The Second *Booke* of Sir Thomas *Malory*, donated to the Library by the Hon. Mr. Wm. Landsdowne. MDCCCLXIII."

Exactly which library, and how the book made its way from the library to the parish church of St. Barbara and St. Christopher, is still unknown, and a number of researchers are investigating the subject, but investigation into the identity of "Wm. Landsdowne" has suggested a possible connection.

Lansdowne is a field near Bath where a battle was fought in 1643, early in the English Civil War. A Parliamentarian army, led by William Waller, was positioned to defend Bath against Royalist expansion into the southwest. Lord Hopton, leading the Royalists, engaged Waller's forces from an inferior position, and a confused and bloody fight followed, lasting most of the day, with routs on both sides. Finally, Waller retreated from the position, but Hopton was injured and his gunpowder was destroyed in a fire on his ammunition supply, forcing him to withdraw as well.

Sir Bevil Grenville, one of Hopton's officers, was killed in the action, but led one of the more important charges in the battle, and his grandson George Granville was later made Baron Lansdowne in recognition of Sir Bevil's courage and loyalty. The title died with him, but the title Marquess Lansdowne was created a century later for John Petty, husband of Sir Bevil's great-great-granddaughter.

Initial investigation focused on the Lansdowne family, which is still extant, but proved ultimately fruitless; no record could be found of their having owned the book, or being particularly connected to a library. But the connection to the battle is possibly still relevant.

Geoffrey Landsdown was buried in a churchyard in rural Somerset in 1649, with an entry in the parish records stating that he had died "a soldyr of the King," although it's unlikely that he was actually killed in battle, as non-aristocratic soldiers were generally buried where they fell or left on the field rather than transported.

However he died, he is noteworthy in that there is no record of his birth, either in the parish he was buried in – St. Trudpert's near Cheddar – or anywhere nearby. It could be argued that he wasn't a local, especially given his trade, but there *is* a record of his marriage and the birth of his child. "Landsdown was married in St. Trudpert's, his son Charles was born there, and he was buried there," says Dr Celeste Sharp (Bournemouth). "Rather than assuming that he moved there, as is sometimes suggested, I propose that he changed his name. There were a number of reasons someone might change his name at the time: perhaps there were two Geoffreys in the same parish with the same name, and it seemed simplest to change it. Or maybe he just wanted to commemorate a battle he'd fought in."

However they came by the name, the Landsdowns lived in Somerset for generations, only dying out in the first world war. And an old record from a bookbinder's shop, on display at a museum of town life in Taunton, holds the following notation: "rebind. goat lether. 504 pages, irregular folio. W Landsdn, 18s/–" The entry is dated 1863. It seems likely that this is the same "Wm. Landsdowne" who donated the book to the library, and maybe a member of the Landsdown family of St. Trudpert's, who took their name from a battle their ancestor had fought in, in the defence of his King.

APPENDIX II

Dark North

*"Alle that I ever hadde or desired
thy lede toke fram me!"*

There is a thread of bloodthirst in the *Second Book*: already, in the first two stories, Sir Alymere (*The Black Chalice*) has been transformed from a loyal soldier to a hopelessly corrupt boy who dreams of murdering his king, and Sir Dodinal (*The Savage Knight*) has gone from a rather hapless adventurer to a berserk warrior seeking death as an end to his own fury. In that vein, we meet Sir Lucan, once called "The Butler," which in Malory's day was not a household servant but the lord in charge of the court, alongside his brother Bedivere the marshal and Kay the seneschal. In the *Morte*, Lucan is one of Arthur's most stalwart defenders, eventually succumbing to his wounds after bringing him home from his final battle; in the sixteenth-century English ballad *King Arthur's Death*, it is he, rather than his brother, who throws Excalibur into the Lake. In "The Noble Tragedie of Lucan and Trelawna," however, he has become murderous and pitiless, a tortured survivor of a loveless upbringing, bitterly exercising his fury at his dead father upon the bodies of his king's enemies.

Malory – or Pseudo-Malory, if the Herefordian camp is to

be believed – has made of Lucan and Bedivere's father Duke Corneus a veritable monster, who tortured his vanquished foes to death and drove their mother into an early grave. Just as the brothers despised him, for his cruelty and his "might makes right" mentality, and would have gladly killed him had fortune not robbed them of that duty, Lucan fears that he will become him. And though he rails against that fate, he also seems to embrace it: he keeps his father's two bequests – the great sword with which he so brutally slaughtered his foes and the wolfskin cloak that came to be his emblem – as a reminder, and perhaps as a warning to others.

The Romans

"THE NOBLE TRAGEDIE of Lucan and Trelawna" is set against the events of Book II of *Le Morte D'Arthur*, "The Noble Tale Between King Arthur and Lucius the Emperor of Rome," which tells the story of Emperor Lucius's embassy demanding tribute from the former colony, of Arthur's refusal, and of the subsequent war, which Arthur won, placing a regent on the Imperial throne.

This remarkable piece of anachronism sits awkwardly in the midst of a whole fabric of anachronisms. Malory's Arthurian world is set in the fifth century, and yet home to the technology and fashions of his own fifteenth century; of the ideals of chivalry itself, a largely recent creation; and even of countries and cultures that had only come into being a century or two before, such as France. Yet Arthur goes to war on the Roman Empire, whose collapse decades before his career was the only reason fifth-century Britain wasn't Roman in the first place.

In the *Second Book*, Malory (or Pesudo-Malory) brings Rome into his world, making them an Italian state and firmly part of the Renaissance world. It is no longer Rome, but "New Rome," a contemporary Christian kingdom wearing the trappings of its former greatness and attempting to regain the lands and power it once held.

So what is Rome? Lucius Bizerta – Lucius Tiberius, in the *Morte* – is himself evasive. He first appears in Geoffrey of Monmouth's *Historia Regum Britanniae*, and the source is unclear, but there are two possible candidates. Glycerius was the Byzantine emperor from 473 to 474, before being rejected by the court at Constantinople; his name was sometimes rendered Lucerius, which Geoffrey may have shortened or further misspelled. Tiberius II Constantine was the Byzantine emperor another century later, which makes him very late for Arthur, but he was known for his attempt to re-establish an imperial hegemony in the west. Of course, it's possible that Geoffrey invented him. In any case, to Malory, he was the Roman emperor from Arthur's time, established in his most important source.

More than anything, Rome, to Malory, was the antithesis of Britain. The Romans are decadent and corrupt, where Arthur's court are principled and honest; the priests of the Roman church set hierarchies and ceremony above the worship of God, where Britain's virtue is protected by knights, and wise hermits, and pious ladies.

But is British simplicity and virtue so untainted? "The 'Noble Tragedie' is filled with references to clothes, to games and songs and other fine culture, which had come to Britain in Malory's day," says Tamsin Redmore (Roehampton). "Where the Romans expect a land of barbaric savages feasting in smoky halls, they find instead a sophisticated country, where knights dress in the latest fashion and ladies are devoted to the *Cult D'Amor*. It's possible that Malory is just appealing to the interests of his audience, but he may be saying something about British society. Was he simpy saying that the British were every bit as enlightened and cultured as their Roman detractors? Or was he needling his readers, highlighting the similarities between the two peoples? Perhaps suggesting that British society in his own time had become too soft, too interested in finer things? He's judging them, and warning them. The British were complacent in their belief in their own piety, but in fact they were no better than the Romans."

And indeed, as Maximion tells Lucan at the end, the British way is doomed. Roman corruption is the "future" of Lucan's world, the present of Malory's.

Might Makes Right

IF BRITISH CULTURE is being judged, then so is British chivalry. The conflict between Lucan and his father highlights one of Malory's greatest anxieties, and central to the story of Arthur's war with Rome: the legitimacy of force.

The Pentecostal Oath, the code that Arthur and his knights swear, insists that "no man take no battles in a wrongful quarrel for no law, ne for no world's goods." This principle of war pursued only in a just cause is the heart of chivalry, and expressed over and over throughout the story. And yet, in Malory's world, and even in other sources for the life of Arthur, it is often not adhered to.

"Arthur and his court frequently quarrel with their enemies without provocation," says Dominic McDowell-Thomas (Miskatonic), "and the business with Rome is typical. In Monmouth's *Historia*, Arthur throws the Roman embassy out of his court, stating that 'nothing acquired by force and violence is justly possessed by anyone.' Yet he promptly raises an army and sails to France to make war."

Is Arthur justly responding to extreme provocation? Or is he spoiling for a fight? In the *Morte*, Malory observes that Arthur's knights were "many days rested" after a long period of prosperity, and excited at the prospect of war with Rome, "for now shall we have warre and worshype."

In the *Second Book*, through the words of Lucan's father Corneus, Malory is even more explicit. "Theer is no lawe but thine owen," says the dead Duke, in a letter to his son. "Godde regardes him that conquers and makes triumphe in His name." This is the lesson Lucan learned as a boy, and one he struggles against all his life.

The "father's letter" originally appeared in the middle of the "Noble Tragedie," in lines 612-627, after Lucan's discussion with Turold about his decision to don his wolf fur. Lucan reminisces about when he acquired the fur, and what it meant to him; to Malory, it was an indicator that Lucan has transformed from the guardian of civilisation to an avenger, intent on the destruction of those who had wronged him. But in many ways, it serves as the overall theme of the work. "The conventions of Malory's time forbade him from breaking with a linear narrative," says McDowell-Thomas. "He could use reminiscences, prophetic dreams, even intrude with his narrative voice and refer to other events, but he couldn't simply drop in text where he wanted without a narrative reason for it. But Corneus's letter is so central to the story that, had he been able to open with it, he probably would have done. Everything in the story is about the exercise of power. Lucius's intended conquest of Britain, Arthur's siege of Rome, Rufio's seduction of Trelawna and Lucan's vengeance; are all exercises of power, all shows of strength."

Even his marriage to Trelawna tells of the problem of force. The prize of war, taken from her family's household when Lucan destroyed them for his king, she was a good wife and a dutiful one, but never loved him. She never came to be happy in Penharrow, and they never had a child. And when she is stolen away by Rufio, and Lucan tracks him down to be avenged, at the last she is lost to him; she lives, and he bears her home, but he cannot take her back to his home in Penharrow. Again, nothing aquired by force is justly possessed by anyone.

And what does Lucan learn? Upon finally achieving his goal in Castello Malconi, Lucan finds his enemy unworthy of him. Zalmyra's magic brings him face to face, in the end, with his father, and here the true conflict arises. Lucan is confronted with what he rails against in himself, with what he could become. His ersatz father proves indestructible; the lightning that destroys it comes not from Lucan's strength, but from God's will. In the end, it seems, there is only one legitimate authority, and it lies not in the hands of men.

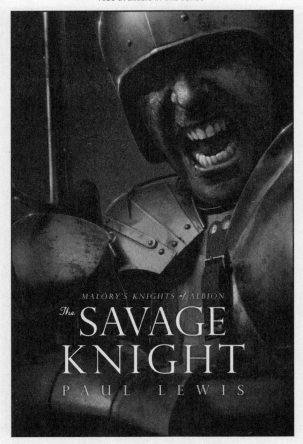

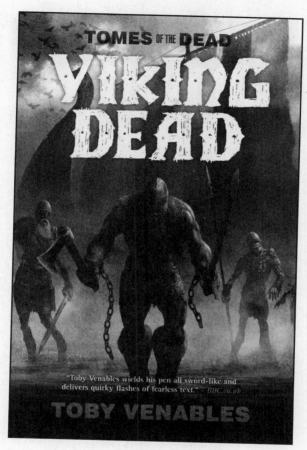

UK ISBN: 978 1 907519 68 0 • US ISBN: 978 1 907519 69 7 • £7.99/$9.99

Northern Europe, 976 AD. Bjólf and the viking crew of the ship *Hrafn* flee up an unknown river after a bitter battle, only to find themselves in a bleak land of pestilence. The dead don't lie down, but become draugr — the undead — returning to feed on the flesh of their kin. Terrible stories are told of a dark castle in a hidden fjord, and of black ships that come raiding with invincible draugr berserkers. And no sooner has Bjólf resolved to leave, than the black ships appear...

Now stranded, his men cursed by the contagion of walking death, Bjólf has one choice: fight his way through a forest teeming with zombies, invade the castle and find the secret of the horrific condition — or submit to an eternity of shambling, soulless undeath!

WWW.ABADDONBOOKS.COM
Follow us on Twitter! www.twitter.com/abaddonbooks

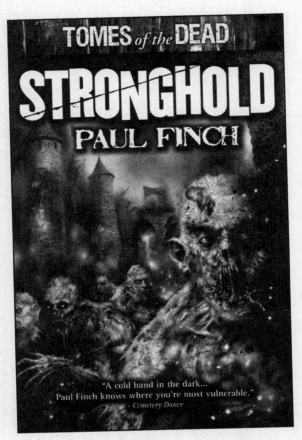

ISBN: 978 1 907519 10 9 • £7.99/$9.99

Ranulf, a young English knight sent to recapture Grogen Castle from Welsh rebels, comes into conflict with his leaders over their brutal methods. Unbeknownst to any of them, the native druids are planning a devastating counterattack, using an ancient artifact to summon an army that even the castle's superstitious medieval defenders could never have imagined.

Grogen Castle, seemingly impregnable to assault – armed with fiendish devices to slaughter would-be attackers in their multitudes – is besieged by countless, tireless soldiers forged from bone and raddled flesh. As lives are held in the balance, Ranulf must defy his masters and rescue the daughter of his enemy, but hope lasts only so long as the stronghold holds out against the legions of the angry dead...